THE SMALL TOWN, U.S.A., COLLECTION

Step onto Main Street of any small town in America and you feel as though you've come home. Here, neighbor knows neighbor, the shops and businesses are familiar, and people take care of their own. It's an idyllic existence, surrounded by those who share our values.

But don't let the slower pace of life fool you! There's always something happening in these small towns and watch out for the surprises around almost every corner. Whether it's the stranger in town, a secret coming to light or discovering love in unexpected places, there is never a dull moment.

So step onto the front porch, sit down and savor this special 2-in-1 collection of classic romance stories that bring you into the heart of America and remind you of what we love about small towns!

If you enjoy these two stories, be sure to look for more romances set in small towns from Harlequin Special Edition and Harlequin Superromance.

ALLISON LEIGH

A frequent name on bestseller lists, Allison Leigh's high point as a writer is hearing from readers that they laughed, cried or lost sleep while reading her books. She credits her family with great patience for the time she's parked at her computer, and for blessing her with the kind of love she wants her readers to share with the characters living in the pages of her books. Contact her at www.allisonleigh.com.

New York Times Bestselling Author

Allison Leigh
and
Liz Talley

WED IN WYOMING

AND

A LITTLE TEXAS

All my Best,

Allison Leigh

⬧ **HARLEQUIN**® SMALL TOWN U.S.A.

Recycling programs
for this product may
not exist in your area.

ISBN-13: 978-0-373-60670-2

Wed in Wyoming and A Little Texas

Copyright © 2014 by Harlequin Books S.A.

The publisher acknowledges the copyright holder
of the individual works as follows:

Wed in Wyoming
Copyright © 2007 by Allison Lee Davidson

A Little Texas
Copyright © 2011 by Amy R. Talley

HARLEQUIN®
www.Harlequin.com

Printed in U.S.A.

CONTENTS

WED IN WYOMING
Allison Leigh

For my editor, Ann Leslie. Thank you for your patience, flexibility and general excellence. I think we've come a long way together!

Prologue

November

"Are you insane? What if someone sees you here?" Angeline Clay looked away from the tall man standing in the shadows of the big house to the wedding reception guests milling around behind her, barely twenty yards away.

"They won't." The man's deep voice was amused. "You forget, sweet cheeks, what I *do* for a living."

She rolled her eyes. They stood outside the circle of pretty lights that had been strung around the enormous awning protecting the tables and the dance floor from the chilly Wyoming weather. Her cousin Leandra and her brand-new husband, Evan Taggart, were in the center of the floor dancing away, surrounded by nearly every other member of Angeline's extensive family. "I'm not likely to forget, Brody," she assured drily.

Since then, her brief encounters with the man had been few and far between, but they'd nevertheless been memorable.

Annoying, really, considering that Angeline prided herself on keeping her focus squarely where it belonged. Which was most assuredly *not* the impossible appeal of the elusive Brody Paine.

She flexed her bare fingers around the empty platter that she had been on her way to the kitchen to refill when Brody had stepped into her path. "How'd you even know I was here, anyway?"

The corner of his lips lifted. "It's a small world, babe. You know that."

Sweet cheeks. Babe.

She stifled a sigh. She couldn't recall Brody *ever* using her actual name. Which was probably one of the reasons why she'd never tried very hard to take the man seriously when it came to anything of a personal nature.

When it came to the work he did, however, she took him quite seriously because Brody Paine was well and truly one of the good guys. Since she'd learned at a particularly early age that the world was definitely on the shy side when it came to such people, she tried to give credit where it was due.

"I'm just visiting Weaver," she reminded him. "For the Thanksgiving holiday and Leandra's wedding. I'm going back to Atlanta soon."

He blandly reeled off her flight number, telling her not very subtly that he was perfectly aware of her schedule. "The agency likes to keep track of its assets."

She looked behind her again, but there was nobody within earshot. Of course. Brody wouldn't be likely to mention the agency if there had been. "I'm hardly an asset," she reminded him needlessly. She was a courier of sorts, true. But in the five years she'd worked for the agency, all she conveyed were pieces of information from one source to another. Even then, she was called on to do so only once or twice a year. It was a schedule that seemed to suit everyone.

"Believe me, hon. You've got more than any woman's fair share of assets," he assured drily. His gaze—she'd never been certain if it was naturally blue or brown because she'd seen his eye color differ over the years—traveled down her body. "Of course for some stubborn reason you keep refusing to share them with *me*."

She'd seen appreciation in men's eyes when they looked at her since she'd hit puberty. She was used to it. But she still felt absurdly grateful for the folds of the cashmere cape that flowed around her taupe-colored dress beneath it. "That's right," she said dismissively. "I assume this *isn't* a social call?"

His lips twitched again. "Only because you're a stubborn case, sweet cheeks."

Her lips tightened. "Brody—"

"Don't get your panties in a twist." He lifted one long-fingered hand. "I'm actually in the middle of another gig." He looked amused again. "But I was asked to give you this."

She realized that a small piece of paper was tucked between his index and middle finger. She plucked it free, careful not to touch him, only to nearly jump out of her skin when his fingers suddenly closed around her wrist.

She gave him a startled look.

The amusement from his face had been wiped away. "This is important."

Nerves tightened her throat. She wasn't used to seeing Brody looking so serious. "Isn't it always?" He'd told her, chapter and verse, from the very beginning just how important and sensitive her work with Hollins-Winword was.

"Like everything else in life, importance can be relative."

Behind them, the deejay was calling for everyone's attention since the bride and groom were preparing to cut their wedding cake. "I need to get back there. Before someone comes looking for me."

He slowly released her wrist. She stopped herself from rubbing the tingling that remained there just in time.

The man was entirely too observant. Which was, undoubtedly, one of the qualities that made him such an excellent agent. But the last thing she wanted him to know was that he had *any* kind of affect on her.

They were occasionally connected business associates and that was all. If the guy knew she'd been infatuated with him for years—well, she simply didn't want him knowing. Period. Maybe the knowledge would make a difference to him, and maybe it wouldn't. But she didn't intend to find out.

Playing immune to him was already hard enough.

She couldn't imagine how hard it would be if she spent any real time with the man.

He gave that small smile of his that had her wondering if mind reading was among his bag of tricks. "See you next time, babe." He lifted his chin in the direction of the partygoers. "Drink some champagne for me."

She glanced back, too. Leandra and Evan were standing in front of the enormous, tiered wedding cake. "I can probably get you a glass without anyone noticing. Cake, too."

She looked back when he didn't answer.

The only thing she saw was the dark, tall form of him disappearing into the cold night.

Chapter One

"I still think you're insane."

Since Angeline had last seen Brody Paine almost six months ago, he'd grown a scruffy brown beard that didn't quite mask the smile he gave at her pronouncement.

His sandy-brown hair hung thick and long around his ears, clearly in desperate need of a cut, and along with that beard, he looked vaguely piratical.

"Seems like you're always telling me that, babe."

Angeline lifted her eyebrows pointedly. They were sitting in a Jeep that was currently stuck lug nut deep in Venezuelan mud. "Take a clue from the theme," she suggested, raising her voice to be heard above the pounding rain.

As usual, he seemed to pay no heed of her opinion.

Instead, he peered through the rain-washed windshield, drumming his thumb on the steering wheel. The vehicle itself looked as if it had been around about a half century.

It no longer possessed such luxuries as doors, and the wind that had been carrying sheets of rain for each of the three days since Angeline had arrived in Venezuela kept up its momentum, throwing a stinging spray across her and Brody.

The enormous weather system that was supposed to have veered away from land and calmly die out over the middle of the ocean hadn't behaved that way at all. Instead, it had squatted over them like some tormenting toad, bringing with it this incessant rain and wind. May might be too early for a hurricane, but Mother Nature didn't seem to care much for the official calendar.

She huddled deeper in the seat. The hood of her khaki-colored rain poncho hid most of her head, but she still felt soaked from head to toe.

That's what she got for racing away from the camp in Puerto Grande the way she had. If she'd stopped to think longer, she might have at least brought along some warmer clothes to wear beneath the rain poncho.

Instead, she'd given All-Med's team leader, Dr. Miguel Chavez, a hasty excuse that a friend in Caracas had an emergency, and off she'd gone with Brody in this miserable excuse of a vehicle. She knew they wouldn't expect her back anytime soon. In *good* weather, Caracas was a day away.

"The convent where the kids were left is up this road," he said, still drumming. If he was as uncomfortable with the conditions as she, he hid it well. "There's no other access to St. Agnes's. Unless a person was airlifted in. And *that* ain't gonna happen in this weather." His head bounced a few times, as if he were mentally agreeing with whatever other insane thoughts were bouncing around inside.

She angled her legs in the hard, ripped seat, turning her back against the driving rain. "If we walked, we could make it back to the camp at Puerto Grande before dark." Though dark was a subjective term, considering the oppressive clouds that hung over their heads.

Since she'd turned twenty, she'd visited Venezuela with All-Med five times, but this was the worst weather she'd ever encountered.

"Only way we're going is forward, sweetie." He sighed loud enough to be heard above the rain that was pounding on the roof of the vehicle. His jeans and rain poncho were caked with mud from his repeated attempts to dislodge the Jeep.

"But the convent is still *miles* away." They were much closer to the camp where she'd been stationed. "We could get some help from the team tomorrow. Work the Jeep free of the mud. They wouldn't have to know that we were trying to get up to St. Agnes instead of to Caracas."

"Can't afford to waste that much time."

She huffed out a breath and stared at the man. He truly gave new meaning to the word stubborn.

She angled her back even farther against the blowing wind. Her knees brushed against the gearshift, and when she tried to avoid that, they brushed against his thigh.

If that fact was even noticeable to him, he gave no indication whatsoever. So she left her knee right where it was, since the contact provided a nice little bit of warmth to her otherwise shivering body.

Shivers caused by cold *and* an uncomfortable suspicion she'd had since he unexpectedly appeared in Puerto Grande.

"What's the rush?" she asked. "You told me we were merely picking up the Stanley kids from the convent for their parents."

"We are."

Her lips tightened. "Brody—"

"I told you to call me Hewitt, remember?"

There was nothing particularly wrong with the name, but he definitely didn't seem a "Hewitt" type to her. Brody was energy itself all contained within long legs, long hands and a hard body. If she had to be stuck in the mud at the base of a mountain in a foreign country, she supposed Brody was about the best companion she could have. She wouldn't go so far as to call the man *safe,* but she did believe he was capably creative when the situation called for it.

"Fine, *Hewitt,*" she returned, "so what's the rush? The children have been at the convent for nearly two months. What's one more night?" He'd already filled her in on the details of how Hewitt Stanley—the real Hewitt Stanley— and his wife, Sophia, had tucked their two children in the small, exceedingly reclusive convent while they trekked deep into the most unreachable portions of Venezuela to further their latest pharmaceutical quest.

Brody had, supposedly, enlisted Angeline's help because he claimed he couldn't manage retrieving both kids on his own.

"The Santina Group kidnapped Hewitt and Sophia two days ago."

"Excuse me?"

Despite the rough beard, his profile as he peered through the deluged windshield could have been chiseled from the mountains around them. "Do you ever wonder about the messages you're asked to dispatch?"

"No."

"Never." He gave her another one of those mind reader looks.

Sometimes, honesty was a darned nuisance.

"Yes. Of course I am curious sometimes," she admitted. "But I don't make any attempt to satisfy that curiosity. That's not my role. I'm just the messenger. And what does that have to do with the Stanleys?"

He raised one eyebrow. "When I gave you that intel back in November, you didn't wonder about it?" He didn't quite sound disbelieving, but the implication was there.

"There are lots of things I wonder about, but I don't have the kind of clearance to know more. Maybe I prefer it that way." The tidbits of information that she dispatched were not enough to give her real knowledge of the issues that Hollins-Winword handled. It was a tried-and-true safety measure, not only for her personal safety, but for those around her, the agency's work and the agency itself.

She knew that. Understood that. Welcomed it, even.

She believed in her involvement with Hollins-Winword. But that didn't mean she was anxious to risk her neck over four sentences, which was generally the size of the puzzle pieces of information with which she was entrusted. Brody's message for her that night at Leandra and Evan's wedding reception had been even briefer.

Stanley experimenting. Sandoval MIA.

She'd memorized the information—hardly difficult in this case—and shortly after she'd returned to Atlanta, she'd relayed the brief missive to the impossibly young-looking boy who'd spilled his backpack on the floor next to her table at a local coffee shop.

She'd knelt down beside him and helped as he'd packed up his textbooks, papers and pens, and three minutes later, he was heading out the door with his cappuccino and the message, and she was sitting back down at her table with her paperback book and her latte.

"You didn't look twice at the name Sandoval."

Somehow, cold water had snuck beneath the neck of her poncho and was dripping down the back of her spine. She tugged the hood of her poncho farther over her forehead but it was about as effective as closing the barn door after the horse was already out, considering the fact that she was already soaked. "Does it matter? Sandoval's not that unusual of a name."

His lips twisted. "How old were you when you left Santo Marguerite?"

The kernel inside her suddenly exploded, turning tense curiosity into a sickening fear that she didn't want to acknowledge. "Four." Old enough to remember that the name of the man who'd destroyed the Central American village where she'd been born, along with nearly everyone else who'd lived there, had been Sandoval.

She reached out and closed her hand over his slick, wet forearm. "I'm no good at guessing games, Brody. Just tell me what you want me to know. Is Sandoval involved with the kidnapping?"

His gaze flicked downward, as if surprised by the contact, and she hastily drew back, curling her cold hands together.

"We haven't been able to prove it, but we believe that he is the money behind the Santina Group. On the other hand, we *know* Santina funds at least two different black market organizations running everything from drugs and weapons to human trafficking. According to the pharma-

ceutical company Hewitt works for, he was on to something huge. Has to do with some little red frog about the
size of my fingernail."

He shook his head, as if the entire matter was unfath-
omable to him. "Anyway, the pharmacy folks will try to
replicate synthetically the properties of this frog spit, or
whatever the *hell* it is." His voice went terse. "And in the
right hands, that's fine. But those properties are *also* the
kind of properties that in the wrong hands, could bring a
whole new meaning to what profit is in the drug trade."

"They've got the parents and now they're after the
kids, too. Sandoval or Santina or whoever," she surmised,
feeling even more appalled.

"We're working on that theory. One of Santina's top
men—Rico Fuentes—was spotted in Caracas yesterday
morning. Sophia Stanley's parents were Venezuelan, and
she inherited a small apartment there when they died.
The place was tossed yesterday afternoon."

"How can you be sure the kids are even at the convent?"

"Because *I* tossed the apartment yesterday *morning* and found Sophia's notes she'd made about getting there, and packing clothes and stuff for the kids. I
didn't leave anything for ol' Rico to find but who knows
who Hewitt and Sophia may have told about their kids'
whereabouts. I've got my people talking to everyone
at the pharmaceutical place, and so far none of them
seems to know anything about the convent, but..." He
shrugged and looked back at the road.

"Hewitt obviously knew they were on to something
that would be just as significant to the bad guys as to
the good," he told her. "Otherwise, why squirrel away
their kids the way they did? They could have just hired

a nanny to mind them while they went exploring in the tepuis." He referred to the unearthly, flattop mountains located in the remote southeast portion of the country. She knew the region was inhabited by some extremely unusual life-forms.

"Instead," he went on, "they used the convent where Sophia's mother once spent time as a girl."

"If this Rico person gets to the children, Santina could use them as leverage to make sure Hewitt cooperates."

"Bingo."

"What about Hewitt and Sophia, though? How will they even know their kids are still safe? Couldn't these Santina group people lie?"

"Hell yeah, they could lie. They *will* lie. But there's another team working on their rescue. Right now, we need to make certain that whatever threats made concerning those kids *are* a lie."

She blew out a long breath. "Why not go to the authorities? Surely they'd be of more help."

"Which local authorities do you think we can implicitly trust?"

She frowned. Miguel had often complained about the thriving black market and its rumored connection to the local police. "Brody, this kind of thing is way beyond me. I'm not a field agent. You know that better than anyone." Her involvement with Hollins-Winword had only ever involved the transmittal of information!

A deep crevice formed down his cheek as the corner of his lips lifted. "You are now, sweet cheeks."

"I do have a name," she reminded.

"Yeah. And until we get the kids outta this country, it's Sophia Stanley."

"I beg your pardon?"

"Beg all you want. There's a packet in the glove box."

She fumbled with the rusting button and managed to open the box. It was stuffed with maps and an assortment of hand tools. The packet, she assumed, was the dingy envelope wedged between a long screwdriver and a bundle of nylon rope. She pulled it out and lifted the flap. Inside was a narrow gold ring with a distinctive pattern engraved on it and several snapshots.

He took the envelope and turned the contents out into his hand. "Here." He handed her the ring. "Put this on."

She gingerly took the ring from him and started to slide it on her right hand.

He shook his head. "Left hand. It's a wedding ring, baby cakes."

Feeling slightly sick to her stomach, she pushed the gold band over her cold wedding-ring finger. It was a little loose. She curled her fingers into her palm, holding it in place.

She'd never put a ring on that particular finger before, and it felt distinctly odd.

"This—" he held up a picture "—is Sophia."

A laughing woman with long dark hair smiled at the camera. She looked older than Angeline, but overall, their coloring was nearly identical, from their olive-toned skin to their dark brown eyes.

"Not a perfect match," Brody said. "You're prettier. But you'll have to do."

She frowned, not sure if that was a compliment or not, but he took no notice.

"These are the kids. Eva's nine. Davey's four." He handed her a few more pictures, barely giving her time to examine one before handing her the next. "And this is papa bear."

If the situation hadn't been as serious as she knew it was, she would have laughed right out loud. The real Hewitt Stanley definitely matched the mental image his name conjured.

Medium height. Gangly and spectacled. Even from the snapshot, slightly blurred though it was, the man's *un*-Brody-ness shined through. Other than the fact that they were both male, there was nothing remotely similar between the two men. "*This* is who you're pretending to be."

"You'd be surprised at the identities I've assumed," he said, taking back the photographs when she handed them to him. He tucked them back in the envelope, which then disappeared beneath his rain poncho.

"Why do we even need to pretend to be the Stanleys, anyway? The nuns at the convent will surely know we're *not* the people who left their children in their safekeeping."

"Generally, the Mother Superior deals with outsiders. She's definitely the only one who would have met with Hewitt and Sophia when they took in the children. And she's currently stuck in Puerto Grande thanks to the weather that *we* are not going to let stop us."

"Maybe we can fool a few nuns—" she hesitated for a moment, rather expecting a bolt of lightning to strike at the very idea of it "—but the kids will know we're not their parents. They will certainly have something to say about going off with two complete strangers."

"The Stanleys had a code word for their kids. Falling waters. When we get that to them, they'll know we're there on behalf of their parents."

The situation could not possibly become any more surreal. "How do you know *that?*"

"Because I do. Believe me, if I thought we could just

walk into that convent up there and tell the nuns we were taking the kids away for their own safety, I would. But there's a reason Hewitt and Sophia chose the place. It's hellacious to reach, even on a good day. It's cloistered. It's small; barely even a dot on the satellite imaging."

Again she felt that panicky feeling starting to crawl up her throat. "W-what if we fail?" The last time she'd failed had been in Atlanta, and it hadn't had anything to do with Hollins-Winword. But it had certainly involved a child.

He gave her a sidelong look. "We won't."

"Why didn't you tell me all this when you showed up at the aid camp?" If he had, she would have found some reason to convince him to find someone else.

"Too many ears." He reached beneath his seat and pulled out a handgun. So great was her surprise, she barely recognized it as a weapon.

In a rapid movement he checked the clip and tucked the gun out of sight where he'd put the envelope of photographs beneath his rain poncho.

She'd grown up on a ranch, so she wasn't unfamiliar with firearms. But the presence of rifles and shotguns hanging in the gun case in her father's den was a far cry from the thing that Brody had just hidden away. "We won't need that though, right?"

"Let's hope not." He gave her a look, as if he knew perfectly well how she felt about getting into a situation where they might. "I don't want to draw down on a nun any more than the next guy. If we can convince them we're Hewitt and Sophia Stanley, we won't have to. But believe me, sweet cheeks, they're better off if I resort to threats than if Santina's guy does. They don't draw the line over hurting innocent people. And if we're not as far ahead of the guy as I hope, you're going to be pretty happy that I've got—" he patted his side "—good old Delilah with us, sweet cheeks."

He named his gun Delilah?

She shook her head, discomfited by more than just the gun.

Sandoval certainly hadn't drawn the line over hurting people, she knew. Not when she'd been four and the man had destroyed her family's village in a power struggle for control of the verdant land. When he'd been in danger of losing the battle, he'd destroyed the land, too, rather than let someone beat him.

"It's not sweet cheeks," she said, and blamed her shaking voice on the cold water still sneaking beneath her poncho. "It's Sophia."

Brody slowly smiled. "That's my girl."

She shivered again and knew, that time, that it wasn't caused entirely by cold or nerves.

It was caused by *him*.

Chapter Two

They abandoned the Jeep where it was mired in the mud and proceeded on foot.

It seemed to take hours before they managed to climb their way up the steep, slick mountainside.

The wind swirled around them, carrying the rain in sheets that were nearly horizontal. Angeline felt grateful for Brody's big body standing so closely to hers, blocking a fair measure of the storm.

She lost all sense of time as they trudged along. Every step she took was an exercise in pain—her thighs, her calves, her shins. No part of her seemed excused until finally—when her brain had simply shut down except for the mental order to keep moving, keep moving, keep moving—Brody stopped.

He lifted his hand, and beat it hard on the wide black plank that barred their path.

A door, her numb mind realized. "They won't hear," she said, but couldn't even hear the words herself over the screaming wind.

His fingers were an iron ring around her wrist as the door creaked open—giving lie to her words—and he pulled her inside. Then he put his shoulder against the door and muscled it closed again, yanking down the old-fashioned wooden beam that served as a lock.

The sudden cessation of battering wind was nearly dizzying.

It was also oddly quiet, she realized. So much so that she could hear the water dripping off her onto the stone floor.

"Señora." A diminutive woman dressed in a full nun's habit held out a white towel.

"Thank you." Angeline took the towel and pressed it to her face. The weave was rough and thin but it was dry and felt positively wonderful. She lowered it to smile at the nun. *"Gracias."*

The woman was speaking rapidly to Brody in Spanish. And though Angeline hadn't spoken the language of her birth in years, she followed along easily enough. The nun was telling Brody that the Mother Superior was not there to welcome the strangers.

"We're not strangers," Brody told her. His accent was nearly flawless, Angeline realized with some vague surprise. "We've come to collect our children."

If Angeline had held any vague notions of other children being at the convent, they were dissolved when the nun nodded. *"Sí. Sí."* The nun turned and began moving away from the door, heading down the middle of the three corridors that led off the vestibule.

Brody gave Angeline a sharp look when she didn't immediately follow along.

She knew she could collapse later, *after* they knew the children were safe. But just then she wanted nothing more than to just sink down on the dark stone floor and rest her head back against the rough, whitewashed wall.

As if he could read her thoughts, Brody wrapped his hand around her wrist again and drew her along the corridor with him in the nun's wake.

Like the vestibule, the hallway had whitewashed walls. Though the wash looked pristine, it didn't mask the rough texture of the wall beneath it. There were no windows, but a multitude of iron sconces situated high up the wall held fat white candles that kept the way well lit. The few electrical sconces spread out less liberally were dark.

Angeline figured they'd walked a good fifty feet before the corridor turned sharply left and opened after another twenty or so feet into a wide, square room occupied by a half-dozen long wooden tables and benches.

The dining hall, the nun informed them briskly. Her feet didn't hesitate, however, as she kept right on walking.

"You catching all that?" Brody asked Angeline in English.

She nodded. She'd come to English only when Daniel and Maggie Clay had adopted her after her family's village was destroyed. And though Angeline had deliberately turned her back on the language of her natural parents, she'd never forgotten it, though she'd once made a valiant effort to do so.

She'd already been different enough from the other people in that small Wyoming town where she'd gone to live with Daniel and Maggie. Even before she'd been old enough to understand her actions, she'd deliberately rid the accent from her diction, and copied the vague drawl that the adults around her had possessed. She'd wanted so badly to belong. Not because any one of her adopted family made her feel different, but because inside, Angeline had known she *was* different.

She'd lived when the rest of her natural family had perished. She'd been rescued from a poor Central American orphanage and been taken to the U.S., where she'd been raised by loving people.

But she'd never forgotten the sight of fire racing through the fields her cousins had tended, licking up the walls and across the roofs of their simple houses. And whatever hadn't been burned had been hacked down with axes, torn apart with knives, shot down with guns.

Nothing had escaped. Not the people. Not the livestock. Not the land.

Only *her.*

It was twenty-five years ago, and she still didn't understand why she'd been spared.

"Sophia." Brody's voice was sharp, cutting through the dark memories. Angeline focused on his deep blue eyes and just that abruptly she was back in the present.

Where two children needed them.

"I'm sorry." How easily she fell back into thinking in Spanish, speaking in Spanish. "The children." She looked at the nun. "Please, where are they?"

The nun looked distressed. "They are well and safe, *señora.* But until the Mother Superior returns and authorizes your access to them, I must continue to keep them secure."

"From me?" Angeline didn't have to work hard at conjuring tears in her eyes. She was cold, exhausted and entirely undone by the plot that Brody had drawn her into.

"I am their mother." The lie came more easily than she'd thought it would.

The nun's ageless face looked pitying, yet resolute. "You were the ones who made the arrangement with Mother. But now, you are weary," she said. "You and your husband need food and rest. We will naturally provide you with both until Mother returns. The storm will pass and soon she will be here to show you to your children."

"But—"

Brody's hand closed around hers. "*Gracias,* Sister. My wife and I thank you for your hospitality, of course. If we could find dry clothes—"

"*Si. Si.*" The nun looked relieved. "Please wait here. I will send Sister Frances to assist you in a moment if that will be satisfactory?"

Brody's fingers squeezed Angeline's in warning. "*Si.*"

She nodded and turned on her heel, gliding back along the corridor. Her long robes swished over the stone floor.

The moment she was out of sight, Brody let go of Angeline's wrist and she sank down onto one of the long wooden benches situated alongside the tables. She rubbed her wrist, flushing a little when she realized he was watching the action. She stopped, telling herself inwardly that her skin wasn't *really* tingling.

What was one more lie there inside that sacred convent, considering the whoppers they were already telling?

Brody sat down beside her and she wanted to put some distance between them given the way he was crowding into her personal space, but another nun—presumably Sister Frances—silently entered the dining area. She gestured for Brody and Angeline to follow, and Brody tucked his hand beneath Angeline's arm as he helped her solicitously to her feet.

They followed the silent nun down another corridor and up several narrow flights of stairs, all lit with those same iron wall sconces. Finally she stopped and opened a heavy wooden door, extending her hand in a welcoming gesture. Clearly they were meant to go inside.

Angeline passed the nun, thanking her quietly as she entered the room. Brody ducked his head to keep from knocking it against the low sill and followed her inside. The dim room contained a single woefully narrow bed, a single straight-backed wooden chair and a dresser with an old-fashioned ceramic pitcher and basin atop it.

The nun reached up to the sconce on the wall outside the door and pulled down the lit candle, handing it to Brody. She waved her hand toward the two sconces inside the bedroom, and Brody reached up, setting the flame to the candles they contained.

Warm light slowly filled the tiny room as the flames caught. Brody handed the feeder candle back to the nun, who nodded and backed two steps out of the room, pulling the wooden door shut as she went.

Which left Angeline alone with Brody.

The room had no windows, and though Angeline was definitely no fan of small, enclosed spaces, the room simply felt cozy. Cozy and surprisingly safe, considering the surreal situation.

"Well," he said in a low tone, "that was easier than I expected."

She gaped. "Easy? They won't even let us *see* the children."

"Shh." He lifted one of the candles from its sconce and began prowling around the room's small confines.

She lowered her voice. "What are you looking for?"

He ignored her. He nudged the bed away from the

wall. Looked behind it. Under it. Pushed it back. He did the same with the dresser. He turned the washbasin and the pitcher upside down, before replacing them atop the dresser. He even pulled the unlit bare lightbulb out of the metal fixture hanging from the low ceiling. Then, evidently with nothing else to examine, he returned the fat candle to the sconce.

"Don't think we're being bugged."

Her lips parted. "Seriously?"

"I'm a big believer in paranoia." He looked up at the steady candle flames. "Walls in this place must be about a foot deep," he said. "Can hardly hear the storm out there."

And she was closed within them with *him* in a room roughly the size of the balcony of her Atlanta apartment. "Sorry if I'm not quick on the uptake here. Is that supposed to be good or bad?"

He shrugged, and began pulling off his rain poncho, doing a decent job of not flinging mud onto the white blanket covering the bed. "It ain't bad," he said when his head reappeared. "At least we probably don't have to worry about that hurricane blowing this place to bits." He dropped the poncho in the corner behind the door. The Rolling Stones T-shirt he wore beneath it was as lamentably wet as her own, and he lifted the hem, pulling the gun and its holster off his waistband.

He tucked them both beneath the mattress.

"Probably," she repeated faintly. "Bro— Hewitt, what about the children?"

"We'll get to them," he said.

She wished she felt even a portion of the confidence he seemed to feel. "What happened to that all-fire rush you were feeling earlier?"

"Believe me, it's still burning. But first things first."

His long arm came up, his hand brushing her poncho, and she nearly jumped out of her skin. "Relax. I was just gonna help you take off your poncho."

She felt her cheeks heat and was grateful for the soft candlelight that would hide her flush. "I knew that."

He snorted softly.

Fortunately, she was saved from further embarrassment when there was a soft knock on the door.

It only took Brody two steps to reach it, and when it swung open, yet another nun stood on the threshold carrying a wooden tray. She smiled faintly and tilted her head, her black veil swishing softly. But like the sister who'd shown them to the room, she remained silent as she set the tray on the dresser top and began unloading it.

A simple woven basket of bread. A hunk of cheese. A cluster of green grapes. Two thick white plates, a knife, two sparkling clear glasses and a fat round pitcher. All of it she left on the dresser top. She didn't look at Brody and Angeline as she bowed her head over the repast.

She was obviously giving a blessing. Then she lifted her head, smiled peacefully again and returned to the door. She knelt down, picked up a bundle she'd left outside, and brought it in, setting it on the bed. Then she let herself out of the room. Like Sister Frances, she pulled the door shut as she went.

"Grub and fresh duds," Brody said, looking happy as a pig in clover. He lifted the off-white bundle from the bed and the items separated as he gave it a little shake. "Pants and top for you. Pants and top for me." He deftly sorted, and tossed the smaller set toward the two thin pillows that sat at the head of the modest bed.

She didn't reach for them, though.

He angled her a look. "Don't worry, beautiful. I'll turn

my back while you change." His lips twitched. "There's
not even a mirror in here for me to take a surreptitious
peek. Now if you feel so compelled, *you're* welcome to
look all you want. After all—" his amused voice was dry
"—we are married."

Her cheeks heated even more. "Stop. Please. My sides
are splitting because you are sooo funny."

His lips twitched again and he pulled his T-shirt over
his head.

Angeline swallowed, not looking away quickly enough
to miss the ripped abdomen and wealth of satin-smooth
golden skin stretched tightly across a chest that hadn't
looked nearly so wide in the shirt he'd worn. When his
hands dropped to the waist of his jeans, she snatched
up the clean, dry clothing and turned her back on him.

Then just when she wished the ground would swallow
her whole, she heard his soft, rumbling chuckle.

She told herself to get a grip. She was a paramedic for
pity's sake. She'd seen nude men, women and children
in all manner of situations.

There's a difference between nude and naked, a tiny
voice inside her head taunted, and Brody's bare chest was
all about being naked.

She silenced the voice and snatched her shirt off over
her head, dropping it in a sopping heap on the floor.
Leaving on her wet bra would only make the dry top
damp, so she snapped it off, too, imaging herself anywhere but in that confining room with Brody Paine. She
pulled the dry top over her head.

She tried imagining that she was a quick-change artist as she yanked the tunic firmly over her hips—grateful that it reached her thighs—then ditched her own wet
jeans and panties for the dry pants.

She immediately felt warmer.

She knelt down and bundled her filthy clothes together, tucking away the scraps of lace and satin lingerie inside.

"Trying to hide the evidence that you like racy undies?"

Her head whipped around and the towel tumbled off her head.

Brody was facing her, hip propped against the dresser, arms crossed over the front of the tunic that strained slightly in the shoulders. He had an unholy look in his eyes that ought to have had the storm centering all of her fury on them considering their surroundings.

"You promised not to look."

His mobile lips stretched, revealing the edge of his very straight, very white teeth. "Babe, you sound prim enough to be one of the sisters cloistered here."

Her cheeks couldn't possibly get any hotter. "Which doesn't change the fact that you promised."

He lifted one shoulder. "Promises are made to be broken."

"You don't really believe that."

"How do you know?"

It couldn't possibly be any more obvious. "It doesn't matter how many lines you give me, because the truth is, you couldn't do the work you do if you didn't believe in keeping your word," she said simply.

Chapter Three

Brody looked at Angeline's face. She looked so...earnest, he thought. Earnest and sexy as hell in a way that had *nothing* to do with those hanks of black lace he'd gotten a glimpse of.

She'd always been a deadly combination, even in the small doses of time they'd ever spent together.

Was it any wonder that he'd been just as interested in consuming a larger dose as he'd been in avoiding just that?

Complications on the job were one thing.

Complications off the job were nonexistent because that's the way he kept it.

Always.

But there she was, watching him with those huge, wide-set brown eyes that had gotten to him even on their first, ridiculously brief encounter five years earlier.

He deliberately lifted one eyebrow. "It's a job, sweet cheeks. A pretty well-paying one."

"Assembling widgets is a job," she countered. "Protecting the innocent? Righting wrongs? That's not just a job and somehow I doubt you do it only for the money."

"You're not just prim, you're a romantic, too," he drawled.

She frowned a little, possibly realizing the topic had gone somewhat awry. "So what's the next step?"

He held up a cluster of grapes. "We eat."

Right on cue, her stomach growled loud enough for him to hear. "Shouldn't we try to find the children?"

"You wanna pull off our own kidnapping?" He wasn't teasing.

"That's essentially what your plan *was*."

"I'd consider it more a case of protective custody."

She pushed her fingers through her hair, holding it back from her face. She didn't have on a lick of makeup, and she was still more beautiful than ninety-nine percent of the world's female population.

"Fine. Call it whatever," she dismissed. "Shouldn't we be doing something to that end?"

"I told you. First things first. How far do you think we'll get if we set out right this second? You're so exhausted I can see the circles under your eyes even in *this* light and I'm not sure who's stomach is growling louder. Yours or mine." He popped a few grapes into his mouth and held up the cluster again. "Come on, darlin'. Eat up."

"I think we should at least try to see the children. What if that password thing doesn't work?" But she plucked a few grapes off the cluster and slid one between her full bow-shaped lips. She chewed and swallowed, and avoiding his eyes, quickly reached for more.

"It will." He tore off a chunk of the bread and handed it to her, and cut the wedge of cheese in half. "Here."

She sat on the foot of the bed and looked as if she was trying not to wolf down the food. He tipped the pitcher over one of the glasses, filling it with pale golden liquid. He took a sniff. "Wine." He took a drink. "Pretty decent wine at that." He poured the second glass and held it out to her.

She took it from him, evidently too thirsty to spend a lot of effort avoiding brushing his fingers the way she usually did. "Wine always goes straight to my head."

"Goody goody." He tossed one of the cloth napkins that had been tucked beneath the bread basket onto her lap. "Drink faster."

She let out an impatient laugh. "Do you *ever* stop with the come-ons?"

"Do you *ever* take me up on one?"

She made a face at him. "Why would I want to be just another notch?"

"Who says that's what you'd be?"

She took another sip of wine. "I'm sure that's the only thing women are to you."

"I'm wounded, babe. You're different than all the others."

She let out a half laugh. "You are so full of it."

"And you are way too serious." He bit into a hunk of bread. He was thirty-eight years old—damn near a decade her senior—but he might as well have been sixteen given the way he kept getting preoccupied with that narrow bed, where she was gingerly perched.

"I'm a serious person," she said around a not-entirely delicate mouthful of bread. "In a serious business."

"The paramedic business or the spy business?"

"I'm not a spy."

He couldn't help smiling again. "Sugar, you're a courier for one of the biggies in the business." He tipped more wine into his glass. "And your family just keeps getting pulled in, one way or the other."

"You ought to know. You're the one who approached me in the first place to be a courier."

He couldn't dispute that. "Still. Don't you think it's a little…unusual?"

She didn't even blink. "You mean how many of us are involved with Hollins-Winword?"

At least she wasn't as in the dark as her cousin Sarah had been. Sarah'd had no clue that she wasn't the only one in her family hooked up with Hollins-Winword; probably wouldn't know even now if her brand-spanking-new husband, Max Scalise, hadn't tramped one of his own investigations right through Brody's assignment to protect a little girl named Megan. They'd been staying in a safe house in Weaver, set up by Sarah, who mostly made her living as a school teacher when she wasn't making an occasional "arrangement" for Hollins-Winword. But she'd only learned that her uncles were involved. She hadn't learned about Angeline.

Or the others in that extensive family tree.

And now, he'd heard that Sarah and Max were in the process of adopting Megan.

The child's parents had been brutally murdered, but she'd at least have some chance at regaining a decent life with decent people raising her.

She'd have a family.

The thought was darker than it should have been and he reached for the wine pitcher again, only to find it empty. Thirty-eight years old, horny, thirsty and feeling envious of some innocent eight-year-old kid.

What the hell was wrong with him? He'd been several years older than Megan had been when his real family had been blown to bits. As for the "family" he'd had after that, he'd hardly term a hard-assed workaholic like Cole as real.

Sitting across from him on the foot of the bed, Angeline had spread out the napkin over her lap, and as he watched, she delicately brushed her fingertips over the cloth.

She had the kind of hourglass figure that men fantasized over, a Madonna's face and fingers that looked like they should have nothing more strenuous to do than hold up beautifully jeweled rings. Yet twice now, he'd found her toiling away in the ass-backward village of Puerto Grande.

That first time, five years ago, his usual courier had missed the meet and Brody had been encouraged to develop a new asset. And oh, by the way, isn't it convenient that there's a pretty American in Puerto Grande whose family is already involved with Hollins-Winword.

The situation had always struck Brody as too convenient for words. But he'd gone ahead and done his job. He'd talked her into the gig, passed off the intel that she was to relay later when she was back in the States and voilà, her career as a courier was born.

The second time he'd found her working like a dog in Puerto Grande had been, of course, just that morning. He'd called in to his handler at Hollins-Winword to find out who he could pull in fast to assist him on getting the kids, only to learn that, lo and behold, once again the lovely Señorita Clay was right there in Puerto

Grande. She would be the closest, quickest—albeit unlikely—assistant. And one he'd had to think hard and
fast whether he wanted joining him or not. Desperate
measures, though, had him going for it.

Not that it had been easy to convince her to join him.
As she'd said, she wasn't a field agent. Not even close.
Her experience in such matters was nil. *And* she had
her commitment to All-Med to honor. The small medical team was administering vaccinations and treating
various ailments of the villagers around Puerto Grande.

He'd had to promise that another volunteer would arrive shortly to replace her before she'd made one single
move toward his Jeep.

She was definitely a woman of contrasts.

When she wasn't pulling some humanitarian aid stint,
she worked the streets of Atlanta as a paramedic, yet
usually talked longingly of the place she'd grown up in:
Wyoming.

And there wasn't a single ring—jeweled or otherwise—on those long, elegant fingers, except the wedding band that had been his mother's.

Usually, he kept it tucked in his wallet. As a reminder
never to get too complacent with life. Too comfortable.
Too settled.

Considering how settled he'd been becoming lately,
maybe it was a timely reminder.

"Do you remember much of Santo Marguerite?"

Her lashes lifted as she gave him a startled look. Just
as quickly, those lush lashes lowered again. She lifted
one shoulder and the crisp fabric of the tunic slipped a
few inches, giving him a better view of the hollow at the
base of that long, lovely throat.

"I remember it a little." She pleated the edge of the

napkin on her lap then leaned forward to retrieve the wineglass that she'd set on the floor. "What do you even know about the place? It no longer exists."

She had a point. What he knew he'd learned from *her* file at Hollins-Winword. The dwellings of the village that had been destroyed were never rebuilt, though Sandoval had been in control of the land for the last few decades, guarding it with the violent zealousness he was known for.

She evidently took his silence as his answer. "Where did *you* grow up?" she asked.

"Here and there." He straightened from his perch and stretched. Talking about her past was one thing. His was off-limits. Even he tried not to think about it. "You figure that bed's strong enough to hold us both?"

Her eyes widened a fraction before she looked away again. "I…I'm used to roughing it in camps and such. I can sleep on the floor."

"Hardly sounds like a wifely thing to do."

She scrunched up the napkin and slid off the bed. "I'm not a wife."

"Shh." There was something wrong with the way he took such pleasure in seeing the dusky color climb into that satin-smooth complexion of hers.

Her lips firmed. "You've already established that these walls don't have ears."

"So I did. Kind of a pity, really. I was looking forward to seeing how well we played mister and missus for the night."

Giving him a frozen look, she polished off the rest of her wine. Then she just stood there, staring at the blank wall ahead of her.

In the candlelight, her hair looked dark as ink against

the pale cloth of her tunic, though he knew in the sunlight, those long gleaming locks were not really black at all, but a deep, lustrous brown.

"Whatcha thinking?"

She didn't look back at him. She folded her arms over her chest. Her fingertips curled around her upper arms and he saw the wink of candlelight catching in the gold wedding band. "I wonder why they don't have windows here."

"Considering the way the weather was blowing out there, that's probably a blessing about now." He watched her back for a moment. The tunic reached well below her hips, and though he'd always had the impression of her being very tall, he knew that it was merely the way she carried herself. Not that she was short, but he had her by a good seven or eight inches. And there, in that tunic and pants, her feet bare, she seemed much less Wonder Woman than usual.

Vulnerable. That was the word.

She looked vulnerable.

It wasn't necessarily a comfortable realization.

"You claustrophobic?"

She stiffened and shot him a suspicious look. "Why?"

"Just curious." Though the walls in the room were probably going to feel mighty closed in the longer they were confined together with that single, narrow bed.

Her hands rubbed up and down her arms. "The electricity here would be from a generator, wouldn't it?"

"I'd think so, though that doesn't explain why it's not running. Maybe they've got concerns with the gas it would take. Why? You cold?"

"Some. You, um, you suppose there's plumbing here?"

He hid a smile. The convent was cloistered, and located in a highly remote location. But it wasn't entirely out of the middle ages. "This is built like a dorm," he said. "I saw the bathroom a floor down."

She dropped her arms, casting him a relieved look. "You did?"

"Probably better facilities here than you had in that hut at Puerto Grande." He reached for the door. "After you, my darling wife."

When they got to the bathroom door, Brody stopped. "Place is built for women," he reminded her. "You'd better go first. Make sure I don't send some poor nun into heart failure."

"I won't be long." She ducked inside.

In his experience, women were forever finding reasons to spend extra time in the bathroom. Lord only knew what they did in there.

But she did open the door again, almost immediately. "All clear." She slipped past him back into the corridor and he went inside.

The halls were still silent when they made their way back up the narrow staircase and to the room. They passed a half-dozen other doors as they went. All closed.

"Where do you suppose the children are?"

He wished that he had a good answer. "We'll find out soon enough."

"I don't understand why you're still feeling so awfully patient, considering your hurry to get up here."

"Honey, I'm not patient. But I am practical."

She stopped. "What's so practical about getting all the way here, with no means of getting back *out* of here?"

"Oh, ye of little faith." He caught a glimpse of swishing black fabric from the corner of his eye.

"Bro—"

He pulled Angeline to him and planted his mouth over hers, cutting off his name.

She gave out a shocked squeak and went ramrod stiff. Her hands found their way to his chest, pushing, and he closed his hands around hers, squeezing them in warning.

She went suddenly soft, and instead of fighting him, she kissed him back.

It took more than a little effort for him to remember the kiss was only for the benefit of the nun, and damned if he didn't feel a few bubbles off center when he managed to drag his mouth from those delectably soft lips and give the sister—Sister Frances, in fact—an embarrassed, Hewitt-type apology.

She tilted her head slightly. "The sacrament of marriage is a blessing, *señor.* There is no need for apology." Her smile took in them both. "You will be comfortable for the night? Is there anything else we can provide for you?"

He kept his hands around Angeline's. "A visit with our children would be nice."

"I'm sorry. The Reverend Mother must return first."

Angeline tugged her hands out of his. "We understand, Sister. But won't you tell them that we're here for them? That we'll be going home just as soon as we can?"

"Of course, *señora.* They will be delighted." She gave them a kind look. "Rest well. The storm will hopefully have passed by morning and Mother will be able to return." She headed down the hall toward the staircase.

Brody tugged Angeline back into their room and closed the door.

The second he did, she turned on him. "You didn't need to do that."

"Do what?"

Her lips parted. She practically sputtered before any actual words came out. "Kiss me."

He slid his hand over her shoulder and lowered his head. "Whatever you say, honey."

She shoved at him, and he stepped back, chuckling. "Relax, Sophia. We have the nun's blessing, remember?"

"Very funny." She put as much distance between them as the small room afforded. "I'm not going to have to remind you that no means *no,* am I?"

He started to laugh, but realized that she was serious. "Lighten up. If I ever get serious about getting you in the sack, you'll know."

"You're impossible."

"Usually," he agreed. He yanked back the cover on the bed, and saw the way she tensed. "And you're acting like some vestal virgin. Relax. You might be the stuff of countless dreams, but I do have *some* control."

Her cheeks weren't just dusky rose now. They were positively red. And her snapping gaze wouldn't meet his as she leaned past him and snatched one of the thin pillows off the mattress. "If you were a gentleman, *you'd* take the floor."

"Babe, I'll be the first one to tell you that I am *not* a gentleman."

"Fine." She tossed the pillow on the floor, and gathered up the top cover from the bed. She flipped it out on the slate by the pillow, and sat down on one edge, drawing the other side over her as she lay down, back toward him.

"You're really going to sleep on the floor."

She twitched the cover up over her shoulder. "Looks that way, doesn't it?"

He didn't know whether to laugh or applaud. "If I

needed a shower despite the one that Mother Nature gave us that badly, you could have just told me."

She didn't respond.

He looked at the bed. A thin beige blanket covered the mattress. The remaining pillow looked even thinner and more Spartan now that its mate was tucked between Angeline's dark head and the cold hard floor.

Brody muttered a mild oath—they *were* in a convent, after all, and even he didn't believe in taunting fate quite that much—and grabbed the pillow and blanket from the bed and tossed them down on the ground.

She twisted her head around. "What are you doing now?"

"Evidently being shamed into sleeping on this god-forsa—blessed floor." He flipped out the blanket and lowered himself onto it. Sad to say, but nearly every muscle inside him protested the motion. He was in pretty decent shape, but climbing the mountain hadn't exactly been a picnic.

"You don't *have* any shame," she countered.

He made a point of turning his back on her as he lay down, scrunching the pillow beneath his head. The area of floor was significantly narrow, but not so narrow that he couldn't have kept his back from touching hers if he'd so chosen.

He didn't choose.

So much for trying to convince the higher powers that he was entirely decent.

She shifted ever so subtly away from him, until he couldn't feel the warmth of her lithe form against him. He rolled onto his back, closing the gap again.

She huffed a little, then sat up and pushed at him to

move over. When he didn't, she scrambled to her feet and stepped over him, reaching back for her bedding.

"Where are you going?" He rolled back onto his side and propped his head on his hand, watching her interestedly.

"Away from *you*," she assured. She flung the cover around her shoulders like an oversized shawl and climbed onto the bed. "When lightning strikes you down, I don't want to be anywhere near."

Brody smiled faintly. "That's good, because I was beginning to think you were afraid of sleeping with little ol' me."

She huffed. "Please. There is *nothing* little about you."

"Babe. I'm flattered."

She gave him a baleful look that made him want to smile even more. "You know they say the larger the ego, the smaller the, um—"

"Id?" he supplied innocently.

She huffed again and threw herself down on the pillow. "Blow out the candles."

"I thought you'd never ask." He got up and did so, turning the small, cozily lit room into one that was dark as pitch.

She was silent. So silent he couldn't even hear her breathe.

"You all right?"

"It's *really* dark."

He wondered how hard it had been for Angeline to admit that. She damn sure wouldn't appreciate him noticing the hint of vulnerability in her smooth, cool voice.

Two steps to his right and he reached the dresser. The small tin of matches was next to the pitcher and bowl and he found that easily, too. A scrape of the match against the wall, a spit of a spark, the flare of sulfur, and the tiny flame seemed to light up the place again. "I can leave one of the candles lit."

"You said you weren't a gentleman."

He set the flame to one of the candles and shook out the match. "I'm not," he assured.

"Then stop acting like one, because now I *have* to give you room on this bed, too." She moved on the mattress, and the iron frame squeaked softly. She groaned and covered her face with her hand.

He laughed softly. "It's just a few squeaky springs. I doubt any of the good sisters are holding glasses against these thick walls hoping for a listen. You act like you've never shared a bed with a guy before."

She didn't move. Not just that she was still, but that she *really* didn't move.

And for a guy who'd generally considered himself quick on the uptake, he realized that this time he'd been mighty damn slow. "Ah. I…see." Though he didn't. Not really. She was twenty-nine years old. How did a woman—a woman who looked like her, yet, with her intelligence, her caring, her…everything—how the hell did she get to be that age and never sleep with a guy?

"Why are you still—why haven't you ever—oh, hell." Disgruntled more at himself than at her, he scraped his hand down his face. "Forget it. It's none of my business."

"No," she agreed. "It's not. Now, are you going to sleep on the bed or not?"

He snatched up the pillow from the floor and tossed it beside her.

She's a virgin. The thought—more like a taunt—kept circling inside his head. Probably what he got for catching a glimpse of that sexy underwear of hers when he'd promised not to look.

He lay down next to her, and the iron bed gave a raucous groan.

"Not one word," she whispered fiercely.

That worked just fine for him.

Chapter Four

Angeline didn't expect to sleep well.

She knew she'd *sleep,* simply because she'd learned long ago to sleep when the opportunity presented itself. And even though Brody's long body was lying next to hers, his weight indenting the mattress just enough that the only way she could keep from rolling toward him was to hang on to the opposite edge of the mattress, she figured she would still manage to catch some z's.

What she didn't expect, however, was to sleep soundly enough, deeply enough, to miss Brody *leaving* the bed.

Or to find that someone had filled the pitcher on the dresser and laid out a freshly folded hand towel on the dresser top.

Okay. So she'd *really* slept soundly.

Not so unusual, she reasoned, as she dashed chilly

water over her face and pressed the towel to her cheeks. Making that climb in the storm had been exhausting.

Or maybe you're more comfortable with Brody than you'd like to admit.

She turned and went out of the room, leaving that annoying voice behind.

As before, the corridor was empty, still lit by candles in the sconces. She went down the stairs, visited the long, vaguely industrial-like restroom and then went searching.

But when she reached the ground floor without encountering the impossible-to-miss dining hall, she knew she'd taken a wrong turn somewhere along the way.

Annoyed with herself, she turned on her heel, intending to head back and make another pass at it, but a muffled sound stopped her in her tracks.

Footsteps?

Nervousness charged through her veins and she tried to shake it off. She was in a convent, for pity's sake. What harm could come to them there?

Even if the nuns realized the identity fraud they were perpetrating, what would they be likely to do about it, other than call the authorities, or kick them out into the storm? It wasn't as if they'd put them in chains in a dungeon.

Nevertheless, Angeline still looked around warily, trying to get her bearings. She went over to the nearest window, but it was too far above her head. She couldn't see out even when she tried to jump up and catch the narrow sill with her fingers. So she stood still, pressing a hand to her thumping heart, willing it to quiet as she listened for another sound, another brush of feet, a swish of long black robes.

But all she heard now was silence. She was listening

so hard that when melodious bells began chiming, she very nearly jumped out of her skin.

She leaned back against the roughly textured wall and waited for the chiming to end.

"If you're praying, there's a chapel within spitting distance."

Her heart seemed to seize up for the eternal moment it took to recognize the deep male voice.

She opened her eyes and looked at Brody. She came from a family of tall, generally oversized men, much like Brody. And she was used to the odd quietness with which most of them moved. But Brody seemed to take that particular skill to an entirely new level. "It's a good thing my heart is healthy," she told him tartly, "because you could give a person a heart attack the way you sneak around!"

"Who needs to sneak?"

"Evidently *you* do," she returned in the same quiet whisper he was using.

Despite the wrinkles in his gender-neutral tunic and pants, he looked revoltingly fresh, particularly compared to the rode-hard-and-put-up-wet way that she felt.

"Did you know you pretty much sleep like the dead?"

She wasn't going to argue the point with him when ordinarily, as a result of her paramedic training, she was quite a light sleeper. "What are you doing sneaking around? Do you know what time it is?"

"It's almost 3:00 a.m. And what are *you* doing sneaking around? I've been trying to find you for ten minutes."

"I needed the restroom," she whispered. A portion of the truth at least.

He cocked his head. "You got your boots on. Good." He closed his long fingers around her wrist and started walking along the hallway, sticking his head through doorways as he went. "While you were dreaming of handsome princes, I was scoping out this place. Hard to believe, but the fine sisters have an interesting collection of vehicles."

Her stomach clenched. "You'll ask to borrow one?"

Despite the dim lighting, she could tell that his expression didn't change one iota.

She swallowed a groan. "We can't steal one of their cars," she said under her breath.

"Babe." He sounded wounded. "Steal is a harsh word." He stopped short and she nearly bumped into him. "I like *borrow* better."

"That only works when you intend to ask permission to do so," she pointed out the obvious.

"Details. You're always getting hung up on details." He reached up and plucked a candle out of one of the sconces, then pulled open the door beside him and nudged her through. "I wanna move fast, but we've gotta stay quiet. Think you can manage that?"

Her lips parted. "Yes, I can be quiet," she assured, a little more loudly than she ought.

He raised his eyebrows and she pressed her lips together, miming the turning of a key next to them.

His lips quirked. "Good girl."

The spurt of nervousness she'd felt before was nothing compared to the way she felt now as Brody drew her through the doorway. He stopped long enough to hold the door as it closed without a sound.

After tramping down a warren of alarmingly narrow halls, the tile floor gave way to hard-packed dirt.

She swallowed again, feeling like they were heading down into the bowels of the mountain. "Did you sleep at *all?* How long did it take you to discover this rat maze? Do you even know where we're going?"

He paused again, letting her catch up, and the candle flame stopped the wild dance of light it cast on the walls. "Yeah, I slept enough. And yeah, I know where we're going. Don't you trust me? We're going to get the kids and get the hell outta Dodge while the going's good."

"But what about your big first-things-first speech?"

"You slept some, didn't you?" His voice was light. "And ate."

She pressed her lips together, determined not to argue. "Your sudden rush just surprised me," she finally managed stiffly.

"Well, along with their various vehicles," he said in such a reasonable tone that she felt like smacking him, "the fine sisters here have a satellite phone system. Hardly the kind of thing one would expect, but hey. Maybe one of the local politicians figures he's buying his way into heaven or something. Anyway, I checked with my handler. The Stanleys have been moved again. And despite the weather, the Mother Superior has found a guide to get her back to her flock. She's supposed to be here shortly after sunup."

"A guide," Angeline echoed. Her irritation dissolved. "What kind of guide?"

"The kind who won't let a washed-out road get in his way."

"You don't think it's that Rico person who searched Sophia and Hewitt's place?"

His gaze didn't waver.

Dismay congealed inside her stomach. "This is a nightmare."

"Nah. Could be worse. Way worse," he assured.

She looked over her shoulder in the direction from which they'd come. What was worse? Going forward or going back? Either way, she really, *really* wanted to get out of this narrow, closed-in tunnel. She looked back at him only to encounter the look he was giving her—sharp eyed *despite* the gloom. *"What?"*

"You tell me. What's bothering you?"

Aside from the entire situation? She moistened her lips. "I, um, I just don't much care for tunnels."

He held the candle above his head, looking up. Then he moved the candle to one side. And the other.

She knew what he was looking at. The ceiling overhead was stucco. The walls on either side of them were stuccoed, as well. And though the floor was dirt, it wasn't as if it were the kind of dirt that had been on the road where the Jeep had gotten stuck. Her boots had encountered no ruts. It seemed perfectly smooth, perfectly compacted.

Not *exactly* a tunnel.

She knew that's what Brody was thinking.

But "We're almost there," was all he said. "Think you can stand it for another couple minutes?"

Pride lifted her chin if nothing else would. This was part of St. Agnes, not a culvert running beneath the city of Atlanta. "Of course."

He didn't smile. Just gave a single nod and turned forward again.

His simple acceptance of her assurance went considerably further than if he'd taken her hand and drawn her along with him like some frightened child. She focused on watching *him,* rather than the confining space, as they continued their brisk pace.

As he'd promised, it was only a few minutes—if

that—before she followed Brody around another corner, up several iron stairs and out into the dark, wet air. A vine-twined trellis overhead kept the drizzling rain from hitting them, though Angeline shivered as the air penetrated her clothes.

Thunder was a steady roll, punctuated by the brilliant flicker of lightning.

She got a quick impression of hedges and rows of plants. The convent's garden? Surely there would have been an easier route to take.

It was then that Brody took her hand in his, lacing his fingers through hers.

She looked up at him, surprise shooting through her.

"Remember, Sophia," he murmured softly, and squeezed her hand. "Falling waters."

She nodded, and right before her very eyes, Brody's expression changed. His shoulders seemed to shrink, and it was as if he no longer towered over her. He even pulled a pair of wire-rimmed glasses from somewhere and stuck them on his face.

Clearly, he wanted to be prepared in case they were discovered.

She wondered suddenly if he had his gun tucked beneath the wrinkled tunic.

Then he drew her from beneath the awning and they dashed across the thick, wet grass toward the building wing on the far side of the garden. They went in through a narrow door, up a flight of stairs and then Brody stopped next to a door. He pushed it open quietly, and pulled her inside.

The room was nearly identical to the one she and Brody had been given, only here, two narrow beds had been pushed against the walls. Small forms were visible beneath the white blankets.

"Let's get her first." Brody nodded toward the bed with the slightly larger hump beneath the covers. He tucked the candle against the basin and pitcher on the dresser and headed to the bed on the right. He touched the covered mound. "Eva—" his voice was soft "—come on, kiddo, rise and shine."

The girl mumbled and shifted, dragging the blanket nearly over her head.

Brody tried again.

This time, the dark head lifted. But at the sight of the strangers, she sucked in a hard breath and opened her mouth.

"Shh." Brody covered her mouth with his hand. "It's okay. Don't scream."

The girl tried scrambling away from Brody, but he held her fast.

"We're here for your parents," Angeline whispered, aching for the child. "Falling waters, right?" She knew from the pictures that Brody had showed her that the girl was pretty with the petite, refined features of her father and the coloring of her mother. But now, in the dark room above the hand Brody still held over her mouth, her eyes were nothing but wide pools of fear.

At the code the Stanleys had instituted, however, the girl's resistance began to ebb.

Angeline knelt beside the bed, closing her hands gently over the fists Eva had made around the edge of the blanket, and willed the girl to trust them.

"Everything is fine," she promised. "Just fine. We're going to take you to your parents just as soon as we can."

She prayed that would come to pass. That the team sent to rescue them would be successful.

Eva slowly blinked.

"You need to stay quiet," Brody told her. "Can you do that?"

Again, she blinked. Finally, she gave a faint nod, and Brody gingerly pulled back his hand.

"Who are you?" Eva's whisper shook.

"He's Brody. I'm Angeline. We're…friends of your parents."

"But Sister Frances told us that our parents were already *here*." She knuckled her eyes. "But she wouldn't let us see them. Davey cried."

"*They* aren't actually here," Angeline explained awkwardly. "We, um, we used your parents' names."

Eva drew her eyebrows together. "But—"

"I need you to wake your brother up," Brody interrupted. He'd moved away from the bed and began silently pulling open dresser drawers. "So he's not so frightened." He pulled out several items of clothing and tossed them onto the bed beside the girl. "Do you two have hiking boots or anything? What about a suitcase?"

She nodded warily. "Under the bed."

Brody dropped down and retrieved the boots. He took one look at the unwieldy suitcase and pushed it back beneath the bed. "Thank God for pillowcases," he muttered, and plucked one of the pillows from behind Eva. He yanked the case off and shoved the clothing inside.

"My parents were working in the tepuis. Why didn't they come themselves? And why did you lie to the sisters?" Eva might only be nine, but she certainly knew how to speak her mind.

"They're still working," Angeline assured, lying right

through her teeth and hating every moment of it. She squeezed Eva's fists. "Come on now. Let's get Davey awake."

Eva pushed back the blankets and slid off the bed. The hem of her long nightgown settled around her bare feet as she crossed to the other bed and sat down beside her brother. "Davey." She jiggled him. "Wake up." Her attention hardly left Brody, though, as he moved back to the dresser and found some more items to add to the pillowcase.

Davey sat up, looking bleary-eyed. However, at the sight of two strangers—who definitely weren't the nuns he was used to—he practically buried his head against his sister's side.

Even though he was more than half her size, Eva pulled him onto her lap, circling her arms around him protectively. "Mom and Daddy aren't here, after all," she told him. "But they want us to go home."

Angeline could have applauded. The child was showing much more adaptability than Angeline felt.

"In the dark?" Davey asked. He was as blond as his sister was dark, though from the pictures, Angeline knew his eyes were the same deep brown. "How come?"

Angeline sent a beseeching look toward Brody. He ignored it as he pushed his latest handful of clothing into the pillowcase and crouched next to the bed.

She stifled a sigh and tried to find an explanation that wouldn't scare the children any more than they already were. "You know that we're here for your parents, but Reverend Mother doesn't know that. She only knows that your folks left you in her care, and she's not to release you to anyone *but* your parents. And that's why we told them we were them."

"So, just tell the truth," Eva said.

Davey weighed in. "Mama says to always tell the truth."

"Mama is right," Angeline said. She looked at Brody. "They need to know."

"No. They really don't. But we've gotta move now."

Angeline crouched in front of Eva. "I know this is probably scary for you and your brother. But it's very important that we leave quickly."

Eva's arms tightened around her brother. "My mom and dad are in trouble, aren't they. That's why you're here."

"They're going to be fine," Brody said with enough calm assurance that even Angeline felt inclined to believe him. "But they need us to get you to a safer place than here."

Eva's eyes widened. "But—"

"We'll talk more on the way," Angeline promised. She ran her hand down the girl's arm. "For now, though, we need to listen to Brody."

"We're not s'posed to talk to strangers," Davey whispered loudly.

"Right," Angeline said quickly. "And you remember that. But we're not quite strangers, are we? Your—your mom and dad, they told us what to tell you so you'd know that."

"Falling waters," Davey said. "'Cause they al-ays wanna take us to see Angel Falls." He named the world's tallest waterfall.

"I think we should stay here," Eva said warily. "With the sisters. Then—"

"We need to get off the mountain before morning,"

Brody said quietly. "Which means we have to go now. Right now."

A very large tear slowly rolled down Eva's cheek. "They're dead, aren't they. They fell off the mountain they were climbing or something."

"Oh, honey. No." Angeline shook her head. "Of course not."

Brody muffled an oath and suddenly plucked Davey off Eva's lap. The boy went even wider-eyed. "Think of this as an adventure," he told the child. "You can be Peter Pan. He was always my favorite. Had his sword. Could even fly."

Angeline knew that Brody's cases usually involved children, but she was nevertheless surprised with the competent way he began stuffing the boy's feet into socks and boots as he began extolling the exciting virtues of Pan as if he really had been his favorite.

And Davey was soaking it all up like a sponge.

"They're not dead?" Eva's voice was choked.

Angeline couldn't help herself. She pulled the girl close, hugging her. "Of course not."

Another set of bells began ringing, and they both jerked, startled at the sound. "That's the four o'clock bell," Eva said. "The sisters will get up for prayers before they fix breakfast."

Brody's eyes met Angeline's. He dropped a piece of paper on Eva's vacated bed. "Just get her boots on," he muttered. "And hurry up about it."

Angeline quickly helped Eva pull on the boots. Then she tugged the sweatshirt Brody tossed her over the girl's head, right on top of the long flannel nightie.

"She's a funny looking Tinkerbell," Davey said, giggling.

Angeline figured that was much better than crying.

Brody tossed the bulging pillowcase to Angeline, blew out the candle and opened the door, cautiously looking out. A moment later, they were hurrying down the hall.

The bells fell silent and almost simultaneously, a dozen doors along the corridor opened.

Angeline held her breath and Brody muttered an oath.

No *wonder* he'd taken such a circuitous route to the children's room.

It was smack in the middle of nun central.

"You said a bad word," Davey piped out clearly.

And Brody said quite a few more as he grabbed Eva off her feet, too. Angeline ran after him as they disappeared down the narrow back staircase and out into the drizzle before any of the nuns spotted them.

Chapter Five

The "interesting collection" of vehicles evidently included a Hummer.

Stalwart and sturdy looking where it sat parked on the other side of the garden.

And though Angeline kept expecting someone to come racing after them across the wet grass, taking them to task for not waiting for the Mother Superior's all clear, no one did.

She supposed that Brody didn't waste time on such concerns. He certainly didn't waste time on manners when they reached the vehicle. He dumped the kids inside through the rear door, leaving Angeline to manage for herself, and he had the engine running by the time she made it around to the passenger's side.

"Buckle up." He didn't wait to make sure they obeyed

before he put the vehicle in gear and slid around in an uneven circle.

"Hold on," he warned, heading straight for a stand of bushes. "This ain't gonna be a smooth ride."

"That's an understatement," Angeline gasped moments later as the vehicle began rocking violently downward. Her head banged the window beside her, and she couldn't tell if they were on the road or not.

Another sharp drop and both Davey and Eva cried out. "We're flying," Davey hooted. "And we don't got no pixie dust even!"

"Seems like it," Brody agreed.

Angeline closed her eyes.

"What're you praying?" Brody's voice was almost as exhilarated as Davey's, and he didn't have the excuse of being four years old and innocent.

"I'm asking forgiveness for *borrowing* this vehicle and…and…oh—" her head knocked the side window again "—and taking the kids the way we did."

"I left the sisters a note. I said someone from All-Med would return the vehicle."

Angeline gaped at him. Now he was pulling the volunteer crew in on this? "But, but that means we'll have to stop in Puerto Grande."

"Just long enough for you to fill in Dr. Chavez about getting the truck back to the convent. Believe me, we won't be staying long, and we won't be doing any rounds of visiting. There's no guarantee that our pal Rico won't have ears around."

"What if Miguel doesn't *want* to help? You know, he and the team are plenty busy without—"

"He will."

If only *she* felt as much certainty as Brody exhibited oh so easily. A tree branch slapped against the windshield and she winced. The windshield wipers were slapping away as much flying mud as rain as they hurtled down the mountain.

He'd said he wanted to get the children out of Venezuela. That wasn't going to happen on foot. "If, um, we leave the Hummer in Puerto Grande, what are we going to use as transportation then?"

"Miguel's got an SUV, doesn't he?"

She frowned. "*All-Med* has an SUV."

"And Miguel Chavez—" he broke off, cursing under his breath as they began sliding sideways. He spun the wheel, the vehicle jerked, smacked another bush straight on and continued downward again. "Like I was saying, Miguel Chavez is the head of All-Med's team. Same difference."

Not exactly. All-Med had a dozen teams that were assigned a dozen different locations.

"You're making my head hurt," she muttered.

He just grinned, and they continued bucking their way over the treacherous terrain.

The sky had begun to lighten when she finally saw from a distance their Jeep. The river of mud had climbed even higher since they'd abandoned it, and the empty vehicle listed to one side.

She swallowed a wave of nausea. If they had tried to walk back to Puerto Grande as she'd wanted, they'd have been on the road that was now fully flooded.

"Guess we won't be going that way," Brody said, clearly seeing the same thing she was.

"And neither will the Reverend Mother," Angeline

pointed out. "There's no way she and her *guide* could get up the road again."

"I imagine a creative person would find a means," he countered.

Goodness knows Brody had.

Nothing like the creativity of *stealing* a Hummer from a bunch of nuns.

She pressed her fingertips to her eyes.

What she wouldn't give to be sitting in a coffee shop about now, doing her *regular* kind of work for Hollins-Winword.

But no, she'd had to spend her two weeks of vacation pulling another stint with All-Med.

"How'd you even find me in Puerto Grande?"

Brody had turned away from the teeming mud flow and, if her sense of direction hadn't gone completely out the window, was heading west, away from the river where the village was located.

"I told you, babe. The agency keeps track of its assets."

Right. He had. She pinched the bridge of her nose, willing away the pain that was centered there.

"You were the closest one they could find for me in a pinch," he added. His lips twitched. "Bet it makes you want to sing for joy, doesn't it?"

She wondered what he'd have done if the nearest Hollins-Winword agent had been a grizzly-looking man. Probably have come up with some other impossible plan.

"You didn't tell us why we have to go somewhere safer," Eva reminded.

The pain in Angeline's head just got worse. She lifted her brows when Brody gave her a look, as if she ought to answer. "You're the expert in these situations."

He looked about as thrilled as she felt.

But he pulled the vehicle to a stop and slung his arm over the seat, looking back at the children. "Because there's a guy—not a nice one—who wants something from your parents and *they* wanted to make sure he didn't come bothering you two at the convent before they could get back. So they asked for us to help them."

Eva swallowed. "What does he want?"

"Some of your dad's research. But that's not going to happen. So all you two need to do is stick with us. We're going to go back to the United States, and then your parents will come to meet you there. But until then, that whole talking to strangers thing? That still goes. Got it?"

Looking scared out of her wits, the girl nodded.

Davey tugged at Eva's arm, whispering something in her ear. "He has to go to the bathroom," she relayed.

Brody raked his fingers through his hair. "Anyone else?"

Eva shook her head.

Angeline felt her face flush a little as Brody looked to her. "No."

"All right, then." Leaving the vehicle running, he climbed out and opened the back door for Davey. "Us men, we got it easy," he said to the boy, who looked pretty amazed at being referred to as a man.

Eva didn't speak until after Brody closed the door and headed away with Davey. "Are you guys married?"

"What?" Angeline looked back at Eva, surprised. The wedding ring on her finger seemed to grow warm. "Oh. No. No, no. We just…work together."

Eva plucked at the nightgown hanging down below her sweatshirt. "The rain got me all wet."

"We'll get you both dried and changed when we stop in Puerto Grande." She hoped that wasn't another promise she might not be able to back up. "It looked like Brody grabbed plenty of your clothing."

"I think he's nice."

Angeline pressed her lips together and she watched Brody lead young Davey off to the side out of their eyesight. "Yes," she said after a moment. "I think you might be right."

Getting to Puerto Grande proved almost as harrowing as getting off the convent's mountain. Particularly when the rain picked up again, gaining almost as much force as it had shown the previous day.

Washed out as it was, they couldn't take the main road. So Brody put the Hummer through some severe paces, carving out their own road, until finally, what seemed hours later, they came upon the small village.

It was comprised mostly of thatched huts, some stilted, clustered along a riverside that was lush with vegetation. Right now, the trees and bushes were swaying madly in the wind, while the river pushed well beyond its banks.

Angeline felt numb surveying the damage as Brody plowed the vehicle through the mud, keeping to higher ground as much as he could in order to reach the shack that All-Med was using.

When they finally made it, Brody pulled to a stop beside an SUV parked behind the shack. The vehicle was covered in mud and was considerably smaller than the one they'd appropriated from the nuns. "If it weren't pouring, I'd have had you leave me with the kids back by the river while you finagled Chavez out of his SUV. Now we're going to have to chance someone seeing the kids."

Angeline still didn't know how she was going to explain the situation to Miguel. She held none of Brody's confidence that the doctor who headed the team would simply hand over his keys to her. He'd been unhappy enough when she'd abandoned the camp the day before.

"You'd better get moving," Brody suggested blandly. "Just tell the guy you've still got an emergency in Caracas, but you need to borrow his truck to get you there."

"Sure. Make it sound easy." She pushed open the door and, ducking her head against the rain, jogged across the rutted ground toward the shack.

She untied the flap of heavy canvas that served as a door and dashed her long sleeve over her forehead before slipping inside, refastening the flap after her.

The shack had three rooms, shotgun style, that not only served as All-Med's temporary clinic, but their sleeping quarters, as well, and she headed through to the very rear section.

"Hey there," she greeted, striving for nonchalance and surely failing miserably. "Look what the wind blew in."

Obviously startled by her appearance, Robert Smythe dropped the cards he was dealing at an ancient folding table. Maria Chavez hopped up from the folding chair on the other side of the table. "Angel! Good heavens, girl, you look like you've been swimming in the river. You and your friend surely haven't made it to Caracas and back, already?"

Along with her doctor husband, Miguel, Maria was in charge of the team. She was lithe and dark haired with skin the color of cream and caramel and, with a decade on Angeline in years, she could have been an even closer "double" for Sophia Stanley.

"No. The storm stopped us." She smiled faintly at the thin blonde girl who made up the third at the table. The replacement Brody had promised?

"Did you at least have some shelter last night?" Maria asked.

"Yeah." Hoping that her lies weren't too transparent, she busied herself with the pile of linens that were stacked on one of the upturned milk crates and picked a towel from the stack. "A local family—I didn't know them— took us in for the night. We, um, we borrowed their truck to get back here."

Maria looked past Angeline, as if she expected to see the man who Angeline had left with the day before.

"Brody's waiting for me in the truck," Angeline said quickly, only to wish that she'd come up with some other name for him.

Evidently, his paranoia was rubbing off on her.

She wrapped the towel around her shoulders and flipped her hair over the top of it. "It's pretty wet out there. Wet enough to keep the visitors away, I see." They'd seen at least a hundred villages despite the weather be- fore Angeline had gone off with Brody.

"A lot of them are heading inland for higher ground." Robert deftly gathered together the cards again. "Should probably introduce you to Persia." He nodded toward the blonde. "She arrived yesterday evening."

Definitely the replacement that Brody had promised. Was this slip of a girl another Hollins-Winword asset? The newcomer looked as if she wasn't even out of her teens.

She crossed the room, her hand out. "Angeline Clay. Nice to meet you."

The girl's handshake was firm. "Persia Newman. I was sorry to hear about your friend's accident. I assume you came back to pick up your stuff?" Persia's gaze stayed steady on Angeline's face.

"Uh, yes. Right. My stuff."

The girl nodded. "I thought so. I hope you don't mind, but since I was using your cot, anyway, I took the liberty of packing up your duffel. You know. Just in case you had to grab it and run."

"Miguel thought we'd maybe have to try running it up to you in Caracas," Maria added. "You'll certainly need your passport along the way."

They were so helpful that Angeline wanted to crawl through the wood floor. "Thanks." She watched Persia move into the center room that housed the cots that made up their sleeping quarters. "So, Maria, what's the plan for the team? Are you still going to head for Los Llanos when you're finished here?"

Maria shook her head. "The plains are flooding too badly. We hear most of the roads are already underwater. Instead, we'll work our way along the coast until we end up in Puerto La Cruz." She named the popular tourist hub. "After that, we'll wait for All-Med to determine where we're best needed. This storm is going to cause some major damage, I fear." She lifted her hand. "But you don't worry about that. You just get yourself to Caracas and tend to your friend there."

Angeline moistened her lips and swallowed. Maria and Miguel and the rest were *used* to rolling with the punches and she had to think about the safety of the Stanley family. But that didn't make lying to this woman whom she considered a friend any easier. "Yes, well. About that."

Persia returned with Angeline's battered blue duffel bag. "You're good to go. Passport is in the zippered pocket inside."

"Thanks."

"How are you even getting there?"

Young she might be, but Persia Newman was definitely better at subterfuge than Angeline was. "Actually, that's another reason we came back. The, um, vehicle we borrowed belongs to the convent at St. Agnes."

Maria's eyebrows shot up. "How on earth did you get it?"

"The family we stayed with last night. Anyway, we—Brody and I—" she almost winced at saying his name yet again "—said we'd try to see that it gets returned for them to the convent, so they wouldn't have to do it themselves."

"Robert and I could drive it there," Persia offered, looking impossibly enthusiastic. "Once the weather clears a little, that is." She looked toward Maria. "You and the doctor could spare us for a few hours, right?"

"Of course." Maria readily agreed. "But that still doesn't solve Angeline's problem of getting to Caracas."

"She will take the Rover, of course." Miguel himself walked into the room, dashing his hand over his wet black hair. "I was out visiting the Zamoras. They even sold their Jeep, evidently, to add to Brisa's college fund." He didn't skip a beat, jumping back to his original topic. "The keys are already in it, as usual. The Rover, that is. Why didn't you tell me that your emergency was so serious?"

"I—"

"I saw your friend, Brody, waiting outside. He told me your college friend in Caracas may not survive." Miguel dropped his hand on Angeline's shoulder. "We will all pray for her, *niña.*"

Miguel had seen Brody, obviously.

But what about the children? It didn't seem as if he'd seen *them*.

"Here." Persia pushed the duffel into Angeline's hands,

as well as a canvas bag of food. "You'll need something to eat along the way."

Angeline eyed the loaves of bread, fresh fruit and the tall steel thermos that filled the bag. It just reminded her that it had been quite some time since she'd supped with Brody the night before. "But what will you guys do without the Rover?"

Manuel smiled easily. "You just leave the Rover at the All-Med office in Caracas. They'll arrange to get it back to us."

"I—I don't know what to say. Thank you."

"Angeline."

She whirled. Brody stood just inside the canvas flap. "Yes?"

"We should hurry."

"Yes." Maria began pushing Angeline toward the front of the shack where Brody waited. "We will work together again, my friend. For now, you take care of what you need."

She returned Maria's fast hug, handed back the towel and once again found herself dashing through the rain, Brody by her side.

It was beginning to feel oddly comfortable.

Chapter Six

The kids, it turned out, had been stowed by Brody out of sight inside the Rover before he'd approached the shack. Now, Eva and Davey stayed huddled down beneath a blanket as Brody took the wheel and headed away, and they didn't come out until they'd left the village of Puerto Grande entirely behind.

Brody didn't worry about finding an out-of-the-way route to Caracas. The weather was so awful that there was hardly any other traffic for them to encounter anyway, so he kept to one of the main—marginally safer—roads as they headed north.

In the backseat, Eva and Davey managed to change into some of the dry clothes that Brody had brought. Then Angeline divvied out the food, and they all took turns drinking the hot soup that filled the thermos.

And showing the resilience of youth, it was only a few

hours before Eva and Davey were hunched against each other in the backseat, sound asleep.

"You should sleep, too," Brody told her when he handed her back the empty thermos lid that they'd used as a cup. She'd already tipped the last of the soup into it, assuring him that he should finish it off.

"You had even less sleep last night than I did." She was tired, but her nerves were still in such high gear that she couldn't have slept if her life depended on it. "I'm used to short nights, anyway."

"Work the late shift in Atlanta a lot?"

She tilted her head back against the headrest. "I'm surprised you don't already know."

He slanted her a look. "Turns out there are a *few* things I didn't know about you."

Her cheeks warmed. Naturally he wasn't going to let her forget his discovery the night before.

That would hardly be Brody's style.

Of course, she hadn't thought it would be his style to play the Peter Pan card in order to keep a little boy from becoming too frightened, either.

"So, talk to me." Brody's attention was square on the road ahead of them once again. "Keep me awake, because that soup is trying to do a number on me."

"Talk about what?" she asked warily.

"Anything. What took you to Georgia in the first place."

She folded her hands together in her lap, surprised even more by his unexpected retreat from a topic that could have given him plenty of entertainment.

She wasn't ashamed of her virginity, but at her age it wasn't necessarily something she felt the need to explain, and she definitely didn't like it being the subject of amusement for someone.

"J.D. moved there first, actually," she said, not bothering to explain that J.D. was her sister when he undoubtedly already knew.

"She's the horsey one. And your brother, Casey, is the bookworm."

Despite herself, she felt a smile tug at her lips at the aptly brief descriptions. Neither sibling was hers by blood, but that hadn't kept her and J.D. from being thick as thieves. The two of them were as different as night and day, and she wasn't only Angeline's sister, she was her best friend. "Casey's finishing his graduate degree in literature—and women," she added wryly. "And J.D. is a trainer on a horse farm in Georgia."

"But she trains Thoroughbreds for racing. Kind of a departure from the whole cattle-herding thing your family does in Wyoming, isn't it?"

"She could train cutting horses just as happily. Doesn't matter to J.D., as long as she's got her beloved equines. Anyway, I followed her to Atlanta about a year after she went there."

"You were already an EMT."

She nodded. "In Casper. I got my paramedic license in Atlanta, though." She worked long hours, and when she wasn't, she was studying, taking other classes and generally trying to decide just what she ought to be doing with her life.

"I imagine Atlanta is a whole different ball game in the medical emergency biz."

"Busier, maybe," Angeline said smoothly. She didn't really want to talk about her work. One of the reasons she'd chosen to spend her vacation time with All-Med was to get entirely away from it.

"So what are you *not* saying?"

"I don't know what you mean," she lied. Since he'd found her in Puerto Grande, she'd been doing a lot of that.

She pushed back her hair, only to have her fingers get caught in the tangles. Nothing like a reminder that she probably looked like the Wicked Witch of the West. And she couldn't easily reach her duffel at the moment, where, presumably, Persia had packed her meager toiletries, because Brody had stowed it in the very rear of the vehicle.

"Yeah, right," he drawled. "Fine. Keep it to yourself. For now."

Her fingers were useless with her hair. "What are we going to do once we get to Caracas?" Focusing on the situation at hand was infinitely more appealing than thinking about Atlanta.

"We're going to get out of the country as unnoticeably as we can."

"By flying? Aside from the storm, which I would think would make that sort of difficult, we don't even have the kids' passports." She certainly hadn't noticed him adding the items when he'd filled the pillowcase with the kids' clothing.

"Yes, we do," he corrected smoothly. "I…appropriated them when I found that satellite phone. They were stored in the desk there."

She had an instant image of him rifling through the Mother Superior's desk and wondered what sort of karmic punishment *that* would deserve.

Endless rain upon an entire country?

"But it doesn't matter," he went on, oblivious to her thoughts. "Can't use them through Customs anyway, because our movements could be traced. At this point we can only hope the sisters at St. Agnes bought our charade. Otherwise they could report us for taking the kids just as much as they could for us borrowing the Hummer. And even if *they* don't send up a hue and cry, it's damn sure that Rico will be watching for any sight of them when he realizes they're *not* at the convent. Which means using the international airport is not even a consideration."

"So we're going to leave the country illegally."

"Creatively," he countered. "Don't let it shock that good-girl head of yours too badly. We're not doing anything immoral. It's not as if we're running drugs or something."

She knew that. But still…. "It just seems like Hollins-Winword should be able to find more official means to get us back to the States."

The corner of his lips lifted and she realized with a start that she was actually beginning to get used to his beard and mustache. "I thought it was only your cousin Sarah who was naive about Hollins-Winword."

"Sarah's not naive," she defended. Her cousin had one of the kindest hearts she knew and was, first and foremost, an elementary school teacher. Learning last November that she'd also been pulling a stint with Hollins-Winword had come as a big surprise. Angeline had been hard pressed not to let slip what *her* work with them involved.

Her family already worried enough about her and J.D. off in Atlanta and away from the bosom of Wyoming. Add into that her cousin Ryan, who was in the Navy and had been missing now for the better part of a year, and the Clays had way more than enough concerns. She wanted to add to that with the truth about her courier sideline about as much as she wanted to beat herself with a stick.

As it was, she was hoping that this current insanity with Brody would be resolved before her vacation was up.

Nobody back home would ever be the wiser.

Brody was snorting softly. "Sarah might set up safe houses now and then, but she definitely puts a kinder face on the powers that be than I would."

Angeline pulled the last apple out of the canvas bag. "Considering that it was those same 'powers that be' who have helped to arrange her and Max adopting Megan— the girl *you* were protecting in Weaver last November— I'd have to say that my cousin seems more on the mark than you."

He'd pulled out a pocket knife earlier so she could use it to cut the apples for the kids, and she flipped the wicked blade open again, deftly slicing the fruit in quarters.

"Yeah, well, said powers don't make a habit of it." His voice went flat.

She leaned across the narrow console separating their seats and held a piece of apple up for him.

Instead of taking it from her fingers, though, he just leaned forward and grabbed it with his strong white teeth, biting off half.

She swallowed and sat back in her seat, the remaining wedge of apple still in her fingers. "We, uh, we're just going to have to agree to disagree. If it weren't for Hollins-Winword and Coleman Black, in particular—" she named the man who'd been at the helm of the underground agency for as long as she'd been alive "—I would have grown up in a Costa Rican orphanage. Instead, I ended up with Dan and Maggie. They were able to adopt me, and I even received citizenship without having to go through the usual channels."

He had an odd expression as he finished the apple piece. One she couldn't possibly hope to read. She fed him the second half, all the while trying to pretend that doing so wasn't sending odd frissons down her nerve endings.

"He was there when Santo Marguerite fell," Brody said abruptly when he'd polished off the second bite.

He referred to her father, Daniel Clay. "I know." He'd been assigned there by none other than Coleman Black. She knew there wasn't a day that passed that he hadn't felt the weight of responsibility for being unable to prevent Sandoval's destruction there. "He's my father. Of course he told me."

"Just don't expect every situation to come up blooming the same kind of daisies."

She swallowed, instinctively looking back at the sleeping children. "Hollins-Winword operations are usually successful," she said.

"You telling me or asking me?" He shot her one of those disturbingly perceptive looks of his.

She looked away from it, focusing on the apple again. She cut another smaller wedge and leaned over, feeding it to him.

Even *that* was easier than feeling like he'd just taken a tiptoe through every fear she possessed.

When there was nothing left but the apple core, she opened the window just enough to toss it out.

"Littering." Brody shook his head, tsking and sounding more like his normal self again. "You're turning into a regular rebel."

She flicked the rainwater that had blown in at him and

told herself that she really did *not* find her insides jigging around a little at the sight of the dimple that showed, despite his disreputable whiskers.

After wiping the knife blade, she folded it again and set it back in one of the cup holders molded into the center console.

She was well aware of the periodic looks that Brody gave to the rearview and side view mirrors.

As if he expected someone to be following them.

But every time she looked back, she saw only empty road.

"Why keep pulling EMT hours when you could make more with a helluva lot less effort by focusing just on Hollins?"

"Being a courier works only because I'm able to fit it *into* my regular life. I don't want it to *become* my regular life." She lifted her hand, trying to encompass everything—the muddy vehicle, the treacherous weather, the children. "Who wants this kind of thing to be their entire life?" She shook her head, dropping her hand back to her lap. "Not me."

"I'll let the dig you just gave me pass," he said drily.

"I didn't mean—"

"Forget it." He reached up and adjusted the rearview mirror. "The truth is, my life isn't too many people's cup of java. And me, hell, I'd be bored stiff if I had to stay in any one place for too long a stretch. But I didn't mean that you should try to be in the field all the time. Just that you could be kept a lot busier as a courier than you are, if you wanted."

She shook her head. "I don't."

"Smart girl," he murmured almost as if to himself.

Then he shot her a look. "As a source of excitement, your job probably gives plenty, right?"

Her fingers strayed to the tangles in her hair again. "I suppose." She'd dealt with everything from delivering babies to people who'd died peacefully in their sleep. And most everything in between.

She knew what it felt like to lose a battle that she couldn't have won no matter what, and that was fine. She still slept at night.

It was the battle that she hadn't *had* to lose that plagued her. The one where she'd hesitated, where she'd made the wrong choice, taken the wrong action. That was the thing she wasn't able to accept. The thing that made her question pretty much everything she'd thought she wanted to do with her life.

Supposedly, knowing any problem—identifying it, putting a name to it—was supposed to be the first step in dealing with it.

So far, the theory hadn't helped her one iota.

She'd still let a fourteen-year-old kid down, in the most final of ways because she'd thought she could get to him without having to climb through a culvert.

Brody flicked the windshield wipers to a higher setting. They swished back and forth so rapidly, they were almost nothing but a blur of motion. He checked the rearview again.

Angeline looked back through the window. All she could see was the misty swirl of water kicked up by the tires as it warred with the rain. "You don't think we're being followed, do you?" The notion tasted acrid.

"No."

She turned forward once more and chewed on her lower lip for a moment. "Are you lying?"

"I've always thought that one of those useless no-win questions." His voice was considering.

She folded her arms. "Well, pardon me."

"Seriously, think about it." His thumb lifted off the steering wheel. "If a person *is* lying, they're hardly going to want to admit it. If they say they're not, why is that any more believable than the original lie? And no matter whether they ever admit that they are lying, the person who asked the question in the first place is going to be no happier knowing it. Because they either want to believe what the person did say or they don't."

She squinted at him. "I'm sorry. Was that supposed to make *any* sense?"

He shrugged.

She propped her elbow on the door and covered her eyes with her hands. "Davey's the one who had it right, anyway. It's just better to tell the truth."

"Maybe in a perfect world." He gave her a look. "This ain't a perfect world, Angeline. The sooner you face that, the better off you'll be."

Angeline.

So he *could* manage her name when he felt like it.

Unfortunately, she now knew—too late of course—that hearing her name roll off his lips was far more disturbing to her peace of mind.

Once they reached Caracas, even with the aid of the city map Angeline found in the glove box, it took two efforts before she was able to direct Brody through the confusing streets to the All-Med office. Naturally, when they got there, the small storefront was locked up tight for the night.

When Brody strolled past, speculatively studying the

assortment of vehicles parked on the street, Angeline was too tired to muster any surprise. "Nobody's going to be at the office until tomorrow morning to do anything about returning this thing to Miguel. Don't you think we might as well keep driving it until then? The kids need to eat, Brody. You and I need to eat. And a shower and some fresh clothes wouldn't necessarily hurt any of us, either."

"How much cash do you have?"

"Not much. Just what I had back at the camp in Puerto Grande. I don't carry a lot cash when I come here; it's easier to use my credit card."

"Can't use that."

She wasn't surprised. Electronic means were too easily traced.

In the rear, Davey was pushing at Eva, complaining that she was hogging too much of the seat. Angeline reached her hand back, automatically trying to separate them. "You two have been great all day today, and I know you're tired. But just have patience for a little while longer," she urged.

Brody raked his hand down his face. "We've already stayed with this SUV too long."

Angeline swallowed. The reality of their situation had hovered beneath the surface throughout the long day of driving. Now it gurgled again to the surface like some dank, oily monster. But throwing up her hands in panic wasn't going to solve anything.

The children still needed food and some chance to stretch their legs before they got some sleep in a proper bed.

Brody turned on the interior light and pulled the map across the steering wheel. "Do you know this area?" he asked, pointing to a spot.

Angeline shook her head. "I don't know much of Caracas at all, except the airport and how to get from there to the All-Med office."

Eva sat forward, poking her head between the seats. "Tell Davey to stop kicking me or I'm gonna *punch* him."

"Nobody is going to kick or punch *anyone*," Angeline said, giving them both a firm look.

Brody pushed the map back toward Angeline, turned off the overhead light and began driving up the narrow street. "We'll find a place to hole up for the night, and get you settled with the kids. Once that's done, I'll ditch the SUV back at All-Med."

Somehow she doubted that he'd be catching a taxi back to the hotel after he'd done so. But she didn't want to delve too deeply into what alternative means he'd likely use.

This time, when it seemed as if they were driving around the city in circles, it wasn't because she'd told him to turn the wrong direction toward All-Med. It was because he was doing it deliberately.

Just in case. The realization was sobering.

Then finally, *finally,* he pulled up to a nondescript hotel that seemed as if it was located about as far from All-Med's office as it could be.

"Amazing," he murmured. "This place is still here." He shot her a quick look. "Stay here. Keep the doors locked. This place is no St. Agnes."

She pressed her lips together. She was perfectly aware that many of the cheap hotels were more in the business of renting by the hour than playing home base for vacationing families. Judging by the few people she saw milling around, she suspected that the hourly rate probably wasn't all that high, either.

"I don't like this place," Eva said once Brody disappeared into the building.

"Neither do I," Angeline murmured. "But it might be the best we can do in a pinch. And Brody will make sure we're safe."

"Are you sure?"

Was she?

She swallowed, ready to offer the lie that would keep the girl from worrying any more than she already was.

But then she saw Brody heading back toward them, his stride long and purposeful. The lamppost nearby cast a circle of light over him, highlighting the sparkle of raindrops catching in his disheveled hair.

A curious calm centered inside her.

"Yes, Eva, I'm sure."

There wasn't an ounce of untruth in her words.

Chapter Seven

"Here." Brody tossed the oversized room key into Angeline's lap as he climbed behind the wheel once more. He was becoming heartily sick of the rain. "It's a room in the very back. Supposed to be more…quiet than some."

She held the key between her long fingers. "You seem familiar with the place. Have you stayed here before?"

"No."

She lifted her eyebrows, clearly expecting more of an explanation.

He was more interested in getting rid of the All-Med vehicle as quickly and thoroughly as possible than he was in satisfying Angeline's curiosity over his sometimes misspent years.

He drove the truck around to the far back side of the building. Habit had him cataloging not only the people loitering about but also the vehicles parked there, as well.

He parked, and took the key back from Angeline. "Let me check the room."

"More paranoia?"

"Paranoia keeps me sane, baby cakes." He opened the door, hit the door locks to lock them in again and crossed the laughable excuse of a sidewalk to room number twenty-nine.

The interior wasn't going to win any awards, but it looked cleaner than he'd expected. The two beds appeared marginally adequate. Unfortunately, both had mirrors mounted on the ceilings above them, but they weren't in a position to be finicky. There was also a television, a couple of chairs and a bathroom.

He stepped into the doorway, gesturing for Angeline and the kids.

Neither Davey nor Eva wasted any time. They raced into the room, jockeying for first dibs on the bathroom.

Eva won.

Brody chucked Davey under the chin as he morosely stomped away from the door that his sister had shut in his face. "Get used to it, son. Girls *always* get dibs on the loo."

Angeline dropped the kids' pillowcase on the table. "Sounds like you speak the voice of experience."

"What's a loo?"

"A bathroom," Angeline told Davey when Brody didn't answer.

Dragging his thoughts away from the experience he *had* once had was difficult. Too difficult.

He must be more tired than he thought. Why the hell else would he keep thinking about Penny? About things that had occurred decades before?

His sister was dead.

Just like the rest of his family.

He didn't let himself think at all about the man who'd taken him in after that. Not when he blamed him for all of it in the first place.

Angeline was walking back and forth in front of him and the boy, evidently well into female mode as she clucked over the ceiling mirrors that Davey had just discovered and seemed fascinated by.

Wondering what kind of thoughts filled Angeline's head about the presence of the mirrors was enough, at least, to help Brody close the door on the past again.

When she noticed him watching her, dusky color filled her cheeks and she quite obviously turned her attention to the thin spreads on the bed, the pillows, the metal hangers hanging in the cupboard. Not even the surface of the dresser missed her examination.

"Sorry I don't have a white glove handy," he drawled.

Angeline pursed her lips together, and she'd probably have been appalled that the look didn't really have the intended effect on him. He didn't exactly feel taken to task when he was more interested in exploring the faint dimple that appeared, just below the corner of those smooth, full, pressed-together lips.

Flirting with Angeline was one thing. She was eminently flirtworthy. The perfect mark: a combination of smarts and wit and innocence—hell, he'd never be able to forget just *how* innocent after he'd stepped onto that particular buried mine—that combined together in one impossibly appealing package.

Fortunately, Eva opened the bathroom door then, ensuring that Brody—plagued with unwanted memories and inconvenient desires—didn't do something really stupid.

The young girl barely had time to get out of the way as Davey bolted inside.

The clothes that Eva had changed into in the SUV all those hours ago were mismatched and wrinkled, and he wasn't all that surprised when she hugged her arms around her thin body, giving wary looks to both him and Angeline, who was now busy trying to make some order out of the pillowcase contents. Eva sidled around the room to sit in one of the chairs near the small window next to the door.

The long ride after their precipitous exit from St. Agnes and then Puerto Grande had lulled her into a quiet acceptance of the situation. But now, her Stanley mind was probably ticking furiously away over everything that had occurred.

Angeline sighed, and pushed nearly all of the newly folded clothing neatly back into the pillowcase. It looked to him like what she'd left out was for the following day. Then she turned and folded her arms over her chest.

She, like he, hadn't had the advantage of changing out of the tunic and pants the nuns had provided and he wondered if she was as aware as he just how thin the linen really was as it closely draped her magnificent curves.

"You didn't manage to grab any pajamas," she told Brody.

He shrugged. That was the least of their worries. "That's what T-shirts are for," he dismissed.

She accepted it without argument.

Which only made his stupid brain drift on down the dangerous avenue of wondering just what Angeline usually wore to bed.

T-shirts?

Little silky nightgowns?

Nothing at all?

He scrubbed his hand down his face. He'd be better off envisioning her in thick flannel from head to toe, but suspected that even that wouldn't derail him. "Food," he said abruptly. "I'm gonna go scavenge up some food for everyone."

Eva couldn't hide the relief on her young face at that idea and Brody felt a pang inside. He'd pushed hard all that day and the kids had been troopers. Angeline, too, for that matter.

But they weren't used to being on the run.

He went to the door, opened it enough to look through the crack, then stepped out. "Angeline."

She joined him.

He pulled her farther out the door, closing it slightly so that Eva couldn't see. Being at the end of the building, he didn't worry much about being seen by any of the guys who were hanging around the hotel.

Angeline eyed him. "What is it?"

He deliberately reached out and grabbed her slender waist, pulling her until she stood less than a foot from him.

Her lips parted, startled. "Brody—"

When he lifted the hem of her tunic, her expression went frosty and she slammed her palms hard against his inner elbows.

"Relax," he muttered, even as he was sort of impressed with the strength behind the movement that had knocked his unprepared hands clean away from her all-too-lovely body.

He lowered his head toward hers, enjoying way too much how she stiffened. Whether it was pride or not that kept her from sliding a step back from him as he invaded her personal space even more, he couldn't tell.

He lifted the hem of her tunic again, drawing it right up over those curving hips. High enough to see the drawstring that held the pants—not very effectively, he noticed—around her very narrow waist.

His fingers brushed against the satin-smooth plane of her belly.

She inhaled on a hiss. "What—"

"Shh," he hushed, and because he was running on no sleep, no food and clearly no smarts, he grazed his lips over hers.

Whether that shocked her more than the Glock he tucked into the front and center waist of her pants or not as he kissed her, he couldn't tell.

Fortunately though, some cells in his brain were still in functioning order, and he brusquely tugged her tunic back down in place, and stepped away. "Take care of Delilah for me."

Her hand slapped against her belly, obviously holding the weapon in place. "I don't want her. *This.*"

"I don't care." He knew she was capable of shooting it, because he knew what kind of training Hollins-Winword had put her through.

Even couriers needed to know how to fire a weapon, whether or not it was ever likely to be necessary.

Besides, she'd grown up on a ranch. She'd probably known way more about firearms at an early age than *he* had.

Kids born to a British barrister and a surgeon didn't have much need to be around weapons.

Or they shouldn't have had a need if Cole would have just kept his distance from Brody's mother.

"Do you really think Rico would show up here?" Angeline lifted one hand, cutting off the pointless speculation going on inside his head. He'd given up years before wondering what would have happened if anything had been different.

"You drove around in so many circles, I don't even have a clue where in the city we are," she went on. "Nobody could possibly have followed us without us noticing."

"What I hope for versus what I know is possible are two very different things. There's an extra clip in your duffel bag. The cash I've got is in there, too."

"When did you put it in there—oh, never mind." She looked resigned. "You *are* just going out to get us some food, right?"

"Now I am. Consider this a run through for when I take the SUV back to All-Med."

"When will that be?"

"Later. The point is, you have to be prepared for anything, Angeline."

She moistened her lips. He saw the swallow she made work its way down her long, lovely throat. "O-okay."

"If I'm not back by dawn—that's *if*," he emphasized when she looked startled, "I want you to go back to the office here, talk to Paloma. She said she'll still be working even in the morning. She used to be sort of trustworthy—"

"*Used* to be?" Her fingers closed over his wrists, only to let go again, to press against her waistband. "I'm really not liking the sound of this."

"Yeah, well, beggars can't be choosers. Necessity is the mother of invent— Hell." He dropped the light tone.

"Just listen. She'll get you to a guy who can get you all to Puerto Rico."

"But what about the storm? There aren't even any flights going right now."

"*Now* is not tomorrow morning. Try not to agree to a price that'll use up all the cash—but do it if you have to. Once you get to Puerto Rico, look up a hotel called Hacienda Paradise. Owner's name is Roger. Think you can remember that?"

She looked insulted. "Of course. Roger. Hacienda Paradise. Hardly complicated."

"Tell him Simon sent you."

Her eyebrows rose. "Simon?"

"Just tell him. He'll get you back into the States."

"Just on the say-so of Simon. What is that? Another one of your aliases?"

He exhaled. "Can you do that?"

"Yes, I can do that. But it's not going to be necessary. Because *you're* going to be back." Her voice lost a little tartness. "Aren't you?"

"I'm going to try like hell," he said evenly. "But even the best situations can fall apart. And, sorry to say, babe, this isn't the best of situations. If I'd had a little more time to prep the op, it would have been kind of helpful. As it is, we're sort of flying by the seat of my pants."

"Well." She tugged at her disheveled hair. "Better your pants, than flying by someone else's."

"Babe." He pressed his hand to his heart. "I'm touched."

She exhaled suddenly, rolling her eyes, and reached for the door again to go back inside. "Just hurry up and get us some food, would you please? My stomach is about ready to eat through itself to the other side." She slipped into the room and closed the door.

He waited until he heard her slide the lock into place. Good girl.

She's not a girl, you twit.

He ignored the voice, perfectly well aware that Angeline was entirely *all* woman.

Then he went in search of the only kind of sustenance he was going to be sharing with his beautiful, virginal partner.

By the time Brody made it back *with* food, Angeline had run the kids through baths and into their improvised pajamas—a pale green scrub top of Angeline's for Eva, and a T-shirt of Eva's for Davey. She supposed that he was just too worn-out to protest the T-shirt with the glittery princess printed on the front.

In any case, they were clean and barely keeping their eyes open as they watched the grainy television channel showing a Spanish-dubbed version of an old American sitcom, when Brody knocked on the door.

Angeline's hand went to Delilah—she couldn't believe she was thinking of the Glock like another woman—that was tucked into her pants. It had been hidden there ever since he'd tucked it in her waistband, well over an hour earlier. She peeked through the dingy orange drape hanging at the window and relief made her feel positively weak-kneed at the sight of him standing on the other side of the door.

She quickly undid the lock and opened it for him.

He pushed the large brown bag into her hands and headed for the bathroom.

"Come on, my dears. Supper time," she said cheerfully.

Davey's tiredness almost miraculously abated at the idea of food. Eva, however, just shuffled silently to the table, slipping into one of the two chairs closest to the wall.

The feast Brody had returned with turned out to be a filling one. There were red beans and rice, and some sort of pork and chicken, tortillas and several bottles of water, as well as a few cans of soda with the easily recognizable kind of logos that transcended translation and a handful of wax-paper-wrapped sweet pastries. Soon Brody joined them.

Like Angeline, he sat on one side of the bed facing the table. And he ignored the paper plate she'd left for him, instead using the foil container that had held the beans and rice as his plate.

He didn't say much of anything as he ate, and when he thanked her for the opened bottle of water she handed him, she knew something was up.

Not from the tone of his voice. Goodness, no. She could hardly ever tell anything from his voice—or not very accurately, anyway. Nor was it his expression, which was as inscrutable as it ever was. His blue eyes—she was almost positive now that they must be his natural color, because she hadn't once seen him take out or put in contact lenses since they'd stared up the mountain to St. Agnes—were unreadable.

And it certainly wasn't anything he expressed in words, which at the moment—around mouthfuls of food—tended to center on answering Davey's questions about how high did Brody think he could jump when using a mattress as a springboard.

Brody gave Angeline a quick look. "Wants to jump on the bed, does he?"

She nodded. "He wants to see his handprints on the mirror up there." It was better than if the boy had expressed too much curiosity over *why* there were mirrors on the ceiling. She hadn't let him jump on the bed, of course, but she'd still considered it a good sign that he wasn't becoming too distressed over their activities. She wished she could believe the same was true about Eva.

The girl was becoming increasingly withdrawn.

She didn't even bat an eye when Davey slid the onions he'd carefully picked out of his chicken concoction onto her paper plate or when he plucked her pastry out of its wrapper and broke a gargantuan piece from it.

"Davey," Brody said, his tone warning.

The boy's shoulders drooped. He handed the pastry back to his sister.

She just shook her head. She'd only eaten half her meal. "You can have it. I'm full, anyway." She began to push herself back from the tiny table. "Oh. May I be excused?"

"Of course." Angeline caught the thin paper napkin that had been on Eva's lap before it fell to the floor as the girl slipped out from between the table and the wall and went over to the far bed.

She climbed onto one side, and lay facedown, burying her head in the pillow.

"She just sleepy?" Brody's voice was low.

Angeline watched the prone girl for a long moment. She couldn't decide what was more worrisome—wondering what was bothering Brody that he wasn't telling her, or Eva's exhaustion. "I hope so."

"Well, sleep is what you all need," he said. He grabbed

the other uneaten half of Eva's fruit-filled pastry, and polished it off in just two bites.

She began wrapping up the trash, setting aside the water and sodas they hadn't yet opened. They wouldn't go to waste because they'd definitely need them sooner or later. Brody stuffed the trash back into the sack. "I'll pitch it in the bin outside," he said.

Which only had disquiet curling through her all over again, because Brody's remaining task for the night had yet to begin.

She told Davey to wipe his hands and face and get into the unoccupied bed. "Brody, wait." She joined him at the door.

"Planning a little segregation of the sexes tonight? Girls in one bed? Guys in the other?" His lips twitched as he lowered his head closer to hers. "They'd be good chaperones, babe, just in case you're worried that two nights in a row with me in the same bed might be more temptation than you can handle."

She felt her face heat. "Get over yourself, would you?"

He chuckled softly, but when he straightened again, his expression was serious. "Don't forget now. Palo—"

"Paloma. Roger, Hacienda Paradise. Simon. I know. I know."

He nodded and turned to go, but she put her hand on his arm, stopping him. "Something's bothering you," she said quietly. "What?"

His expression didn't change. "Nothing new."

"Right. Too bad I don't believe that." She looked over her shoulder at the children. Davey's attention was focused once more on the television set, and all she could see of Eva was the back of her head. "What happened when you went out for the food?"

"Nothing."

"And I believe that like I believe in Santa Claus."

"Well, you are as untouched as an eight-year-old," he drawled, "so it wouldn't surprise me at all to find you sitting in front of the fireplace every Christmas Eve ready to greet the jolly old dude with milk and cookies warm from your oven."

Her lips tightened. "Don't patronize me."

He sighed roughly. "There's nothing you can do about it anyway, so forget about it."

Her fingers tightened on his uncompromisingly hard arm. "Do...about...*what?*"

"I couldn't reach my handler."

She frowned a little. "So?"

He looked upward. "So. So, that's a problem."

"Because someone didn't answer a phone just once when you expected them to? Maybe he was busy."

"She."

"Fine. Maybe *she* was busy."

"Handlers don't do *busy.* They're available 24/7. Period."

She rubbed her neck. "Well, you'll just have to try again," she stated the obvious, and received a wry "you think?" look right back from him as a result.

"Getting us all back to the States is going to be a helluva lot easier with some help than without," he told her. "I'm not saying it's impossible without it. What I am saying is that it's...unusual...not to be able to reach her. Plus, no contact means no updates on the Stanleys' situation."

It was a sobering thought. "Who is your handler, anyway?" The world that Hollins-Winword operated in was often murky and ill defined. They didn't operate counter to the federal government, of course, who often found it helpful that the agency was able to move where official means were impossible. Nor did it matter if the problem was small and domestic, or invasive and international. The people involved with the agency were sometimes far-flung, and they certainly didn't operate out of any typical office building.

"You know I'm not gonna tell you." Brody was looking amused again. "No offense, babe, but that's strictly need to know."

"But what if I did need to know?" She hugged her arms to herself. "Theoretically speaking, I mean. Would you ever break *those* rules?" She was acutely aware of his propensity for breaking others.

"It's pretty obvious there are plenty of rules I'm willing to break." His gaze drifted downward, seeming to hesitate around her mouth. "But there are a few—probably too few to make much of a saint out of me—that I won't." Then he closed the door.

She swallowed, her mouth suddenly dry. She wasn't sure just exactly what they were talking about, but she feared it had nothing to do with her question about his handler.

Chapter Eight

Angeline was awake and sitting in the chair, facing the door, when the fingers of dawn light crept eerily around the edges of the ill-fitted orange window drape.

In one bed, Eva slept soundly. She hadn't stirred once all night long.

In the other bed, Davey slept, too, though he'd tossed and turned enough for both himself and his sister.

Climbing into bed herself was just not something she could make herself do. Not with Brody's "in case of emergency" instructions circling in her head.

Brody hadn't returned.

Which meant that, if she were a good Hollins-Winword agent, she'd get the children up and dressed and race down to the office and this Paloma whom Brody *thought* might be trustworthy.

She rubbed her eyes and the dim light just grew stronger.

Problem was, she *wasn't* a particularly good Hollins-Winword agent. She wasn't cut out for this cloak-and-dagger stuff. She was just a courier of information for them. That's all she'd *ever* been!

And he expected her to get the kids, ultimately, back to the United States and just leave him behind?

How on earth was she supposed to make herself do that?

Not even during her worst shifts in Atlanta had she felt so tired. So rattled. So unsure of herself.

It was even worse than—

The doorknob jiggled and she sat up like a shot, dragging her feet off the second chair so quickly that it tipped onto its back, bouncing softly on the threadbare carpet.

She tossed aside the bright blue towel she'd draped over her lap and Delilah after she'd raced through her own shower, and scrambled over the chair, nearly tripping on the legs as she made for the door.

She threw open the lock and yanked open the door.

Brody stood there, looking furious. "What the *hell* are you still doing here?"

"Be quiet," she muttered, "just be quiet." And she wasn't sure who she shocked more when she reached up and wrapped her arms around his neck. "Don't *ever* scare me like that again."

His arms had come around her back. "Angel—"

"You were gone *hours!*" She squeezed his neck again. For some reason she couldn't seem to stop herself from clinging.

"Okay. Ohhh-kay." He sounded a little strangled, and his hands went from her back to unhook the ones she'd locked around his neck like some manic noose. He worked the Glock she still held out of her clenched fingers, and tucked it in the small of his back, then closed his hands around her fists and pulled them between them. "Breathe, would you?"

She drew in a huge breath, hardly aware that she'd been holding it in the first place.

"Better." He reached over her shoulder and pushed the door wider. "At least you were armed," he said gruffly. "Get inside."

She backed up as he headed forward enough that he could close the door once more. "Wake them up."

He was still furious, she realized.

And though she felt some compunction for not having followed his exact instructions, she didn't feel overly apologetic, either.

After all, he'd arrived, hadn't he?

He'd arrived, she realized belatedly, wearing a completely different set of clothing than the disheveled tunic and pants that he'd left wearing.

"You've got different clothes."

He was righting the chair that she'd tipped over. *"Now."* He was clearly not referring to her observation.

She sidled past him, heading for Eva. The girl, when she finally sat up, looked glassy-eyed and pale.

Angeline frowned a little, pressing her palm against Eva's forehead. It didn't feel overly warm, though. "Come on, sweetie, it's time for us to get moving again." She pulled over the clothing that she'd set out the night before. "Can you get yourself changed?"

Eva nodded and without argument began exchanging the scrub top for her own jeans and sweatshirt.

Brody had disappeared into the bathroom. She heard

the shower come on, and made a face at the closed door. Obviously he wasn't in such a hurry that he couldn't manage a few minutes for that particular necessity.

She turned her attention to Davey. Like the previous day, he didn't wake quite as easily as his sister. But when he did, he began dressing himself, assuring Angeline quite indignantly that he did not need help.

She hadn't even finished tucking the kids' improvised nightwear back into the pillowcase when Brody came out, dressed again in the unexpected blue jeans and dark blue T-shirt. His hair was wet and slicked back from his face, and without looking at her, he picked up her small toiletry bag sitting on the edge of the chipped white sink and began rummaging through it.

"Can I help you find something?"

His gaze met hers briefly in the mirror above the sink as he pulled out her toothpaste and her toothbrush and began brushing his teeth.

She didn't know what disturbed her more.

The fact that he was using her toothbrush, or the fact that she wasn't absolutely appalled that he was using her toothbrush.

He was still watching her through the reflection of the mirror.

She swallowed and bundled up the towel she'd been using as a lap blanket and stuck it back inside her duffel. She pulled on her sturdy boots again, and when she looked toward Brody again, he'd finished brushing his teeth and had soaped up his face with bar soap and was stroking her narrow pink razor over his jaw, muttering an oath with every pass.

Her eyes drifted down from the way the T-shirt stretched tight over his shoulders to the way it was nearly loose at his narrow waist, where it—along with the grip of the weapon—was tucked into his jeans.

She quickly looked away again before he could catch her ogling his undeniably *fine* backside, and helped Davey tie his tennis shoes.

When she was finished, Brody was wiping the last bit of soap suds from his newly revealed jawline.

She turned her eyes from the bead of blood on his angular chin and told the kids to be sure to use the restroom before they left.

Once again, Eva—finally showing some energy—darted in first.

Davey's shoulders hunched forward and his head tilted back. "Gaaawwwwwl."

Angeline handed him the pastry that she hadn't eaten from the night before. "Maybe this'll help." She caught Brody's look. "What?" she said defensively. "It's basically a fruit Danish."

"Did I say something?"

She narrowed her eyes. "You didn't have to."

He moved toward her and dropped the toiletry bag in her hand. "Yet when I really *do* say something, you ignore it completely."

Her lips parted. "That is not fair."

His eyebrows rose. His jaw was still shiny and damp and his raked back hair looked nearly black with water. He looked like some archangel, fallen to earth.

And was mighty peeved about the entire process.

"Just how is it *not* fair, love? Did you head out at dawn, like I told you to? Did you speak with Paloma? Did you buy your way across the water to Puerto Rico? Did you do any…single…thing…I told you to do?" His voice dropped with every word, only succeeding in making his anger even more evident. "Dammit, Angeline, I trusted you to—"

"To what?" She refused to back away, but keeping her chin up in the face of that dark, blue-eyed glower was no small feat. She was also aware of Davey's avid attention, but couldn't seem to stop her tongue. "To leave you behind?" She propped her hands on her hips. "How could you really think I could leave you behind?"

He exhaled, sounding aggravated beyond measure. "Believe me, I think I could have managed to keep my head above water, even without your help."

She sniffed imperiously, though the sarcastic words stung. Deeply. "Well, next time, I won't make the same mistake, I assure you."

"You'd better not."

She turned away and since both Eva and Davey had taken their turns with the bathroom, she stomped across the room and shut herself behind the door.

Only there did she let her shoulders relax.

She pressed her hand to her heart, willing its thunderous pounding to still, for the shudders working down her spine to cease.

But she nearly jumped out of her skin a moment later when he wrapped his knuckles on the other side of the wood panel. "Hurry it up," he told her brusquely. "We're rolling in five minutes."

She stared at the door. Stuck her tongue out at it and felt both foolish and better.

But before five minutes had passed, she'd finished the most necessary of her morning ablutions, and the four of them left the cheap hotel room behind, toting their ragtag belongings with them.

The air outside was chilly and damp; the sky above

a heavy, dull gray that was turning to silver with every centimeter of sunlight that rose.

But it wasn't raining. At least not at the moment. It was one bright spot, she thought, as she took Davey's hand in hers and followed after Brody.

He did not, as she had expected, head for the office to consult with the still-unseen Paloma. Brody crossed the street, heading for the corner, where he stopped beside a mustard-yellow taxicab. Despite the lack of a driver sitting behind the wheel, he pulled open the back door, tossed in Angeline's duffel that he'd evidently decided she was too inept to carry herself and nudged Eva in after. Davey ran ahead to join his sister, and Angeline quickly broke into a jog herself.

Brody shut the door after Davey and flung open the passenger's door, then rounded to the driver's side.

She ought to have known not to be surprised by anything, but she couldn't help herself when she sat down in the front seat next to Brody. "Where's the driver?"

He shrugged. "Hopefully sleeping for another few hours so we can ditch this someplace before he even realizes it's gone."

Another stolen car.

She sank her teeth into her tongue, determined to remain silent on the matter. He *was* supposed to be the expert here.

It was strictly her problem that she immediately had visions of the two of them being forever incarcerated in some horrible jail cell on multiple counts of grand theft auto, and kidnapping. And the children—

She couldn't think that way. As long as Brody was around, the children would be safe.

The man in question was weaving through the streets

that seemed congested even at such an early hour and Angeline faced the irony in her cogitations.

She was riddled with anxiety over his disregard for legalities, yet she still trusted that he'd see them all safely through this.

But then that's the way it had always been with Brody.

Equal measures of wary fascination and instinctive trust. Both of which she'd been wise to refrain from examining too closely.

Up until now, that had been fairly easy to do, considering how rare and brief their encounters had always been.

He slammed on the brakes suddenly, throwing his arm up to keep her from falling forward.

She pressed her lips together, painfully aware of his palm pressed hard against her sternum as the car shuddered to a stop.

She imagined she could feel each centimeter of those long fingers burning a tattoo into her skin.

So much for easy.

"You okay?"

She nodded even though she was aware that it was the children he'd addressed. Assured that they were, his gaze slid over Angeline and he pulled his palm away from her chest, wrapping it once more around the steering wheel.

Ahead of them, she spotted a three-car pileup. Judging by the trio of men standing around yelling and gesturing, she was fairly certain that nobody had been hurt. At least she couldn't see anybody still inside the vehicles.

Nevertheless, she threw open her door and ran forward, hardly aware of Brody's oath behind her.

She went first to the car that had been hit on both sides, looking through the windows. A woman was lying on her side across the backseat, her hands pressed to her distended abdomen.

Angeline scrambled with the door, but it was too badly crunched to open. She knocked on the window drawing the woman's attention. "Are you hurt?" She repeated it in Spanish when the woman gave her a confused look.

"My baby is coming too fast," she replied.

Naturally. Life wasn't giving any easy outs these days. Angeline smiled encouragingly and promised to return in a moment. She ran to the other cars that were thankfully empty now and headed back to the pregnant woman, trying the opposite door this time with no better results.

Brody was storming toward the cars and she ignored him as she managed to wriggle her arm through the window of the door that seemed to have less damage, and twisted her arm around enough to roll the window down farther. She was amazed it moved at all, given the sharp dent in the door. When it was down, she ducked through, running her hands cautiously along the woman's legs, which were bared by the bright red dress she wore. *"Mi nombre es Angeline,"* she told the woman calmly.

"Soledad," the woman replied around panting breaths. "The other car, it came from nowhere. My husband—"

"He's out calling for help," Angeline blithely lied the assurance. As far as she could tell, the three men weren't doing a single productive thing but yelling obscenities at each other. "How far apart are your pains?"

"Minutes."

No easy outs and hellacious innings to boot, she thought. "I'll be right back," she promised the woman, and pulled her torso back out of the window. She turned, nearly bumping into Brody, who was standing behind her, looking thoroughly maddened.

"What the bloody hell do you think you're doing?" His voice was calm. Pleasant even.

She actually felt herself start to quail. But a cry from the woman trapped in the car stiffened her resolve. "She's in labor," she told him hurriedly. "Both doors are jammed. You need to see if any one of those guys—" she threw out her arm "—has called for help."

"In case you've forgotten, we are sort of in the middle of our *own* emergency."

She lifted her hands at her sides. "Is Ri—our friend on our tail right this minute? Have you seen him?" She didn't wait for an answer. "What would you really have me do, Brody? Ignore that poor woman? Good heavens, at least *this* sort of thing I'm trained to handle!"

"Deliver a lot of babies on the side of roads do you?"

"This will be my tenth, if you must know! Now make yourself useful and find some way to get one of those doors open." She pushed past him and hurried back to the taxi.

Eva and Davey were sitting with their arms crossed over the back of the front seat as they watched the action unfold in front of them. Angeline managed a quick look into Eva's face and felt a little better about the girl—she'd worried when she'd woken her that she might be coming down with something. But now, she looked more like her regular self again.

Angeline dragged open her duffel, rooting past the clothes and the small toiletry bag. She dragged out the blue towel again and her bottle of waterless antibacterial soap. Then, at the very bottom of the bag, she found her first-aid kit. She tucked the webbed strap of its holder over her shoulder. "Eva, can you hand me one of the water bottles?"

Eva pulled one out of her pillowcase-luggage and handed it over. "What're you doing?"

"There's a woman about to have a baby in that blue car," she said. "I'm going to help her. You two wait here in the taxi, okay?"

"Brody looks mad," Eva said.

"He's just concerned that we get you two back to the States as quickly as possible." The last part was truthful, at least. "Hopefully, this won't take too long and we'll be doing just that before you can say Jack Sprat."

"Huh?"

She smiled and shook her head before hurrying back to the vehicle. Brody had evidently convinced the arguing parties to pool their efforts in more productive ways since two of them were leaning their weight against a crowbar, trying to work the least mangled door free.

"Wait." Angeline waved off their work for a moment. She tossed her collection of supplies through the window onto the front seat. "Help me climb inside first," she told Brody in English. "I'm worried that she's too far along to wait until you get the door jimmied."

The distinctive wail of sirens suddenly filled the air.

"Great," Brody muttered. "You're playing Nurse Nightingale and the freaking police are getting ready to join the party."

"You're the one used to adapting to the situation. Adapt." She tucked her head and torso through the window as far as she could. "You'll have to push me the rest of the way." She'd do it herself, but she simply couldn't gain enough leverage to either pull or push herself through.

His hands circled her waist and he nudged her inches forward. She wasn't exactly a wide load, but her hips had always been more curvaceous than she'd have liked, and the window was hardly generous. She shimmied and sucked in a hard breath when Brody's hands moved from her waist to plant square against her derriere.

"Desperate situations necessitate desperate measures," he said, sounding amused as her rear cleared the window's confines and she pretty much landed on her face on the front seat.

She dragged her feet in after her. "Keep working on the door," she said, not looking at him as she maneuvered her way awkwardly into the backseat.

The woman was drenched in sweat and amniotic fluid.

Angeline smiled again as she started to draw the woman's soaked skirt upward.

"Are you a doctor?"

"Sort of." Angeline didn't hesitate. "Have you had other babies?"

The woman nodded. *"Tres."*

"Ah. Then you're an old hand at this," Angeline said brightly. She kept up a running conversation in Spanish with the woman—as much as her panting would allow, at any rate—to keep her distracted from the pain. She doused her hands liberally with the antibiotic soap, and reminded herself as she checked the woman for dilation that Miguel and Maria Chavez had delivered children with even fewer sanitary conveniences.

Soledad was not just fully dilated, the baby was already crowning.

With the sirens drawing ever nearer, Angeline reached over the seat to drag open her meager medical kit. She had a few packages of sterile gloves but didn't bother at this late stage. She did, however, rip open an alcohol pad to drag it over her sharp little scissors, which were all she had in the kit to cut the umbilical cord with.

"Madre de dios," she heard one of the men breathe outside the windows.

Ignoring them all, Angeline kept encouraging Soledad not to push just quite yet. "Pant, one, two, three, that's right. Good, good." She grabbed a paper-wrapped spool of sterile gauze from the kit, as well as the small blue aspirator bulb, and dropped both on the crumpled dress covering Soledad's belly. "Okay, now, push. That's it. *Push,* Soledad." The baby's head emerged and Angeline caught her breath at the awesomeness of the moment.

No matter how many babies she'd helped delivered it always seemed a miracle to her.

"Keep panting, Soledad. Hold off on pushing for just a moment." She grabbed the bulb and gently, quickly suctioned the infant's nose and mouth. "All right, now. Let's finish the job now. Come on, you can do it. Push!"

The woman gave a mighty yell, hunching forward, and the rest of the baby seemed to nearly squirt right into Angeline's hands.

Soledad's head fell back against the door behind her, exhausted. Angeline joggled the slippery infant in her hands, clearing the mucus again. Already the tiny girl's skin was pinkening and she let out a mewling, very healthy howl.

Soledad cried, pressing her hands against her chest.

"Congratulations, Mama. You have a beautiful daughter," Angeline told the woman, and wrapped the baby in the blue towel that had so recently, she realized surreally, hidden a Glock in her lap. She settled the baby on the woman's belly and ripped open the gauze, cutting off a length to tie around the umbilical cord.

Behind her, the door to the car suddenly sprang open and the men began yelling again as if they'd never stopped. If it weren't for the hands Brody held out for her, Angeline would have tumbled out onto her backside.

"Easy does it," he said, holding her in place. His chin hooked over her shoulder, his chest pressed against her back. "Amazing," he murmured, looking at the tiny baby swathed in terry cloth.

Angeline finished making the knot. She could see the ambulance that had finally pulled up, so she didn't bother tying off the cord a second time in order to cut it. She'd leave that, as well as the afterbirth and washing up the baby, to the emergency crew.

As it was, Angeline's wonderfully clean clothing that she'd donned after her shower were—once again—somewhat less than pristine.

With her adrenaline finally slowing, Angeline leaned closer to the baby again. "God speed to you both," she told Soledad.

"*Gracias,* Angeline." The new mother caught Angeline's hand with her own. *"Gracias."*

"We'd better move out of the way," Brody told her softly. The ambulance crew had wheeled a stretcher alongside the wreck.

She ducked her head inside the car just long enough to retrieve her kit, and then they were heading toward the taxi.

It was Soledad's husband who provided the distraction they needed. When he spotted the officer, he ran forward, his hands gesturing wildly as he continued sharing the tale that, Angeline suspected, would just grow in scope with each telling.

They climbed into the cab and, showing great decorum, Brody backed up and turned around, pulling into the first side street he came to. Only then did he allow himself to put on some speed.

"Was it gross?" Davey was bouncing in the backseat, where there was a lamentable lack of seat belts. "You sure *look* kinda gross, Angeline."

Angeline laughed a little, though her nerves were beginning to set in, making her feel shaky.

"I don't think she looks gross at all," Brody countered.

She gave him a surprised look only to have her gaze captured for a long moment by his.

"In fact, I think she looks pretty amazing."

She swallowed. Hard.

Then he turned that disturbing intensity back onto the road in front of him and it was as if that tight, breathless connection had never occurred. "But you should ditch the T-shirt right now for something less noticeable." His voice was brusque. "God only knows whose attention we've earned *now*."

Chapter Nine

Whether or not their detour drew attention, Brody managed to drive through the city without further delay or mishap. Angeline, calling on every pragmatic cell she possessed, exchanged her soiled top right there in the front seat next to Brody for a fresh T-shirt that Eva pulled out of the duffel for her. And the shirt was left crumpled on the floorboard right along with the taxi that he parked in a teeming lot near the airport. The lot was already congested with cars—what was one more, even if it was big, bright and yellow?

Before they caught one of the city buses that carried them to yet another corner of Caracas, Brody instructed the kids to address him and Angeline as Mom and Dad from here on out. It seemed to bother them much less than it did Angeline, who sat there twisting the mock wedding ring around and around her finger.

Once more, they were showing more resilience than she felt. And if they were feeling paralyzed with worry over their *real* parents, they weren't showing it.

The first bus was followed by three others until finally, they walked into a small, dusty building that sat at the end of an airstrip.

The International Airport it most certainly was *not*.

Fortunately, Angeline had had her share of experiences with small planes back in Wyoming, so she wasn't completely thrown when in short order they were taking off in a minuscule six-seater piloted by a smiling young man who talked a mile a minute.

He didn't seem to notice or care that Brody's responses to his nonstop dialogue were few and far between. Calling them curt would have been charitable.

As for Angeline, she was kept plenty busy keeping Davey from squirming out of his safety belt because he was insatiably curious about everything. Keeping Davey contained was better than looking out the window, though, at the expanse of water beneath them.

When they landed, without incident, in Puerto Rico, Angeline had a strong, *strong* desire to drop to her knees and kiss the dusty unpaved runway on which they'd landed. Instead, she kept the children's attention diverted from the exchange of money between Brody and the pilot.

Then it was a hair-raising cab ride—this time with the proper driver—and more money exchanged hands before they landed on the doorstep of Hacienda Paradise.

It was considerably smaller than even the hotel in Caracas had been, yet *this* one looked as if it had been designed as a vacation home away from home.

Pristine stucco looked particularly white with the vivid ochre arches over the doors and windows and the wealth of flowering bushes planted against the walls. Situated on a hillside, she could see the ocean beyond and despite the pervasively gray, cloudy sky, it was still a beautiful sight.

They went in through the colorful main door, where the interior was as lovely and welcoming as the exterior. There was an expanse of gleaming terra-cotta tile, dozens of potted plants and warm rattan furnishings—all covered with cushions in varying patterns and colors that combined as a whole in pleasing results.

"Wait here," Brody said, gesturing at the collection of tropical-print-upholstered sofas in the lobby. "I haven't seen Roger in a long time and let's just say that we didn't part on the best of terms."

Angeline was too tired to let that little revelation rock her, and she was happy enough to sit and wait for whatever reception they received. The truth was, the run of sleepless nights was beginning to catch up with her. And the rattan sofas were *so* comfortable. She let out a long, soft sigh.

Beside her, Eva made a similar sound. Davey, however, was beyond overtired. He was in constant motion.

Brody crossed the tile heading toward the shining wood reception desk, but before he made it halfway, an exceedingly handsome black man, dressed completely in white, headed for him, a smile wreathing his face.

"Simon," he greeted, his English tinged with an islander's lilt. Without a moment's hesitation, he grabbed Brody in a massive bear hug, slapping him on the back.

Angeline tucked her tongue in the roof of her mouth.

Looked to her like the men were on pretty good terms.

And obviously, she'd been right about "Simon" being another one of Brody's aliases. She watched him turn toward her, extending his long arm. "Darling," he called, using the most perfect British accent she'd ever heard, "come and meet my old friend, Roger."

"Why'd he call him *Simon,*" Davey whispered.

Angeline gave Eva a look as she slowly rose.

"That's his name for now," Eva whispered to her brother, pulling him onto her lap. "Don't forget."

"But I thought we was supposed to call him Mr. Dad."

"Just Dad. We are. Shh. We don't want anyone to hear."

Angeline gave them an encouraging smile and continued forward. Her conscience niggled at her for approving of the quick way they adapted to deception. It was disquieting how easily she stomped out that niggling, too.

She reached Brody and Roger and pinned what she hoped was a natural-looking smile on her face. Keeping it firmly in place when Brody slung his arm around her shoulders and pulled her up snug against his side took even more effort.

"Roger Sterling, this is my beautiful wife, Angie. Darling, this old reprobate is an old…friend of mine."

Roger clasped her hand in both of his, bending low to kiss the back of it. "Beautiful Angie. Welcome to my Hacienda. But what your Simon isn't telling you is that we used to work together."

Brody squeezed her shoulder when she gave a little start. "Oh?" She managed to look enquiringly up at her "husband."

"That was aeons ago, Rog." Brody smiled at her. "Back in our ideological youth."

"Youth?" Roger tossed back his head and laughed. "Not even those ten—no, it's twelve years ago now—could you or I claim youthfulness. Now, who are those young ones over there watching us with big brown eyes? Surely not—"

"Angie's kids," Simon-Brody said. "I'm afraid her first husband—"

"—don't bore the man with that old tale, darling," Angeline interrupted. She looked up at Roger, who was nearly as tall as Brody. "Simon's a wonderful father," she lied as if she'd been doing it all her life. And it wasn't all a lie, because the fact was, Brody was good with the children. "He even insists on bringing them with us every time we go on vacation."

"So this *is* a holiday?" Roger looked back at Simon. "I'm wounded, old man. You should have given me some notice. As it is, I have only two rooms available."

"We're actually on our way back to the States. If you can let us hole up for one night, we'll be—"

"Sure, sure." Roger lifted his hand, cutting off Simon's words as he went back to the reception desk. He produced an old-fashioned key and came back, dropping it into Brody's palm. "Nothing but the best for my old debating partner. Do you have luggage?"

"Nothing we can't manage," Simon-Brody assured. He looked at the room key, on which Angeline could see engraved in gold the number ten. "This have a good location?"

"The best," Roger assured. "Perfect view of the pool in one direction and the ocean in the other. I'll have one of my boys show you back."

"No need." Brody slid his hand down Angeline's arm, linking his fingers through hers. "We'll catch up later, after we've had a chance to settle the kids."

Roger's smile was still in place as Brody collected the children in their wake and they all headed back out the front door and around to the side where he'd left her duffel and the children's purloined pillowcase.

"So, *Simon,* you worked with him, did you?"

He ignored her soft comment, and continued striding along the flower-lined sidewalk until they reached the end of the lovely building.

The door Brody stopped at was in the very rear of the courtyard. He unlocked it, quickly set their ragtag belongings inside and then ushered them in. He pressed his fingers to his lips as he shut the door and fastened the locks.

All four of them.

She frowned a little at the sight of so many locks, and then leaned back against the door as he went into the same hunt-and-seek mode that he'd used at the convent.

Since this room was not a room at all, but a suite, she expected that it might take him some time to appease his paranoia.

Eva pointed to the couch, silently checking with Brody before throwing herself down on it when he nodded. Brody had already turned on the television, and she picked up the remote, slowly flipping through the channels that offered a seemingly dizzying assortment of options.

Angeline unlatched Davey from her hip and picked him up. His head snuggled down into the crook of her neck. "Come on, bud," she whispered. "Let's you and I go have a lie down." She peeked through the open doorways. The first was a bathroom—standard, albeit well-appointed.

She passed it by for the next doorway. A bedroom. Two twin beds, each with its own chair, table and lamp beside it. The last doorway, separated from the other two by a neatly appointed kitchenette, contained only one bed, which looked wide enough to sail home on. Attached to that was another bathroom, this time with a tub large enough for a party.

At least a party of two.

The guilty thought taunted her as she turned tail and headed back to the twin beds.

There, she curled up on the wonderfully soft mattress with Davey tucked against her. She felt reasonably confident that if she kept him still for even five minutes, he'd get the nap he badly needed.

Sleep dragged enticingly at her, and she told herself she'd just grab a nap. A little one.

Then she could face whatever was next on Brody's plan.

While Angeline napped, Brody finished searching every inch of the bedroom right around them.

He added the surveillance bugs he found there to the small pile of them that was growing on the top of the fancy, satellite-fed television.

On the couch, Eva was sleeping, too. She'd lasted all of ten minutes after Angeline and Davey had hit the mattress.

Catching some shut-eye himself was mighty appealing, but first he'd finish searching out the rest of the suite.

One advantage was that Roger hadn't changed his style over the past decade. When Brody felt reasonably confident that he'd discovered every listening device, he dropped them by handfuls into a glass pitcher that he found conveniently provided in the nicely equipped kitchenette.

Then he filled the pitcher with water and stuck the entire thing inside the refrigerator.

Roger would be pissed, but Brody didn't care.

Then he went into the main bedroom with its decadent bathroom en suite. He tossed Angeline's duffel on the dresser and rooted shamelessly through it until he found her first-aid kit. He flipped it open, cataloging the contents, and then worked the T-shirt over his head, managing not to dislodge the bandage that he'd taped there what seemed days earlier.

It hadn't been days, though.

It had just been that morning, before dawn.

"Oh, my *God*."

He whipped his head around, wincing as the adhesive tape he'd slapped copiously around the mound of gauze pads over his rib cage pulled. "I thought you were sleeping," he groused.

Angeline's lips were parted, her gaze trained on the less-than-professional work he'd made of the bandage. She stopped next to him and prodded her fingers none too gently against his shoulder. "Turn so I can see better. Good Lord, Br—Simon, who taped up this mess?"

"*I* did," he admitted grumpily. He didn't assure her that the suite was safe to speak openly, though.

She huffed, and began picking at the edge of one long strip. "It clearly didn't occur to you to say something about this earlier." Her voice was snippy, a perfect accompaniment to her withering expression. She freed the edge finally and took definite delight in yanking it off his skin.

He winced. "Hells bells, woman. Go a little easy there."

She tore another strip, literally, off his hide. "Why? You're the big macho man who doesn't have to admit to any sort of weakness." She yanked a third off.

He yelped and covered her hand with his. "Dammit!

What is this? Nurse Ratchet has replaced the saintly Florence?"

But he realized that her hand beneath his was trembling.

"Dammit," he said again, only this time with far less heat.

He slid his arm around her shoulders as she turned into him, burying her face against his chest, inches above where the gauze had done a reasonable job of keeping the seeping knife wound from staining his shirt.

Her hand swept up his spine. "What happened?" Her voice was muffled, her words warm puffs against his flesh. "*Was* it our, uh, our friend? No wonder you were so furious when I insisted on stopping to help Soledad."

"It wasn't him." He circled her braid with his fingers; it was thick as her wrist and silkier than anything he'd ever felt in his life. So much for thinking that he'd keep her at a distance if she thought they might be listened in on. "Merely a couple blokes who didn't appreciate me interrupting their drug deal."

"Merely." She shuddered against him. "God. You should have said something sooner. Like when you came back to the hotel this morning."

"We were already running late. Too late."

She tilted back her head, her dark eyebrows pulling together. Her hand settled over his bandaging as gently as a whisper.

In its way, that soft touch was more painful than her wrenching off the sticking adhesive strips.

"This is why you weren't back before dawn."

"Yes."

She moistened her lips and ducked her forehead against his chest again. Ground it softly against him.

A whole new set of pain surged; the kind he couldn't—wouldn't—allay.

As if realizing it, she went still for a gut-twisting moment. Then she took a step back. The thick ridges of her braid slid smoothly out of his hand.

She gathered up the first-aid kit. "Come into the bathroom," she said. "There's probably better light in there." She led the way, turning on every light—and there were a good half-dozen of them.

"Sit there." She gestured at the wide plank of earthtoned granite that spanned the distance between the two hammered copper sinks.

He sat.

She ran water until it was hot in one of the sinks, and wet one of the thick washcloths, which she then held over the adhesive, helping to loosen what he now considered an overly effective death grip. Then patiently, she managed to coax the strips loose until she could peel away the gauze that he'd bunched together over the slash.

She sucked in a hard breath when she saw the extent of the wound. She tossed the gauze into the other unused sink. "This should have been sutured."

"I didn't have a lot of free time," he reminded, trying not to wince like a damn baby.

But, *Christ,* it hurt.

Her slender, deft fingers moving on him were causing plenty of their own torment, too.

She made a soft hmming sound, and wet another cloth with warm water, which she used to clean away the dried blood around the perimeter of the gash. "How, exactly, did this happen? There were two of them?"

"Three."

She hmmed again. It reminded him of his mother, actually, whenever she was withholding judgment over his defense of some mischief he and Penny had gotten into.

For once, thinking of his sister didn't make everything inside him want to shut down. Maybe it was just because it seemed to be happening more often lately.

Maybe it was just the company he was keeping of late.

She cast a look up at him through her lashes. The compress carefully moved over the gash and drizzled warm water over it. "And?"

She was using plenty of water. It slid down his belly, soaking into his jeans. At the rate she was going, he'd be out of dry pants for the rest of the day.

"And nothing. They didn't like me interrupting them."

"But where were you? Where'd this happen? At the All-Med office, or after?"

"After."

She pursed her lips, bringing into evidence that little dimple below her lips—situated there like some pretty birthmark on a long-ago pinup girl. "I don't suppose you went to the police."

"No." His voice was dry.

"How'd you get the supplies to bandage yourself up?"

"You mean the stellar example of proper first aid that you so admire?"

The dimple disappeared as she smiled. "Ah, now there's the wit I know." She dropped the sopping cloth back into the water in the sink, sending a small cascade over the edge, where it soaked into his jeans.

"I'm going to need to use Roger's damn laundry service," he muttered.

"Where *did* you get the clothes?"

"In the same drugstore where I pinched the gauze and tape."

"You actually found a drugstore that was open at that hour?"

He gave her a look.

"Oh, dear." She sighed faintly. "Does it not bother you *at all* to avail yourself of…of…things that don't belong to you?"

"Nobody's going out of business as a result of it," he defended drily. "And the trucks have all gone back to their rightful owners, assuming that your peeps at All-Med made it up to St. Agnes already." When things got back to normal, he might just have to satisfy his curiosity over who'd donated that unusual equipment to the convent…and why.

"There's the Jeep we left stuck in the mud."

"Hey. I'll have you know that I purchased that decrepit transport, and paid a few bucks *more* than I ought to have, considering its deplorable condition."

"Really." She stepped back, holding the tube of antiseptic aloft. "Who'd you buy it from then?"

"Some lad in Puerto Grande, if you must know." If he'd heard that defensive tone in anyone else's voice he'd have laughed uproariously. As it was, he was considerably annoyed by it. "His whole family was trying to sell off nearly all their belongings," he finished. "A bicycle missing a wheel, a radio that was a good twenty years old, a swaybacked excuse of a mule. They were trying to get enough together to pay for the kid's sister's first—"

"—first semester of college," she finished, taking the words right out of his mouth.

He frowned. "Yeah."

"Puerto Grande is a small village," she murmured. "We all knew about the Zamora family. Brisa is the youngest and will be the first member of their family ever to go to college. *You're* the one who bought their Jeep."

"Isn't that what I've been trying to say?"

She smiled softly and stepped forward again, right into the vee of his legs. Her chocolate-brown eyes were on a level with his mouth, and their focus seemed to be fixated there. "What am I going to do about you, Mr. Simon?"

He dug his fingers into the granite on either side of him.

Of course, the stone didn't have a helluva lot of give.

Not like the gilded skin stretched taut over her supple arms would.

He deliberately racked his head against the expanse of mirror behind him.

"You're going to bandage me up," he said, but his voice was gruff. Damn near hoarse.

"In a minute," she whispered. She leaned into him, tilting her head, and light as a whisper, she rubbed her lips over his.

Chapter Ten

She'd started out feeling tenderness.

That was all, Angeline assured herself. Just tenderness for this man, whose unexpected acts of kindness touched her just as much as his more "creative" stunts shocked her.

But tenderness was abruptly eaten up in the incendiary flames that rose far too rapidly for her to fight.

Instead, she stood there, caught, as a wildfire seemed to lick through both of them.

His arm came around her shoulders, an iron band holding her needlessly in place, his mouth as hungry as hers. A sound, raw and full of want, rose in her throat—or was it his?

She couldn't tell, and didn't much care, as he pulled her tighter against him, tighter until she felt the heat of his bare chest burning through her T-shirt, tighter until she felt that undeniably hard ridge rising and pushing against her, making her want to writhe against him in response.

Her fingers pressed greedily into the sinewy muscles cording his bare shoulders and she dragged in a hoarse breath when his lips burned from hers, down over her cheek. Her jaw. Her neck.

His hand curled around her braid, tugging her head back more, until he touched his tongue to the pulse beating frantically at the base of her throat. Again that needful moan filled the room.

It was definitely coming from her. A thoroughly unfamiliar sound—one that was vaguely shocking in some far distant reach of her mind.

She stared up blindly at the gleaming light fixture above their heads. Pinpoints of light shone in her mind, less from the bulbs than from the dazzling wonder of his touch.

Without conscious direction, her hands slid over those wide, wide shoulders, around his neck, into his brown hair that slipped, smooth and thick, through her sifting fingers.

Her braid bunched in his hand, he cupped the back of her head, pulling her mouth back to his. His other hand swept down her spine, around her hip, between them, urging her closer, closer—

"Ouch, oh, sh—" He yanked his head back, knocking his head against the mirror again, this time far less intentionally. "*Bloody* hell."

Angeline froze, reason returning with one swift, hard kick.

She stared at his chest, at the hideous knife wound running parallel to his ribs that looked as if it would bleed again at any moment, at his large hand still cupped over her breast.

His thumb moved, rubbing over the tight hard crest that only rose even more greedily for him.

Horrified at herself, she jerked back, snatching up the antiseptic tube from the floor that she'd dropped somewhere along the way.

Like when she'd been dragging her hands all over his body, completely forgetting the basic fact that the poor man was wounded!

"I'm sorry," she said quickly. She fumbled with the threaded top on the tube. She got it off, only to have the tiny top slip through her shaking fingers. "I...I don't know what I was thinking."

"I know what *I* was thinking." His voice was even deeper than usual. Huskier.

And it sent another ribbon of desire bolting through the ribbon parade already working from her heart down to knees that felt as substantial as jelly.

"I shouldn't have done that." She licked her lips, forcing her attention to stay on his wound as she squeezed an uneven glob of antibiotic cream over it.

He sucked in a hard breath, the ridged muscles of his abdomen jerking. "No, *that* you shouldn't have done," he muttered, and caught the hand delivering the cream and dragged it away before she could do more damage.

She sank her teeth into her tongue for a long moment, trying to master the burning behind her eyes before she did something even more embarrassing than throwing herself at him. "I need to d-dress your wound."

His teeth bared slightly. His eyes were slits of blue between his narrowed lashes. "Pardon me if I tell you that I'd rather *you* just simply undress."

Angeline felt as if she'd lost her ability to speak.

So she just stood there.

Staring at him.

Wanting him.

He looked like an oversized jungle cat, lying in wait for his prey to draw near. And *she* was the prey.

"Here."

She blinked, looking stupidly at the packet of gauze pads he'd picked up from the kit beside him.

"Come on, Angie. Finish the job."

Angie. And spoken in that perfectly British accent that she realized, belatedly, he hadn't dropped for even one moment.

She sucked in another hard breath, this one formed of cold, hard mortification.

He suspected they were being listened in on. He'd done his usual search and destroy, but had he found some sort of bug, after all?

Had someone really been *listening* to them?

To her? To that utterly sexual moan that had flowed out of her, more than once?

She racked her brains, trying to think if she'd said his name, as well—God, it had been screaming through her mind, her body—

She snatched the packet from him and tore it open. Tossed the sterile packaging aside to gently fit the gauze over his wound. "It would be better if I had a few butterflies instead of just this gauze to pull it together more tightly." The hoarseness of her voice went a long way toward diffusing her brusque words.

"Keep talking, babe." He'd tilted his head back slightly, watching her from beneath his lashes. "I'm getting hotter by the second."

She flushed and layered on more gauze, creating a cushioned dressing. He pulled the spool of tape from the kit and held it looped over his finger.

Unfortunately, his finger was attached to his hand that was resting on the very firm bulge of thigh covered in somewhat damp denim.

She swallowed on her dry throat again, and slid the tape off his finger, trying to pretend that she wasn't perfectly aware of his erection mere inches away.

She tore off a length of tape and carefully sealed the edges of the dressing. "This is paper tape. It won't hurt when we have to change it," she assured, putting all of her effort into keeping her voice steady and smooth, and failing miserably. "But you'll want to keep it dry, so when you shower, we'll cover it with plastic first."

"Easier to take a bath. You can wash my back."

Her gaze slid guiltily to the enormous built-for-two tub and she knew, if he told her to turn on the taps right that instant, she'd have been hard pressed not to do just that. No matter that the walls might have ears, no matter that Eva was sound asleep in one room on the couch and Davey in another.

No matter that she'd never shared a bath with any man, much less shared her body.

When it came to Brody-Hewitt-Simon Paine, she feared she was excruciatingly willing to share *everything*.

She pressed her palms together, feeling the wedding ring on her finger. It no longer felt so strange wearing the gold band.

Which was a realization that on its own was enough to make her feel somewhat daunted.

"Do, uh, do you need something for the pain? I've only

got over-the-counter stuff, I'm afraid, but you could take a prescription dosage of it."

"Is that the only pain you're willing to take care of?"

She opened her mouth. Closed it again before the assurance came out that she didn't really mean, anyway. Instead, she admitted the raw truth. "No."

His eyes narrowed again. He let out a hiss between his teeth. "You know how to make it hard on a man, don't you." His voice seemed to come up from somewhere deep inside him.

She flushed all over again.

"No pun intended," he added.

The flush grew even hotter.

He sat forward, wincing a little as he pressed his palm against the new dressing, and straightened from the granite countertop. "You know, it's a lot easier to resist you when I think you're going to be strong enough for the both of us. If you're going to look at me with those eyes a man could drown in and be *honest* like that, I don't know what the hell to do with you."

Her eyebrows rose with sudden boldness. "You don't *know?*"

He gave a short laugh. "Angeli—" He bit off the rest of her name.

She pressed her lips together.

"I don't often forget myself," he murmured. He lifted his hand and brushed the back of his finger down her cheek. "But you sure do have a way of getting me right to that point."

Her knees evidently decided jelly was too substantial, and dissolved into water instead.

Then he closed his hand around hers and drew her out of the sinful bathroom, past the bed she couldn't bring herself to look at and back into the main room, where he opened the door of the refrigerator and gestured.

Angeline peered at the pitcher of water, which was the only thing inside, except for the gleaming shelves. "Good grief. Are those—?" At least three inches of metallic-looking discs—each no larger than a watch battery— were sunk in the water, filling the bottom of the pitcher.

Brody nodded.

He'd told her that paranoia kept him sane, but she'd sort of taken that as an exaggeration.

Looking at those dozens of discs now, she wasn't so sure it was an exaggeration.

Not when they were dauntingly real.

He pushed the refrigerator door closed again.

Angeline folded her arms tightly over her chest and looked around, as if she'd be able to see if there were any more bugs still hidden around. That, of course, was as likely as her being able to jump over the moon.

If Brody hadn't found them, why on earth would she?

"You think there might be others?" She looked back at him, only to find his gaze fixed on her arms, folded across her breasts.

The ribbon parade inside her jumped right back into action, sliding into an all-out rumba.

"Possibly."

She dropped her arms and deliberately turned her back on him, looking over at Eva, who still slept, sprawled facedown on the sofa. The television remote control sat on the rattan table next to the sofa. The device wouldn't be very useful, unless Brody saw fit to put the parts back together.

"Is this how Roger always greets you? With such, well, such *nice* accommodations?"

"Pretty much."

"But he said you worked together. With—" She didn't know what she could dare to say—whether she ought not to mention Hollins-Winword—but Brody, showing his usual perception, understood, anyway.

He shook his head.

Roger had talked about their association being twelve years past. But Angeline had been quite sure Brody had been with Hollins-Winword since his very early twenties. He'd told her that the very first time they'd met. She'd told him about coming from Wyoming and he'd told her he didn't come from anywhere.

And then he'd given her a gargantuan flirtatious grin and told her that if she needed anyone to show her the ropes, he had plenty that he'd be willing to lasso around her.

"Then what did you and he…" She trailed off when he lifted his hand. The universal *stop* sign.

She sighed. Her curiosity would have to go unappeased, obviously. At least for now. But later, she fully intended to discover more about the things that made Brody tick.

"I'm going to go out and stretch my legs," he said abruptly. "You'll be fine here, though. If you need anything, just ring Roger."

She looked toward the door again, with its four substantial locks. Not even in her apartment in Atlanta did she have that much security on her door. "Are you, uh, going to take the girl?"

He smiled suddenly. "Delilah, you mean? Yes."

Obviously, he didn't worry about someone wondering who Delilah was. "Are you going to try to reach your—" handler "—friend about our travel arrangements?"

"That's the plan."

"Will you be gone long?"

"Why? You going to miss me?" He tilted his head closer to hers, his voice dropping even lower. "Go swim in that big tub while I'm gone," he suggested. "Think of me."

She pursed her lips together, giving him an annoyed look that didn't fool him for a solitary second, if the un-holy gleam in his eyes was anything to go by.

He disappeared into the bedroom and came out a min-ute later, the blue T-shirt back in place. He hadn't tucked it in, though, and she assumed that was all the better to hide Delilah with.

"The children will need to eat when they wake," she told him, wondering if whoever was listening—*if* anyone was listening—thought she sounded like a proper wife.

"Then eat," he said simply.

Which made her feel idiotic. As if he thought she couldn't make a simple decision like that. "I *meant,* would you prefer that we wait for you to return, so we can all eat together." That's what families did mostly. At least in her experience.

Her parents had sat down at the dinner table nearly every night with her and J.D. and Casey while they'd been growing up. They'd talk about their day, some-times they'd argue, but far more often than that, there was laughter.

And always there had been the security of knowing their roots were set in an unshakeable foundation.

It was the kind of home she'd wanted to make some-day for *her* children, if she ever had any. These days, that desire had come less and less frequently, though. Not be-cause she still didn't want it someday, but because it had become more difficult to see herself sitting across her own dinner table from the man of her dreams.

"Touching," he said, which made her search his expression for amusement.

But she found none and realized that was even more disturbing.

"I'll probably be back in an hour or so. If I'm not, go on down to the restaurant. Have Roger charge it to the room." At *that,* he did look amused.

Which made her wonder if he intended to finagle his way out of paying for their lodgings altogether. She'd have asked, but assumed that was probably not one of those things he'd want to be possibly overheard.

"And if you're longer than that?" She couldn't help but think about his cautions back in Caracas.

She didn't need to elaborate. He understood, perfectly. "Same thing I said before still stands."

They were staying in a room that had been bugged, presumably by the owner himself. Yet he nevertheless believed the man would get her and the children back to the States, just because "Simon" had asked him to.

"I think there's an interesting story in there somewhere," she murmured.

"Not one worth the effort of retelling." He headed for the door, stopped short and backtracked, surprising her right out of her sanity again when he pressed a hard, fast kiss to her mouth.

She swayed unsteadily when he straightened and stepped away from her. His sharp eyes, of course, noticed her swaying around like a tree in a hurricane, and he gave a little nod. "Good," he murmured. "Glad I'm not the only one thrown for a loop." Then he strode to the door, flipped open the multiple locks and peered out.

Evidently, *some* things didn't change, just because they were currently ensconced in considerably nicer—albeit possibly surveilled—digs. "Lock these after me."

She was already heading for the door to do so.

A moment later, he was gone.

She slid the substantial locks into place and turned back to face the lovely suite. She suddenly felt cold, and it wasn't only the reminder that their purpose there at all wasn't a lighthearted one.

Hewitt and Sophia Stanley were still out there somewhere, being held against their will, and their children *were* in danger, as well.

What also had Angeline shivering, though, was the realization that for the first time in her life, she could put a face on the man who sat on the other side of the dinner table from her, with their children scattered along in between in that lovely image of the future.

Brody's face.

Yet he was the man who had—within the last forty-eight hours, no less—admitted that he had no yearning desire to stay in any one place for any particular length of time.

He was the least likely person she knew who'd ever even want that dinnertime ritual with the family, who'd want to see the sun rise and set day after day over the same horizon, much less the same home.

So what was she doing?

Was she keeping the man at arm's length, never taking his flirtations seriously, never letting herself get swept into the wake of his appeal?

No.

She was throwing herself right into his arms, and no amount of reminding herself all the reasons why doing so again would be a monumental mistake seemed to be enough to keep her from taking that flight again. Because, right or wrong, Angeline finally faced the truth.

She was in love with Brody Paine.

Chapter Eleven

Considerably more than an "hour or two" had passed before Brody returned later that day.

As Angeline had predicted, the kids had been ravenous when they'd awakened. Very aware of the bugs that Brody might not have discovered, she decided it was better to take Eva and Davey down to the restaurant.

She'd been afraid that the kids might slip—call her by her name or something, but they never did. Not even when Roger, insisting on meeting their every culinary desire—right up to and including Davey's requested deep-fried macaroni and cheese—had sat down at the table with them had they given anything away.

If anything, she was as wary of something coming out of *her* mouth. Squelching her curiosity over just how Brody and Roger were connected was nigh impossible, though she managed.

Just.

While Roger, on the other hand, seemed to feel free in asking plenty of his own questions about her relationship with Simon.

She tap danced her way around, giving the man direct answers as much as she could, but feared she wasn't really fooling anyone.

Then, when Roger had turned his focus on the children, and asked how they thought their stepfather rated, she sat forward, giving Eva and Davey steady looks in return to the startled ones they gave her.

"They think he's wonderful, obviously," she assured Roger on their behalf. "Of course they love their father, as they should. But Simon has been good to all of us." She turned and smiled, full wattage, into his face, knowing perfectly well the effect that usually had on most members of the male species. "And what about you, Roger? Any woman and child keeping your home fire burning?"

His speculative smile turned regretful. "If there were a beautiful woman such as you who wished to burn any fires with me, I'd certainly consider setting several."

"Stop flattering my wife, old man," Brody said, appearing almost out of nowhere beside their table. He slid his hand, deliberately proprietary, over Angeline's shoulder, and left it there. "Just because you haven't found a woman of your own is no reason to go poaching in my territory."

"What is this accusation of flattery about?" Roger pressed his hand across his heart. "I speak only the truth."

Angeline just laughed lightly, and pushed her chair back, rising from the table. "My head spins," she assured. "But you'll have to excuse us. The children get restless if they sit too long at the dinner table." It was a blatant exaggeration and one that she felt slightly guilty for offering.

But only slightly.

Eva, Angeline noticed as the girl tucked her napkin under the edge of her half-empty plate, was looking a little flushed again. "The meal was very good," she said politely. "Thank you." She elbowed Davey.

"Thank you," he echoed, rubbing his side and giving her an aggrieved look.

"I'll join you in a few, love," Simon-Brody told her. "Roger and I have some catching up to do."

"Of course." She sent a smile Roger's way again, and ushered the children away from the table. She couldn't help wondering if the "catching up" had to do with the matter of getting the four of them back to the States.

"Can we swim?" Davey asked as they left the restaurant. They could see the pool through the gleaming windows overlooking the courtyard area of the hotel.

Angeline resisted the urge to look back at Brody. "Do you know how to swim?"

"My dad taught us," Davey said.

"We're s'posed to wait an hour after eating before swimming," Eva said, giving him a severe look.

"I think that's an old wives' tale," Angeline murmured.

"And besides, we don't have our swimsuits with us," the girl reminded.

They left the lobby behind and headed across the courtyard. "You've got a T-shirt and shorts," Angeline said. "You could wear that. In fact, let's just stop at the swimming pool, right now. You can roll up your jeans and dangle your legs over the side, at the very least."

"Yippee." Davey grabbed Angeline around the thighs and hugged her. He darted toward the pool.

Muffling an oath, Angeline nudged Eva ahead of her, hurrying after his precipitous race for the pool. In contrast to Davey's energy, Eva, however, was showing very little.

Angeline slipped her hand along Eva's ponytail. "Everything is going to be all right," she told her softly.

"I'm not a baby. You don't have to say things that might not be true." Eva sounded fierce, but Angeline still recognized the need beneath that begged for reassurance.

Her heart squeezed. She stopped there in the middle of the narrow sidewalk, facing Eva. Amidst the profusion of lovely flowering shrubs, it seemed hard to believe that anything terrible could touch them.

But Angeline had seen too much in her work to let herself believe that "prettiness" provided any sort of substantial barrier against disaster.

"I don't think you're a baby, Eva," she said with perfect truthfulness. "And I'm not lying because I think you can't handle the truth. I truly believe that this all will turn out fine in the end."

"Because of, um, Simon."

Angeline smiled faintly. She smoothed her hand along Eva's ponytail again. "Between him and the three of us, I think we've made a pretty good team." She slipped her hand beneath Eva's small, pointed chin. "Keep your faith strong, sweetheart. Amazing things can result."

Her eyes shimmered. "My mom says stuff like that," she whispered.

Angeline let out a long sigh, and leaned down, hugging the girl's narrow shoulders. She knew she'd made the right move when Eva hugged her back. Tightly.

Her throat closed a little. What brave children the Stanleys were. "And I can't wait to meet her and tell both her and your dad what a fabulous pair of kids they've got," she said just as softly.

"I just wish I could talk to them." Eva's fists pounded against Angeline's shoulders in frustration.

"I know, honey. I know."

From his vantage point in Roger's second-floor office, Brody had a clear view of the courtyard and the pool. He saw Davey yanking off his tennis shoes and rolling up his pants. Saw Angeline stop and talk with solemn-faced Eva, then after a while, not looking quite so serious, they joined Davey poolside.

Soon all three of them were sitting on the edge of the pool, their pants up around their knees, as they kicked and splashed each other.

"You haven't told her, have you." Roger sat at his desk, where he'd just finished making the arrangements to help get them out of the country.

Brody leaned his shoulder against the tall window, taking his gaze off Angeline and the kids only long enough to scan the courtyard. Seeing nothing unusual among the lush landscape, he looked back at his *family*. "No point."

"You and I go back a long way, Simon."

"Too long," Brody drawled.

"We would have made a great team," Roger continued, ignoring the interruption. "If you hadn't bailed on me."

"I didn't bail."

"We didn't exactly hang out our shingle, either, my friend." Roger's voice never lost the gait of his native Jamaica, but now it sounded pretty dry. "Sterling and Brody," he reminded. "Attorneys at Law."

"Brody and Sterling," he corrected blandly. "And just

because I didn't keep with the plan didn't mean *you* had to ditch it for all this." He gestured out the window. "You were never with Hollins as long as I was, anyway."

"True." Brody heard, rather than saw, the fatalistic shrug his one-time partner gave. "I was recruited out of university, while you—"

"I was recruited out of grade school," Brody muttered, exaggerating only slightly. He'd been fifteen when his family was killed, and fifteen when he'd been taken under the wing of Hollins-Winword's main man, the infamous Coleman Black.

Warm and fuzzy, though, it had not been.

"I never did understand why you stay with the agency when you hate them as much as you do."

"The agency makes freaks out of us all," Brody murmured. Not even Roger knew just how "close" a relationship Brody'd had with Cole. "That's not hate. That's plain fact. Look at the way you decorate your suites around this place." He shot Roger a dry look.

"You don't have to worry about your privacy," Roger added, drolly. "I only monitor the room when I have something to gain from it."

"Sounding like your pirate roots are showing, there, Rog."

Roger's teeth flashed, but his expression stayed sober. "If you didn't like what the agency was making of us, then you shouldn't have gone back in. You left it, Simon. You were free of it all. So was I."

Yet Brody had walked away from the legal practice they'd planned. He'd had a taste of what life—normal life—could be like, and he'd bolted just when he'd been on the verge of feasting on all that normalcy. He'd gone right back to the agency that had failed in keeping his family safe.

He was well aware of the twisted reasoning and wasn't sure if it was better or worse than the other reason he'd gone back.

Because Cole had asked him to.

"You should tell her."

Trust Roger not to let an issue drop. He'd obviously never lost his liking for tenacity. "Why didn't *you* stick with the legal career? Why go into the hotel business? *Here?*" Brody and Sterling, Attorneys at Law, was supposed to have been located in Connecticut, not co-incidentally very far from the factory that fronted Hollins-Winword's center of operations.

"We all have our paths to walk, my friend. My path brought me back here."

"The woman you loved died here," Brody said. He knew that Brigitte's death during her and Roger's last year of college had been the incident that propelled him into the cold bosom of Hollins-Winword. They'd wanted to close the human trafficking ring in which Roger's girl-friend had unknowingly strayed during a spring break vacation with two of her friends.

All three young women had disappeared, their bodies never recovered.

"The last place Brigitte was seen was in the hellhole of a place right on this very location," Roger agreed evenly. "So when it came up for sale eight years ago, I tore it down and built paradise for her, instead. That's my path. Tell Angie who you are, Simon. I recognize that ring she's wearing."

He wished he'd been more sparing with the details of their situation. He'd known Roger would help, he just hadn't wanted to have to ask for it. But the situation was definitely turning for the worse. The sooner Brody got them all back in the U.S., where he could squirrel them away in a location that he *could* trust, the better.

"Every *case* matters to me," he countered flatly. "And who I *am* is Brody Paine. Simon Brody should have died a long time ago."

"Just because your family did, doesn't mean *you* should have, as well."

He didn't bother answering. The argument was old and hadn't been worth fighting even when it was new. "When's the pilot going to be ready to leave?"

"As soon as the ink is dry on the passports." Roger may have left the agency behind, but he hadn't lost some of his more creative talents. "You'll be welcomed back into the States with opened arms and nary a question," he assured. "If Santina's guy is on your trail, he's not going to follow it beyond here."

"The agency could still use you."

Roger just shook his head. "I've made my place here. And my peace. I am content. You should try it."

"Not cut out for it, I'm afraid." Brody finally turned away from the bird's-eye-view window. "I appreciate the assistance."

"What are old partners for?"

Roger's voice rang in Brody's ears as he headed down to join Angeline by the pool. To hear Roger talk, one would think they'd been partners for decades rather than just two years.

But, he was also the only regular partner that Brody had ever been assigned.

Look how well *that* had turned out.

They'd both decided to leave the agency and open a

law practice. Some stupid-ass dream of following in their fathers' footsteps.

Funny how it had turned out. Or not so funny, really, since it turned out that Brody pretty much *was* following in his father's footsteps.

Just not the man that, for the first fifteen years of his life, he'd thought had been his father.

He pushed away the memories at the same time he pushed through the glass doors and entered the courtyard. The sky was still heavy and thick with clouds, but the afternoon air felt warm and sultry.

And when Angeline lifted her head, watching his approach with a faint smile on her face, it wasn't only the air that felt warm.

Tell her, Roger had said.

But what would be the point? He didn't talk about his past with anyone. Roger only knew part of it because Brody had clued him in one drunken night. Roger had told Brody about Brigitte's death. And Brody had told Rog about his parents, the barrister and the surgeon.

Angeline had drawn her legs out of the water, and she pushed to her bare feet, watching him with those dark, melted-chocolate eyes. "You're looking very serious," she murmured when his steps carried him to her side. "Did you reach your friend?"

Translate that to handler, he knew.

Admitting that he hadn't would only emphasize to her what a deep kettle of stinking fish they'd landed in. But he was coming to realize that voicing the lies he was used to wasn't as easy when he was looking square into her lovely oval face.

It was almost laughable, really, when Brody's entire

existence for nearly as long as she'd been alive had been a string of lies, one right after another.

The only truth had been the agency—and the man who ran it—who held in its grip the end of all of those strings. Like some damn collection of balloons.

Only if there had ever been any cheery balloons being held aloft on the end of all those strings, they'd long ago popped, leaving nothing but tatters in their place.

"No," he said, opting for truth in at least this one thing.

She drew her brows together. Her concern evident, she touched his arm, only to press her lips together and pull away again. She crossed her arms and the ring on her finger glinted softly. "You think something's gone wrong."

There were two reasons why a handler would maintain silence like this. Because their security was broken, in which case the agent was on his own, or because the agency found itself in the rare position of needing deniability. In which case, the agent was on his own.

Either way, the agent was on his own.

Even Brody wasn't protected from that protocol.

He pushed his fingers through his hair. There were a few scenarios he could think of that would prompt either option, and none of them were pretty.

"Simon?" She was still waiting.

"The last woman to call me Simon was my mother," he murmured.

Her eyes went wide. "I—" She shook her head a little, as if to dislodge whatever words were stuck in that long throat of hers that just begged for him to taste.

"Come on." Proving that he was still a coward when it came to dealing with anything really personal, he turned toward the kids, who were splashing at the edge of the pool. "Move it out," he told them. "We've got a plane to catch."

He looked back at Angeline.

She was still staring at him as if she'd never seen him before. "Where are we flying to?" Her voice was faint.

"The one place that I actually trust we'll all be safe," he said quietly. "Wyoming."

Chapter Twelve

Angeline had expected that they would be flying on another small private plane.

Brody…Simon…what*ever* his name really was, was full of his usual surprises though. After she'd gathered the children from the pool and they'd cleaned up once more, Roger had driven them to the airport himself. Before he'd dropped them off, though, he'd handed Brody a manila envelope.

The false passports that Brody produced for the four of them from that envelope didn't garner so much as a second glance from airport security. With a few minutes to spare, Simon and Angie Black, along with their two children, Eva and Davey, were boarding the jet bound for home.

Roger had even managed first-class seats.

The day seemed as if it had been going on forever, but

when they landed in Miami, the sun was still hanging over the horizon, though barely. Brody bought them all pizza in one of the airport food courts. His cash reserve, she suspected, had to be nearly depleted, just from the cost of getting them out of Caracas. How he'd purchased the four first-class tickets back to Florida was a mystery.

Maybe he'd borrowed from Roger.

Her curiosity had to go unanswered, however, as they barely had time to finish eating before they were boarding another flight.

This time bound for Seattle.

As a route to Wyoming, it was definitely going around the long way.

What followed was the most exhausting, circuitous route that Angeline could never have imagined even in her worst nightmares. More than thirty-six hours had passed since they'd left Miami when Brody finally, finally picked up the duffel bag from the baggage claim and headed, not to another airline ticket counter, but to the exit.

Davey was fitfully asleep, hanging over Brody's shoulder like a limp sack of potatoes. Eva looked flushed and glassy-eyed, as she dragged herself along beside Angeline, who *felt* flushed and glassy eyed.

She honestly didn't feel like she could even string two coherent thoughts together, as she—keeping an instinctive grip on Eva's hand—blindly followed Brody onto a small shuttle van outside the airport. Even though the van was empty and they could each have had their own long seat, they sat three abreast, with Davey still on Brody's lap.

Angeline thought it was morning, but she couldn't be certain. Her eyes felt like there were glass shards in them from lack of sleep. She couldn't even be sure where they were.

"Almost there," Brody murmured beside her.

She jerked a little, realizing her head had been sinking down onto his shoulder in the same way that Eva's head had found her lap.

The shuttle driver—a middle-aged man wearing a John Deere ball cap and a grin—looked over his shoulder at them. "You folks look like you've had a long trip. This the front end of your trip or the back?"

"Back," Brody said, his drawl an exact imitation of the driver's. "Took the family to Hawaii." He shook his head, sounding rueful. "Damn glad to be back on my own turf, if you know what I mean."

The driver chuckled. "Yessir, I do." He turned into a long-term parking lot.

Angeline would have smiled at the irony, too, if she'd had the energy. Seemed as if Hawaii was one of the very few States in which they hadn't managed to cross over or land.

The shuttle stopped and let them off, and Angeline braced herself against the weight as Brody transferred Davey to her arms. "Wait here," he said.

Angeline wouldn't have had the gumption to *not* wait. She braced her feet apart, holding the boy in her arms while Eva leaned heavily against her side and watched Brody disappear down a row of parked cars. Within minutes, a dark-colored SUV stopped beside them.

Brody came around and lifted Davey out of her arms again and strapped him into one of the rear seats. Angeline helped Eva in after her brother before taking the front seat beside Brody. She fumbled with the seat belt and he pushed her fingers away, clicking it into place himself.

"Don't worry," he murmured. "I *own* this one."

She blinked, trying to find the sense in his words. "Really?"

"Would I lie?" His hand brushed down her cheek and she felt herself pressing into his warm palm.

"Yes."

He made a soft sound. "Hang in there, toots. We'll be home soon."

"I don't even know where we are."

"Billings."

"I thought we were heading to Wyoming."

"We are."

"Then why'd we land in Montana?"

His hand finally left her cheek. "Because that's where this was." He patted the steering wheel.

"You always keep a truck parked in the long-term lot in Billings?"

"Pretty much." He sounded remarkably cheerful considering that he had to be just as tired as she was.

"It'll take us hours to get to Weaver from here."

"I never said we were going to Weaver."

She forced her eyes wider at that. They had already left the airport behind. "When you said Wyoming, I assumed—"

"Wrong."

Her lips compressed. She couldn't believe the wave of disappointment that seemed to engulf her. She'd wanted to go back to Weaver. Far more than she'd realized until knowing that it wasn't, in fact, where they were heading at all. "I should have known enough by now to ask you exactly what your intentions were."

"My intentions are always honorable," he assured, looking amused.

She closed her eyes and turned her head, resting it against the seat.

"I have a place near Sheridan," he said.

That brought her eyes right open again. She looked at him, lost for words.

"Nobody knows about it. I mean nobody who can connect it to me and what I do. We'll be safe there until I can figure out…everything."

"Oh," she managed faintly. "Is it really yours?"

"The truck or the place?"

"Both."

"Yeah. They're both really mine."

She swallowed. Moistened her lips. "So what, um, what name does it say on the ownership papers?"

"Does it matter?"

Did it? She felt oddly close to tears and blamed it on exhaustion. "No," she lied. "As long as there is an immoveable horizontal surface to sleep on, I don't much care."

"What if I told you there was no furniture?"

"Is there a floor?"

He laughed softly. "Yes."

"Then we're good to go," she murmured and closed her eyes again. Keeping them open simply took too much effort.

She didn't open them again until the shuddering of the SUV jarred her awake.

They weren't still pelting down the mountain after St. Agnes. They weren't still racing toward Venezuela. She wasn't still inhaling Brody's entire being in that heavenly hotel suite that had been overrun with bugs of an electronic variety.

"Honey, we're home." Brody singsonged in his low,

deep voice. He turned off the engine and they sat there for a moment, the utter silence broken only by Davey's soft, snuffling snores.

Angeline's curiosity would kick in before long, she knew. But just then all she felt was utter relief at the sight of a long stone-fronted ranch house that sat in the crook of a small hill, with nothing but open field currently covered in undulating waves of green lying around it for nearly as far as the eye could see.

"You planning to sit here for the rest of the day?"

She realized that Brody was watching her curiously. He'd unhooked his seat belt and his door was open. Fresh air was pouring into the SUV. "No." She unsnapped her safety belt and climbed out of the truck, stretching hugely.

There was an entrance to the house on this side. Just a plain door painted a warm ivory to match the other painted portions of the structure. Those were minimal at best; most of the house was faced in rustic stone.

Brody hadn't needed to wake Davey. The boy was already climbing the concrete steps that led up to that side door. He tried the latch, and looked back at the truck. "It's locked, Mr. Dad."

"Yup." Brody took the steps in a couple bounds. He didn't pull out a key, though, she noticed. Instead, he flipped up an invisible panel near the door, punched in something, and then closed the panel up once again. "Try it now."

Davey turned the knob. The door swung open without a sound. "Cool," he breathed, and without a second's hesitation, headed inside.

"Should you let him go on ahead like that?"

"This is about the only place that I feel confident to

let him explore. He's a kid." Brody shrugged. "Let him go adventuring when he can."

Something soft and sweet curled inside of her. "You'd make a good father," she murmured.

His eyebrows shot up into the brown hair that tumbled, unkempt, across his forehead. "Perish the thought." He practically shuddered as he followed the boy inside.

Soft and sweet turned crisp and dry.

She reached behind her and joggled Eva's knee. "Hey there, sweetie. Rise and shine."

Eva slowly peeled open one weary eye, and the girl fairly tumbled out of the truck. Angeline caught her arm, and together they made their way up the steps and inside.

Not knowing what to expect about the interior—maybe all he really did have were bare floors and unfurnished rooms, after all—the sight that greeted them came as a welcome surprise.

The door they'd come in through opened onto a tidy, slightly austere laundry room. On one side was another door, open to reveal a half bath, and on the other was a kitchen that could have popped from the pages of a decorating magazine. Lots of gleaming granite countertop and stainless steel appliances built into warm wood cabinets.

Off to one side, surrounded by a bay of windows that overlooked the—her tired mind tried to orient herself—the rear of the property, she decided, sat a large square walnut table, surrounded by four chairs. It even held a wooden bowl of fruit in the center of it.

From overhead, she could hear the faint thump of rapid footsteps. Undoubtedly Davey's as he continued his intrepid exploration. She followed Eva from the kitchen into a hallway that wasn't really a hall at all but more of an open circle. The staircase—pretty much a masterpiece

of carved wood—curved up the wall to the second floor.
There were a few closed doors and the other side of the
round area opened into a giant great room.

The house *definitely* didn't look so large from the outside.

Davey popped his head over the landing above them.
"Eva, come *see*. There's a room for you and a room for
me."

Showing a little more life, Eva went up the stairs to
join her brother.

Angeline crossed the great room, drawn by the view
from the windows on the far wall of the not-so-distant
mountains. Something about that view had everything
inside her seeming to sigh in relief and missing Weaver.

"Come on."

She looked over her shoulder. Standing amid the collection of leather couches and nubby upholstered chairs,
Brody looked surprisingly "in" place. Which made her
realize that she'd never let herself think about whether
or not the man even *had* a home. He'd always been just
"Brody"—an entire entity, complete and intact all on his
own—as if he had no need or desire for the usual things
that most people wanted in their lives.

"Where?"

"You wanted a horizontal surface, didn't you?"

The thought that swept into her mind had absolutely
nothing to do with the act of sleeping upon one. She
tucked her tongue behind her teeth and nodded. "Sleep."
The word sounded forced.

And if the way Brody's lips twitched was any indication, he was well aware of the direction of her unruly
thoughts. He turned, but instead of heading toward the
staircase, he opened one of the doors in that circular

nonhallway, and waited, clearly expecting Angeline to precede him.

She passed through the doorway and went a little limp inside at the perfection of the master suite that waited on the other side. At least she assumed it was the master suite. As a guest bedroom, it would definitely border on overkill.

The bed was massive, owing a good portion of that impression to the rich, deep gleam of the wooden bed frame. The mattress was even covered with a thoroughly unbachelor-like comforter. All golds and reds and browns that were complemented by coordinating pillows—again oversized and beautiful without managing to be frilly or fussy. The tall narrow windows that flanked the bed were dressed with wooden shutters, currently open, and cornices over the top finished with fabric that matched the bedding. There were two chairs sitting alongside each other in another corner with a table tucked between. The perfect spot for coffee in the morning. Aside from them, there was no other freestanding furniture in the room at all. Everything else—shelves and drawers—was constructed of wood that looked similar to the bed and was built into the wall facing it. And in the center of all that detailed woodwork was a fireplace. One of the most perfectly beautiful fireplaces she'd ever seen.

"Who, um, who did the decorating for you?"

He looked wounded. "What? You think I couldn't have done it?"

She walked to the fireplace and reached up to pluck a fat, squat red candle off the mantel. She sniffed it. "You picked out bayberry candles?"

His dimple flashed. "Okay. I hired an outfit to take care of things for me. They *did* follow my instructions," he added defensively. "Do you think I have no taste whatsoever?"

She sat on the edge of the bed and the mattress was so high that her toes actually cleared the floor. "I think," she said slowly, "that I don't really know you at all. I thought I did, but…" She shook her head, her voice trailing away.

He stood with his back to the fireplace. Above the mantel with its artful collection of candles and an engraved wooden box, a large oil painting of a handsome couple posed with two small children was propped against the stone chimney. "But now you don't? What is it you want to know?"

What *did* she want to know? Besides everything?

She looked from Brody's face to the family portrait. There wasn't really a resemblance that she could spot between the faces there and his, but what other purpose would he have for displaying it in his private bedroom if they were strangers?

She realized she was pressing her thumb against the wedding ring that she still hadn't taken off her finger, turning it in a slow circle. "How long have you lived here?" It wasn't at all the deep, meaningful questions that plagued her where he was concerned.

"I had this house built nearly five years ago."

More surprises. For some reason she'd had the sense he'd acquired it more recently. "Built," she said slowly. "But how *long* have you lived here?"

He smiled faintly. "About six months, give or take. I… made more permanent arrangements to be here when I was pulling the gig in Weaver last November."

He meant when he was protecting little Megan.

"Why then?"

He lifted a shoulder. "I was in the vicinity. Easier to take care of the details."

"No. I mean *why* then? If you hadn't really lived here in all the time since you built it, what prompted you to do something about it in November?"

His lashes narrowed. His blue eyes were bloodshot and his jaw was shaded with whiskers. His jeans seemed to hang a little loosely on his tight hips and the blue shirt was definitely looking travel weary.

She could only imagine what state his bandage was in.

He looked, frankly, like hell, yet he was still the most beautiful man she'd ever seen.

"That's not really a question you want to be asking right now," he said.

She shifted, pressing her palms flat on the mattress beside her hips. "Why?" Her voice turned wry. "Don't I have a high enough security clearance to hear the details?"

"No. Because everything I've ever done about this place has been prompted by you."

Chapter Thirteen

Brody's words swirled inside Angeline's head, making her dizzy. Or maybe it was her heart, shuddering around inside without an even beat to save its soul, that was causing her curious light-headededness.

How could *she* have ever influenced something in Brody's personal life?

They'd barely known one another.

That didn't stop you from falling for him.

She ignored the voice inside her head. Moistened her lips and swallowed against the sudden constriction there. "I don't understand."

He rubbed his chin, looking oddly uneasy. And when, less than a moment later, Davey bolted into the room, he looked happy for the interruption.

He leaned over and scooped the boy up by the waist, leaving his arms and legs dangling.

Davey gave a squeal of laughter and squirmed.

Angeline's heart lurched all over again. She looked from Brody and the boy to the portrait once more.

"Where's your sister?" Brody was asking the giggling boy.

"In the bathroom," Davey managed to impart between laughs. *"Again."* He tried to reach Brody's torso with his little fingers, intent on tickling, but couldn't. "Are we gonna stay here until my mom and dad come to get us?"

"That's the plan. Which means we've got to get some food into this place so we don't starve." Brody swung the boy from one side to the other.

Davey went into peals of laughter again.

Clearly, *he* wasn't upset by the latest turn of events.

Angeline pushed herself off the bed, ignoring the weak feeling that still plagued her knees, and started for the doorway.

"Where you going?"

"To figure out what you need in your kitchen."

He shook his head, waving away the idea. "No need. I'll just call up Mrs. Bedford."

"Who's that?" Davey asked curiously, beating Angeline to the punch.

"She—" Brody swung the kid upright finally, and brought their noses close "—is my housekeeper," he told him. "And she'll have us set up with plenty of food in just two shakes."

"Two shakes of what?"

"Of you." Brody jiggled the boy again, sending him into another spasm of laughter.

Angeline smiled faintly, as entranced by the un-guarded grin on Brody's face as she was by the idea that

Brody had something as unlikely as a housekeeper. "I'll just make sure the kids get settled in, then," she said.

"Take a nap," Brody told her, nodding toward the bed. His bed. "I can handle them on my own for a bit."

She pressed her lips together. The truth was, after the last few days she believed that Brody was capable of handling them for a lot more than a "bit." He wasn't just good at protecting children. No matter how much he shuddered over the idea of having his own, he was good *with* children.

It shamed her that she was so surprised by the fact. As if she'd given him short shrift when she—coming from the family that she did—should know just exactly how multifaceted a caring man could be.

"Maybe I should use one of the other rooms," she suggested.

Davey had looped his arm around Brody's shoulder. "But then I'd gotta share with Eva. And I *al-ays* gotta share with her."

Brody's gaze slanted toward Angeline, full of sudden devilry. "Think of his sacrifice, babe. We can't have that."

She swallowed. *That* was the Brody she knew and loved.

Unfortunately, she was well aware that thought had become less a turn of phrase than reality with every passing hour they'd spent together.

"Fine." She headed back toward the bed, watching Brody from the corner of her eyes as she slowly reached for one of the large decorative pillows at the head of it. She pushed it aside, and turned back the comforter, revealing the smooth chocolate-brown sheets beneath.

He suddenly looked less goading and more…disconcerted. "All right, then. Let's leave her to it, Dave, my man." He tossed the boy over his shoulder, setting off more giggles, and headed to the door. When Angeline caught him looking back at her, she deliberately drew back the top sheet and sat down on the bed. She leaned back and slowly toed off one boot. Then the other.

Brody shook his head. "You're dangerous," he muttered, and closed the door on her, leaving her alone in the room.

She flopped back on the bed, her palm pressed to her thundering heart. What was dangerous was thinking that she could ever play with the fire that was Brody Paine and come out unscorched.

She rolled over, tucking the down bed pillow that had been hidden behind the sham beneath her cheek, and wondered how many nights—and with how many women—Brody had spent in the wide, comfortable bed.

Her gaze slid to the portrait yet again.

Whatever had come before didn't necessarily matter, she knew. Because she was only there as a result of the Stanley situation.

She'd do well to remember that particular fact.

Then she deliberately closed her eyes. If she didn't sleep, she'd at least pretend to.

But it wasn't long before pretense became reality. When next Angeline opened her eyes, there was nothing but moonlight shining through the opened shutters.

The fat pillows had all been removed from the bed and were sitting, stacked haphazardly on the two chairs by the other windows. The comforter had been pulled back across the bed, as if it had been shoved aside by a tall, warm body.

The evidence that Brody, too, must have slept at some

point right there beside her made something inside her heat. And it wasn't at all the uneasy kind of feeling she'd had when they'd shared that narrow mattress at St. Agnes.

Now, though, there as no sign of him.

She rolled onto her back, stretching luxuriously. She felt quite refreshed, even given the fact that she'd been sleeping fully dressed. She pushed off the bed and padded across the thick rug that covered much of the hardwood floors and went into the adjoining bathroom.

As appealing as soaking herself in hot bubbling water sounded, she contented herself with a shower instead, dragging the opaque burgundy and gold striped curtain around the circular rod that hung over the tub. The water was hot and plentiful and was almost as welcoming as Brody's bed had been. She used his soap, which smelled like some sort of spicy forest, and his shampoo, which smelled like babies and made her want to giggle.

Brody Paine used baby shampoo on that thick sandy hair of his.

Finally, feeling squeaky clean for the first time in days, she turned off the water and yanked back the curtain.

Brody was sitting there on the closed commode facing the tub.

She yelped and grabbed the edge of the curtain, dragging it across her torso. Her face felt flushed, and her body felt even hotter. "What on earth are you doing?" He'd obviously showered, too, because his hair was still damp and he'd exchanged his blue jeans and blue T-shirt for clean ones, this time both in black.

"Hey," he defended. "I'm covering my eyes."

He was. With one hand that she didn't trust in the least spread across the upper portion of his face.

She slowly let the curtain drop, almost but not quite revealing her nipples that had gone appallingly tight at the unexpected sight of him, and twisted her lips when the coffee cup he was holding nearly spilled right onto his lap. "As I suspected," she said, managing a tart tone only through sheer effort.

He dropped the hand and extended the coffee toward her. "I was just thinking of you," he drawled.

She shoved the edge of the curtain beneath her arms holding it tight there, and reached for the white mug. Less than a week ago, she would have dismissed his words as pure blarney.

Now, after all the things he'd done, said, she was no longer sure about anything.

She sipped at the coffee, hot, fragrant and strong just how she liked it, and eyed him. His feet were bare and that, more than anything—even her barely protected nudity—made her feel shaky inside.

They were so intimate, she realized. Those bare feet of his. Lightly dusted with dark hair. High arches. Long, vaguely knobby toes. She pressed her lips together for a moment. "Did you keep your bandage dry when you showered?" The words sort of blurted out of her.

His lips tilted. "I put a brand new one on, ma'am."

She could only imagine the results of that, given the first bandage she'd witnessed. "Where are the children?"

"Snug as bugs in their beds."

"What about supper? Did they eat? I should probably check—"

He lifted his head, cutting off her litany. "I fixed them mac and cheese. Evidently not some fried variety that Davey thinks is the bomb, but it filled their stomachs. At least his. Eva did more picking than anything. They had baths, a few minutes of television and then they had bed. Only thing they didn't have was a story read to them by yours truly," he added drily. "Satisfied?"

She narrowed her eyes at him. "What time is it now?"

"Almost eight. And no, that isn't decaf in case you're about ready to ask that, too."

"I wasn't. I would never make the mistake of thinking you might let a little thing like caffeine stop you, even at eight o'clock at night. Um—" she gestured with the mug toward the towels hanging on the wall opposite him "—mind handing me a towel?"

He hooked a long toffee-colored towel off the rod and held it out to her. She exchanged the mug for the towel, careful to remain behind the protection of the curtain as she dashed it over her wet limbs before wrapping it sarongwise around her, tucking the ends in above her breasts. "Any luck reaching your handler?"

"Not exactly."

She peeked out from the curtain again. "What does that mean?"

"I reached someone," he said. "The situation hasn't changed."

Which could mean anything, she supposed, but since he wasn't looking like they needed to bug out, she'd follow his lead. "It's, um, it's pretty rude of you to just bust in like this, you know. Didn't your parents teach you some manners?"

"My parents were British. They were *all* about manners," he assured. His gaze drifted downward, from her wet hair to her hands clutching the shielding curtain. "Why are you still a virgin?"

She stared at him. The porcelain of the tub was losing its heat without the water pounding on it, and her toes curled against the slick surface. "I thought we agreed that was none of your business."

"It wasn't." He leaned forward, his hands folded loosely between his knees, looking thoroughly casual. As if he held conversations like this in his bathroom most every day. "Now it is."

"*Now?* Why now?"

His casual mien abruptly slipped and her mouth dried at the hunger darkening his eyes. "Because the plan to keep my hands off you isn't going to work much longer."

No amount of effort seemed enough to propel a single word past her lips.

He pushed to his feet. "Do you really think I make a habit of busting in, uninvited, on women in the shower? That I don't know how the bloody hell to wait for an invite?"

She swallowed. "Brody," she whispered.

"So you'd better tell me *why,* love, and make it a good one while you're at it." He stopped when his legs encountered the side of the tub. "One that even my damned conscience can manage to heed."

She sucked in a breath. Moistened her lips. And still nothing emerged but his name. Husky. Soft.

His eyes darkened even more, the blue looking nearly as black as the shirt stretched across his wide shoulders. "That's not helping me any here, Angeline. Are you waiting for marriage? For—" his mobile lips twisted slightly "—hell, I don't know. True love?"

She lifted her chin. "Something wrong with that?"

He muttered an oath. "I should have known."

She slicked her hand over her hair, pushing the tangles behind her ear. "I just never…trusted anyone enough to believe they cared all that much about me. About what was behind—" She waved her hand, feeling herself flush. "You know. Behind the genetics. The looks. The, um, the—"

"Body?"

She nodded, feeling foolish.

"I'm sorry to break it to you, babe, but you've got more than your share of both going on," he murmured.

She pressed her lips together. "So men have been telling me since I was barely a teenager. All I ever heard were catcalls and wolf whistles by the idiots. The nice guys, well, they didn't ever call because they figured I was already out living it up, or they didn't want to get turned down. Leaving Weaver didn't help. If anything, it got worse."

She flinched a little when Brody's hand came up and touched her shoulder.

The hunger was still in his eyes, but it was the gentleness in his touch that stole her breath all over again. "And I behaved the same way."

She sank her teeth into her lip. "S-sometimes."

"It was the only way I knew how to keep you at arm's length," he murmured. "You think I didn't know that flirting with you was the quickest road to keeping things simple where you were concerned? That I didn't recognize the stop signs that always came up in those brown eyes of yours?" His thumb traced a slow circle around her shoulder. "I needed those signs, Angeline."

The edge of the curtain wrinkled even more in her tight grip. "Why?"

His thumb slowly, so slowly, dragged down her arm toward her elbow. "Because being with you made me want things I gave up wanting a long time ago." He reached her wrist and stopped, resting over the vein that pulsed there. "You remember when we first met?"

"I could hardly forget."

"You told me about Wyoming. And everything about you—inside here—" he let go of her wrist long enough to tap the center of her forehead "—and here—" he drew his finger in a short, burning line from the base of her throat to her cleavage that wasn't exactly hidden by the thick folds of towel tucked there "—shined out like a homing beacon."

He looked up at the curtain hanging from the rod, and seemed to study it for a moment. "I always thought it was interesting that you'd chosen to go to Atlanta considering the way you always talked about Wyoming. For a long time, I figured that it must have had something to do with a man."

She shook her head. "I was just sticking close to my sister. We missed each other."

"I know how that feels." His gaze slowly dropped again, still studying the curtain, only this time where she held it gripped in her fist. "I bought this land shortly after you and I met and had the house built within less than a year. And I've already told you I started actually living here late last year." He breathed out a half laugh. "Not because I ever expected us to be standing here like this someday, that's for certain."

She waited for his low voice to continue, barely daring to breathe. "Then why?"

"Because I wanted to feel what you felt that first day we met. I wanted to see if I *could*. If it was still in me, or if it had been burned out of me when I was still a kid."

Her eyes went damp. "What happened, Brody? Or is it really Simon after all?"

"It used to be," he murmured. "But it doesn't matter anymore."

The curtain slipped in her loosened grip. "Of course it matters. It's your past." The portrait over his fireplace hung in her mind's eye. "You had a sister. What was her name?"

"Penelope. Penny."

"What happened to her?"

He shook his head. "This isn't about my past. This is about why you've chosen to remain a virgin."

"I think," she began softly, cautiously, "that this is about both." She let the curtain fall away between them. "You want me to give you an inviolate reason why I've never slept with a man. One that will convince you once and for all that I'm off-limits. Not because you're worried that I might be compromising some deeply held belief about sex before marriage or any of that. But because you're afraid that it wouldn't *be* just sex. Because it might open that door on emotions that you like to keep closed because if you don't," her voice was strained, "everything that you've been able to pretend no longer affected you will come tumbling down on you. Like one of those closets that people keep shoving stuff into, again and again and again only to find, one day, they forget themselves and open the door and—" she waved her hand "—whoosh. There are all our issues piled up, nice and unresolved, around our ears."

"Maybe," he countered, "I just like a woman with more experience."

She shook her head and slowly stepped out of the tub. "Are you expecting that to hurt?" Level on the floor with him, she had to tilt her head back to keep her eyes on his. "To push me away? It might work if I believed you.

Maybe—" she lifted her hands and settled them softly on his chest "—you just feel safer with a woman who doesn't make you feel anything."

His eyes narrowed. He caught her wrists in his hands as if to pull them away from him. "Brave words," he cautioned.

She didn't feel particularly brave. She felt out on a limb in every possible way. "Prove me wrong, then," she whispered.

His jaw seemed to tighten as she twisted her wrists out of his light hold. She reached for the towel and flipped the knot loose.

The towel dropped to her bare feet.

He exhaled roughly. "Thought you were all about playing by the rules."

She stepped out from the folds of terry, closing the last few inches remaining between them, almost but not quite smiling when the man actually took a step back.

"And you're the one who thinks rules were just made to be broken." She inched forward again, until her bare toes touched his, and her breasts brushed the soft fabric of his T-shirt.

"I don't want the thing that gets broken to be you."

There were already too many emotions swirling inside her to examine the way his rough admission made her want to cry, as much for him as for her. "I'm a big girl," she assured softly. She slid her hand behind his neck, tugging his head toward hers. "All grown up."

"I didn't have any doubts about that." His assurance murmured against her lips and his hands finally came around her back, pressing warm and hot against her spine.

She still shivered, but not with cold.

Not when his body felt like a furnace burning through

his clothes to her flesh. Not when her blood seemed to expand inside her veins and her nerve endings set off sparks wherever he touched.

"You deserve a bed," he muttered, his mouth dragging down the column of her throat. "Some romance or something. Not tedious flights and questionable hotels."

"This isn't a hotel." She sucked in a harsh breath when his hands dragged over her hips, his fingers kneading. "I'll reserve judgment on the questionable part for now, if you don't mind."

He laughed softly and pulled her right off her feet, until her mouth met his. His hands slid down her thighs, pulling them around his waist, and he carried her out of the bathroom into the bedroom.

She swung her legs down when he stopped next to the bed. He pressed his forehead to hers for a long moment, then shook his head a little, straightening. His fingers threaded through the wet skeins of her hair, spreading it out past her shoulders. "I can't not tell you that you're beautiful," he murmured. "Because you are."

She swallowed. His hands drifted from her shoulders, skimmed over the full jut of her breasts only to stop and torment the hard crests into even tighter points, while need shot through her veins, all collecting in the center of her until she felt weak from it.

Her fingers flexed, desperate for something more substantial to grab on to than air. She satisfied them with handfuls of his shirt that she dragged loose from the waist of his jeans. "What did you do with Delilah?"

He snorted. "You want to know that *now?* God, I am getting old."

She finally got her hands beneath his shirt, and ran them up his long spine, swept out over his wide back.

"I've wondered ever since we left San Juan," she murmured.

"I left her with Roger. Compensation for the bugs of his I drowned." He caught her waist again and covered her mouth, kissing any more silly questions she might have uttered into nonexistence.

She pulled in gulps of air when he finally lifted his head.

"Anything else you want to discuss?"

She pushed his shirt higher and he finally yanked it off over his head. As she'd suspected, the bandage he'd covered himself with was almost as much a disaster as the first one had been.

She vowed to change it for him. Later.

She slid her fingers through his, pulling his hands boldly back to her breasts. "Does this feel as good to you as it does to me?"

"That'll take further examination." He dragged his thumbs over and around, again and again as he backed her inexorably against the side of the bed until, off balanced, she tumbled backward.

He must have turned on the lamp near the chairs while she'd been in the shower, because it hadn't been burning when she'd wakened. Now, she was glad for its soft glow as he stood there above her, his eyes dark and full of intent. He undid his jeans and pushed them off, and Angeline let her eyes take their glorious fill.

"*I* can't not tell you you're beautiful," she whispered huskily and slowly lifted her hand toward him.

The mattress dipped when he bent his knee against it. He took her hand, pressed his mouth to the palm of it. Her other hand found his hip, drifted over the unbelievably hard glute that flexed in answer to her touch.

He suddenly grabbed that exploratory hand and pressed it, along with the other above her head.

Her breath came faster, so much emotion rocketing around inside her that she thought she might burst. "What about your chest? I don't want you to undo whatever healing has already occurred."

"If my heart can withstand this, I think that damn knife wound can," he muttered, and pressed his mouth to the pulse beating wildly at the base of her throat. "I could spend a lifetime exploring you."

"I don't want to wait that long," she assured, twining her legs impatiently around his, trying to pull him down to her. She knew he wanted her. There was no hiding that particularly evident, impressive, fact.

"For a virgin, you're quite the demanding little thing, aren't you?" He dropped his mouth even farther, exploring the rise of her breasts.

"Brody—" She pressed her head back in the soft bedding, writhing against his tormenting tongue.

"That's my name," he whispered, as he continued southward. "Feel free to wear it out." And when his mouth reached her *there,* and everything inside her splintered outward, she was afraid she well might, as she cried out his name. Again. And again.

Tears streaked from her eyes when he finally worked his way back up her trembling body. "Now," he said, his body settling in the cradle of her thighs. "Are you sure?"

She arched against him, winding herself around him and answered the question once and for all as she took him into her body. "God," he gritted, "Angeline."

"That's my name," she returned breathlessly, full of wonder. Full of him. "Feel free to—"

He pulled her more tightly beneath him, and the words

died in her throat as heat and pleasure and everything that was right and beautiful in the world came screaming together in the collision of their bodies. And when that pleasure was more than she could bear yet again and she exploded apart in his arms, he groaned her name, following her headlong into the fire.

Eventually, when their hearts finally stopped pounding against each other, he lifted his head.

He looked just as undone as she felt and she sighed softly. Contentedly. "You were worth the wait," she whispered.

His eyes darkened. He slowly kissed her lips.

Then he looked over at the portrait across from the bed that they'd nearly destroyed. "I was born in London. They named me Simon Brody," he murmured. "After him. Until I was fifteen and I learned otherwise, I thought he was my father. Only it turns out that my mother didn't meet Simon until Penny was two and my mother was pregnant with me. They married right after I was born."

She curled her arms around him and his head lowered to her breast. "How did you find out?"

"I found my birth certificate. I was grounded for smoking and bored, so I was snooping. I never expected to find *that*."

"I learned a long time ago that it doesn't take blood for a man to be a father. Did you love him?"

He was silent for so long that she wasn't sure he'd answer. She sifted her fingers slowly through his hair and finally, he did. "Yes."

"Then that's all that matters, Brody. Love is always the thing that matters most."

His hand slid down and caught hers. She knew he felt the wedding ring that she still hadn't bothered to remove.

And when he folded her fingers in his, and kissed them, she couldn't stop herself from wishing—just for a moment—that the ring was real.

Chapter Fourteen

"Mr. Dad. Angeline."

The voice was faint, but Angeline sat bolt upright and nearly screamed when she heard a crash from some distant part of the house.

"Stay here." Beside her, Brody was already pushing back the covers. He stopped only long enough to hitch his jeans over his hips and pull something from a hidden panel in the wall as he left the room.

Angeline scrambled out of bed, nearly tripping over the tangle of bedding they'd made. She fumbled her way into the scrubs that were the first thing her hands encountered in the duffel she'd yet to unpack. Her heart was in her throat, waiting for God knew what.

Another cry from Davey?

Another crash?

A gunshot?

Heedless of Brody's instruction, she headed out of the room, stopping short at the panel that was still open. With only the lamp on the far side of the room as her guide, she peered into the wall safe. Stuck her hand in, sweeping it around the walls inside.

Even in the dark hole of the safe, she recognized what her fingers found. Guns. And plenty of them.

She closed her palm around one grip and pulled it off the bracket holding it in place and stuck her head out the bedroom door that Brody had left ajar.

All she heard was the banging of her heartbeat inside her head.

Could Santina's thug have found them even after all their precautions?

She quietly padded across the floor toward the base of the staircase.

"Angeline."

She nearly jumped out of her skin at the sound of Brody calling her name. Loudly.

"What is it? What's wrong?" She started up the stairs.

"Eva's sick. She's burning up." He met her in the hallway and muttered an oath when he saw the gun she held. "Give me that."

He plucked it out of her unresisting hand and Angeline dashed into the room. Davey was huddled at the foot of the bed, looking scared. Eva was curled up in a fetal position, and was definitely fevered. The heat practically rolled off her in waves.

Angeline sat down beside her. "Honey, how long have you felt like this?" She surreptitiously found Eva's wrist and felt her pulse.

"I dunno." The girl shifted away, as if she couldn't

bear the touch. "My stomach hurts," she added hoarsely, and promptly threw up across Angeline's lap.

Davey jumped back. "Eeuuww." But he sounded more tearful than anything.

"Run in the bathroom across the hall and grab the towels," Brody told Davey.

The boy dashed out of the room.

"She needs the hospital," Angeline said, looking up at Brody. Everything inside her felt seized up by guilt as she cradled the girl against her. She'd slept the day away after they'd arrived, and after that, she and Brody had—

She shied away from thinking about the hours spent in his arms.

"This could be anything from a bug she's picked up to appendicitis," she told him.

"Here." Davey returned with the towels tumbling out of his arms.

Brody took one and gave it back to him. "Go get this one really wet." Again the boy dashed out and Brody, without turning a single hair, began mopping up the mess.

"I'm sorry," Eva cried.

Angeline lifted the girl's dark hair out of the way for Brody. "Nothing for you to be sorry about, sweetie." She, on the other hand, had plenty. If she'd been paying more attention to the children and less to Brody—

"I want my mom."

Angeline's eyes burned. "I know you do, Eva. She'd be here too, if she could." She took the soaked towel that Davey came back with and smoothed the corner of it over Eva's flushed face. "I want to get you out of these pj's, okay?" The pajamas in question were comprised of the same scrub shirt that Eva had worn in Caracas and Angeline drew it over the girl's head.

Brody added it to the soiled sheets that he'd managed to slide out from beneath Angeline and Eva.

One portion of Angeline's mind wondered how many times he'd had to deal with vomiting children because he was more than a little adept at it.

"All she's got left that are clean are jeans." He was staring into the top drawer of the bureau. "No way are you getting those on her. I'll grab a shirt of mine." He headed out of the room, though she could easily hear his voice as he went. "Come on, Davey. You better get your shoes on so we can take your sister to the doctor."

"Is she gonna be okay?"

"Heck, yeah. You think Angeline and I would let anything happen to either one of you?"

She bit her lip. She wished she felt that sort of confidence. That she *deserved* that sort of confidence. "I'm going to have Brody carry you down to the car when he gets back, okay?"

Eva nodded slightly. "What if I throw up again?"

"Then you do." Angeline pressed her lips to the girl's sweaty forehead. "It's not the end of the world." Brody came back into the room a few minutes later. Not only did he bring a T-shirt for Eva, but one for Angeline, as well as her jeans and boots.

While he helped Eva maneuver into the shirt, Angeline hurriedly exchanged her ruined scrubs for the clean clothes.

"You finish dressing. I'm going to take her down to the truck." Brody gingerly lifted the girl into his arms and headed out of the bedroom.

Angeline fumbled with the boots, only to realize he'd tucked socks inside them.

And he'd accused *her* of getting caught up in details.

She pulled them on, shoved her feet into the boots and hurriedly caught up to them on the staircase, where Davey was already waiting, clinging to the banister. Angeline took his hand and within minutes they were in the SUV, racing away from the house.

Fortunately, when they reached the town, traffic at that hour was nil and they arrived at the hospital in short order. Brody pulled right up in the emergency entrance by the door and carried Eva inside. Angeline barely managed to pull the keys from the ignition before she and Davey followed.

The waiting room was empty and with one look at Eva's condition, the nurse standing by the reception desk waved Brody through a set of double doors behind her.

"Use the passport," Brody told Angeline before the doors closed between them.

She blinked.

"Ma'am? I'll need you to complete just a few things and you can go back with your husband and daughter."

She focused in on the receptionist, who was holding a pen and clipboard out toward her. "Right." As a paramedic, she ought to have been intimately familiar with the process of checking in a patient through the E.R., yet she really wasn't. Their end of the paperwork was considerably different than the patient's end.

So she scribbled one of her names of the day—Angie Black—where the receptionist pointed, and filled in the only address that her frantic mind could remember—the one she'd grown up with in Weaver. "We, um, we just moved here," she told the receptionist, as if that would explain her complete and utter inadequacy when it came to answering the simple questions.

Beside her, Davey was standing on his tiptoes, trying to see over the desk. "Where'd Mr. Dad and my sister go?"

The reception smiled at the term. Angeline supposed she must have heard just about anything and everything in her position. "They went back to have the doctor look at your sister and see what he can do to make her feel better." The woman produced a plastic-wrapped sucker and handed it over. "It's sugar free," she assured Angeline.

Davey didn't let that bother him as he whipped off the plastic and started sucking on it.

Then Brody stuck his head through the double doors. "Angeline." His head disappeared again.

She started to call Davey, but the receptionist shook her head. "Let him stay out with me," she advised. "It's a slow night. I don't mind."

Torn, Angeline looked at the boy. What was the likelihood of any harm coming to him there? "Davey, you stay right here with—" She looked toward the receptionist.

"Bonny."

"—Bonny," she repeated to Davey. "No going off and exploring, okay?"

He shrugged and sat down on one of the chairs near the television set. "Can I watch cartoons?"

"We'll find some for you," Bonny assured. "We'll pop in a videotape if need be."

Angeline hurried through the swinging doors.

There was no question where Eva had been taken because she could see Brody standing not far down the hall.

Eva was already on a hospital gurney. One nurse was drawing blood. Another was attaching an IV. And the doctor, a young man who looked old enough to be a grade schooler, introduced himself as Dr. Thomas.

He pulled the curtain shielding the bed closed somewhat and stepped out with them on the other side. "The blood test will confirm it, but I believe your daughter's appendix has decided to create a fuss. The surgeon on duty tonight is Dr. Campbell. He's already scrubbing in. We don't want to waste any time and chance it rupturing. We'll need you to sign the consent papers as soon as they're ready."

Angeline looked at Brody, lost for words. Of course she'd known it could come to this; she wasn't a fool. But knowing and doing were two very different things.

"I'll sign whatever you need," Brody said evenly. His hand closed around Angeline's shoulder. "Just make sure she's all right."

Dr. Thomas smiled reassuringly. "Better that you brought her now, than a few hours from now." He tugged back the curtain again. "Eva, the nurse is going to give you something that's going to make you really sleepy, and then we're going to get rid of that nasty pain in your tummy. Okay?"

Eva's dark eyes were tightly shut. "I wanna go home."

Angeline went to her side, closing that small fist in her hands. She pressed her lips to the girl's temple. "We all want that," she assured her. "You're going to be all right, though. A little while from now you're going to be feeling a whole lot better."

"We need to move her," one of the nurses said in a kind voice.

Angeline nodded and stepped back from the gurney. "We'll be right here waiting for you, Eva."

The dark head managed a small nod of acknowledgment.

Then the nurses were rolling the gurney quickly along the hall.

"She'll be fine," Dr. Thomas assured. "All her symptoms say there's been no rupture yet." He pushed open the doors back out to the waiting area. "Once you finish with the forms, Bonny can tell you how to get to the waiting area outside surgery. It'll be a little more comfortable for you there."

"Thanks," Brody said, turning toward Bonny and the waiting forms. He picked up the pen and with an efficiency that Angeline envied, completed the form. Then he pulled out a cell phone that he must have brought from the house, because she'd certainly never seen it before, and punched in a few numbers. "Mrs. Bedford? Simon Black here, again. I have a bit of an emergency."

Angeline started. She'd thought he'd just made up the name of Black for the purpose of the passports that Roger had produced for them. But obviously, if his housekeeper knew him by that name, he was used to using that particular alias.

"Ma'am?" Bonny drew her attention away from Brody, who was asking Mrs. Bedford if she'd mind coming to pick up Davey from the hospital. "I need your signature, as well." She held out the pen that Brody had used.

Angeline slowly took it and wrote in her name next to his. Only after she'd finished did she realize she'd not used the diminutive of Angie, but Angeline.

She eyed the names, side by side, feeling distinctly off balanced. Simon and Angeline Black.

"Okay." Brody had pocketed his phone. "Mrs. Bedford will be here shortly. Timing couldn't be better, actually. When she dropped off the groceries earlier today—all of you were snoozing like Rip Van Winkle—she had her grandson with her. Cute kid. Davey will like him."

"I can direct you to the other waiting room now if you'd like," Bonny suggested.

A short while later, they found themselves seats in the much smaller, but much more comfortable waiting room. Angeline couldn't make herself sit in one of the upholstered chairs, though, and paced slowly around the room, conscientiously giving the other couple who was also in the waiting room their space and privacy, as well.

Davey sat on Brody's lap, his blond head resting against that chest that Angeline knew from experience was wide and comforting.

Her pacing feet took her back to them. "You should get a tetanus shot while we're here," she told him.

"What's tet-nus?"

"Like a vaccine," Brody told Davey. "I had one a year ago."

"Still." Angeline paced away again. Every time she looked at the clock on the wall, she expected hours to have passed, but instead, it was only minutes.

Before too long, a woman in her fifties, Angeline guessed, arrived. "Angeline, this is Mrs. Bedford," Brody introduced them. "She's the one who keeps the house looking like the Pope himself will be dropping by any minute."

Mrs. Bedford's cheeks flushed with pleasure. "Oh, you and your teasing." She turned her bright gaze on Angeline. "We'd have met earlier but I know you were all just tuckered right out. I'm so glad I'm able to help now, though. How's the girl?"

"She's in surgery."

"Oh, my. Bless her heart. What a miracle that you were here when it happened." Mrs. Bedford sighed a little but then patted Angeline's shoulder as if she'd known her since she was a tot. "Don't you worry, though. The doctors here are just fine. Kept my Joe going when he had a heart attack a few years ago, that's for sure."

Angeline managed a smile. If she'd held any suspicion that the housekeeper might really be associated with Hollins-Winword, they pretty much dissolved in the face of her kindly ordinariness.

The woman was holding out her hand for Davey. "You can call me Mrs. B.," she told him. "How'd you like to go to my house and have some ice cream with me? My husband and my grandson, Tyson, are there, too."

Evidently, the notion of ice cream at midnight was enough to overcome whatever reservations Davey might have. He took the woman's hand and waved as he left with her.

Angeline rubbed her hands up and down her arms. "You're not worried about…you know?"

Brody shook his head. "She's more capable than you give her credit for."

Which just had Angeline wondering all over again.

She began pacing once more, only sitting next to Brody when a surgeon came in to speak to the other couple.

Judging by their devastated expressions, the news was not good.

She looked away. Brody reached over and closed his hand around hers and the urge to pace finally died.

The waiting room was empty except for them when a middle-aged man wearing a white coat over green scrubs entered and looked around. "Mr. and Mrs. Black?"

Angeline and Brody rose from their chairs. She swallowed, and felt Brody's hand slide around her shoulders. "That's us," he said.

Angeline tried and failed to decipher the man's expression as he crossed the waiting room toward them. Her stomach felt tight, her nerves shredded.

"I'm Dr. Campbell," he introduced himself without preamble. "Eva's surgery went very well. She's doing fine."

The relief was nearly overwhelming. Angeline's knees started to shake. Brody held her even tighter, as if he were trying to lend some strength to her.

"We got the appendix before it ruptured," Dr. Campbell was saying, "which is a very good thing. Her recovery time should be minimal."

"When can we see her?"

"She'll be moved from the recovery room to her own room within the next hour or so. Go get yourselves some coffee. Something to eat. Stretch your legs. That'll help take up the time," he advised, "until she's settled in her room. Unless you have any questions?" He lifted his eyebrows.

Angeline had a million of them, but couldn't seem to marshal her thoughts enough to voice a single one.

And Brody was decidedly silent, as well.

The surgeon didn't seem to notice anything amiss in their reactions, though. As if he were used to it. "I'll be along to check on her again in a few hours. We can talk then, too. And of course you can call at any time. Just ask one of the nurses."

"Thank you."

Brody stuck out his hand, shaking the surgeon's before the man walked back out of the waiting room.

Angeline sank down onto the edge of the chair, pressing her fingertips to her forehead. "This is all my fault." If she'd paid more attention to Eva she might have realized that the girl was suffering from more than just worry over her parents. "She's probably been working on this for days."

"Whether she was or not, it's hardly your *fault*." Brody pulled her hands, tugging her up from the seat. "People get sick, babe. It happens. The doc's right. Let's get some air."

"I should wait here," she resisted.

"For what?" Brody's voice was soft. Reasonable. His head dropped closer to hers. "Even if Hewitt and Sophia were here, they'd need to eat. They'd have to wait until the doctor cleared Eva for seeing them."

He was right. Knowing it did little to make up for the guilt that swamped her.

"I can't do this," she whispered hoarsely. "I just can't."

She had only a glimpse of Brody's narrowed eyes as she tugged her hands free of his, and slid past him, intent on escaping the waiting room.

She made it out into the corridor before he closed his hands over her shoulders, halting her from behind. Her throat ached and her eyes burned deep down inside her head. "Let me go."

He made a sound she couldn't interpret, and pulled her back into the waiting room, pushing closed the door that had been standing open.

"What's this really about?"

She hugged her arms around herself, feeling chilled. "I'm just tired. And relieved."

His lips twisted. "In the past week, I've seen you in pretty much every state a person can achieve. *Every* state."

She flushed miserably. "This isn't the time to joke."

"Who's joking?" His serious expression told her that

he certainly wasn't. "I'm tired and relieved, too, and whatever is nagging at you is more than that."

"Brody—"

"Just spit it out, Angeline."

"I just…I just can't bear to make another wrong decision. The last time I did—" She broke off, shaking her head. "The last time," she tried again, "a boy died."

Brody sighed. He ran his hands down her arms, circling her wrists, lifting her palms until he could slide his fingers between hers. "You're a paramedic, love. Not even you can save everyone."

"I know. But this time, I should have. Just like now. With Eva. I should have recognized earlier that she was really ill! Instead, I was…you and I were…" She slid her hands free of his and raked back her hair. "We're supposed to be *protecting* Eva and Davey." She wasn't supposed to be falling in love with a completely unsuitable man.

"You think Eva's appendix would have been just dandy if she'd been with her parents, or with another bodyguard? Dream on, Angeline. Sometimes the best-laid plans get shot to hell, particularly when there are kids involved. But even if she were nineteen instead of nine, she could have gotten sick like this. There's no telling, and there's sure in hell no blaming."

"*You* would have noticed," she said thickly.

His eyebrows shot up. "Did you see me yanking her to a doctor any more quickly than we did?" He lowered his voice. "Tell me what happened with the boy."

"There's nothing to tell." She felt brittle. "He was only a kid. A gang member, they told me. And there was a shooting. I thought I could reach him from the rear side where the culvert wasn't so narrow." She swallowed. "I was wrong. By the time my partner and I reached him from the front side, the side *I* should have used in the first place, he'd bled out."

"And now you don't like going through tunnels," he murmured.

"I've *never* liked tunnels," she corrected. "Caves. None of that kind of thing."

"Caves." He let out a sigh. "I read in your file that you were hidden in one when Santo Marguerite was attacked."

She pressed her lips together, disconcerted that she had a file, much less one that he'd read. "The cave wasn't much for size. I was always told to stay out of it. But then someone—a cousin, maybe, because I don't remember my mother doing it—pushed me down into it." Not quickly enough for her to miss the attack on the village, though. "Davey's four," she murmured. "The same age I was when it happened. You suppose he's going to remember the madness we've put those children through these past few days?"

"If he does, his parents will help him deal with it, just like Maggie and Daniel helped *you*."

"That boy still died, Brody. Because I hesitated. Because I knew if I went in that culvert, I'd freeze up."

"But you *did* go in the culvert."

"Too late."

"What about your partner?"

"He was a rookie. He was following my lead."

"So you were human and something went wrong. Are you going to keep beating yourself with it or are you going to pull it together and keep on keeping on? Angeline, I swear I have yet to see you hesitate even when I think you should. You see something that needs doing, and God. You do it. If you'd gotten to the kid any faster than you had would he have lived?"

She swallowed. Pressed her palms together. Shook her head. "Probably not." That's what her supervisor had said. That's what the emergency room doctors had said. "That's the only reason I have a job to go back to when my vacation is up." She waited a long beat, and finally admitted the truth. "If I go back at all. I just…I want to come back to Wyoming. I just don't want to come back feeling like I failed."

"You can't stop helping people, Angeline. You're a natural at it. So who the hell cares if you're doing it in Atlanta or in Weaver. Or Venezuela, or Sheridan for that matter?"

She jerked a little at that. "I put my fear ahead of my job, Brody, and that kid never had a chance. Today, with Eva, I put my…my need ahead of her." She waved her hand, encompassing the hospital waiting room around them. "And look where we are!"

"You made me feel human again," he said quietly. "You knew Eva and Davey were fed and bedded because *I* told you they were. So if you want to blame anyone, babe, it had better be me. Not yourself. You're a paramedic, for God's sake. Not a doctor. You're trained to respond to emergencies, which you've done pretty damn well as far as I'm concerned."

Her throat tightened. "But if I don't go back to Atlanta—"

"—then you don't go back," he said simply. He slid his hand through her hair. "The world's not gonna stop spinning, love, if you change courses. But that guilt?" He looked regretful. "Even when it's deserved, it doesn't do anything but dry a person up from the inside out. Let it go, Angeline."

"What do *you* know about guilt? You've probably never made a misstep in your entire life."

He slowly picked up her hand. The one with Sophia's wedding band. "I know that if I had kept quiet when I learned that Simon Brody wasn't my real father, he and my mother and Penny would all probably still be alive. Instead—" he broke off and looked grim. "Instead, word got out to the wrong person that the man who *was* my real father had two kids and an ex-wife whose existence he'd managed to keep hidden for fifteen years. My mother broke the silence between them because of *me*. Because I wanted to know the man who'd really fathered me and Penny. And just like Santina would use Davey and Eva to manipulate their parents if they could, Sandoval tried using my family to manipulate *him*."

Shock swirled through her, thick and engulfing. "Oh, Brody. No. I'm so sorry. Sandoval? The same monster who destroyed Santo Marguerite? London's a far cry from Central and South America. Those were his stomping grounds, I thought. Why would he have reason to go after *your* family?"

"London had nothing to do with anything except that's where we lived. On the other hand, my father, the one who contributed his genes to me that is, was the one person who kept thwarting Sandoval's actions *wherever* they occurred," he said flatly. "And that's why my parents and sister died in a car bombing one fine spring afternoon. It was a total fluke that I wasn't with them."

Her stomach dropped. She stared at Brody's lips, waiting for him to continue.

But the door to the waiting room burst open and a tall,

silver-haired man stood there, looking almost as surprised at the sight of *them*. But it wasn't surprise in his deep voice when he spoke. It was annoyance. Pure and simple. "*There* you are. Bloody hell, Simon. You don't make it easy to find you, do you."

Brody's expression had grown, if anything, even more grim. His lips twisted. "I don't believe you've ever officially met," he told her, startling her out of her surprised stupor. "So let me have the honors. Angeline—" he angled his head toward the older man "—meet Coleman Black."

Her stomach dropped to her toes, knowing what was coming even before Brody finished speaking.

"My father."

Chapter Fifteen

Brody watched the color drain from Angeline's face as she looked from him to Cole and back again. Her lips moved, as if she were struggling to find something appropriate to say, which only made Brody feel more like the slug he was for tossing her without preparation into the sordidness that was his life.

Cole gave him an annoyed look and crossed the room, his hand outstretched toward Angeline. "Simon isn't *quite* correct," he said smoothly. "We have met. But you were so small you wouldn't remember." He caught her hand in his, raising it to his lips. "You're as lovely as I would have expected, my dear."

Angeline looked disarmed, color coming back into her cheeks. Cole might be finally pushing retirement but that didn't mean the old man didn't have his charms.

As a father, however, he'd been pretty damn miserable.

"You saw me when I was a child?"

"All long hair and enormous brown eyes with barely a word of English to your name," he assured. "And now, you and my son here have been leading us all around in a merry chase. Needless to say, it was quite a surprise to actually have him call me for assistance." His gaze cut from Angeline to Brody, and there was no charm in the look for him.

It was pure steel.

Of course, the old man wouldn't be pleased that Brody had contacted him. It was entirely outside of protocol.

Brody deliberately smiled. He might be closing the gap to forty by leaps and bounds, but he still knew how to goad the guy, just as he had when he wasn't yet sixteen and Cole had pretty much dragged him, kicking and sullen, from London and taken him back with him to Connecticut.

He'd never sent out announcements that his son had come to live with him, that's for damn sure. Not hard when Brody hadn't actually lived *with* Cole. He'd been in a well-secured house, tended by well-trained agents, none of whom knew the entire story.

Nobody, not a single soul inside or outside of Hollins-Winword knew that Brody Paine was anything other than one more survivor taken under the protective wing of the agency until the suspected terrorist who'd targeted his family could be caught.

Which they never were, since Sandoval was still out there.

To this day, he didn't know if Cole had ever grieved over the loss of the woman he'd been married to for so brief a time. Or his daughter.

He'd never said.

And Brody sure in hell had never asked.

What they did do was exist in a sort of vacuum where Brody did his job and Cole did his, and rarely the twain ever met.

"Brody called you?" Angeline was looking at him with surprise. "He didn't tell me that."

"I told you I reached someone," he defended.

Her lips compressed.

"If you'd shown a lot less stubbornness and more sense," Cole told him, "you would have contacted me the first time you couldn't reach Persia, protocol be damned."

"Persia!" Angeline gave them both a horrified look. "That...that, *girl* who replaced me at the All-Med site is your handler?"

"Was," Cole said. "She's been...replaced."

"But why?"

"Don't bother asking, babe. He doesn't answer questions like that."

"Miguel Chavez discovered she was playing both ends from the middle when she made a few unwise calls while returning that Hummer to St. Agnes. Hewitt was the one who donated that to the nuns, by the way."

Brody felt sure that Cole wouldn't have provided the information about Persia if not for the pleasure of proving him wrong. And he didn't much like that the old man had shown the same curiosity he'd felt about the presence of that expensive truck at the convent in the first place.

"Miguel." Angeline looked dazed. She sat down on the nearest chair. "*He* is involved with Hollins, too?"

"On occasion," Cole said briefly. "As he got to know you through your volunteer work with All-Med he thought you might be a good asset, and that's when I sent Brody to meet you there five years ago."

She shook her head. "Most people would just pick up the phone and set a meeting," she murmured.

Cole laughed.

"Sweet as this reunion is," Brody drawled, "why didn't someone replace Persia sooner?"

His father's laughter died. He looked irritated all over again. "We didn't know where the hell you were. The only trace we found of either of you was an All-Med T-shirt covered in blood on the floor of a cab that was riddled with your fingerprints in Caracas. That's when we were positive it was the two of you, and not Santina's man, who managed to get the Stanley children out of St. Agnes. Until then, we had no confirmation either way. You can imagine the difficulties that has presented."

"Good grief." Angeline hopped back to her feet. "My family doesn't know about the shirt, do they?"

"Unfortunately, yes. The media down there got wind of an aid volunteer seeming to disappear off the planet, with nothing left behind but her bloody shirt. Damn reporters. Always messing things around when they shouldn't. If you'd ever turn on a television and watch the international news, Simon, you might know these things."

Angeline groaned. Any television viewing for them of late had been geared toward Davey's four-year-old tastes.

"But I've let your folks know that you're safe," Cole assured. "I notified them earlier as soon as I heard from Simon."

She pressed her hand to her forehead. "They must have been going mad." She eyed them both. "This is *exactly* why I didn't want them knowing I was involved with Hollins. We're all worried enough about my cousin who's still missing!"

Cole stayed silent on that and Brody wanted to kick

him. But the fact was, Ryan Clay *was* missing. Not even the agency had been able to unearth him, and they'd been quietly trying for months. That news wasn't likely to make any one of them feel better.

"Your parents will see for themselves soon enough that you're safe and well," Cole warned. "Daniel told me he and Maggie would be here by morning."

Angeline's hands flopped down to her sides. "Well, great. I never mind seeing my parents. I, um, I have to go check on Eva. I don't suppose in all these revelations you can tell me that her parents are free?"

"I wish I could," Cole told her. "We're working on it," he added. "We know where they're being held in Rio, and that they're very much alive. Getting them out, however, has been proving problematic."

From experience, Brody knew that term could mean just about anything.

"I'll go with you to see Eva," he told her and ignored the eyebrow his father lifted in surprise.

Angeline nodded, moistened her lips and turned toward Cole. "It's been an…eventful night, I must say." She leaned up and pressed a kiss to his cheek. "Thank you. For everything that you've done for me. For my family. It's nice to have an opportunity to tell you that, in person, after all these years."

He smiled faintly. "I like to see a happy ending as much as anyone. That's what keeps me in this business. Sadly, the people closest to me weren't able to find that." His gaze cut to Brody's, and for once, he let his regret show. "But now I have hope again."

Brody didn't even want to know what that was supposed to mean.

He closed his hand around Angeline's elbow and drew

her toward the door. Eva would surely be settled in her room by now.

"Simon. A word, please."

He should have known. Cole always had liked to have the last word.

"Stay," Angeline murmured. "Talk with him. Come to Eva's room when you're finished." She looked around him. "Mr. Black, I hope we see one another again."

"Coleman. Or Cole, if you choose." He looked slightly amused. "And I feel certain that we will."

Brody waited until she'd disappeared down the hall and around the corner before he looked back at his father. *"What?"*

"Are you willing to stay on the Stanley children until that situation is resolved? I've already arranged for a team to keep watch over the hospital, either way."

Brody's lips thinned. When had he ever let go of an op before it was completed? "Do you need to ask?"

"I suppose not. You're good at what you do, Simon. Too good when it comes down to it."

"Is there a point in there somewhere? Because I'd kind of like to see how Eva's doing after they've cut her open."

Cole's lips compressed. "Touché," he said evenly. "I was never there when you were in the hospital being patched up from your various escapades. Of which there were *many*. So maybe my point is moot, after all."

He didn't want to care what the man had to say. But he did. For the same reasons that he'd gone back to the agency even after he'd planned to hang out his shingle with Roger.

He *was* like Cole.

Dammit all to hell.

So he stood there. Waiting. "Well?"

"Don't turn into me," Cole said simply. "If Angeline matters to you, and it seems that she does, change your ways and make a life with her. Hang out that law degree you worked so hard to get. Do anything but this. You can't combine being a field agent with a family."

"Tristan Clay did." Hell, Angeline's uncle was pretty high up the Hollins food chain of command.

Cole's expression didn't change. "I could easily name fifty other agents who have not. So what odds would you lay your money on? Whether you want to admit it or not, Simon, you're too much like me. I'm just suggesting you not make the same choices that I did. The cost is too high. You're old enough to recognize what matters in life, and young enough still to do something about it."

"Don't pretend that you know me all that well, Cole. We both know otherwise."

The other man pulled out a pipe, looked around the waiting room that was clearly marked "no smoking" and tucked it away again. "I know enough to recognize the ring that Angeline is wearing."

"It was my mother's first wedding ring from Simon," Brody said tightly. Before she'd been buried, he'd taken it from her favorite jewelry box, the one where she'd kept her dearest possessions. "It has nothing to do with you."

"Did she tell you that?"

"Yes." He bit out the word.

Cole smiled, but there was no happiness in it. Only years of weariness and a sadness that seemed to go a mile deep. "Actually," he said quietly, "it was the ring that *I* gave her."

Then he turned and walked out of the waiting room.

* * *

When Angeline found the room the nurse directed her to, Eva was sound asleep.

She sat down beside the bed and rested her hands lightly on the mattress.

The ring on her finger winked up at her.

She toyed with it. Slipped it off easily, for it *was* loose. Yet, in all the madness of the past several days, she'd managed to keep it in place.

"You kept wearing it."

She looked up to see Brody standing in the doorway. "You kept telling people we were married," she pointed out truthfully enough.

His gaze slanted toward the bed, as if he'd already lost interest in the subject. "How's she doing?"

"Sound asleep, as you can see." She curled her fingers, wanting to hide the ring from his too-seeing eyes. "How are *you* doing?"

He exhaled. "Does it matter?"

She pushed back the chair and rose. "Of course it matters, Brody."

"How much?"

She wavered. "What do you want me to say? I don't know what you're asking."

His eyes were nearly black. "I think you know."

Her spine stiffened. Did he want her to lay her soul bare merely for pure entertainment value? "Just what did you and your father talk about?"

"How much like him I am."

"Don't make that sound like such a death sentence," she chided softly. "I know you have your reasons for feeling differently, *good* reasons, but if it weren't for him…" She lifted her shoulders. What more could she say?

"Santo Marguerite might still be standing if Hollins-Winword hadn't tried to intervene."

"You mean if your father hadn't tried." She sighed. "Sandoval is the monster in this story, Brody. Not your—not Coleman Black."

She could see the resistance in his eyes and stepped closer, folding her hands around his. "It wasn't anyone but Sandoval who wanted the land around my family's village. The likelihood that he'd have done something terrible regardless of your father's presence there—of any kind of Hollins-Winword involvement for that matter—is extremely high. If it didn't happen when I was four, it could have happened before I was born, or twenty years after. Am I right? *Am I?*"

"He's still active, obviously," he allowed grimly.

"Exactly. And Sandoval still controls that land, even to this day. My father told me long ago that there's no reasoning with a man like him. My surviving what happened there makes no more sense than you not being in the car that day with your family. We survived. They didn't. That's reality and you and I get to live with it. And maybe—" she swallowed "—maybe it's time we stop questioning why, and just accept the blessing for what it is. Your father—I'm sorry—*Coleman* helped me to a new life as a Clay. And I'm assuming he played some role in your life after your parents and sister died?"

"Only enough to make sure nobody else got wind of who I really was. He put a roof over my head in Connecticut and guards on my tail and the only thing we ever talked about was the agency."

"Why would he do that? Because you think he didn't care? Don't you think it might be because he didn't want to lose you, too? It's your past, Brody. You know it better than I, obviously. But regardless of how or why any-thing happened with your childhood or with mine, here we are. Survivors." She looked over at the bed. "Did he say anything more about them?"

"Just made sure I wasn't going to bail on the situation."

"He wouldn't think that."

He snorted softly. "Like you said once. We're going to have to agree to disagree where Coleman Black is concerned. You don't have to worry about any Santina folks showing up here, though. He told me there's a team watching the hospital now."

"If *he* and all of Hollins-Winword that he has at his command weren't able to track us here until you con-tacted him, I don't think Santina would be able to find us, either. But now that everything's out in the open, more or less, I guess there's no more need for me to be here. Or, like you said, for this." She slipped off the ring and held it out to him, wanting with everything she possessed for him to tell her that she was wrong.

To tell her that *she* mattered.

That he wanted her to stay for reasons that had noth-ing to do with Eva or Davey or anything but what had gone between them.

He slowly lifted his palm.

It was not the answer she wanted.

She sucked down the pain inside her, and prayed that it didn't show on her face.

No woman wanted to face the fact that the man she'd fallen in love with didn't return the feeling.

Without touching him, she dropped the ring into his palm.

His fingers slowly curled around it. "The ring wasn't what I thought it was," he murmured.

"It wasn't what I thought, either." Despite herself, the words emerged. She pressed her lips together, keeping her composure together with an effort.

She turned to the bed, wrapping her hands around the iron rail at the foot of it. "So, um, what now? I still h-have a week of vacation left. I'd like to spend it with, um, with Davey and Eva. If you don't mind." Her eyes burned and she blinked furiously, determined not to cry in front of him.

"And after your week is up?"

"Then I'll go back h-home." In all of the time they'd spent together, he'd never before been cruel like this.

"In Atlanta?"

"What do you want from me, Brody? Maybe I'll stay in Atlanta. Maybe I'll go back to Weaver. *I don't know.*"

"Is there anything that you *do* know?"

Stung, she slapped her hands on the rail. Eva didn't so much as stir. "I know I must have been a fool to let myself love you," she snapped. "So if you want to know how much you matter, *now* you do. Are you quite satisfied?"

"I don't know. I haven't been loved in a long time." His voice sounded rusty. "I'm out of practice."

And just that simply, her anger eased out of her, leaving nothing but her heart that ached for him.

"I think you've been loved all along, you just haven't wanted to face it."

"I don't want to talk about Cole."

She angled her chin, looking up at him. "Then who do you want to talk about?"

"You. Me." His blue eyes were steady on her face. "It's been a crazy week."

"It hasn't even been a week," she whispered, feeling choked.

"But it's been years of foreplay."

She flushed and opened her mouth. Caught the faint smile playing around his lips and closed it again.

"I love you, Angeline Reyes Clay. I know that seems fast, but it's been a long time in the making. And maybe I'm not so far gone that I can't heed good advice when I hear it even if I don't care much for the person delivering it. Maybe I'm just tired of making my way alone. Or maybe the fact that we both survived, like you said, meant we were supposed to find our way here to each other. But what I do know is that I don't want you to walk away from me when your vacation is done. Fact is, I don't want you to walk away from me ever."

A tear slid down her cheek. "Brody."

"I don't want you to go back to Atlanta unless that's really where you want to be. And then, hell, I don't know. I guess I'd follow you there. But then I'd have to drag you back here, because, *babe.* A city? When we've got all of Wyoming at our disposal? If you don't like the house I built, I'll build you another. A dozen if I have to. One thing I can say about Hollins is that it does pay well. I could even start a law practice. But if I didn't, I can still support you. And, you know. Kids. If you wanted."

She laughed, the tears coming faster. "You'd want kids? *You?* Not long ago you shuddered at the idea!"

"I'm a guy," he dismissed. "Don't you think I'd be good at it?"

She tilted her head, tsking. "Brody."

"So?" He looked oddly unsure of himself.

"You're really serious," she breathed, hardly daring to believe that he didn't want just the here and now. He wanted…more.

"I'm a serious man," he said gruffly, pulling her into

his arms. "In the serious business of loving you." He held up his hand and she saw the ring tucked on the end of his index finger. "This was my mother's," he said. "I thought it was the ring my dad—Simon—gave her. She treasured it," he murmured. "But it was from Cole."

"Why didn't you say something before? I thought you'd gotten it from the Stanleys' apartment."

"It was easier to let you think that than let you know that, even then, you mattered to me." His hand shook a little as he drew it down her cheek, and she leaned into his touch, the tears sliding down her cheek.

"I love you, Brody. And I don't want to go anywhere that you're not."

"I'll get you your own ring," he said huskily.

She pressed her lips to his for a long, long moment. Then she drew his hand with the ring to her, clasping it against her heart. "Do you think that Coleman didn't love your mother when he gave this to her?"

A shadow came and went in his eyes. "I don't know anymore."

"I think he did," she whispered. "And you know she treasured it, because you said so. So maybe this *is* the ring I'm meant to have, Brody. Maybe we're all just finally coming full circle. Like the ring itself. No beginning. No end."

"If you want this ring, just say so, Angeline." But the sudden sheen in his eyes gave lie to his wry words, and her heart slipped open even more to him.

This utterly *good* man in his heart, who was a positive whirlwind. Who shocked her and delighted her, who challenged her and had faith in her, even when she didn't have it in herself.

"I want your ring, Brody Paine," she whispered surely.

"And even if there were no ring at all, I'd still want you. I'd still love you."

"You think this has been a crazy few days? Be sure, Angeline. Because I won't let you go."

She slid her hand up his chest, over the bunch of bandage she could feel beneath, until she found his heartbeat, pulsing against her palm. "What's a few crazy days when we've got a lifetime of them yet to live?"

His head came down to hers. "Together." The word whispered over her lips.

She closed the distance, her heart as full as it could possibly ever be. "Together."

Epilogue

"Where are the boutonnieres?" Casey Clay sauntered into the room where the groom's half of the wedding party was assembling before the wedding.

"Davey's guarding them on the counter there." Brody pointed to the boy, who wore a miniature black suit like his. Davey, looking important, handed over the sprig when Casey went to him.

Stephanotis or some such thing, Brody knew. He'd been hearing about flowers for the past month. Ever since his and Angeline's plans for a simple elopement flew right out the window.

She hadn't wanted to disappoint her family, she'd told him. And he'd caved rather than see any disappointment darken her eyes. He figured she deserved the wedding of her dreams. It was the least he could do to make up for proposing in a damn hospital room after five of the most insane days of their lives.

Now, he stared at himself in the mirror, trying to get the knot in his damned tie straight. Thank God he had insisted on no bow ties.

As it was, the wedding that he'd figured he could slide Angeline quickly through had turned into a regular circus. They couldn't hold it at the house in Sheridan, because the entire family was in Weaver. Angeline had been raised in the church there, so of course she ought to be married there.

On and on and on.

"How're you holding up?" Max Scalise held out a tall glass of champagne. Brody took it, though he'd have preferred a beer.

"Fine, if I could get this bloody tie straight."

"Just think about the honeymoon," Max advised, thoroughly amused. He reached over and yanked the long silver tie front and center. "You look real pretty."

"Don't make me regret asking you to be my best man," he muttered, polishing off the champagne all too quickly. Roger had sent his regrets that he couldn't make the wedding, so the position had needed filling. And now that Max was the sheriff and married to Sarah, he evidently no longer had reason to loathe the ground that Brody walked. Brody had even begun to actually like the other guy. He was a good cop.

"Don't make me regret agreeing," the other man returned. "What're you so grouchy about? You've got a beautiful woman, and I mean *seriously* beautiful, ready to commit the rest of her life to you. Most folks would just think she needed committing."

"Hilarious."

"This is just a day, Brody. It's the marriage that counts."

"I know. Believe me. I know. It's just all this…" He waved his hand at the flowers, the champagne. "Never in my life did I figure I'd ever be doing this."

"Did you ever figure you'd have someone like Angeline in your life?"

"No." He turned back to the mirror. Started to reach for the tie only to decide it looked fine the way it was. "She's been staying in Weaver for the past week," he finally said under his breath. While he'd been in Sheridan with Davey and Eva and Mrs. B. making plans to open that law practice. Finally. "We're going bloody insane without her. What's it going to be like ten years down the road and she wants to go away for a week or something?"

"God. You do have it bad." Max clapped him over the shoulder. "Suck it up," he advised, obviously amused. "Be a man."

From the sanctuary, Brody heard the organ music begin playing.

"Here." Casey held out the boutonniere. He, like Evan Taggart and young Davey, was serving as Brody's groomsmen. "Don't want to forget your posies."

Brody managed to pin the thing into place without stabbing himself to death and then, just as they'd rehearsed the evening before, they filed into the church.

His eyes drifted over the guests. No "his" and "her" sides, Angeline had said. Because everything from here on out was an "our" situation.

Mostly, he figured, she knew his side would be pretty damn empty otherwise, and soft heart that she had, she thought that would bother him.

He watched Casey escort his mother, Maggie, up the

aisle, where orchids dripped from the sides of each pew. Her blond hair was twisted in a sleek knot, her slender figure accentuated by the dark blue dress she wore. Next to her hulking son Casey—who'd definitely inherited the tall-blond-Clay thing—she looked even more petite.

Her eyes met Brody's and she smiled as she took her seat in the front pew. Once she'd taken him to task for dragging his daughter around the world and scaring the life out of them the way he had, she'd welcomed him with more generosity than he deserved.

Clearly, Angeline took after her.

Sitting behind Maggie were Angeline's grandparents, Squire and Gloria. And behind *them,* the rows on both sides of the church were jammed with more relatives. Angeline had counted them off for him one day and the number had been staggering, particularly for a guy who had only his quasi father to claim.

He was sitting in the front row on Brody's nonside.

Again, Angeline's doing. She'd insisted he invite Cole. Brody hadn't believed the man would even show up, but there he was. Just another surprise in his life since Angeline.

The organ music changed suddenly and everyone turned expectantly toward the rear of the church.

Brody realized he was holding his breath.

Sarah came first, and beside him, he heard Max sigh a little at the sight of his wife, who was noticeably pregnant in her long blue dress. And Max had said that Brody had it bad? He shot his best man a look. Max just shrugged. He was thoroughly besotted and didn't care who knew it.

Close on Sarah's heels was Leandra. As small as Sarah was tall, she came up the aisle, not seeming to look at anyone but her husband, Evan.

"She's pregnant," Max murmured to Brody. "Just told him before they got to the church."

Which would explain the vaguely dazed look on the vet's face, Brody suspected, and felt a definite envy. He'd told Angeline just a week ago that he wasn't getting any younger; they needed to get cracking.

Of course, at the time, he'd mostly just wanted to get her into bed, but she'd blushed and looked so suddenly shy that he hadn't been able to get the hope out of his head.

Davey and Eva headed up the aisle. The boy held a pillow with the rings tied to it in ribbon, and it was a good thing because he kept tipping the pillow back and forth as he grinned widely, happy to be the center of attention. And Eva—fully recuperated in the past six weeks since her appendectomy—looked pretty as a picture with her hair up in curls, wearing the same blue as the women. She had a smile on her face, too, and Brody was glad to see it, since Hewitt and Sophia's absence had been hitting her harder than Davey.

He gave Eva a subtle wink and she wrinkled her nose, smiling wider. Lord, but he was going to miss them. He, the guy who had always preached never getting too attached.

J.D. was sauntering up the aisle, and Brody's mouth dried a little, because he knew Angeline came after her. As if she could read his mind, J.D.'s green gaze was full of laughter as she passed him, and took her place in line. She gave him an audacious wink. Since she'd given Brody the third degree at the rehearsal the night before, evidently she'd decided she could be sparing with her good humor now.

He grinned back at her. Yeah, he liked J.D. She was a good kid.

And then he saw her. The only woman he'd ever loved. Angeline.

Standing in the rear of the church looking so beautiful he thought his heart might lurch out of his throat.

The afternoon sun slanted through the high windows above their heads, as the organ swelled and she slowly started forward, her hand on her father's arm. She'd told him she wasn't going to wear white, but the long dress she wore looked pretty white to him. The soft-looking lace clung to her figure, looking innocent and sexy all at once.

Her long dark hair was pulled back from her face, only a single, exotic flower tucked in the gleaming waves, and when she finally reached him, she angled a look up at him. She slowly, softly smiled. "You ready for a wedding, Brody Paine?"

As long as she kept smiling at him, there was nothing in life that he couldn't face, he thought. Even a wedding in Wyoming.

"Only with you," he promised and knew he'd do the whole thing a dozen times over, just to see the shining in her eyes.

She tucked her hand surely in his, and handed off her bouquet of orchids to J.D., and the two of them stepped up into the chancel with the minister, who beamed a smile over all of them and opened his bible.

"Dearly beloved," he began, only to be interrupted when Davey suddenly bolted for the rear of the church.

"Mom! Dad!" His voice filled the rafters. Eva suddenly dropped her bouquet and pelted after him.

Angeline's startled eyes met Brody's and they all turned.

Sophia and Hewitt Stanley were rushing up the aisle, grabbing their kids up and swinging them around.

Angeline bit her lip. She looked up at Brody, who didn't look as surprised as everyone else. Nor did Coleman, when she gave him an inquiring look.

He smiled. Lifted his hands.

In their pew, Angeline's parents were holding hands and looking amused. After all, twenty-five years earlier, Angeline's arrival had very nearly interrupted *their* nuptials.

"I suppose you knew they were coming," Angeline whispered to Brody.

"I wasn't sure when they would get here. They were extracted two days ago," he told her. "There was a lot of debriefing. At least a few of the Santina group are going to be out of commission for a long while."

"And Sandoval?"

He shook his head. "Not everything can be solved, sometimes."

Davey was dragging his parents by their hands toward them. "Mr. Dad, this is my *real* dad."

Both Hewitt and his wife were pale from their ordeal, but the hand he extended was steady. "Thank you," he said simply.

Sophia's eyes were wet. She held Eva tight against her.

Angeline crouched down and touched the girl's cheek. "I told you faith could do amazing things." She felt Brody's hand squeeze her shoulder.

Eva's face was wet with tears as she twisted an arm around Angeline's neck, too. "I love you, Angeline."

"I love you, too, sweetie. And I'm going to miss you, but we'll see each other again." Her eyes blurred with the promise as she rose and faced Sophia. "I feel like I know you."

"And I feel like we will never have truer friends," Sophia returned, looking just as tearful as her daughter. She hugged Angeline tightly. "But we are interrupting. We would have waited outside if we'd realized the ceremony had already begun. But there was a message from a Mrs. Bedford that the children were *here*."

"Of course you had to come. Right away," Angeline assured. She brushed her hand down her antique gown. "So now you'll stay…find a seat," she suggested, laughing.

Coleman gestured, and the four of them joined him in that front pew. He rescued the pillow with the rings that Davey had dropped on the floor. His gaze hesitated for a moment on the smaller of the two bands. Then he handed it to Brody. "You'll be happy," he told him gruffly.

"I know," Brody replied simply. He took the pillow and handed it off to Max. Then he turned to Angeline. "Shall we try this again?"

She dashed her fingers over her cheeks and nodded. She folded her hand through his arm again, and they stepped up into the chancel, where the minister was looking slightly bewildered. He opened his bible once again.

"House is going to feel empty without them," Brody murmured before the man could begin speaking.

Angeline huffed out a puff of air. "You know, don't you. Are you going to *ever* let me surprise you?"

He gave a bark of laughter and caught her around her waist, lifting her right off her toes. "Brody," she gasped, but she was smiling and looped her arms around his shoulders.

"Every day with you is a surprise, Angeline," he told

her and kissed her deeply. The guests were laughing. Some cheering. She barely heard any of it.

Oh, she loved this man who loved her.

The minister cleared his throat. Loudly. "If we could have a little order, here?"

Brody set Angeline on her feet again. He reached out and opened the bible for the minister, pointing at the pages. "Right there," he said.

The minister's lips thinned. But there was a definite twinkle in his eyes that even *he* couldn't hide. "Never a dull moment when there's a Clay around," he murmured. "All right then." He lifted the bible higher. Looked at Angeline and Brody, then at the congregation behind them. "Dearly beloved…"

* * * * *

LIZ TALLEY

Liz Talley writes romance because falling in love is the best feeling a person can experience. A 2009 Golden Heart finalist in Regency romance, she's since found her niche with Harlequin Superromance writing sassy contemporaries with down-home warmth and Southern charm. She lives in North Louisiana surrounded by a loving family, a passel of animals and towering loads of laundry. Visit her website at www.liztalleybooks.com.

Look for more books from Liz Talley in Harlequin Superromance—the ultimate destination for more story, more romance! There are six new Harlequin Superromance titles available every month. Check one out today!

A LITTLE TEXAS
Liz Talley

Where would I be without friends?
This one is for a few good ones:
for Dianna for suggesting I write;
for Rachel, the most generous person I know
(who else would take me to Commander's
on her dad's dime?);
for Connie, who keeps me on track
and should own stock in Starbucks;
and Sandy, who I'm convinced
really can run the world better.
There's a bit of each of you in this book.

Chapter One

"You did what?" Kate Newman asked, tossing aside the letter from the IRS and shuffling through the papers piled on her desk. Maybe she would find something to negate what she'd read. Something that would magically make the whole tax mess disappear. "Tell me this is some kind of joke. Please."

No sound came from the chair across from her. She stopped and looked up. "Jeremy?"

Her friend and business partner sat defeated, shoulders slumped, head drooping like a withered sunflower. Even his ever jittering leg was still.

She picked up the letter again. Only one question left to ask. "How?"

A tear dripped onto his silk shirt before he lifted his head and met her gaze with the saddest puppy-dog eyes she'd ever seen. Jeremy enjoyed being a drama queen, but this time the theatrics were absent. He shook his head. "It's Victor."

"Victor?" she repeated, dumbly. "What does he have to do with the salon? With paying our taxes?"

The small office at the rear of their salon seemed to rock as the reality of the situation sank in. IRS. Taxes not paid. Future in peril. Kate grabbed the edge of the desk and focused on her business partner.

He swallowed before replying in a near whisper, "He's got cancer. It's in his bones now."

"Cancer?"

"He's dying."

Her legs collapsed and she fell into her swivel chair. "Oh, my God. What kind?"

More tears slid down Jeremy's tanned cheeks. He closed his eyes, but not before she saw the torturous pain present within their honey depths. "He was diagnosed with testicular cancer two years ago. He underwent treatment, and the doctors said he was in the clear. We didn't think it was a big deal. We never even told anyone. But six months ago, the cancer came back. And you know when he lost his job, he lost his insurance."

Kate couldn't think of a thing to say. Her feelings were swirling inside her, tangling into a knot of sorrow and outrage. How could this happen? How could Jeremy's life partner be sick and her business at risk? The world had tipped upside down and now Kate was hanging on by her fingernails.

"I didn't know what to do. He was so sick...*is* so sick, and there was all that money sitting there in the bank. I thought I could pay it back in time. Kate, he's my life." Jeremy's last words emerged as a strangled plea before he broke into gut-wrenching sobs. "Please forgive me,

Kate. I needed the money for his chemo. To stop the cancer. It didn't work."

She closed her eyes and leaned her head against the leather chair. She wanted to cry, to express some emotion, or punch Jeremy in the mouth. But all she felt was emptiness. Then fear crowded her heart, choking her with the sour taste of failure. How could she have let this happen? Why had she assumed Jeremy was taking care of their taxes?

"I don't know what to say, Jeremy. I'm seriously contemplating murder."

His shoulders shook harder.

Shit. As angry as she was with him, she knew she'd have done the same thing.

The sunlight pouring in the window seemed way too cheerful for such a day. It pissed her off, so she jerked the blinds shut. "Why didn't you tell me? Let me help you before it came to this?"

His sobs subsided into an occasional sniffle. She knew he hurt badly. His partner meant everything to him. The two men had been together for four years—they'd met at the launch of Fantabulous, Jeremy and Kate's high-energy salon located on the outskirts of Las Vegas. Jeremy and Victor had hit it off immediately, acting like an old married couple almost from the beginning. They were the happiest couple she knew.

"I couldn't. Victor is so private and didn't want anyone to know. He was adamant about it. You're my friend, but he's my partner. I promised, and until now, I kept the promise."

His eyes were plaintive. He could offer no other explanation and Kate couldn't blame him. She'd felt much the same way her whole life. Private. Elusive. Never one to offer up a motive.

"I don't expect you to forgive me, Kate, but there was nowhere else I could go for the money. I even called my parents." Jeremy's long fingers spread in a plea.

"They wouldn't help you," she said, shifting the colorful glass paperweight her friend had given her for Christmas. She wanted to yell at this particular friend, get it through his gel-spiked head, that somehow she would have helped, but it was too late.

"No. Didn't even return my call."

"So what are we going to do? Can't we stop this? Put the IRS off somehow?" Kate knew she sounded desperate. She felt frantic, sick. Vomit perched in the back of her throat. Although Vegas had taken a huge hit economically, they'd been making it, but money wasn't flowing the way it had when they'd first opened.

"I talked to my friend Wendell. He's a bankruptcy lawyer. He said if we could scratch up ten thousand, we might hold them off then see where we stand. He also said we might cut a deal with the IRS and pay a lesser amount on the back taxes."

"Ten thousand?" she echoed. She only had about three thousand in savings and she'd been dipping in to cover extra expenses for the past few months. She didn't own anything she could use for collateral, and they'd put a second mortgage on the salon for an expansion right before the economy tanked. She looked down at the three-hundred-dollar boots she'd bought before the holidays and thought she might be ill on them. She felt stupid. Dumb. She should have been better at saving her money.

Jeremy dropped his head into his hands.

"That feels like a fortune. I don't have it right now. No

one does in this economy. The banks won't give us free suckers anymore, much less a loan," Kate said.

"I don't have the cash, either," he said. "I mean, obviously."

She pushed her hands through her hair and looked at the IRS letter. It ridiculed her with its tyrannical words. She wanted to rip it up, pretend it was a silly nightmare. Lose her business? *Ha. Ha. Joke's on you, Kate, baby.*

But no laughter came. Only the heavy silence of defeat.

Like a bolt of lightning, desperation struck. Once again she was a girl lying in the small bed inside her grandmother's tinfoil trailer, praying she'd have enough to make the payment on her class ring. Praying she'd have enough to buy a secondhand prom dress. Praying no one would find out exactly how poor Katie Newman was.

Her unfortunate beginning had made her hungry, determined to never feel so insignificant again.

She had to get out of the salon.

She snatched her Prada handbag from the desk drawer.

"Where you going?" Jeremy's head popped up. He swiveled to watch her stalk out of the small office.

"Anywhere but here," she said, trying to keep the panic from her voice. She felt as if someone had her around the throat, closing off her oxygen. She could hardly take in the temperate air that hit her when she flung open the back door.

"Kate! Wait! We have to tell Wendell something."

"Tell him to go to hell. I'll rot before they take the salon," Kate managed to say through clenched teeth. And she meant it. She didn't care what Jeremy had done. She wasn't going to lose her business. She'd go Scarlett O'Hara on them if she had to. The image of her clutching a fistful of deposit slips in the bank lobby crying out, "As God is my witness, I shall never go hungry again!" popped into her mind. She saw herself sinking onto the bank's cheap Oriental rug, tears streaming down her face.

She yanked open the door of her cute-as-a-button powder-blue VW Bug, plopped her purse on the seat and slid her sunglasses into place. "Screw 'em. I ain't giving in. Even if I have to sew a dress from my stupid-ass curtains, I'll get that money."

She wasn't making sense. She didn't care that she wasn't making sense. She needed money. She needed it fast.

And there was only one way for her to make money fast in Vegas.

Blackjack.

Three hours later, Kate slid onto a leather stool in the casino lounge. For all the clanging and clinking going on outside the bar, it was eerily quiet in here. Curved lamps threw soft light on the polished dark walnut tables scattered around the room. Kate had chosen the nearly empty bar over a cozy table. She needed to be close to the liquor.

Blackjack had not been her friend. In fact, blackjack had taken her last hundred dollars and bitch slapped her.

"What'll it be?" said the bartender. He wore an old-fashioned white apron that suited the Old World ambience of the place. Soft music piping from the speakers settled over the few patrons.

Kate pursed her lips. "Grey Goose, twist of lime, three cubes of ice."

"Nice. I like a woman who drinks like a man." The voice came from her left. She glanced over at the guy.

"I wasn't aware vodka was a man's drink," she responded with a lift of one eyebrow, a move she'd perfected in junior high school.

"Touché," he said, sliding a predatory smile her way. He looked good. Toothy grin, disheveled brown hair, five o'clock stubble designed to make him doubly irresistible. Any other time and Kate might bite.

But not tonight.

She gave him a flashbulb smile and turned ever so slightly to her right. *Stay away, buddy.*

But he was like any other man—couldn't read a woman's body language.

She felt him scoot closer.

The bartender set the glass in front of her. Without hesitating, she picked it up and downed the vodka in one swallow. It felt good sliding down her throat, burning a path to her stomach.

"And you drink like a man, too," her unwanted companion said.

Kate turned toward him, not bothering to toss him a smile this time. "How do you know I'm not a man? We're in Vegas."

His eyes raked her body. "I can see you're not a man."

Kate narrowed her eyes. "Good vision, huh? Well, don't trust your eyes. Don't trust anybody, for that matter."

She didn't say anything else, just turned from him and studied the way the light illuminated the bottles lining the mirrored bar. It made their contents glow, made them seductive.

Bars of "Sweet Caroline" erupted from her purse and she rifled through it until she found her cell phone. A quick glance at the screen and she knew her friend Billie had finally got around to returning her earlier call.

Finally. She could seriously use a sympathetic shoulder. And not of the rumpled, sexy, "can I buy you a drink" variety.

She punched the answer button on her iPhone. "Where the hell have you been?"

"Oh, my God, I'm like *so* having an emergency here." Billie's normally sarcastic tone sounded like neurotic chicken. A whispery neurotic chicken.

"What's going on?"

"He freakin' proposed!"

"Nick?" Kate asked, picking up the fresh drink in front of her.

"No, the Easter Bunny," Billie huffed into the phone. "I'm in the bathroom. Oh, God. I don't know what to say…I think I'm hyperventilating."

Kate pulled the phone from her ear and stared at it. Where was her calm, self-assured friend? The one she needed now that her business was doomed? "Okay, first thing, head between your knees."

"The toilet area's not real clean. I'm gonna stand."

Kate wanted to scream that she'd lost everything today and didn't need to hear about Nick and his damned proposal. But she didn't. Instead she said, "Okay."

"Kate, he has a ring and everything. He actually got down on one knee." Billie's voice now sounded shell-shocked. "I didn't know what to do."

Kate picked up the vodka and tossed it back. It felt as good going down as the first one. "So you said…"

"I said I had to go pee," Billie whispered.

Kate couldn't help it. She laughed.

"Don't you dare laugh, Kate Newman!" Billie snapped. "This is not funny."

Kate sobered. Well, kinda sobered. The vodka was

working its magic. "You're right. It's not funny. It's sweet."

"You can't be serious," Billie whispered. "He's talking marriage. *Marriage,* Kate!"

Kate heard something muffled in the background, then Billie's quick intake of breath. Then she heard Billie call, presumably to Nick, that she'd be right out.

"Okay, stop chewing your hair."

"What?"

"Do you love him?" Kate asked.

"Yes. I totally love him," Billie whispered.

"Then say yes."

"Are you joking?" Billie said. "Did you just tell me to say yes? You don't believe in marriage."

It was true, she didn't—well, at least not for herself. Love was fairy-tale bullshit. She shouldn't be giving relationship advice to a dead cockroach, much less a living, breathing friend. "I don't. But you do."

The line remained silent.

"Can you imagine waking up with him every morning even when he's old and wrinkly and…impotent? Can you imagine watching your grandchildren together? Filing joint taxes? Painting a nursery?" Kate couldn't seem to stop the scenarios tumbling from her lips. "How about picking out china patterns or cleaning up your kids' vomit—"

"Okay. I get it. Yes," Billie said.

"Then hang up, open the door and take that ring."

Kate punched the end button and tossed the phone on the bar. If Billie was so stupid as to reject a man who loved her despite her seriously weird attributes, then she deserved to stay locked in Nick's bathroom. With pee on the floor.

When she looked up, the bartender and her previously pushy friend stared at her as if she'd lost her mind. Well, she had. And her business along with it. And now Billie wasn't even available to her. Kate was on her own.

Like always.

Before she'd hit the ATM machine several hours earlier, she'd contemplated borrowing the money she needed from Billie. As a successful glass artist with international acclaim, her friend had steady cash flow even in a bad economy. But Kate never asked for help. And to do so now, with a friend, felt not cool. With a possible wedding on the horizon for Billie, ten thousand would be hard to spare. Besides, if she were going to borrow money, it would be from her absolute best friend, who lived in Texas and was loaded to the gills with old oil money. But Kate had never asked Nellie to help her before, not even when Kate had dropped out of college her freshman year to go to beauty school and spent three months eating bologna and ramen noodles.

She couldn't bring herself to do it. Kate had always relied on herself to make it through whatever problem arose, and this was no different.

But what *would* she do? There was no way the salon could generate extra income in the coming months. It was post-Christmas and debt squashed unnecessary services for regular customers. Many spas had closed their doors and many friends had gone from esthetician to cocktail waitress in the past few months.

The bartender finally moseyed toward her. He eyed her a moment before asking, "You want another?"

Kate waved her hand over the empty tumbler. "No thanks. If I have any more, I might go home with Pushy over there."

"In that case, I'd like to buy her another drink," the bed-rumpled hunk deadpanned.

Kate laughed. What else could she do? Her life was falling apart and someone wanted to pick her up. Just not in the way she needed.

She turned to the guy. He stared back, amusement in his brown eyes. She almost rethought her position on taking him up on his not stated, but obviously intended offer. "Listen, you don't want to deal with me tonight. It's been a hell of a day, and I just lost eight hundred dollars at the blackjack table. Unless you've got ten thousand dollars in your pocket, there isn't much else I want out of those pants."

The bartender laughed. "She's got you there, partner."

The hunk joined in on the laughter. "Not only sexy, but a smart-ass mouth. Damn, if I don't want to take you home right now."

"How much are you worth?" Kate asked, raising her eyebrows.

"Not nearly enough." He slid his own empty glass toward the bartender. "But I figure I can at least afford to buy you another drink."

Kate smiled. "Well, I'm gonna pass. It's almost midnight and that's when my car turns into a pumpkin."

She rummaged through her bag, found her matching Prada wallet, flipped it open and tossed her credit card onto the counter. As she snapped her wallet closed a small, yellowed piece of paper caught her eye. She'd carried it with her for years and years.

She pulled it from the pocket in which it had been nestled. Written in her grandmother's shaky handwriting before she'd died was a name. It hadn't mattered that Kate already knew the truth about him. That nearly everybody in her hometown had known the truth about the man. Her grandmother insisted on putting it in writing. Like that mattered.

Justus Mitchell.

The name of her biological father.

The man who refused to claim her.

The man she hated.

She fingered the timeworn edges of the paper. Justus Mitchell had once been the richest man in East Texas. His lands had stretched as far as the eye could see and his oil money went as deep as the earth that sheltered the precious commodity. The man was rich, powerful and politically connected. In his heyday, he'd owned everyone from cocktail waitresses to governors. He still held influence, or had the last time she'd checked. But even the powerful were vulnerable to hidden truths. Look what illegitimate children and mistresses had done to politicians.

Kate had morals. She had character. But she wasn't beyond blackmail in order to save her salon. And a lowdown snake like Justus had mounds of money sitting in the bank.

So…if she needed money, he might as well provide what he'd refused to give her so many years ago.

Child support.

He owed her. She'd feel no guilt because Justus wasn't a victim.

And neither was she.

Chapter Two

Rick Mendez swallowed the words he wanted to say as he watched Justus Mitchell roll his way. He shouldn't be here. There was no need. Rick could handle the center without the old man's meddling.

Rick watched as Justus navigated the maze of the recreation room. The sloped shoulders, withered legs and blue-veined hands betrayed the power of the man halting his wheelchair before a table set with dominoes. He could no longer walk, but he still commanded any room he entered.

"So how are things progressing, Enrique?"

Rick set the bill for the sprinkler system on the Ping-Pong table and moved toward the older man. Only Justus called him Enrique. "No problems yet."

"You know, I've launched many ventures over the years, but none of them have been as important as this one. This one is for Ryan." His chin jutted forward emphatically, as if Rick could forget how intricately involved Justus's son had been in the initial idea of Phoenix, the Hispanic gang rehabilitation center. Ryan had given it the name, believing that, like Rick, others could rise from the ashes and become new again.

Rick looked at the old white man staring at him with violet-blue eyes. They were Ryan's eyes…yet different. At that moment, Rick missed Ryan as keenly as he ever had.

"I haven't forgotten, but I'm not doing this because of Ryan. This center isn't a memorial. It's vital. And working with gang members isn't going to be easy. Theirs is a different world." Rick unconsciously rubbed a hand across the tattoos on his chest before catching himself. "There will be resistance in the gang community, resistance that might not be pleasant."

"We can deal with thugs. You of all people should know that."

Rick raised an eyebrow. Justus shifted his gaze away, a small measure of retreat. Old Man Mitchell knew better than to remind him of who he'd been. "You'll have to trust me. I can do this."

"I want to be involved."

Rick tamped down his anger. "You are involved."

Justus snorted. "I'm only the bank."

"Si," he said, just to remind Justus of how different they still were. "That has been your role since the beginning, and it is a most worthy role. You can't relate to the men who will come here. I can. I know the path they've walked. I know the pain and regret."

Justus didn't flinch. "I know regret, too."

Rick nodded. "I know, but that doesn't change the fact

that the men who come here will have almost nothing in common with you. Other than wanting to shake free from the life they now lead."

"Fine. I didn't come here to oversee you."

Rick felt a moment's relief, then a prickling arose on his neck. Justus wanted something.

"I have a request. It's quite, ahem, delicate."

Rick crossed his arms. He didn't need this now. Justus had employed Rick when he'd first come to live at Cottonwood and since then he'd done many things for the man before him. Nothing illegal, but some of those tasks made him feel uncomfortable in his skin. Of course that had been before Ryan died. Before Justus's stroke. Before he had changed. Before Rick had tired of being Justus Mitchell's lackey. Yet, Rick owed Justus more than he liked to admit.

And he owed the man's late son.

If it hadn't been for Ryan, Rick would not be the man he was today. Ryan's death had bound him to the Mitchells with invisible ties that would never be severed.

"What?"

Justus's eyes closed for a moment, before opening and piercing him with their intensity. "I have a daughter."

"You have a daughter?"

"Si," he said to be annoying. Satisfaction flashed across his face before he continued, "No one knows about her. Well, rather, they don't talk about her."

"Why?"

The old man rolled a bit closer, banging into the foosball table and causing the little soccer men to spin. The low pendant light cast a gray pall on his pasty skin. "Her mother was a waitress over in Oak Stand. I'd been with her five or six times, but there could have been others.

She didn't seem the choosy type. The child could have been mine, or not. I never bothered to find out."

"Then why worry about her now?" Rick eased himself onto the corner of the new pool table. The green felt was stiff beneath his fingers—very different from the one at the deli in the barrio where he'd won money off leathery broken men. He'd been a ten-year-old hustler with the instincts of a shark.

"Because of this." Justus's eyes shifted to the tray on the motorized wheelchair. The debilitating stroke had caused him to lose mobility in his right arm. His left arm was weak, but he could use it.

Rick picked up the folded paper. The heaviness of the paper spoke much about the sender of the letter. This woman meant business.

He unfolded it and read silently while the old man watched him. The note was brief and to the point. The woman wanted money to keep quiet.

"Well?" Rick said, refolding the paper. "You want me to kill her?"

Justus laughed at his jest. It was a running joke between them. Justus didn't need a Hispanic jack-of-all-trades to take out his competition. The old man could crush whomever got in his way. Money was his weapon, always had been, and Rick knew the power of that particular sword.

"No, I want you to bring her to me."

Rick stiffened. He didn't have time to play nursemaid to some upstart claim to the Mitchell fortune. He had a center to open. The rehabilitation center was the promise Justus had made him the year after Ryan died, and starting next week, Rick would be attempting the near impossible—bringing gang members from the streets of

Dallas to the countryside of East Texas for a chance to change their live's direction. It was a bold undertaking, but Rick wanted to give others what had been given to him. A second chance.

"I can't. I'm no longer employed by you. My focus is on the center."

"I can't trust anyone else." The old man rolled even closer. So close Rick could smell his Aramis cologne, see the deep grooves around his shocking blue eyes. "Please."

"I have to focus on Phoenix."

"You must do this for me, Enrique. This is all I shall ask. One last favor and I will sign the land over to the foundation. Think about it. The center would be secure."

Rick felt his heart pound. Mitchell did not part with much in life. The center was funded through Ryan's foundation. They'd received some federal money, but much of it came through the foundation. Justus was now offering something more. "All for finding this woman and bringing her to you?"

The old man smiled. White veneers flashed, a gold crown winked. "Finding the girl won't be hard. She used a post office box. Probably thought I hadn't kept tabs on her, but, of course, I always have."

Rick glanced at the folded note in his hand. It had not been signed. Just a post office box number given. The girl lived in Las Vegas. "Of course you would. You always know your enemies."

Something flashed again in Justus's eyes. It was an emotion Rick had seen before in those blue depths, and he knew it well. Regret stared at him in his mirror each and every morning.

"She's not an enemy. There is much of me in this girl. She's determined."

"And underhanded," Rick said. "How can you admire a girl who would threaten to ruin you unless you give her money?"

"It's not so different than what I would have done once. She's got her back against a wall. Otherwise, I wouldn't have heard from her. Besides, there's not much left to ruin, is there? Other than the money, of course." The smile Justus gave reminded Rick of a clown in a fun house. He supposed the atrophy on the man's right side was to blame, but still, he couldn't help the prickles that crept along his skin.

The only sound in the room was the hum of the restored soda machine in the corner. Rick wasn't sure he wanted to tangle with this woman, but the allure of owning the hilly land surrounding the center won over the doubt embedded in his gut.

He'd started trusting Justus Mitchell long ago and hadn't regretted it yet. The man had been ruthless, conniving and dangerous, but the day Ryan died had changed everything about Justus.

Nothing defeated a man like the death of his son. And nothing gave a man purpose like finishing the job his dead son had started. Justus had lost Ryan but found Jesus, and he'd declared himself transformed. From that day on, he had tried to perpetuate Ryan's legacy of seeing value in helping others.

"Fine. I'll go to Vegas, but it has to be tomorrow. The center opens next week and I've got five guys coming. That's more important than this girl."

Justus frowned but didn't disagree. "Good. I'll arrange for the flight. She's expecting me to send the money with no questions, but she'll have to give me more than some contrived claim. When you show up, we'll see how serious she is about this venture. The girl will dance to my tune if she wants something from me."

"Don't we all?" Rick said.

A laugh blasted past Justus's lips. "You learned long ago, didn't you? I'm a hard man, there's little doubt of that, Enrique, but I have a heart somewhere in here. I think." The old man moved his left hand jerkily toward his shrunken chest.

Rick nodded. "What's her name?"

"Kate Newman."

"She's gonna be trouble," Rick said, slipping off the pool table.

"All women are."

Kate balanced on her toes in order to check the box at the post office. Why they'd given her one in the highest row she couldn't guess. At barely five feet, it was obvious she'd have a hard time obtaining the mail. Must have been retaliation from the clerk, whose invitation to the movies she'd turned down. Some guys couldn't handle even the gentlest of brush-offs. Jeez. She'd been nice about it. Or as nice as she could be.

She tottered on her toes, her hand barely brushing the inside of the empty box. Damn. Nothing.

"Can I help you, *chavala?*" The low-accented question came from over her shoulder.

She dropped back onto her three-inch heels. "Nope."

She turned around and met eyes as dark as sin.

The man stood with one arm against the tiled wall. His posture affected ease, but she could tell there was nothing easy about him. Energy radiated from him like a wave of heat off the Vegas desert.

"You sure?"

Kate bristled. "Yeah, I'm sure."

His gaze slid down her body, but she was used to men looking her over. She waited while he took in her high-heeled boots, textured black tights, ruffled blue taffeta skirt, skin-tight lycra turtleneck, hoop earrings and short raven hair. "Get your fill?"

A quick smile crossed his lips. "Not quite."

A strange heat gathered inside her at his words. They were spoken quietly, with a hint of a Spanish accent. "Well, too bad."

She spun and stalked toward the glass doors at the front of the post office. She could feel him following her. Alarm curled around her gut.

She faced him. "Listen, buddy. That wasn't an invitation. Back off."

The man stopped, crossed his arms and grinned. "Oh, man. You're a live one."

Kate swallowed. He acted as though he knew her. "Whatever."

She turned around. He followed her. Alarm shrieked in her head. This dude, though seriously sexy, was off his rocker. What kind of lowlife stalked women in a post office? She tried to ignore him, but it was hard. He seemed right on her heels. In fact, she could smell his spicy warmth. It was dark and delicious. Forbidden.

She pushed through the doors and emerged into the blinding Nevada sunlight. Her car was parked under a withered palm tree, right beside an economy rental car. The man still trailed her. She didn't know what to do. It was broad daylight—surely he wouldn't try to abduct her. There were people crawling over the whole complex. It would be lunacy. Stupid. And the man didn't look stupid.

She slowed and watched as he passed her. He pressed

a button on his key ring and the rental honked a greeting. Relief washed over her.

She unlocked her own car and tossed her purse onto the passenger seat.

"Kate."

She froze, one leg in the car, one still on the pavement. The guy knew her name. Her heart pounded and the first thing that popped into her mind was that the IRS had found her.

Which was ridiculous. Wendell had said she and Jeremy would have a month before any action should take place. And the IRS didn't have field agents, did they?

So how did this guy know her?

She looked at him. He rested a forearm on the top of the silver rental and pierced her with his dark eyes. She eased into the depths of the VW, not sure what to do next.

"How do you know my name?"

He smiled. White teeth flashed in the brightness of the afternoon. "There's much I know about you, Miss Newman. But the most important thing I know is that if you want to carry through with your threat against Justus Mitchell, you'll have to get through me first."

Not much shook Kate, but his words made her shiver in the temperate Vegas air. "Wh-what?"

"I read the letter. I know what you want."

"Who are you?" Her legs quaked as adrenaline surged through her. Time to decide—fight or flight?

"Let's just say I'm a good friend of Mr. Mitchell."

Jeez, Louise. Who did her father employ? Henchmen? She looked around. A security officer sat in his little clown car about thirty yards away. She climbed from the car, slamming the door behind her. She knew how to stand up to men like this.

"Well, good friend of Mr. Mitchell, I guess you already know my father is a low-down, no-good bastard who spreads his seed all over Texas and leaves it to sprout with no help. He never acknowledged me or helped my family. I figure he owes me."

She advanced on the man. She could tell he hadn't expected much of a fight from her. What did he think she'd do? Squeak like a mouse, hop in her car and speed away? She'd sent the letter. She wanted the money. The bastard owed her that much. Likely more, but she wouldn't be greedy.

He watched her as she stalked around his car.

She stopped in front of him and planted her fists on her hips. "So, does that get the attention of his majesty? Or do I have to write Mrs. Vera a little note signed 'Kate Mitchell, your husband's illegitimate daughter'? Or maybe I can take out an ad in the *Houston Chronicle?* Bet that'd get the governor's attention."

The man blinked. Then he smiled. "You *are* his daughter."

She narrowed her eyes and waited.

"Justus wants you to come to Texas."

"No. I don't take orders from him. I'll go to a lab and have blood drawn. I know he's my biological father. I've known it for years. My mother and grandmother were not liars."

The man crossed his arms and released a sigh. Though he was slightly under six feet, he towered over her. His shoulders were sinewy and tight, his body trim and coiled. He reminded her of a soldier. Perhaps he was one. "Mr. Mitchell's instructions were firm. You want the money. You come to him."

There was no way she could go to Texas. She needed

to be at the salon raking in all she could, and if she canceled her appointments, she'd likely lose her clients. That was something she couldn't do. She needed steady customers—her future depended on it. It was one of the reasons she hadn't gone to Texas in the first place. That and the killer airfare.

"I can't. I have responsibilities."

"The salon?"

A thread of unease snaked up her spine. Did her father know about her financial troubles? Surely not. "Yes, if you must know. I can't pack up a suitcase and head to Texas to satisfy some old man's whim. I—"

"But you expect him to satisfy yours? Meet your demands with no proof? It's more than reasonable to expect to meet you face-to-face. That was his offer. Take it or leave him be."

Kate chewed on his words. "If he wanted to meet me face-to-face, why send you? Why not come himself?"

The man swallowed what she assumed to be aggravation. "You evidently didn't do your research well. Mr. Mitchell is ill and confined to a wheelchair."

Now, that was something she'd never expected. The powerful Justus Mitchell confined to a chair, crippled and sick? Something stabbed her insides. She was certain it was guilt. After all, she stood there ready to blackmail an ailing man and his reputed angel of a wife with dirty laundry from years past.

But Justus Mitchell wasn't a victim.

Kate didn't consider herself a victim, either. But she'd also grown up without the necessities of life while her father and his wife ate Chateaubriand and drank Perrier. She'd lived in castoffs from the Oak Stand Pentecostal Church while their precious Ryan had galloped upon a pristine lawn in a smocked John-John suit. She'd crawled into a used single-wide trailer each night praying it wouldn't storm while the Mitchells tucked into plush beds in one of the seven bedrooms at the family estate, Cottonwood. And worse still was that everyone knew she was his daughter...and felt sorry for her.

Kate deserved the money.

But she'd rather face a firing squad than go to Texas.

"Here's a plane ticket for tomorrow morning. Either you get on the plane or Mr. Mitchell will fix it so you never see a dime from him. Your choice." He shoved an envelope into her hand.

"You're threatening me?" Kate felt her toes sweat in her boots. They always did when she felt scared. Damn it.

"Turnabout is fair play, Kate."

With those words, the man opened his car door and climbed inside. Kate barely had time to step back before he pulled out of the narrow parking space. She couldn't tell if he watched her in his rearview mirror, standing bereft in the parking lot holding the envelope. He'd put on dark sunglasses that made him look even more menacing.

"I didn't even get your name," Kate muttered to the taillights of the car. "Rude ass."

There was nothing left to do but climb into the comfort of the VW. She blinked back desperate tears. Justus played hardball.

But what had she expected? The man hadn't risen to the top of Texas by letting people run roughshod over him. Of course he'd be as tough as the West Texas landscape that held his oil wells.

So now she had no choice. She'd have to go to him if

she wanted to get the money for Fantabulous. She only hoped she could pull it off. Everything depended on her playing the game well.

Chapter Three

Rick drove out of the parking lot as his cell phone jittered beside him. He glanced at Kate in the rearview mirror. She stared after him looking not the least bit happy, her lips forming words he couldn't hear. He could only imagine the curses being shot his way.

Who could blame her? The tables had been turned on her little blackmail game. And strangely enough, it hadn't amused him to get beneath her skin. He knew how it felt to be jacked around. But she'd brought it on herself.

The phone vibrated again. And again. He glanced down at the persistent humming. Justus's number flashed on the BlackBerry's screen.

He didn't want to talk to the old man right now. He needed to process Kate Newman.

She was a smart-mouthed, sexy piece of work. He liked her style—the edgy look she wore like an attitude.

She'd responded to him. He hadn't missed that. And she didn't seem afraid of him like other women were. There was little doubt she was Justus's biological daughter—not because her manner was as brash as his, but because she had his eyes.

Ryan's eyes.

Justus had stamped his mark on his two children.

Kate's eyes were like an exotic sea glittering at sunset. They dominated her delicate face, even overshadowed her tempting lips. He imagined men tripped over each other for a shot at her. She had a daring vibe, an appeal that would make people draw near to see what she'd do or say next.

Something stirred inside him. He wanted to tell Kate to stay in Vegas and not worry about Justus. There was a pall hanging over Cottonwood. It would suck her in and suffocate her.

Mind your own business, he told himself.

But logic couldn't stop the feelings rising inside him. The one that said "protect her" and the other he didn't even want to acknowledge. The one that whispered "bed her." Those responses were asinine. Kate didn't need protecting—he hadn't seen so much as a hint of fear or regret in those Mitchell-blue eyes. And as to the other, well, he wasn't that man anymore.

The phone sounded again.

He stopped arguing with himself and pulled into an empty lot, pressing the answer button. "Rick."

"Where the hell have you been?"

"Yes, I'm having a nice day. And you, Justus?"

"Skip the bullshit. You're in Vegas. You've seen her."

Rick grimaced. "Yes, I've seen her."

"And?"

"And I think she'll come to Texas, but I can't be certain. She's not what I expected." Even as the words left his mouth, he knew he shouldn't have said anything about Kate. He should let the man draw his own conclusions about his biological daughter. *Don't involve yourself. Keep your distance. The less said, the better.*

"What do you mean?"

"She's…salty. She won't be pushed around easily."

"So she *is* my daughter."

Rick's gaze roamed the lot surrounding his car. It was empty. Yellowed weeds poked through zigzag cracks. Boards covered the windows of a vacuum cleaner repair shop and a series of blue graffiti marked the boards. Staking territory. The number thirteen was displayed prominently, as was the letter *M*. He'd parked on Sureño turf, the street gang that had once been his sworn enemy. "You keep saying she's your daughter, so why go through all this? Just give her some money. You owe her at least that."

But Rick knew why Justus wanted Kate to come to Texas. He'd lost Ryan three years ago, then he'd had the stroke that nearly killed him. His wife, Vera, clung to the past, drowning herself in grief. Things were bad at Cottonwood. Justus needed deliverance. He thought he could get that in Kate.

"I need to see her. For proof."

Just look at her eyes. The words sprang to his lips but he didn't give voice to them. "I'll be back tomorrow, with or without her."

The old man sighed. For a brief moment the silence sat heavy on the line. "Okay. Tomorrow."

The line went dead. No platitudes about having a safe trip back. No polite farewell. Justus had never used niceties on Rick.

He shifted the car into gear and eased toward the road. From the corner of his eye he caught sight of two young guys crossing the back of the empty lot. Young Hispanic men. Flat-billed caps, thigh-length jerseys, baggy jeans, blue bandannas in pocket. Tattoos covered their forearms. Gang members.

The guys laughed, punching each other on the arm, but their laughter died when they saw him. He could feel them stiffen, grow aware.

He drove from the lot, leaving only sympathy behind. Sadness for a childhood lost. He wasn't sure if it was for the two bangers or for himself.

His mind cut to the center. The true test was about to begin. Next week, he'd find out if he'd bitten off more than he could chew. Reality was he didn't know squat about rehabilitating gang members. He only knew how to be one.

Maybe knowing the life would be enough.

The next morning Kate pushed her sunglasses to the top of her head as she entered McCarran International Airport. She glanced through the sliding doors to where Jeremy sat in her car. She gave him a wave and he saluted before pulling away from passenger drop-off.

She wanted to run after him, tell him *he* screwed up, *he* should have to fix everything. But she didn't. Because Jeremy didn't care about Fantabulous as much as she did. And because his partner had taken a turn for the worst and was under hospice care. And because that morning, the IRS letter had mocked her from its position on her fridge. She swore it even gave a snicker when she opened the door to grab a bottle of water and a yogurt. Two weeks ago, life had been much easier.

Now she had a mere three weeks to get ten thousand dollars to Wendell.

Or lose her salon.

That made her throat tighten. She tried her best to ignore the gut-clenching thoughts tumbling in her head as she stepped into a security line that seemed to be moving as slowly as the Vegas economy. One step every two minutes. At this rate, she'd likely miss her flight.

She scoured the crowd for the man who'd confronted her in the post office parking lot the day before. She didn't know if she would see him again. It didn't take a genius to figure out that he'd tracked her down through the post office box. If she really didn't want her father finding her, then she should have devised a more anonymous method of contact.

She should have known this whole blackmail thing was a stupid idea. Blackmailing a man who took pleasure in crushing anyone who got in his way—who did that? She knew the answer. Only someone who was desperate. And now look where it had landed her. She'd set something into motion. Could she handle what was about to happen?

A woman tapped her on the shoulder, pulling her from her thoughts, and pointed toward the moving line.

Finally, Kate made it through the checkpoint, reassembled everything in her purse and carry-on, and headed for the gate. The ticket was in her hand. It was one-way, and that made her nervous.

"Kate."

Her name sounded like a caress on his lips. She turned to face the man who'd shadowed her dreams the night before. He looked calm, as though he'd actually slept. The bags under her eyes sagged lower. "I'd say hello, but you never introduced yourself."

His lips twitched. "Enrique Mendez, but everyone calls me Rick."

He offered his hand. She ignored it. "Do you work for Justus, or just stalk random women at post offices for fun?"

Amusement flashed in his dark eyes before his face went blank. "Not necessarily."

The man was totally vague, but at least she knew his name. "Are you local or are you from Texas?"

His eyes scanned the crowded airport. He took her elbow and started walking toward the gate. "I'm from Texas. I'm flying back with you."

Kate tugged her arm from his grasp. "I can walk by myself."

He didn't react. Simply kept moving toward Gate D-13. She followed, but put space in between them. She studied him from behind as he moved purposefully toward the Delta Air Lines desk. He wore his dark hair clipped close, military-style and had on a black Nike athletic jacket, jeans and hiking boots. The boots didn't fit the look, but she imagined he didn't care. They were probably comfortable. Rick was one of those guys.

He stood in line behind two other people. She didn't bother. She already had a seat on the plane. Instead, she plopped into one of the bucket seats next to a dapper Asian guy reading on a Kindle, parked her stuffed-to-the-max suitcase next to her and watched Rick.

The man who'd made her so uneasy at the post office smiled at the attendant. The dour-looking older lady was forty pounds overweight with a horrible dye job, but she melted like a Popsicle in July at Rick's coaxing.

She wondered what he was trying to get from her. She also wondered why she hadn't been treated to such a smile.

The woman nodded, fluttered her lashes a little and took his boarding pass. She studied the screen before her, tapped a few buttons on the keyboard and looked up with a triumphant smile. She pulled something from a machine beside the computer and handed it to Rick.

The ass had obviously been upgraded.

The woman grabbed the intercom and asked all passengers seated in business class to please begin boarding.

Rick didn't even glance Kate's way as he stepped into the line.

Great.

By the time Kate had stowed her carry-on, popped a Xanax and sank into her seat, she decided she didn't like Rick Mendez one bit. He was chatting with an attractive flight attendant, his legs stretched out in front of him, while Kate had the sharp elbows of the guy to her left to look forward to. Not good.

She blew away the pieces of hair hanging in her eyes and settled into the not-so-comfortable seat. She had forgotten her iPod, so she'd spent her last bit of cash on a book at Walgreens. She hoped the legal thriller could take her mind off the jitteriness she felt at sitting inside the metal bird of death. If that didn't do the trick, the medication would likely kick in to soften takeoff.

She didn't like to fly. She did it when she had to, but only when it was absolutely necessary. Given a chance, she'd have elected to put the top down on her VW convertible, flood the car with her new Pink album and set out for Texas. Nothing better than the wind in her hair, but it was the end of January and she didn't think icicles forming on her nose would be a good look.

She took another peek at business class, but the flight attendant jerked the partition closed, throwing a knowing look at the people sitting in coach. Kate sighed. *Yeah, yeah, sister. We all want to be in there.*

"'Scuse me," Sharp Elbows said as he nearly pierced one of her lungs.

"No problem," she muttered, shifting aside and praying no one would take the seat to her right.

Her prayers went unanswered when a granny toddled toward her, counting off the seat numbers. Sure enough, she was 23E. The woman wore a floating caftan, had poofy hair and carried a purse so big it threatened to topple her forward onto Pokey Elbows's lap as she passed him. She grinned at Kate, showing her silver-framed partial and yellowed teeth smudged with fuchsia lipstick. No doubt she had jeweled sunshades and a brag book of grandchildren lurking in her purse.

"Honey, I'm over there next to you."

Kate lifted herself so the woman could slide into her seat. The ginormous purse smacked her on the thigh.

"Sorry, honey. I'll get settled…right…here." The elderly lady huffed and puffed as she adjusted her seat and tucked tissues in the pouch in front of her.

Kate really hated Rick Mendez. He was getting free liquor. While she was tucked in tight between Lemony Snicket and Mrs. Roper. Kate yawned. The Xanax was kicking in, leaving her feeling sleepy and foggy. She only used the medication for flights. Okay, and when she couldn't stop the merciless anxiety that sometimes swamped her and kept her pacing the floors at all hours of the night. Jeremy had forced her into getting some when she'd let it slip that she suffered from periodic anxiety.

Jeremy.

He wasn't so bad, even if he *had* risked her future without asking. She still loved her flamboyantly gay friend. Besides, she was as unsinkable as Molly Brown. She wasn't going to throw their friendship away over his moment of insanity. After her ill-fated blackjack game, she'd phoned him, listened as he threw himself a pity party, then told him her plan.

Part of the blame fell on her. She'd gotten lax in double-checking the books. Lord knew her accountant had harped on it enough. But she'd never thought Jeremy would endanger their business or friendship. Never. Which went to prove what she'd known all along. She had to rely on herself. No one else.

"Ma'am?"

A smartly dressed flight attendant with a fake smile and a platinum bob jarred Kate from her musings.

"Huh? I mean, what?"

"You can follow me. I've cleared you for business class."

Kate couldn't stop the smile that sprang to her lips, the first one she'd hatched in weeks. Hell, yeah. "Absolutely."

She turned the smile on her former seatmates. "Well, I'm outta here."

"I don't blame you, honey. I wish I'd had the time to show you pictures of my Pomeranians. You know I show them all over the country. Little Boy Blue just won the Hanover."

Kate nodded at the prattling granny. "Sorry I didn't get to see them. Have a good flight."

Then Kate followed the lithe attendant toward the Holy

Grail of the plane. If the plane went down, at least she would die in first class.

It was small consolation.

But it was consolation.

"You look groggy." Rick didn't mean for his words to sound accusatory. Hell, he didn't really know Kate. And shouldn't care. But he knew she was on something. Her eyes showed it.

"I'm fine. Just took a little pill to help me fly," she said, sinking into the seat next to him. "Wait. That didn't sound right. What I meant is I get kinda nervous when I fly, so I took a Xanax."

He eyed her. *Xanax?* "Should you be taking that?"

She raised her perfectly sculpted eyebrows. "I only take it when I feel anxious."

"You want a drink?"

"It's nine o'clock in the morning." Her voice sounded sleepy, reminding him of rumpled bedsheets and lazy morning sex. Not good. This was Justus's daughter. No sense in fantasizing about her.

"I meant a Coke or something."

Kate laughed. It was a smoky laugh. He felt himself grow semierect. Shit. What was wrong with him?

"Now I know you're from Texas. You called a soda a *Coke*."

He blinked at her. She was an odd one. Or maybe the medication was making her loopy. And talkative. He could have sworn she hated his guts.

She fell silent and fumbled for her lap belt. Rooting around, her hand bumped his thigh, which only served to heighten the flash of desire he felt for her. He reached down and grabbed the belt before she could slip her hand beneath his ass and pull it out.

"Sorry," he commented, reaching over and snapping the belt into the end she held against her stomach. He got a whiff of her perfume as he pulled away. Something expensive. And sexy. It made him want to dip his head closer and smell her hair or the silkiness of her collarbone where the perfume had no doubt been applied.

"Thanks," she muttered before opening a book.

He spent several minutes studying her out of the corner of his eye as she read. She'd shown up in tight jeans and an even tighter yellow shirt that wrapped her torso and cupped her small breasts. Yesterday, her hair had been spiky, tinted blue. Today, it was a mass of raven curls, making her look younger and softer. Dangly earrings brushed her shoulders. Her legs, encased in brown high-heeled boots, were crossed at her ankles.

Finally the engines roared to life, causing the huge 737 to thrum with power. He glanced at Kate's book. The cover showcased shadowy figures behind a blood splattered dagger. Horror? Thriller? He couldn't decide, but he'd never seen anyone so engrossed in a book. She hadn't moved.

Then he looked at her face.

Her eyes were closed. Not reading. Her nostrils flared lightly as she took calm measured breaths. Her knuckles weren't white from the suspense in the book.

He pried her fingers from the book, closing it and tossing it toward her crinkled-looking bag. Her eyes flew open.

"What are you—"

"Shh," he said, wrapping one of her cold hands in his. Her small hand felt delicate. It also seemed clammy. He threaded his fingers through hers and gave her hand a squeeze.

She opened her mouth to speak but closed it when he gave her a nod.

"Thanks," she whispered as the plane began its taxi down the long expanse of runway.

Rick thought about winding an arm about her, but that would be stepping over a boundary he shouldn't cross. He shouldn't care about this woman who'd stooped to blackmail her own father. He shouldn't enjoy the feel of her hand in his so much.

But he did.

Even as his rational mind threw up a roadblock, he squeezed her hand again as the wheels left the ground. She glanced at him.

Her blue eyes were twin pools of vulnerability.

"No problem," he said.

She pressed her lips together and nodded.

The plane hit a pocket of air and tilted ever so slightly. Kate took deep breaths as they climbed higher and higher. He rubbed small circles on her wrist with his thumb, offering what little comfort he could, but enjoying the hell out of her tender skin.

They hit one final air pocket before leveling out. Kate let loose her breath. "Okay. Okay. We made it."

"Yep, we made it." He released her hand.

Kate looked at him. "No problem."

But he couldn't respond because he knew there was a problem. And her name was Kate. And she was Justus's daughter. And she had Ryan's eyes. And she stirred some tucked away feeling of protection.

It didn't help that she wore tight-ass jeans and low-cut sexy shirts. That she pranced around in teetering heels, smelling of spicy earthiness. That she knew how to handle a man.

He had to resist her, so he didn't say a word. Because he knew.

Big problem.

Chapter Four

Arriving in Oak Stand, Texas, felt like being tossed into a game of pickup at a state prison. At the end of the day, someone would likely get shanked. The bucolic Texas countryside framed ten square miles of hypocrites and busybodies all wrapped up in a Norman Rockwell-style package with a gingham bow. Kate felt the prying eyes and raised eyebrows as she climbed from Jack Darby's massive pickup.

Yep. The bitch was back.

She stretched, glad the two-hour ride from the Dallas airport was over. She'd been cooped up far too long and needed to move her legs.

"You sure you want to walk to Tucker House? I don't mind dropping you by after I make this deposit," her friend's husband said, doffing his baseball cap and tucking it into his back pocket. Jack looked around as if he too felt the curiosity of the townsfolk. They'd parked in front of the Oak Stand Bank and Trust, the hometown bank with a friendly smile. Service you can bank on.

"I need the walk," Kate said, refusing to remove her sunglasses. She didn't need the protection from the graying sky—she needed it from the prying eyes.

Jack's brow crinkled as he eyed her high-heeled boots. "You sure?"

"I started walking in these when I was five."

"You had big feet, huh?" Jack chuckled.

"Yeah, that's it. And all the kids called me Bozo," Kate drawled, grabbing her purple Balenciaga handbag and slamming the truck door. "I know the way."

Nellie's husband threw her a salute much as Jeremy had earlier that day. Kate never minded a man saluting her. Even a smart-ass like Jack. The man lived to get under her skin, even though she knew he held a grudging affection for her. "See you back at the house, Katie."

"Kate," she said as she yanked the belt of her Burberry raincoat tighter and looked around.

Oak Stand looked about the same as it had the last time she'd visited except The Curlique Salon had gotten a new sign out front and the town square's grass was faded yellow. That was pretty much it for change.

Tucker House wasn't far. She could see the huge white structure across the square, right behind the statue of Rufus Tucker, founder of Oak Stand and great-great-grandfather to Nellie. She could cross through the park on the flagstone-paved path easily enough, but she decided to take the long way around to decompress a bit. Prepare herself. Everything had happened so quickly, she felt cut loose. Floating above herself.

It didn't help that the plane ride seemed a misty memory. The Xanax she'd taken had calmed her too much. She could barely remember the journey. But she remembered Rick, the way he smelled, the way he felt next to her.

She looked down at her bare hand. She'd forgotten her gloves at home, but she hadn't forgotten his touch. The way his thumb had stroked the skin on her wrist as the plane had climbed into the sky. Then once again as the plane prepared to land. Kate had had guys do lots of things to her hands—hold them, squeeze them, kiss them, suck her fingers—but she'd never had a man comfort them.

She tucked her hand into her coat pocket. She didn't have time to think about Rick Mendez and the weird tingling his touch had awakened in her. She'd bought herself some time, but she needed a plan.

When Jack had pulled up to baggage claim at the airport and tossed Kate's carry-on into the cab of his truck, she thought Rick might protest, but he held back, nodding to Jack as he passed him. Rick had told her Justus was expecting her, but she wanted to meet her biological father on her own terms. If this were some sort of a game Justus was playing, she needed home field advantage. Nellie, not Oak Stand, had always been that for her.

She approached the steps of Tucker House feeling as if she'd stepped back through time. As always, the porch was freshly painted and Margo met her at the door.

"Well, I do declare, Miss Katiebug Newman, as I live and die."

"Hey, Margo. And it's Kate, by the way."

The diminutive woman grinned. "I know. Just like to ruffle your feathers is all."

Kate rolled her eyes. Margo had worked for Nellie's grandmother when Nellie was a child, cleaning house and ironing all those Peter Pan collars Nellie had had to wear. Margo had taken a break to help raise her own grandchild, but returned to Tucker House when Nellie had started the senior care center a few years ago. It was good to see Margo holding the door open again.

"Come on in. Nellie's out back with Mae trying to dig up some bulb she wants to plant at her place."

Kate stepped into the heat of Tucker House. The walk had made her plenty warm, and several older ladies and gentlemen peered unabashedly at her as she shrugged out of her coat and hung it on a peg by the beveled glass door.

"You're Myrtle Newman's granddaughter," a spry silver-headed lady said, rising from the couch. The woman wore lavender yoga pants and a sweatshirt that said Hot Yoga Mama.

Kate felt herself stiffen even as she smiled. "Yes."

"Myrtle made a good pie," the lady said, her eyes twinkling in a friendly manner. "I tried to make her chocolate pie one year. Just wasn't the same. I'm Ester."

"Oh, yes, Ester. You taught Sunday school." Kate tried to smile, but it felt stuck. Something about Oak Stand made her feel claustrophobic. As though she was knotted up and couldn't move or breathe.

"Yep. Taught it for twenty-eight years before I got too tired to deal with kids kicking my shins. But you never kicked me, Katie."

"Kate."

"Kate. Of course." Ester beamed at her.

Kate needed to get out of here. Other ladies were creeping closer. "Well, I need to find Nellie."

Kate bolted before anyone could ask her anything else about her late grandmother, her past, her future or her dietary habits. She could never live in Oak Stand. Too many nosy people. Margo laughed at her as she scurried through the kitchen and out the back door.

Kate let the screen door bang against the house as she exited. Nellie dropped the shovel and turned. "Kate!"

"Finally, someone gets my name right," Kate grumbled as she trotted down the stairs toward the only person who felt like family.

Nellie looked terrific. Her blond-streaked hair was in a lopsided ponytail and dirt smudged one cheek. She wore tight jeans tucked into polka-dotted rubber boots and a hooded sweatshirt that hung midthigh. A chubby baby in a pink knitted parka and matching cap clung to her knees. The smile Nellie gave her made the cloudy day seem brighter.

Kate gave her friend a hard hug before dropping to one knee. "Hi, Mae flower, it's Auntie Kate."

Mae blinked green eyes at Kate, then hid her face between Nellie's knees.

Nellie patted her daughter's head. "She's going through a stage. She won't look at people. No one. Not even Margo."

Kate rose. "That's okay. I'm not good with kids anyway."

Nellie sighed and shook her head. "Kate, how would you know? You're probably brilliant with kids. She loves the boots you sent her. Don't you, Mae?"

They both looked down at the baby, who still clutched Nellie like a street peddler would clutch a shiny penny.

"Here's the bucket you wanted," a voice came from behind Kate. A voice with a soft Hispanic accent.

Kate spun around. "What the hell are you doing here? I told you I'd meet with Justus when I'm ready and not before."

Rick shrugged, a slow smile spreading across his face. "I didn't know you were here. I stopped by to talk to Nellie."

Kate faced her friend. "You know this creep?"

"Kate!" Nellie said, scooping up Mae and taking the pail from Rick. "Rick's not a creep. He's a friend. And why are you meeting Justus Mitchell? What is all this about? You never come to Oak Stand."

Kate opened her mouth then closed it. She turned to Rick. "What are you doing here?"

"He came about Phoenix." Nellie said, dropping an absentminded kiss on her daughter's forehead. Mae peeked out at Rick and gave him a drooling smile. Kate guessed Mae looked at good-looking, sneaky guys. Traitor.

She pulled her eyes from the baby. No matter what Rick said, he'd come to Tucker House because she was here. She'd irritated him when she'd turned the tables on him at the airport. He'd seemed to handle her leaving with Jack calmly, but she'd be willing to bet he didn't like it one bit.

"Phoenix is a gang rehabilitation center," he explained. "A place to help gang members make a break from the life and get an education and job training. The rehab center is right outside Oak Stand. Nellie's on the foundation board and I'm the director." Rick's eyes met hers. They were powerful, those dark eyes. Full of mystery and determination. They were obsidian chips of intent. Strong intent. And they made her toes sweat.

"Oh," Kate said.

Nellie looked confused. Kate felt something sink in her stomach. She hadn't told Nellie about trying to blackmail Justus. She hadn't told her friend much of anything except she was coming to town and needed a place to stay. Perhaps Rick had already told Nellie what Kate had done. Or what Justus wanted from her. But she didn't think so. He didn't seem the type to spread anyone's business around town.

"How do you know Rick?" Nellie asked her. "And what's this have to do with Justus?"

Rick smiled at Mae and chucked her on the chin. Kate averted her eyes and watched some small gray birds hop between barren branches before dive-bombing a bird feeder. She didn't say anything. Finally, she met Nellie's gaze and gave her the signal they'd developed when they'd been girls. Two blinks meant "later."

"Okay," Nellie said, shifting Mae to her other hip and dropping some strange-looking potato things in the bucket Rick had brought her. "Let me wash my hands and get those papers."

Nellie shoved Mae into Kate's arms and stalked up the stairs. The baby immediately began kicking and crying, and one of her little boots caught Kate in the upper thigh. This was her punishment for lying to Nellie.

Rick glanced at the squirming child. "Want me to take her?"

She set Mae down. "No, she can walk."

Mae immediately dropped to the ground and wailed. Kate could have sworn it was on purpose, but surely fifteen-month-old babies couldn't be so devious.

He bent down. "Mae, come see what I have in my pocket."

"Bet you say that to all the girls," Kate drawled.

He shot her a look before focusing on Mae. The baby sat up and studied him. Her cries stopped as abruptly as they'd started.

"Here," Rick said, pulling a package from his pocket.

Kate blinked. It was a package of crackers from the airplane.

"Crackers? I hope that's not what you actually give all the girls."

Mae reached out a grubby little hand and grunted.

"Babies love crackers," Rick said, opening the package and handing one to Mae. Sure enough, the baby took it and crammed it in her mouth. "And if I have something in my pocket for you, it won't be crackers."

She frowned at the double entendre, but she *had* started it.

Kate stooped so she could see the baby's mouth. She didn't know how to do the Heimlich maneuver on an infant. "Does she even have teeth?"

"Yeah, she has teeth. Not all of them but enough to gum a cracker." He lifted the baby and gave her the sweetest of smiles.

Something plinked in Kate's chest. She wasn't sure what it was because she'd never felt anything like it before.

Nellie returned holding an envelope. She shoved it toward Rick and gathered Mae in her arms. "Everything is signed and notarized. I'll come by Phoenix sometime soon. I can't wait to see the guys there. You've worked so hard, Rick. It's going to be fantastic."

"Let's hope so." Rick tucked the missive under his arm before turning to Kate. "I'll pick you up at Nellie's at 9:00 tomorrow morning. Justus will expect you before lunch. Bye, ladies."

He headed around the corner of the house.

Nellie shook her head. "What the hell is going on, Kate?"

Rick turned before she could bustle Nellie up the

stairs. His eyes flashed something almost naughty, but he didn't say a word. Just nodded and then he was gone.

Kate closed her eyes and blurted, "Oh, nothing. I just have to go meet dear old dad about a blackmailing scheme."

Her friend didn't say a thing, so Kate cracked one eye open. Poor Nellie looked like she'd swallowed a bug. Her mouth opened then closed. Finally, she managed to choke out, "What?"

"What can I say except what you already know? I'm a bastard child." Kate shrugged, trying to pretend she blackmailed reluctant biological fathers every day.

"You're admitting Justus Mitchell is your father?" Nellie asked, shaking her head.

"Shh!" Kate clamped a hand over her friend's mouth. Mae contemplated her with blank green eyes. Gooey cracker mush dripped from her mouth and landed on Kate's arm. "Don't."

Nellie pulled Kate's hand from her mouth. "Holy shit!"

Kate looked at Mae. "She didn't mean that, Mae flower. She meant holy shuckins."

Nellie swiped at the baby's chin while Kate scraped off the mess. She was glad she hadn't worn her Burberry outside.

"Would you be serious about this?" Nellie huffed.

"I am."

Mae squirmed in her mother's arms. Nellie set her down and studied Kate. "Kate, how is this… I mean, why haven't you ever said anything? And blackmail? I don't understand."

"Look, I'll tell you about it when we get to the ranch. Now's not the time."

"Kate—"

"Please. Let it ride, Nell." She stalked up the steps without looking at her friend again. She'd tell Nellie that night. After dinner. After Mae had toddled off to bed. After Jack had dozed off in the recliner. But not now. Not when her nerves felt shredded and her stomach felt like it harbored rocks. Really heavy rocks.

She'd screwed up when she'd devised this plan.

She should have let the salon go. It was just a business. People lost businesses every day. She could start over, get a job in L.A. She'd done it before.

But it was too late. What she'd put in motion had to be ridden out. She'd poked the devil with a stick, and messing with the devil was dangerous, especially when he had huge stockpiles of supplies and a sexy henchman who made her pulse flutter. And that was the scariest thing about facing the battle that would come in the morning. Something about the devil's henchman made her want to sleep with the enemy. And that couldn't be good.

War really was hell.

Rick pulled his car into the drive of Cottonwood Ranch, Justus's colossal spread. The drive leading up to the enormous white house was long and straight. No meandering for a man like Justus. Direct and to the point.

Rick knew Justus would be irate with him for not bringing Kate directly to the ranch, but he'd rather deal with Justus's anger than deal with being thrown into prison for binding and gagging Kate Newman then shoving her into the backseat of his car.

The thought of controlling Kate appealed to him. He envisioned her under his power, and desire stirred inside him. That was seriously whacked, so he checked that feeling as he parked on the checkerboard grass-and-stone parking area.

Justus's wife, Vera, dabbled in gardening and landscaping, so she'd designed this parking area declaring it more welcoming than concrete. Every time his foot crushed the low-growing thyme in between the pavers, a sweet aroma filled the air. Leave it to Vera to deliver an unexpected gift to the person parking outside her home.

"Rick," Vera called out from the prayer garden she'd built behind the carriage-style garage. "Come see what I've found."

Rick could no more ignore the hint of pleasure in Vera's voice than he could turn out a hungry stray. Grains of happiness were few and far between for the woman Justus had brought to Cottonwood and made his bride over twenty years ago.

He rounded the corner and found her kneeling in a patch of withered canna lily stalks. He looked around at the garden they'd neglected during the holidays. "I guess I need to clear all this dead stuff away and put down another layer of mulch."

Vera looked up at him, her hair falling over her shoulders, brown eyes crinkled with a haunting smile. "I know, but look what I found."

He bent and pushed a hand through the matted pine straw. Small green stalks barely cleared the fertile loam. "Crocus?"

"Yes," she breathed, passing a bare hand over the tiny new growth rising in the grayness. "Ryan planted them when he was a child. Some years they don't come up. I don't know why, but this year they're making an appearance."

"A sign of good fortune, I bet. Better cover them well,"

he said, straightening and eyeing the low, dark clouds. "Those clouds carry rain and with temperatures dipping tonight, we might have a freeze."

She carefully covered the plants then stood. She brushed her hands on her worn jeans and pulled her hair to the side. She looked much younger than her fifty years.

"Did you bring her back?"

Rick stiffened, dread uncoiling in his stomach. How did Vera know about Kate?

"He can't keep secrets from me, Rick," she said softly, tucking her hands into her back pockets and shivering. The wind had picked up and the jacket she wore afforded little protection against the air sweeping across the hilled pasture.

"Don't get involved in this, Vera."

She shrugged. "I know my husband. Knew what kind of man he was before I married him. A secret love child comes as no surprise to me."

Love child? Rick didn't think the term could be applied to Kate. Not the way Justus had talked about her mother. Rick didn't sense any tenderness where Susie Newman was concerned. She'd been just another woman who'd thought she could catch the mighty Justus Mitchell and failed.

Rick studied the woman who hadn't. Her face bore the tale of losing her only child and surviving her husband's declining health, yet, she was lovely. Touched by time and misfortune, Vera still held traces of that Alabama Southern belle she'd been. She was a woman who could serve up coffee and pound cake with the hands she'd just used to transplant a hydrangea or nurse a sick child. She'd been Rick's only friend for a while…aside from the gangly boy who'd dogged his heels when he'd first come to live at Cottonwood.

"You've talked to him about this girl?" he asked as he walked toward the rear of the house.

She followed, tossing her gardening gloves onto a bench outside the mudroom. "Not exactly, no. But I always know what's going on, Rick."

"So you're just pretending not to?"

Vera smiled. "Of course. Justus will tell me when he's ready. He thinks I'm weak. That I have to be protected."

For good reason. Vera had been hovering on the edge of severe depression since Ryan's passing. Few things brought her joy.

They entered the kitchen where Rick's grandmother Rosa ruled. Rosa had been with Justus for over forty years. She ran Cottonwood, and she was the reason for every good thing in Rick's life.

"Hola," Rosa said, her accent still thick despite the years she'd spent in the United States. His grandmother stood at the stove stirring something in a pot. It seemed he could always find her there. The kitchen smelled like barbecue and made his stomach growl. "Mr. Justus said to go to his office. He just called down, upset you weren't here."

Rick shrugged. "He's going to get even more upset. Put antacid next to his plate tonight, *abuela*."

Vera disappeared before he could say goodbye.

Leaving Rick to tell Justus that Kate played by her own rules.

Chapter Five

Kate hadn't gotten much sleep. Mostly because she'd stayed up late listening to Nellie lecture her. Eventually she'd fallen into a fitful, shadowy sleep. When she'd woken this morning, her head pounded and she could barely swallow. A suspicious substance dripped from her nose. The pine trees of East Texas had done their job. Her allergies were going haywire.

Even so, she'd staggered from Nellie's guest bedroom, managed a long shower and pulled on a tight sweater-dress with black kick-ass Tory Burch boots. Of course, her slightly red nose didn't match the violet minidress, but at least it was in color range.

The kitchen was empty. Kate made herself at home, grabbing a cup of black coffee and a Pop-Tart. After three bites of the pastry, she remembered why she never bought them—they tasted like flavored cardboard. Her

half-eaten breakfast hit the trash can just as the doorbell sounded.

Rick had not forgotten. Damn.

She took another sip of coffee with an unsteady hand.
She'd once read an Emily Dickinson poem in college
where Death had politely rung the doorbell. When answered, Death had taken the dude on a trip that ended at
the cemetery. This felt a little like that.

The doorbell sounded again.

"I've got it," Kate called out, forcing herself to move.
She didn't want Nellie to answer. Almost always re-
served, Nellie left the outlandishness to Kate, but if and
when Nellie got her dander up, there was no subtlety
about it. And last night, Nellie had been as mad as Kate
had ever seen her. She wasn't sure if the fury was at her,
Justus or Rick.

Kate threw the door open, and Rick jumped back before giving her a quasi grin. "Good morning, cupcake."

She snorted. "I've been called lots of names before,
but never *cupcake*. Come in. I'll grab my purse and gun."

"Bring plenty of ammunition. His wheelchair is motorized and he's pretty fast in it."

"I have a whole box," she said as she turned toward
the kitchen where she'd left her purse. Nellie hadn't appeared. Thank the Lord. She figured her friend didn't
trust herself not to lash out at Rick for carrying out Justus's heinous mission. Kate hadn't been able to reason
with her over this whole fiasco. And it was a fiasco, but
Nellie didn't seem to understand Kate had asked for this
when she'd written that damn letter. Nor did she understand why Kate hadn't come to her for the money.

Kate had thought Nellie would get why she hadn't
made that call. Everyone in Oak Stand knew Kate and her

grandmother had lived off donations and cast-off cloth-ing, and everyone knew Kate was embarrassed by that fact. Kate had never asked Nellie for anything. Ever. No matter how desperate she felt, it was an unwritten code they never talked about. Another elephant in the room of Kate's life, one that had so many pachyderms in it, it was a wonder she had air left to breathe.

Kate wouldn't take charity. Not from a friend.

But she would take Justus's hush money.

She scooped up her purse and checked herself in the den mirror. She looked good for someone who had a raging sinus headache. She'd made up her eyes a little too heavily, but the blue streaks in her hair balanced the look. She'd finger-combed her hair into a straight edgy look and added dangly hoop earrings. The outfit was cutting-edge fashion. Overall, she looked like Jus-tus's worst nightmare—something like Posh Spice meets Reno prostitute.

She sauntered to the foyer, where Rick studied a col-lage of Mae. The whole damned house was Ode to Mae. Nellie must have taken a picture of the baby every single day of her fifteen months of life.

"She's a cute kid," Rick said as he turned to her. His gaze swept her length, lingering on the high points. Namely her small breasts. She hadn't worn a bra because she didn't really need one. She felt her nipples harden under his perusal. The friction of the sweater dress only served to incite the heat in the pit of her stomach.

Rick Mendez was a nice piece of work. He'd look good on her, no doubt.

"Yeah, she is," Kate said, crossing her arms over her chest. "But they could give the camera a rest. Jeez."

"Ready to go?" Rick stepped back to let her pass through the door he'd left open. The last day in January felt cool and rain-soaked.

"Yeah. You have the blindfold ready?" She shrugged into her coat and tugged the ties.

"Blindfold?"

"For the firing squad."

He narrowed his eyes. They were nice eyes. Chocolaty-brown, but forceful all the same. Like they'd seen and endured much.

She shot him a brave smile and trotted down the steps toward the '66 convertible Mustang parked in the curved drive. The car was salsa-red with a white top. A muscle car to match the intensity of the man walking behind her.

"I carry the blindfolds in my glove box," Rick said, following her to the passenger door. He pushed a key into the lock, pulled the door open for her, then walked around to slip into the car beside her. His shoulder brushed hers as he pulled the modified seat belt over his chest and she got a whiff of him. He smelled clean. His short hair looked damp, as though he'd climbed from the shower only moments ago.

"So you *are* into kinky stuff. Nice."

For a moment, the air ignited. Heat came off Rick in waves. He wanted her. She knew that. But what would he do about it?

"Damn straight," he said, his accent low and dangerous. Kate's stomach prickled. "But they're only for the really bad girls. You're not a bad girl, are you, Kate?"

Kate snorted. "I think you know the answer to that."

His response was to rev the engine. But he wore a smile.

* * *

Cottonwood loomed in front of them like the dream of a nine-year-old girl. Its stately columns and fanciful curved front steps ignited visions of hooped dresses and shiny carriages. Kate had stood outside the gates before, peering through the cold bars where an intricate *M* was carved. She'd dreamed of walking down those stairs, lifting the edge of her wedding gown and stepping into a limousine.

Once she'd imagined herself crossing the trimmed lawn to her smiling father. Imagined him lifting her veil and giving her a gentle kiss. It was a kid's dream. Utter make-believe.

She glanced at Rick as they approached the house. Even he seemed tense. His shoulders were bunched beneath the same jacket he'd worn yesterday and his jaw looked set. Rock hard. That image of Rick was both titillating and off-putting.

"Honey, I'm home." Her voice sounded on edge to her own ears.

Rick glanced at her.

She gave him a shaky smile. "Too soon to call it home?"

At this his lips twitched. Something in his smile gave her comfort. She wanted to thank him for that, for offering her some solace in this moment she faced. That comfort shouldn't have meant anything to her. Justus Mitchell had denied her once—it was entirely conceivable he'd do it again.

She had carried her hatred of him around with her because it had made her who she was. She didn't take crap from anybody and she lived by her own rules. That was what Justus had given her. That and nothing else.

But now she wanted money from him. Money that was way past due.

Rick pulled onto an odd patterned parking area adjacent to the house and cut the engine. "I'll walk you in, then I'm running over to Phoenix. It's not far. My grandmother will call me when you're ready and I'll pick you up."

He was leaving her. For some reason, she didn't want him to. Even though he worked for Justus, he felt like the only guy on her team.

Which was stupid.

He touched her on the shoulder. "Hey."

She lifted her gaze to his, afraid he might see how much she wanted him to stay. He wasn't smiling. He looked as intense as the first time she'd met him, but there was a tinge of softness now.

"You're strong."

His words wrapped round her, doing as he intended, strengthening her, bolstering the courage she'd felt she'd lost for a moment as they'd driven up the lane.

Kate closed her eyes, then she leaned over and kissed him.

Not a peck, like she was thanking him.

But a full-fledged kiss.

At first he drew back, surprised her mouth was on his. But then he leaned in and allowed his lips to soften beneath hers. She opened slightly, tasting him. He tasted like spearmint gum and warm male, so she tilted her head and opened her mouth a bit more. He took advantage, deepening the kiss, sliding his hand to her jawline.

His hands were big and calloused. Something dangerous slithered inside Kate, a flash of desire.

She broke the kiss. "I *am* strong."

Then she threw open the door, grabbed her purse and climbed from the car. She didn't need Rick to walk her inside. She'd deal with whatever waited behind the back door. No sexy Hispanic crutch need apply.

As she lifted her hand to knock, she paused. The Mustang roared to life. She glanced over to where it idled. Rick watched her in the rearview mirror. She wondered what he thought about the kiss, but before she could search for his gaze again, the car pulled away.

She knocked on the door.

An older Hispanic woman answered. A smile curved her broad face, wrinkling the skin around her dark eyes as she said, "*Adelante*. You use the back door? My grandson leaves you here?"

"Oh, hello." Kate pulled her bag higher on her shoulder and tried to discern if the woman fussed at her or Rick. "Um, Rick went to Phoenix. He said you would call him when I'm ready to return to my friend's house."

The woman stood aside so Kate could enter, tsking all the while. "What manners he shows. Dropping you at the back door like a laborer. A man should walk a lady inside."

The phrase "I'm no lady" popped into Kate's mind, but she wisely held the snappy comeback inside. "No, it's fine. I'm a big girl."

"I fuss at him, but I am rude, too. I'm Rosa Mendez. And you are not such a big girl. A *chiquitita*. Very, very tiny. And so lovely."

Kate never blushed, but she felt heat suffuse her face. "Thank you, Rosa."

"It's true." Rosa bustled into the kitchen. Kate followed behind like a puppy on a leash, ogling the cavernous kitchen. Modern appliances gleamed and houseplants overgrew their planters. The smell of herbs and bread permeated the air. Spanish tiles flashed blue and russet upon the counters and a small television sat in the corner playing a Spanish soap opera.

Rosa picked up a handheld radio. "Mr. Justus, Miss Kate is here."

The radio crackled, but she heard his words. "Send her up."

Just like a job interview. *Yes, Ms. Mendez, please send the applicant up.*

Rosa smiled, showing a large gap between her teeth. "*Si,* Mr. Justus wants you to go up."

"I heard," Kate said, looking about the kitchen trying to buy some time.

Rosa wiped her hands on a dish towel. "Don't worry. I'll take you."

"Don't bother, Rosa. I'll do the honors."

The voice came from the opposite doorway.

Kate turned as an older woman—presumably Vera Mitchell—stepped into the room. For a moment, Kate felt as though she'd been dropped onto a remote island with no food or water. *Survivor.* Trust no one.

Vera looked like what she was—a rich Texan's wife with an expensive haircut, manicured nails and clothes from Neiman Marcus. Her expression was measured, as if she were prepared to serve tea to a bastard daughter and not even break a sweat. Kate watched her as she approached.

"I'm Vera Mitchell. Justus's wife. Welcome to Cottonwood." Kate took the extended hand. It was as cool as she'd expected.

"I'm Kate Newman. I have a—" what was it exactly? "—meeting with Mr. Mitchell."

The older woman released her hand. "Yes, I know. Follow me and I'll show you to his office."

Kate glanced at Rosa. Rick's grandmother stood watching, her mouth slightly agape. She assumed the woman hadn't expected Vera to greet the usurper to the throne. Of course, she wasn't really interested in anything from either of the Mitchells. Only a bit of money owed for all the times she'd eaten leftovers from the diner because her grandmother couldn't afford groceries.

She followed Vera to the foyer—noting the modern elevator sitting like an anachronism in the traditional elegance of the mansion. They climbed to the second floor and Kate scanned the massive oil paintings of barren Texas landscapes, the impression of them as cold and imposing as the miles of marble they walked upon.

"Here we are." Vera swept her hand toward an ornately carved door.

"Thank you," Kate muttered, trying not to squirm under the other woman's scrutiny. She'd be damned if she felt remorse about what she was about to do.

"You're welcome," Vera said, catching Kate's gaze with her own. She held it for a moment before nodding. "Yes, you have his eyes."

Kate didn't know what to say. She waited, but Vera didn't say anything else. Instead, she melted away, leaving Kate standing there, feeling weird and out of place.

So Kate gave herself a mental pep talk. Vera didn't matter, Rick didn't matter, no one mattered. Justus Mitchell had denied her. This time, his chick had come home to roost. And this chick wasn't a scared little girl. This chick was a ballbuster.

She didn't bother with knocking—he didn't deserve the courtesy. She opened the door and walked inside as if she owned the place.

Rick made it all the way to Phoenix before turning the car around and heading back toward Cottonwood.

What had he been thinking, leaving Kate alone to deal with Justus by herself? He hadn't discussed anything regarding Kate with the old man, and Justus could be erratic. And, frankly, manipulative. He had come to Christ, but he was still a sinner as much as any man. Rick didn't trust him to not trick Kate.

And what about that kiss? The saucy little salon owner's taste still lingered on his lips.

He passed a hand over his face.

Damn, that kiss had felt good. Good in a scary way, because something had moved inside him again. Like when he'd watched her in Vegas, and again on the plane. What was she doing to him?

He didn't want to think about the compulsion that drove him to return to the ranch.

The Texas countryside passed him, dull and gray. This last day of January was grim, harsh and cool with little to no lacy snow to hide the hibernating earth. Yellowing grass and naked sweetgum trees mingled with the dusky green of the pines. The bright red of his hood was the only brilliance to meet the eye. The only gang-related color he allowed himself in his life.

It had been Ryan's car. The car they'd restored together, right before he'd died.

How they'd both loved the vibrant red paint—the original color, painstakingly researched and tracked down. It had gleamed beneath the many coats of wax they'd applied while nursing warm beers and listening to Santana's sweet licks. Sometimes it seemed like only yesterday they'd stood in the garage and joked about Ryan's girlfriends and the failure of the Cowboys to draft a good quarterback.

Tony Romo had proven them both wrong, but what had it mattered? His young friend would never watch another game with him.

And that haunted him more than any of his past mistakes. Rick should have believed Ryan. He should have known Ryan was telling the truth, but he'd refused to listen.

Rick rolled down the window and allowed the memories to be sucked out the car. The cold air hit his face. Reality had teeth.

Ryan was gone, but Kate was not.

He took the drive fast, kicking up crushed rock and causing dust to boil into the interior.

His grandmother met him at the door. "You shouldn't have dropped her off that way. Left her to face him alone—"

"I know," he interrupted as he beelined toward the door that led into the bowels of the house. "Did you take her to Justus?"

"No, Vera did."

"Shit," he muttered under his breath as he wound through the downstairs and took the stairs two at a time. Vera was nowhere to be seen. In fact, the house was eerily quiet. He stopped outside Justus's office and listened.

He didn't hear anything.

He eased the door open, not knowing what to expect. Then he stared in surprise.

Justus sat in his chair near the window, silent and solemn as Rick had ever seen him, and Kate stood about ten feet from him, hands propped on her hips. Her narrow shoulders were thrown back and her chin jutted high. She didn't see him enter the study. Neither did Justus.

"You're right, of course," Justus said. He did not pull his eyes from the window. He seemed to be looking out at Ryan's garden. No doubt Vera was rambling about. She went there daily to pray, to mourn and to celebrate the son she loved. Justus observed her grief from above.

"You're damned straight I'm right." Outrage laced her words. Only the slightest tremble of emotion in her voice gave any indication the conversation meant more to her than some random argument over a parking spot.

"Yes." Justus nodded before tearing his eyes from the scene below. His gaze met Rick's.

Kate spun around. "What are you doing here? This is a private conversation. I don't need your help."

Her violet-blue eyes flashed, much as Justus's did when he was irate. "Yes, I'm sure you don't. But Justus might."

A choking sound came from Justus. It sounded rusty and was seldom heard around Cottonwood, but was definitely a laugh. "True. She puts up a lot of fight, considering she's no bigger than a dust mite."

This seemed to bother Kate more than it should have. "Being small does not mean being without resource. I can handle myself fine. Now if you will just hand over my child support payment, I'll get out of your life."

A smile hovered on Justus's thinning lips. "Child support? I suppose one could call it that. But…"

A furrow popped up between Kate's eyes. Her brow lowered, like a dog smelling a trap. "But what?"

"I'm first and foremost a businessman, and I can see the apple doesn't fall far from the tree."

"What are you getting at?"

Rick remained silent and watched Kate. He knew Justus well enough to know he had a reason for summoning Kate to Cottonwood and it had nothing to do with money. It was something bigger.

"I have an offer to counter your illegal demand for money, Kate."

She advanced on Justus and stuck a finger in the middle of his chest. "Bullshit. Call it whatever you want, but you owe me."

The old man merely looked up at Kate. His wheelchair whirred as he moved it forward. His daughter stepped back. "If you want child support, I think it only fair to give me something."

"Wrong." Her word cut the air.

"No, hear me out. I'll give you child support, but I want my visitation."

Rick averted his eyes to the painting adjacent to where he stood. He couldn't look at Kate because he knew Justus had done what he always did. Pulled the rug out and left his victim gasping on the floor. It wouldn't be wise to get involved. She'd unleash on him, and Hurricane Kate could pack a punch.

Hell, what was he doing here, anyway? His head said, "run." But his gut said, "stay." Finally, he looked at Kate, whose mouth was open and he knew.

She needed him even though she didn't realize it. And for some reason beyond his understanding, he was going to help her.

Chapter Six

Kate nearly choked on her rage. What the hell did the old man mean, *visitation?*

She put a hold on her anger long enough to glance over at Rick. His expression seemed composed. Had he expected to hear those words come from Justus's mouth? For the umpteenth time, she wondered what he was doing at Cottonwood. Why was he dancing to Justus's fiddle?

"What do you mean?" she asked, directing her attention to Justus. Her fingernails pressed into her palms hard enough to draw blood.

"I want to spend some time with you. Get to know you. It's simple, really. And makes this whole thing an agreement, rather than blackmail."

"No." Kate shook her head. He couldn't control her. Or change the rules. She'd come to Texas at his behest to settle what she'd started. Two days. That was all she was willing to give him.

"You want back payment on child support with no absolute proof that you are my daughter. I think it's only fair I get something in return." Justus's face was placid, calm. The man knew how to play a boardroom. He hadn't climbed to the top of a financial empire by showing his cards.

"*Fair?* You want to talk *fair?*" She couldn't stop her voice from rising, no matter how much she wanted to show indifference. For the second time in her life, she felt absolutely helpless to stop a wave of sheer anguish from crashing over her. She'd felt this way before…the first time she'd confronted Justus.

She'd been but nine years old, a feeble babe under the paw of a wolf. Yet that vulnerability had forged steel in her. She'd never forgotten.

She put aside that memory and concentrated on simply breathing. Why had she done this? Why had she sought out the only man who made her feel so worthless? "You cannot talk to me of fairness. You know what you did."

His face showed the first crack. He wasn't indifferent to her words. She saw this. Rick did, too.

"I'm not sure this conversation involves me. I just wanted to check on you, Kate. Make sure you were okay." His words were comforting. Someone cared, even if he wasn't supposed to.

"I—"

"I don't see why you can't stay, Enrique. I've never kept secrets from you." Justus's words interrupted her.

Rick stopped in his progress toward the door. His mouth turned down slightly. "I'd say that's not necessarily true."

For a moment silence hung over them, a wet blanket, cold, clingy, stifling.

"What do you mean by 'spending time' with me?" Her words brought both men's gazes to her.

Justus swung his one good hand toward the tray upon his wheelchair. He moved a piece of paper toward her. "Take this."

She didn't want to get that close to him again, but she made herself move forward and take the paper. It was a check.

A check for fifty thousand dollars.

"It's postdated two weeks from today. It's yours free and clear as long as you stay for that duration and allow me the chance to change your mind about me."

Kate looked at all those zeroes and swallowed.

This little piece of paper was her salvation.

But was it worth two weeks in Oak Stand? Two weeks with the man she swore she'd hate forever and a year? "Change my mind?"

"About having a relationship with me. Trying to repair the fences that have been broken. I am, after all, your father."

"That's not what you implied earlier," Rick pointed out. "You said she had no proof."

Justus gave a heavy sigh. "I employ you as my assistant for good reason. Nothing slips by you, boy."

"So, you're his assistant? I thought you were the director of that center." She pressed her hand against the throb in her head, trying like mad to figure out why Justus kept a Hispanic tough guy for a right-hand man while also planning on how to wrangle out of the old man's demands.

"I *was* his assistant. One with a vast job description."

Justus snorted, but it was humorless. She couldn't get a handle on their relationship. There were undercurrents, but then again, the room pulsed with undercurrents. She was a hapless traveler clinging to a tree branch in the middle of a raging river.

"I can't stay here," she said. "I have responsibilities in Vegas." She'd lose customers if she canceled any more appointments. Jeremy had already whined about having to be away from Victor so much. Of course, after she reminded him she was saving his ass, too, he shut up. But she couldn't expect him to handle the salon and her customers while she sat at the feet of her long-lost dad so the man could tell her bedtime stories and buy her pretty ribbons for her hair.

Justus was delusional if he thought he'd win any smidgeon of respect or crumb of affection.

"It can be arranged," Justus said, with the assurance of a man who could make almost anything happen. Money and power cleared his path.

She shook her head. "No. You can keep the check. I only want the amount I originally asked for."

The man who sired her looked her straight in the eye. His eyes were a mirror image of her own, and it discomfited her. "No. You can have the amount on that check, but you have to give me the two weeks. That's the offer."

"I can get an attorney. We can do a paternity test, and then I can sue you for what you owe me. Owe my grandmother for raising me all those years." She lifted her chin, glared at him.

"Sure, you can hire an attorney. But there is the matter of the letter you sent." Her father pulled a paper from his shirt pocket and waved it. "I'm not sure a judge would look favorably on blackmail. Besides, a lawsuit will take years and there *is* always the chance I'm not your father. Presently, I'm not asking for proof. You can have the money and you wouldn't even have to be my real daughter. The odds are in your favor."

Kate felt the trap slam shut. He was right. She didn't have the time or money for a lawsuit. She needed the money now.

And Justus knew it.

She took her hands from her hips and crossed her arms across her chest. If she did what Justus wanted her to do, she'd be letting go of that tenuous branch and immersing herself in that raging river. She could only hope that there was dry ground ahead. And that she wouldn't get sucked beneath the surface and end up broken on the rocks below.

It was only two weeks of her life. She could handle anything for two weeks even if it would be a bitch to arrange…and endure.

She let go. "Fine."

Rick moved behind her. She could smell his cologne, feel his warmth. She wanted to lean against him. Or turn and bury her head in his chest. Which was dog-ass stupid. She didn't need anyone to take care of her. Certainly not a man she'd only known for seventy-two hours.

"Excellent," Justus said, moving his chair from the window toward the desk anchoring the room. "I'll have Rosa prepare a room for you."

"I can't stay here," Kate said, stepping back. Her back bumped Rick's chest. His hands slid to her elbows, bracing her.

"How will I get to know you if you aren't at Cottonwood?"

Kate panicked for a moment. He wanted her here alone in this house with him and his cold wife? The thought made her stomach twist into ropes. "If I stay here, you have to give me something to do. I can't just ramble around this house. I need a job. Cover. People talk about me enough in Oak Stand."

"A job?" Justus repeated. "I don't have a job for you."

"The center," Rick said. "We need to hire an administrative assistant to handle things like therapist appointments and grant paperwork. It's really piling up."

Justus frowned, but she felt a niggling sense of satisfaction. Rick had helped her. And there was a flash of something else. Something to do with spending her days with the sexy man. A sort of anticipation. "Good. I'll help at the center and then spend some, ah, time with you in the evenings. That's my deal. Take it or leave it."

Justus's eyes moved between the two of them. Several seconds passed before he muttered, "I suppose that will be acceptable."

Kate felt a string snap inside of her as relief flooded her body. She wasn't absolutely alone in this.

"Okay, I'll stay here with you." She swallowed the acid that had welled in the back of her throat. She could do this. Do it for her future. For the salon's future. "But first, I have to pick up my things. And I'll need to buy more clothes and toiletries. I only planned to stay a few days."

"Give her a credit card, Enrique," Justus said, without a single blink.

She lifted her chin. "I can pay for my own things." She glanced at Rick. "Although a ride into town would be nice."

"I'll be glad to take you into Longview after I stop at Phoenix. I've got a few things to do there."

"Well, then. I'll see myself out." She slipped from the room as quickly as she could manage. Though she still felt partially victorious for setting her own terms of surrender, she could feel a migraine headache start-ing. Little zigzaggy things were already shadowing her vision. When she got to the hallway, she pressed her-self against the polished wainscoting and took several cleansing breaths.

Had she waved the white flag? Or was the battle only beginning? She wasn't sure, but she was certain of two things. Something big loomed ahead of her, and her toes were sweating in her designer half boots.

"Do you think this is wise?" Rick asked as Justus maneuvered his wheelchair behind the colossal antique desk. "What about Vera?"

He shrugged, although it was a rather distorted shrug. "What about her? This doesn't concern her."

"The hell it doesn't." Rick walked to the window. Vera stood among the dead plantings, staring at the marble angel in the center of the circular garden. He could see her lips moving in silent prayer. "She's still hurting over Ryan. And bringing Kate—"

"Why do you care?" Justus's words were tinged with anger. "Vera's not your concern. She's mine. It's been three years. It's time she stopped wandering around this ranch like some shadow of a woman. She's like a Dick-ens character. All she needs is a moldering bridal gown and an old wedding cake. It's absurd."

Rick didn't know Dickens. He'd dropped out of school before the tenth grade, but he knew what Justus meant. Vera had spent long enough mourning, but Rick couldn't abandon the woman who'd first accepted him as some-thing other than a thug. Besides he owed it to Ryan to look out for Vera.

"You're throwing Kate in her face."

"The hell I am." Justus used his good hand to slam a thick book of Irish folklore upon the desk. It caused the picture of a smiling Ryan clad in his graduation gown to fall forward. "I didn't go looking for Kate. She found me. For reprehensible purposes, true, but I've prayed for months for God to send me something, some answer, some way to bring us all back among the living. I think He sent me Kate."

Rick grew still. He'd never thought about the feisty Kate being someone destined to come to Cottonwood. And he certainly hadn't seen her as someone who could breathe life into a house that had folded into itself with grief. But maybe Justus was right.

Maybe Kate had a bigger purpose.

"Okay, I get what you're saying, but you have to promise to tread lightly." He walked toward the door.

"I don't have to promise you a thing," Justus said, staring at the fallen picture frame.

Rick paused with his hand on the knob. "That may be, but this time, I'm not going to allow you to pull all the strings. There are too many people with a stake in this for you to bulldoze over as if they were small saplings."

Justus's laugh was sharp. Biting. "Do you honestly think I'd let you scare me away from a girl who is my own flesh and blood?"

Rick knew Kate was Justus's daughter, but he used the old man's argument against him. "You said you didn't know if she were really your daughter."

"The girl's mine. I've known it for thirty years."

Rick flinched. The admission made his stomach turn. "Then why the hell didn't you acknowledge her?"

Justus's eyes met his. They were as frigid as an Alaskan lake. The way they'd been before Ryan died, before the stroke. The old Justus lurked inside the shell some-where. "I've never had cause to."

"But now you do?"

"I do."

Anger welled in Rick. This man did what he did for his own selfish purposes. He did not have Kate's best in-terests in mind. But Rick would look out for her. Justus Mitchell mowed over many people, but Enrique Mendez was no damned sapling.

He masked his annoyance, nodded and left the room. There was nothing more to say.

He found Kate standing outside the office door, staring at an original Remington bronze of a Cherokee warrior. The piece was poised between two of the artist's original sketches. Justus loved the art of the Old West.

"Is that a real Remington?" Kate asked.

"I think so."

"My friend Billie would love to see it. She's a glass artist, but has a thing for cowboys and Indians." Kate's words sounded detached. She was trying to distance her-self from her emotions. He understood.

"You ready to go?"

"Yeah. I couldn't remember how to get around this mausoleum, so I waited on you." Finally, her eyes met his. They were no longer distant. They were determined. "So let's go. I got myself into this, and there's only one direction I can head now."

Rick moved down the hallway toward the staircase, but then stopped. "You don't have to agree to his terms, Kate. I can get you a ticket back to Vegas. You can go home and forget about everything. It might be for the best."

He didn't want her to go, and that surprised him. But in her interest, she should head for Vegas.

She stopped in the middle of the hall. "You think he'll let me do that? I poked the hornets' nest, Rick. He's not going to let me slink away with my tail tucked. Plus, I don't work that way. He wants me around? Fine. I'll be around. But he can't control me. No one can. I play by my own rules, so that man back there may regret the hell out of wanting me here."

He couldn't help it. He smiled.

"What?" she asked.

He loved her eyes, which was weird, because they looked so much like Ryan's and Justus's. But they were different. He could get lost in hers. Sometimes he hated the romance in his soul. Lost in a woman's eyes? What a bunch of crap. "Nothing. I just…nothing."

She cocked her head, making her look like an inquisitive little mouse. But she didn't push it. She spread her small hands apart, palms up. "Okay, then. Let's go."

He led her down the stairs and out of the house, pausing only to shout a farewell to his grandmother, who sat in front of the TV, immersed in a Mexican soap opera. Vera was nowhere in sight. He was glad. Justus needed to tell his wife about Kate coming to stay.

He stepped out into the blustery day, swamped with the need for separation from the Mitchells. He needed to cut the string that bound him to Justus. He watched Kate cross the drive and knew she'd taken hold of one of those invisible threads and pulled him in even closer.

And he'd gone willingly.

Chapter Seven

Rick didn't say anything as they drove away. Kate was relieved because her emotions were tied into one giant knot that had parked itself in her stomach. It felt like a bowling ball. But she didn't want to acknowledge it. She wanted to pretend the scene in Justus's office meant nothing to her.

The window was open and the cool air tousled her short hair and caused goose bumps to rise on her arms. She pulled the three-quarter sleeves of her sweaterdress lower.

"Roll up the window," Rick said as he turned onto the county highway that would take them toward Phoenix and eventually Longview.

"No, it feels good. Kinda cleansing." She stared at the barren landscape, watching cows munching on clumps of clover that dotted the pastures. "Thanks for coming back."

Such simple words of gratitude were hard for her. She didn't like accepting the kindness of others, especially virtual strangers. But he deserved that much. He'd stood beside her as she faced her father for the first time in years, and he hadn't been obliged to do so. In fact, he shouldn't have. He'd picked the wrong side, considering his history with her father. But having him there had softened the trap that had closed around her.

Justus. She didn't miss the irony in his given name. He was a man who meted his own brand of justice. Was being trapped with him for two weeks fair? Was this nature's joke on her for waking the monster of her past?

She sighed. Rick glanced at her before focusing on the highway. He left her alone with her thoughts.

Facing her father had been more difficult than she'd thought it would be. Seeing the man crippled, a shell of his former self, had been tough, had made her feel quite small for the act she was perpetuating against him. Like she was a bad person.

Then he'd turned the tables. Made her boiling mad. And she hadn't felt so very sorry for him after all. She'd felt absolutely warranted in demanding the money from him.

She pinched the bridge of her nose with her fingers. The roller coaster of emotions she'd just climbed from had sucked the wind from her sails and the shadow of the migraine lingered.

Rick chuckled. "You know, I didn't come back for you. I came back to protect the old man. You're fierce."

Kate allowed a smile to curve her lips. "I think he proved he didn't need you after all. He's got tricks in that bag of his that don't disappear with a stroke or some spiritual transformation. You can't change a leopard's spots."

"Yeah, but you can shoot the leopard and make a coat of him."

Kate summoned a laugh. "I've always wanted a leopard coat. It would look fabulous with my new Manolos."

"What are Manolos?"

And that made Kate laugh for real. "Shoes. But I'm kidding. I don't wear animal skins."

"Sure you do. You wear leather, don't you?"

Kate rolled her eyes. "I guess I should have said I don't wear furs harvested for the purpose of making women look haughty."

Rick looked over at her. "I don't wear furs, either."

"No full-length pimp-daddy coats in your closet?"

"Not anymore." His words sounded heavy, not teasingly light. Something dark tinged his words.

Change of subject needed. "So tell me about Phoenix. How did you come up with the idea for the place?"

The slight tension emanating from Rick vanished. "It's something I'd been thinking about for a long time. Actually, the idea came from Ryan."

"Ryan Mitchell?"

A new emotion touched Rick's face. Kate thought it was tenderness. "Yeah, he…well, we were friends of a sort. I started working for Justus eight years ago, when Ryan was a freshman in high school. When I first came to Cottonwood, I worked as a gardener. Justus gave me a job as a favor to my grandmother."

"Because of your past?" It seemed a touchy subject, but she asked it anyway.

"Si," he said, offering a smile, a mixed bag this time. Acceptance, regret, shame, pride—all rolled into one. "I think you've already guessed my past was something I'm not so proud of. I was in a gang, rolling with the

Norteños, doing all sorts of things that still weigh on me when I have time to think. Phoenix is my penance, my salvation."

His expression turned sheepish, as if the poetics of his words embarrassed him. "What I mean is that the center is my way to pay it forward. Give others the chance I was given. Oddly enough, your father gave me the ability to do that. The center is his tribute to Ryan."

It explained a lot about why Rick had worked for Justus. Still, she sensed he had hidden issues with the man. It wasn't apparent at first, but she suspected there was a mire of complicated feelings between the two. "So Justus pulled you out of a gang?"

"Not exactly pulled me out. I didn't have much of a choice." He propped his elbow on the open window and leaned back into his seat, settling into his story. "I was in my early twenties and got picked up for possession of stolen property. I made bail and waited on my guys to pick me up. Instead, Rosa waited outside. With Justus. She'd actually shooed the gang members off the steps of the city jail."

Kate smiled at the thought of the diminutive Mexican grandmother taking a bunch of gang members to task.

"So I stepped out into the sunshine and she hit me with that look. I couldn't duplicate it if I tried. It was so disappointed and angry looking. When I walked up to her, she said, 'You've got one chance, *cholo*.' I didn't want to, but I climbed into Justus's truck."

His face seemed so worn. He'd seen and done things that had etched a mark on him.

"That was a pretty brave thing, walking away like that. I mean, it's hard getting out of a gang. Isn't it something like once in, always in?" Kate lightly touched his arm before withdrawing and tucking her hand into her lap. She had no right to touch him, even if her fingers itched to stroke the muscles beneath the cloth of his jacket. She'd seen the ink, peeking out of his T-shirt collar. Did it stretch across his chest? She wanted to know what lurked beneath.

"Yeah, it's hard when you go it alone. But I wasn't alone. Rosa had convinced Justus to give me a way out. He pulled some strings and got me probation for the third time. Still don't know how he managed it, but if he hadn't, I'd be lost. I came to Cottonwood, and it was far enough away to give me a chance."

He paused for a moment, his mind obviously in the past. "So that's what Phoenix is about. It's about giving guys who want out of the life a way to get out. They come here, away from the streets, away from the temptation and the danger. That's going to make the difference."

"So by coming here, the gang can't get to them?"

"Well, sort of. Many gangs are ambivalent about centers like Phoenix. They don't like them, but some of the guys understand, like if they could give up the life, they would. I put the word out on the streets about the center at churches and community centers."

"In Dallas?"

He laughed. "Yeah. Oak Stand isn't exactly a hotbed of gang activity. Unless you count the Junior League. Those gals don't mess around."

"You're preaching to the choir," Kate mumbled.

"So, anyway, word is out there's a place you can go if you want out, want to get your GED or get a job. It's started some trouble. A few threatening messages, that kind of thing. But it's going to work."

"Hmm, so the gang leaders think Phoenix is going to steal their workers?"

Rick smiled. "Pretty much. They're a business like any other. There are leaders—shot callers—then there are the guys who carry out the mission. Basic business structure. But their business is drugs, fencing, even prostitution."

Rick turned the car onto a drive. Ahead she could see a massive structure built to look like a lodge. The building was made of stacked stone and cedar planks with a long, low porch covered with rockers along the front. Pulling up to Phoenix felt like arriving at an old home place.

"It's fabulous," she breathed. "I mean, seriously, warm and welcoming. Awesome."

Rick took her hand and squeezed it. "Exactly what I was going for."

The pride in his voice was so evident it made her heart swell. And his hand on hers took on new meaning, new intimacy, and she rubbed her lips together as if trying to remember his taste. He'd tasted good when she kissed him. She wanted to do it again.

He looked at her and she met his eyes. They were a mysterious brown, dark and weighty. His broad cheekbones stretched above a chiseled jaw. This man was all hard edges, masculine and clean lines. His skin looked like aged honey, like she could run her fingers over it and feel the power beneath.

She leaned toward him, unable to stop herself from inhaling his scent. His cologne was woodsy, musky and reminded her she hadn't had sex in a long time.

He watched her, his lids lowered slightly. She could sense the hitch in his breath, feel the electricity uncork between them.

But suddenly he stiffened.

And pulled away.

"Let me show you the center and see what you think. You'll be working here, after all."

Kate blinked and watched him climb from the car. She felt a twinge of displeasure, as if he'd taken a toy from her and put it out of reach. She muttered a curse to the empty interior and climbed out.

The center sat on a hill, crushed granite surrounding the side and back parking area. Her boots slid in the loose rock as she scrambled after him. When she turned the corner, she found Rick, arms akimbo, staring at the back porch. A mangy looking dog sat on the sissel door mat next to an empty food bowl.

"Get out of here," he shouted at the dog, waving his hands in a shooing motion.

"I'm guessing that's not your dog?" she said, kneeling and motioning for the dog to come to her. It truly was a scrawny thing, with matted brown fur and rheumy eyes. Just pitiful. The dog wouldn't come to her. It looked at Rick.

"No, it's not my dog. It keeps hanging around here. The last thing I need is a stray crapping all over the yard and barking at every leaf that blows by."

"Then why are you feeding it?"

Rick tried to look disgusted. "Because it's hungry."

The dog yawned and looked bored. He turned a lazy circle and lay down.

"Hate to tell you this, but if you feed it, it's your dog." Kate walked up the back steps and knelt, extending her hand for the dog to sniff. The mutt lifted his head and licked her fingers. "What's his name?"

Rick stared at her and the stray. "I don't know. Banjo?"

Kate laughed, scaring the dog. The mutt ran straight

to Rick and hid behind his splayed legs. "Yep, Banjo is your dog. An ugly dog at that."

Rick looked down at where the animal cowered at his knees. "I don't know. He's not that ugly. Maybe with a bath, he'd clean up okay."

Kate rose and looked around the area where she stood. Newly planted ornamental grasses flanked the back porch. A bird feeder sat at the back of the large bricked patio that extended off the porch. Adirondack chairs and matching benches scattered the patio and a fire pit sat in the center. Barren Texas countryside surrounded the building, presently desolate, but in the spring, it would be gorgeous.

Rick passed her, leaving the dog to sniff the bushes. He unlocked the center and stepped inside. She followed. The first thing she noticed was the smell. Fresh pine and cedar. The room was large and had a huge fireplace with a moose head over the mantel.

"Do they have moose in Texas?" Kate asked, as she took in the wagon wheel candelabras that hung by iron chains from the ceiling and the rustic leather sectionals. A cowhide rug centered the room. Whoever had come up with the vision for the rehabilitation center had done an excellent job. Kate felt as though she could wrap herself in a woolen throw, grab a hot chocolate and stare out at the countryside for hours.

"That's Winston. Grady Hart donated him. He killed him in Canada on a hunt with your father." Rick's words came from over her shoulder. He stood in the doorway of what was likely the kitchen. An enormous pine table sat in an area just past the large community room.

"It sounds weird for you to say *my father*. I don't really think of him like that," she commented as she moved around the room glancing at the framed photographs of Texas landmarks mounted on the wall.

"But he thinks of you as his."

"Well, I'm not one of his possessions."

Rick considered her. "No, you're not, are you."

Her exploration led her to one of the wide front windows. The Mustang sat forlorn in the drive. The dog had wandered around and now hiked his leg on the tires. She wouldn't tell Rick. Probably wouldn't sit well with him.

"Let me grab some things I have to take back to the office supply store. Might as well do the return while we're picking up things you need in Longview."

Kate nodded. "Don't worry about me. I'll poke around the center."

"Let me show you where everything is."

Kate could tell he enjoyed showing off the place, so she let him play tour guide, following him, past the moose head into a long hallway that stretched over fifty feet. Four rough pine doors sat on each side. Rick opened each, sticking his head inside for a quick survey. The rooms were each sparsely furnished with an iron bed, cheerful quilt and simple pine bureau beside a single window. The only other object inside was a small desk.

"These are the rooms for the clients. Our facility is different from other programs around the country. Some of those programs sit in the middle of the barrios and hoods. They provide therapy, job training, tattoo removals, things like that. There's a program in Los Angeles that even runs a restaurant. We want to give our clients the chance to remove themselves from the destructive environment before taking on the programs that will help them build new lives."

Kate watched him as he spoke. His face changed, took

on a purposeful look. "That sounds like a good thing. It's got to be hard to enroll in a neighborhood program only to go home each night knowing the people you roll with are outside your window. Like too much temptation."

Rick's hand stilled on the doorknob. He faced her. "How did you know?"

"Know what?"

He set his hands on her shoulders, pulling her closer to him. "Have you faced addiction in your past or something?"

Kate didn't know why he'd asked her that. Strange question. "No. I just know there's a reason someone joins a gang. It's not to steal, run drugs or bang chicks. It's for companionship. For purpose. And if you are lying in your bed thinking about how you've got to rip yourself away from something like that, it has to be like a dieter sitting in front of a piece of cheesecake. Really hard to shove away."

Kate had just closed her mouth when his covered it. Warm, soft and as delicious as melted marshmallows on hot chocolate, the kiss curled her toes in those boots.

Rick's hands slid up from her shoulders to cup her head. It felt as though he drank from her, which really turned her on. She allowed him, pushed herself against him, encouraged him.

Her hands fluttered against his chest before sliding lower. The man had a serious six-pack. Nice. She curled her arms around his back and jerked him toward her.

She felt his smile against her lips.

"Bruja."

"Hmm?" Kate murmured, unwilling to tear her mouth from his for even a moment.

He drew back, his brown eyes glinting with a mixture of humor and passion. "You've bewitched me."

She smiled. Then lifted onto her tiptoes and jerked his head back to hers. "I don't want to talk about it."

This time she covered his mouth with hers. He reacted by hauling her against him. He felt so good. Hard. All man. Kate allowed her hands to brush through his close-clipped hair as she opened her mouth to him.

"Well, ain't this the way I last saw you?"

Kate jumped, banging Rick in the nose, and looked over at the man lurking in the hallway.

"Bubba!" Kate shrieked, disentangling herself from Rick and throwing herself into the arms of the man laughing at her. The last time she'd seen Bubba Malone, he'd tripped over her and Brent Hamilton making out by the old dam out on Camp Lease Road. She'd been half-drunk on wine coolers and poor Bubba had been night fishing. He'd hit his head against a tree when he'd tripped and broken his best fishing pole.

"Didn't know you were in town, Katie. Do I need to lock down the liquor stores? Alert the Baptist church?"

She punched him on his beefy arm. "Whatever we need to do to protect folks around here."

Bubba laughed. It sounded like a donkey braying. "You're somethin' else, Katie. Ain't never seen anyone like you. Don't reckon I ever will, neither."

There was no way to describe Bubba other than Texas redneck. He stood about six foot four and wore the most god-awful clothing. Case in point, he was clad in a ratty long-sleeved T-shirt with a Carhartt vest. His jeans were splattered with red clay and his boots were untied with the laces frayed. His nose looked like a kid had shaped it out of modeling clay and stuck it to his face. But his bright blue eyes were friendly and his red beard reminiscent of Yukon Cornelius in the old children's holiday movies.

"Bubba." Rick nodded, drawing their attention to him. "Didn't know you were stopping by today."

Rick looked perturbed. Was he embarrassed to be caught kissing her in the center? She assumed he was. She got the sense he wanted to portray himself as absolutely professional. Making out with the town rebel in the middle of the day was not professional. It was impulsive.

"I saw your car in the drive. I got that generator Jack said he'd give you. Thought I'd drop it by. I knocked but I guess you was busy." Bubba delivered a sly smile, then wiggled his eyebrows.

Rick ignored it, though she could have sworn a bit of color appeared on his cheeks. It was hard to tell on that smooth, golden skin. The yummy warmth emanating from him had disappeared. The interruption had reminded him of who he was and of what he had at stake. "I appreciate your bringing it by. We can put it in the storage building. I'll give you a hand."

Bubba pulled Kate into another hug. "Good to see you, Katie. Don't stay gone so long."

Kate gave him a squeeze before wriggling from beneath his heavy arm. "It's Kate, Bubba. And I don't have much reason to come back to Oak Stand. It can't compare to Vegas."

"You'll always be Katie to me. And just go watch the sun set over them hills out there. Vegas ain't got nothing on us."

Bubba disappeared and Rick followed, leaving Kate alone in the hallway, feeling a little small for being so defensive about her name and where she now lived. Everyone in Oak Stand knew her as Katie Newman and the people in this neck of the woods were proud of the quaint beauty of the little town, even if it did make them backwoods and small-minded. Kate was glad she didn't live here. And for the record, sunsets were spectacular against the Vegas skyline.

Who needed fresh air when there was excitement to replace it?

Rick's head appeared at the entrance to the hall. "You coming, Kate?"

"You bet your sweet ass."

And it was a sweet ass.

Chapter Eight

Kate scanned the racks of clothes at the Longview Target. Usually she loved to shop, even at a chain store, but at present her head felt achy and her gut like an outboard motor running at full throttle. Life had slammed her upside her head.

And it was no one's fault but hers. She'd written that letter. And, God, she wished she hadn't.

"I'm going to the book section. Meet me at the coffee bar in thirty." Rick didn't bother waiting. He swerved around a woman cajoling a toddler in a cart and disappeared. She didn't blame him. The kid was wailing about wanting princess lip gloss and she had a set of lungs.

"Chicken," Kate murmured as she pulled a knit sundress from a rack. It was cute, but a season too early. She needed jeans and sweaters. Texas weather was notoriously fickle. Heck, it could toss out a seventy-degree day after one with light snow. But, for once in her life, she had to be sensible about her clothing. She headed to the clearance rack.

Just after she dumped two red-tag sweaters and a cardigan into her basket, her phone erupted in a Ke$ha tune. She pulled it from her bag. Jeremy.

"Hey, how's my favorite queen diva?"

"Fa-bu-lous!" Jeremy responded in a singsongy voice.

Kate smiled. He always made her feel better. "Great. How's the salon?"

"I hate to tell you, darling, but it's fantabulous."

"That's the name of the place, dummy," she said, squinting at a pair of skinny jeans. They weren't True Religion, but they weren't bad. "Seriously, how's it going?"

"Seriously, it's going well. Mandy brought a couple of new clients along and not one peep out of your peeps. It's, like, totally working, doll."

"Well, that's a relief because I'm not coming back for a couple of weeks."

"Hello!" Jeremy cried, doing his impression of a gay Robin Williams. "What's with?"

Kate sighed. "Dear old Dad wants some baby girl time."

"You're joking," her friend said. "You mean he won't give you the money unless you stay in Texas?"

"Bingo. You're a smart puppy."

"I'm also a good puppy, and if you scratch me where I like it, I'll roll over for you." His tone was light. Maybe Victor felt better today. She didn't want to ask, though. When she'd called him yesterday, Jeremy had been in tears.

"You wish, gay boy," Kate said, studying the packaged panties on an end cap. They were assorted colors with lit-

tle cherries on them. At least they weren't granny panties.
And five pairs for under ten dollars. Cool. She snatched
a package of bikini-style and tossed them in the basket.

"Don't worry, Kate the Great. I've got this covered.
You do your thing and get that money. I'll focus on bringing in the clients. We'll be okay."

She eyed a black lace garter belt. It had hot pink ribbons and a matching bra. She loved sexy undies as much
as she loved comfy sweats and flip-flops. She plucked
both from the display and held them aloft, eyeing them
critically. Not her typical luxurious lingerie, but still...

"Wanna try it on for me?" Rick's voice came from
over her shoulder.

Kate never blushed. Never. But she could feel heat
creeping into her cheeks.

"Who's that?" Jeremy asked in her ear. "He sounds
yummy."

She spun around. Rick stood, one arm extended above
her so it stretched his gray T-shirt over his abs. He was
close enough that she had to retreat from the heat he was
putting off. The sexual static that had erupted between
them earlier at the center buzzed again.

She cheekily rolled her eyes. "Jer, I gotta go. I'll call
you tonight."

She punched End, even though she could hear her
friend protesting.

Rick watched her with hawk eyes as she lowered the
sexy bra and garter. She wanted to play with him. Taste
him. Touch him. Indulge in him. She wanted him. That
much was certain. But things right now were way bi-
zarre and letting lust or whatever she felt with Rick swirl
around within the confusion seemed pretty stupid. She
had enough complication. Still, flirting with him made

her feel like her old self. Like the Kate who could handle everything with a snappy comeback and the toss of her head.

She shrugged one shoulder. "Sorry, they won't let you in the dressing room."

With that she turned, scooped up the clothes she'd chosen—including the lingerie—and sauntered into the dressing room. She knew she shouldn't tease, but she couldn't resist the power she had. So before she disappeared into the depths, she leaned back and gave him a flirtatious smile.

"Let me know if you need any help," he called.

Her response was a wink.

Rick watched Kate disappear into the dressing room. What the hell was he doing? He needed to get his ass back to the book section. Standing in the middle of a grouping of thongs watching the sexiest little number he'd seen in ages strutting around waggling her tight ass in front of him was not the best idea at this juncture.

But she was the first woman who'd seriously tempted him in a long time. At Phoenix, he hadn't been able to resist the temptation to taste her again. And the whole way to Longview, he'd kept daydreaming about her skin sliding against his, her mouth opening to him, her hips clasped in his hands as he sank into her.

She made him want to put aside his vow of no more casual relationships, no more treating women like furniture. He'd retired that life when he'd turned over a new leaf. But Kate…Kate made him doubt himself.

And that should send him running, because he didn't need any more obstacles in his life. The center was opening in a matter of days. He had a lot to do. A list a mile long. And Kate Newman wasn't on the list.

But he felt powerless to stop himself.

He stood in the women's intimates section for several more minutes contemplating how wrong it was for him to want Kate before he noticed a few ladies giving him odd looks. Realizing he looked like a perv, he moved to where socks and scarves hung among purses.

Kate appeared at his elbow. "Okay, I gotta grab some toiletries and I'll be ready."

He started toward the other half of the store just as the kid crying over the lip gloss escaped from the shopping cart. He watched as the child tore away from her mother, shrieking about it "not being fair." He wanted to tell the little girl to get used to it, but that really wasn't his job. He knew nothing about wearing fluffy skirts and rubber boots. Little girls were alien.

Just like Kate was.

He watched the girl run toward him, her boots slapping the newly polished aisle. The mother, holding a pacifier between her teeth, shot a look at the shopping cart where a baby carrier sat before darting after her daughter. The little girl loped past Kate, collided with his knees and wrapped her arms about his legs.

Rick looked at Kate in alarm. The little girl, who wore pigtails, turned her face up to him and in a most desperate voice said, "Will you please buy me princess lip gloss?"

Kate started laughing as the harried mother peeled her daughter from Rick's legs.

"Audrey! Tell the man you're sorry," the woman said, looking back at the cart she'd left a few yards away. "Now."

The girl poked out a lip. "I just wanted the princess—"

"Now," the mother said more firmly.

The girl's shoulders slumped. He figured she knew when she'd been beat. "Sorry."

He patted her on the head. It felt awkward. "That's okay."

"Wow," Kate said, watching the mother march the child back to the cart. "You have girls throwing themselves at you."

"Yeah, but not really the kind I need."

Kate's eyes twinkled. "Oh, I don't know. Give her fifteen years. She's pretty cute."

"Look, I'll loan you some toothpaste," he said, eyeing another mother approaching from the opposite direction. Her cart held two squabbling kids. "I think I'm ready to get out of here."

"But you were good with Mae," she said, cocking her head in a questioning manner.

"She's a baby. She can't talk," he said, pushing her cart toward the front of the store.

"Oh, you just don't like your women to talk. Okay. I'll remember that. Let me just pay for these and we'll go before any more children tackle you and take you down." She swung the clothes in front of him. He didn't fail to notice she'd bought panties with cherries on them. Damn. Why had he noticed? Now all he'd be thinking about were those hot-pink cherries…and what lay beneath them.

Hell.

Kate stared at the striped walls surrounding the antique iron bed. They felt like bars. Prison bars.

Then again, she was doing time. At Cottonwood.

The room was elegantly furnished with a beautiful quilted coverlet in soft blues and greens. The hardwood beneath her feet was softened by a plush Oriental rug that complemented the ivory-and-periwinkle-striped walls. A fireplace anchored the room, bathing the cherry furniture in a soft glow. Dusk fell outside windows framed by tasteful drapes.

Kate couldn't help but think she'd rather be anywhere than facing dinner with her sperm-donor father and his deflated wife.

She spun and checked her image in the mirror. She'd pulled one of the cardigans she'd bought at Target over a white Hugo Boss shirt, pairing it with pants that looked painted on and a pair of soft blue leg warmers. She shoved her feet into a pair of snakeskin flats she'd bought on sale at Nordstrom's and hooked some Gerard Yosca glass stone earrings in her ears. Thank goodness she always overpacked. She hadn't had to spend too much at Target after all.

She took one last glance before blowing a kiss at her reflection and leaving the confines of her room.

Cottonwood was an enormous house and it took her a few wrong turns before she found the dining room.

Justus and Vera were already there, seated at a huge table gleaming with crystal glasses and shiny china. Weird. She felt as though she'd fallen into the TV and appeared on the set of *Dallas*. The theme song played in her head as she pulled a chair from the exact center of the table and sat.

"Evening," Vera murmured, her hand quaking as she lifted a glass of wine to her lips.

"Good evening, Miss Ellie," Kate said, pulling a snowy napkin from her right and placing it in her lap.

Justus frowned, but Vera actually laughed.

"It does seem like *Dallas,* doesn't it? I thought so myself when I first visited. Couldn't get that song out of my head for a good week."

Kate didn't expect Vera to catch on to her reference. It made her feel sorta petty. Time to play the guest. "Thank you for waiting on me. It took longer than expected to get back from Longview. There was an accident on the interstate, so Rick had to take a few side roads."

The whole situation was awkward. No way around it. She looked to her right at Justus. He stared at his empty plate like a grumpy bullfrog. She looked to her left at Vera, who smiled a brilliant fake smile. Kate didn't miss that Vera's hands still trembled as she cradled the goblet of wine. And when Kate looked to the center, she found Ryan Mitchell staring at her.

It was an enormous portrait of the half brother she'd never known. He had to have been around eighteen. His smile held hope, his eyes humor. Boyish charm oozed from the palette of muted paint. Unlike the other paintings scattered through the halls of Cottonwood, this painting had no windswept Texas background. No cowboys or grit. No horses or cows. Just a boy framed against a blue background, smiling as if he knew the answers to life.

As she noted they shared the same cheeky smile, a strange feeling washed over her. It could have been regret, or portent, or déjà vu. She wasn't sure, but it was something.

Before she could ask about the portrait, Rosa bustled in with several platters.

"Here I am. I made special dinner for Ms. Kate. *Chile verde con puerco,* and to start, *caldo de res.* And flan for dessert, Mr. Mitchell."

Justus visibly brightened as Rosa sat a steaming bowl

of soup before him. "Well, now, it's been forever since you've gone to such trouble, Rosa. If I'd known all you needed was a guest, I would have brought someone sooner."

"Si," Rosa said. "We've had no one. When Mr. Ryan was here, we overflowed."

"I miss him so," Vera said, her eyes finding the monument to her son.

"No, no, Mrs. Vera. Ryan would say no," Rosa said, bustling toward Vera and setting down sweet corn cakes and fragrant corn tortillas. "You enjoy Miss Kate being here. Mr. Ryan brought her here."

Kate's hand hit her wineglass and knocked it over. Thankfully, she'd downed most of it. Still, burgundy spread like blood on the snowy cloth. "Sorry. I—"

"I get it, Miss Kate. You eat the corn cakes. They are made the way my grandmother made them. God rest her soul," Rosa said, crossing herself and pulling a towel from the pocket of her apron. She pressed the cloth to the spreading stain, soaking up the spill.

Kate glanced up at Vera. The woman's brow was furrowed and her expression perplexed. She wasn't going to let Rosa's comment slide. "Rosa, why would you say such a thing?"

The housekeeper looked up from her dabbing. Kate stiffened because she knew Rosa would say something about fate. Or God. Or some mystical Mexican superstition. Kate didn't make a habit of running from confrontation, but damned if she didn't want to flee the table.

"I saw your note to God. You asked him to heal you. To send you an angel like Mr. Ryan to make the hurt stop."

Vera flinched and Kate started a litany deep inside of

"no, please, no," but Rosa charged ahead. "I found the paper when I was putting the hose back into the carriage house. Sitting right by the angel. And the next day, Miss Kate gets here. See, he answered your prayer."

Kate swallowed. Hard. Then she looked at Justus to see if he might put a stop to Rosa's words, but he calmly slurped the soup before him, using his good hand. A trickle of the broth dripped from his chin. The bastard wasn't going to say a thing.

"You think Ryan sent her?" Vera's words were harsh. The woman pointed a slender finger at her. "Her? An angel?"

Rosa paused. Kate could feel the housekeeper's alarm. *"Si."*

Vera threw her napkin on the table. "This whole dinner is preposterous. Why don't you say something, Justus?"

He looked up. His blue eyes iced over. "Rosa is free to believe what she wishes."

Vera's mouth twisted. "You sit me at a table with your bastard and allow a crazy Mexican woman to spew garbage and say nothing. You have no respect for me. You don't care about me."

Vera started to rise.

"Sit down," Kate said.

The older woman paused. "What did you say to me?"

"Sit down." Kate pushed her chair back. "This is your table. I don't belong at it. I don't want to be here. The only thing that brought me here was justice. And I mean the word, not the man."

Rosa drew back. "But you are a guest."

"No, as Vera so accurately pointed out, I'm the bastard child. The one who has no place at this table. Let's stop pretending anything different."

"The hell you don't," Justus roared. He launched his spoon at the soup bowl. It clattered against the china and fell onto the tablecloth. "You are staying right there."

He used his good arm to point to the chair Kate had pushed forward.

"And you—" he pointed to Vera "—are going to be polite to my daughter."

Vera blanched but hesitated. "I don't march to your drum, Justus Mitchell. You may control everyone else. But not me."

He leveled her with his eyes. Kate watched as the woman visibly weakened under the duress of his stare. "Sit. Please."

Vera sank onto the upholstered chair.

Kate held on to the back of the chair. All she wanted to do was get out of here. She wondered if Rick would come get her. She didn't know where he was. Didn't have a number for him. Then she recognized where her thoughts were taking her. Did she really want a knight in red Mustang to swoop in and save her?

Hell, no.

She could handle it herself.

Vera spoke first. "Kate, please. I've forgotten my manners. Rosa has prepared a special meal. Surely we can put our feelings aside to enjoy something so generously wrought?"

Kate nodded. What else could she do? She hadn't eaten all day and had no way of leaving Cottonwood, save phoning Nellie. All she had to do was get through dinner. Besides, she didn't want to hurt Rosa's feelings.

Rick's grandmother pretended that Vera hadn't insulted her and handed Kate the napkin that had fallen to the floor and lifted her wineglass to refill it.

"No, thank you, Rosa." Kate rose. But not to leave. Instead she headed for the elegant sideboard holding assorted crystal decanters. She reached for a tumbler and a bottle of Scotch. She'd get through dinner with the help of Islay malt.

The first sip burned a path to her stomach. She nodded and returned to her seat. With a glint of approval in his eye, Justus lifted his own tumbler in her direction.

The approval made her wish she'd stuck with the cabernet.

Vera ignored him and placed her discarded napkin in her lap. She picked up the plate of corn cakes and passed them to Kate. "I'd love to hear about your salon. What is the name?"

Kate blinked. So they were going to pretend nothing had been said. Pretend she'd not just been called a bastard. She looked at Rosa as she lifted the stained towel from the table. The housekeeper shrugged. "Oh, um, it's called Fantabulous."

Vera passed her the container of tortillas. "Well, that's an unusual name. How did you come up with it?"

Kate took a tortilla and slathered it with verde sauce. "My partner came up with it. We didn't want a salon that played 'loons at daybreak.' We made it high energy. More Red Bull than green tea, if you know what I mean."

Even as Kate made polite conversation, she could feel the tension in the air. It was so thick that if an imaginary finger poked it, they'd all tumble to the side from the power of the explosion. But everyone ignored it. It was the strangest meal she'd ever had. And as she spooned the last bite of flan into her mouth, she looked at the portrait of her half brother.

If she'd been the slightest bit open to paranormal happenings, she would have sworn the boy winked at her.

But Kate didn't believe in divine intervention.

And she knew Ryan hadn't brought her to Cottonwood.

Money had. And that was something she could believe in.

Chapter Nine

Kate arrived at Phoenix in a truck Justus had loaned her. Their conversation had been stilted at best, but her father had called his caretaker to bring the truck around. It was a huge Ford F-250 and ran like a tank. She'd had to slide the seat all the way forward and sit on a phone book, but she'd made it without wiping out any roadside bushes or boundary fences.

The first thing she saw as she drove up the lane was a huge lady climbing from a small car parked in front of the center. The woman's skirt rode up higher on one hip than the other and she visibly huffed as she balanced several boxes in her arms. She even carried a stapler under her chin.

Kate jumped from the truck, tucking the keys into the front pocket of her sweater. "Here. Let me help you with that."

"Oh, thank you, sugar." Puff. Puff. "I still gotta get that bag. Would you?"

Kate reached past the woman and scooped up a plastic bag full of office supplies. "I'm Kate, by the way."

"Trudy Cox," the woman huffed as she climbed the stairs. "I'm the GED instructor."

"Cool," she said as she followed the woman onto the wide porch and through the open front door. Again, the smell of cedar and pine tickled Kate's nose. It was a fresh scent, like a new car. She took in several deep breaths.

"Come on in here, sweet," Trudy said as she turned to the right and disappeared into the hallway. Kate followed her, entered a brand-new classroom that she hadn't seen the day before.

The room had pine walls covered with maps and grammar posters. A large whiteboard was mounted on one wall and the desktops shone like patent leather shoes on Easter Sunday. A potted plant draped itself over the massive desk, where Trudy dumped the boxes she carried. "Whew. Those about killed me."

Kate set the plastic bag on one of the desk chairs. "Glad I only volunteered to bring the bag in. I haven't worked out in over a week. I can already feel the burn."

Trudy snorted as she began opening the boxes. "Girl, I could sit on you and nobody would find you for a week."

Kate laughed. "Nobody would come looking."

Trudy stopped and peered over her bifocals. Her black eyes pierced Kate. Maybe the woman had worked as an interrogator for the FBI or CIA. She looked as though she could smell bullshit from three counties over. "Huh. I haven't known you but a minute, yet somehow I didn't take you for a gal who'd feel sorry for herself."

The woman smiled in order to soften her words. All

Kate could think was Trudy hadn't had dinner with Vera last night. Perhaps sitting at that table with a woman with an identity crisis and a biological father who annoyingly slurped his soup had given her license to throw herself a pity party, complete with streamers and a bad attitude.

"I'm over myself. Thanks for the reminder," she said, lifting the bag from the chair. "I'm assisting Rick for the next couple of weeks. Anything I can do to help you while we're waiting on sleeping beauty?"

"Oh, he ain't sleeping, that's for sure. Probably out running or picking up this and that. He's always moving, that man," Trudy said, lifting several books from the box, squinting at the spines and setting them in two separate stacks. "But I guess I won't turn down any help. Would you mind alphabetizing these books on that bookshelf under the window?"

Kate took the first stack and headed to the bookshelf as Rick stepped inside the room. Uncanny how she felt him before he spoke.

"Morning, ladies." His words were like slipping on a favorite robe. Kate felt herself relax. This was even stranger than feeling him before seeing him. She never felt easy with a man. She felt angry, turned-on, interested, but never like she fit with him.

"You been out running in only that little bit of clothing? Are you crazy, boy? It's cold out."

Kate turned to look. Rick's nicely toned arms braced the door. He was wearing a sleeveless light blue workout shirt and dark blue running shorts. She could see some of his ink curving up his neck and scrolling down his arms. She wanted to know what his tats looked like. Wanted to trace them with her finger across his golden sweaty skin.

The man made perspiration look sexy hot. Scratch that comfortable feeling. Replace with turned-on.

"Not that cold. You know I can't function without a run and a cup of coffee." His eyes swung from Trudy to Kate. "You're here early."

Kate tried to stop mentally undressing the man, but it was hard to stop imagining his flat stomach against hers, the way his thighs would nudge hers apart. She swallowed and diverted her thoughts from naughty to nice. "Thought I would make a good impression on my first day. And, like I wanted to stay any longer than I had to at the haunted mausoleum on the hill."

He tossed out a laugh. "So I'm guessing there were no family-fun pillow fights or board games at Cottonwood last night?"

Kate shot him a go-to-hell look. "Not exactly. More like *Jerry Springer.*"

Trudy kept pulling books from the boxes, but Kate could tell her ears were tuning in like a satellite dish.

So she looked at the woman pretending she wasn't soaking up the words between her and Rick. "Trudy, just so you know, I'm staying at Cottonwood with Justus and Vera Mitchell."

She didn't say she was staying because she was Justus's daughter. And no way her mouth even formed the word *blackmail*. She didn't know the GED instructor, but she knew Oak Stand. The town was talking about Katie Newman showing up and ensconcing herself in the mansion outside the city limits. No way in *H-E*-double hockey sticks the subject hadn't been discussed from the Dairy Barn to the hardware store. So she knew Trudy knew who she was. If she didn't, the woman had been in a hole for the past forty-eight hours.

"I'm Margo's cousin on her momma's side," Trudy said, as if that explained everything. And it did. That connection meant she knew all about Kate, Justus and every person in between.

"Heading to the shower. See you later."

Kate shifted her eyes from the overly wise ones of the GED instructor. She desperately tried not to imagine Rick standing naked beneath the stinging jets of the shower. She could just see him moving languidly as the water sheeted down his body, head tipped back as he lathered his hair.

"Kate?" Rick's voice interrupted.

"Hmm?"

"I asked if you'd had breakfast. Grandmother doesn't work on Wednesday mornings, so…"

"So?" Kate asked, rubbing her thumb along the creased spine of a thesaurus, still caught in the fantasy. "You asking me to—"

"Breakfast. That is if you want cinnamon rolls," he finished. She'd been hoping he'd say something more interesting, like scrubbing his back. Too bad. She'd rather have him than pastries. "Okay."

"I guess I just lost my helper, and don't think I didn't notice I didn't get an invitation to eat," Trudy said as she placed a stapler on her desk at a perfect ninety-degree angle from her tape dispenser.

Rick grinned. "I know Ernie got up and made you homemade biscuits this morning. I saw him at the gas station."

The older woman actually giggled. "You right, sugar. I got that man trained."

Kate rose, brushed off the new jeans she'd donned that morning and gave Trudy a salute. "Don't worry, I eat fast.

I'll be back to help you get set up. That is, if Rick doesn't need me for anything else."

She didn't intend her words to sound seductive, but they did.

Trudy raised her eyebrows then grinned as she plopped into her straight-backed wooden chair and started opening drawers. Rick simply vanished from the doorway.

She followed him down the hall and out the back door. The wind had her snuggling into the fleece pullover she'd gotten on clearance for under twenty bucks. Rick should have been freezing, but he ignored the cold and jogged down the steps, hooking to the right toward a small cedar-and-stone bungalow that sat below the hill line.

"I never noticed this cottage yesterday," she called as she followed him. The house was a smaller version of the main building.

"Home sweet home," he called back over his shoulder. "Sorry I'm not waiting, but my pulse dropped and I'm cold."

She hopped across the stepping stones, glad she'd bought some inexpensive sneakers. Her flats would have been soaked by the cold morning dew.

Rick unlocked the door and ushered her inside.

A blast of warm air hit her, along with the smell of cinnamon.

"Holy cow," she breathed. His cottage was awesome. Modern mixed with Mission. Glass tabletops, streamlined aged wood and chrome lamps. It was Harley-Davidson meets *This Old House*.

Rick shrugged. "I like it."

"Did you do this yourself? I mean, you're not gay, are you?"

He shot her a look. "Are you serious?"

"Do you think I'm serious?"

He gave her a big, bad wolf smile. "I think you want me to show you."

She felt heat flood her body. It had nothing to do with the air blowing from the vents above her and everything to do with the Hispanic hunk who stood arm's length away. "I think you're a mind reader."

Kate didn't wait on him. She moved closer, allowing her fingers to brush the Dri-FIT fabric of his shirt, to feel the power of the man beneath the clothes. She wanted to feel his bare flesh even if her stomach was gurgling over the prospect of cinnamon rolls.

But Rick didn't give her the opportunity. His mood shifted, and he caught her hands and gave them a shake. "Go pour yourself a cup of coffee while I grab a quick shower. Cinnamon rolls are in the warmer."

He gave each of her cold hands a brush of his lips before disappearing into the dark hallway behind her.

Well, hell. So much for scrubbing his back.

Or maybe…

But Kate nixed the idea. She wanted Rick, and any other time she'd do something about it, but she could see something held him back, so she resigned herself to eating.

The kitchen was galley-style, tucked beside a small breakfast nook. With light pine cabinets, black granite counters and stainless steel, upscale appliances, it was a masculine kitchen. But it was also well used. Rick liked to cook, if the complicated tools in the sink and the fluffy rolls were any indication.

She didn't drink coffee, so she opened the fridge to look for a soda. No soda. Lots of fruit, soy milk and organic eggs. The man was a health freak. She shivered and grabbed a carton of organic orange juice with extra pulp.

By the time she'd consumed almost two cinnamon rolls and a glass of orange juice, Rick appeared smelling clean and filling up the small kitchen.

"These cinnamon rolls are, like, really good," she managed to say around the last bite.

"Thanks. Rosa taught me."

He reached past her to open the fridge. She didn't bother moving. Better chance of him rubbing up against her. She felt primed for him. What better way to forget the knots in her life than a hot session of sex with a fine specimen of manhood? For an hour—or if she were lucky, two—she could forget and simply feel.

He sidestepped her and grabbed a carton of soy milk.

"They say that stuff is full of estrogen. Sure you really want to drink that?"

He poured a glass and took a big gulp before smiling at her. "I'm not afraid to get in touch with my feminine side."

"I'll let you get in touch with my feminine side if you want to," Kate said, sliding against him like a cat.

He grabbed her arm. "Hey, about that. You know I find you hot—"

She froze. "I can hear a *but* in that sentence."

He set the glass on the counter. "Thing is, Kate, I feel not myself around you, and you make me want to toss out the promise I made to myself."

"Don't tell me you've made some sort of vow of chastity or something. Because that's so wasteful. And so passé."

His eyes shuttered. "It's not a vow of chastity. It's a promise to not engage in casual sex."

Kate cocked her head. She'd never heard of a guy actually wanting a relationship before hitting the sheets. Okay, she was sure there were guys like that. Sensitive guys. Guys who spent their Friday nights watching noir films and sipping espresso. Or guys who spent their weekends at self-help retreats. "Why?"

He gave a humorless bark of laughter. "Do you know how many women I slept with when I was rolling with my gang? I can't even count. When I wanted one, I took her. Didn't matter her name. Or her feelings. Or how wasted she was. I used her."

Kate swallowed. The juice felt sour on her stomach. "Oh."

"I'm not that man anymore. When I have sex, it will be with someone I care about. Someone I'm in a relationship with. Someone I have a future with. No more flings."

His words jabbed at her heart. For some reason, it hurt. So she crossed her arms over her chest as if that would protect her. She wanted to say something funny, saucy, but couldn't think for the life of her how to respond. He didn't want to have sex with her and he didn't care about her. Which one was worse?

He swallowed. "I shouldn't have invited you down here. It was a mixed signal. Things are hot between us. We don't need to stoke any embers."

Kate wrinkled her nose. "What? You think I have no self-control? You think I jump every guy I see and beg him to do me?"

"No. That's not what I—"

"'Cause I can resist you, buddy. I can." She moved away from him, toward the door.

He didn't say anything further. Just tore a roll from the pan and took a bite.

She cocked an eyebrow at him. "I'm surprised you eat that. From the looks of your fridge, I'd expect you to be eating tuna fish or coddled egg whites."

He smiled. It made him look as yummy as the sweet he crammed in his mouth, and it made Kate's stomach twist with regret. "Yeah, but some things are worth it, you know?"

She studied him framed against the sophisticated backdrop of the kitchen. He'd pulled on worn jeans and a tight long-sleeved Henley shirt. His chest was like a fullback's, his legs those of a runner. He was golden, dark and decadent. What a waste.

"Yeah, I know."

He smiled.

"Just so you know," she said, crossing her arms again, "I don't believe in love. And if I did, two weeks is not enough time to fall in love with you."

He choked on his soy milk. "Who said anything about love?"

"No one," she said, turning into the living room. "See you at the center. Thanks for breakfast."

She didn't wait for a response. She left. It was the only way she could uphold her promise not to jump his bones. Maybe cinnamon rolls made her horny. Or maybe it was simply Rick.

Kate stomped up the graded hill. She was a little pissed and she wasn't sure why. She thought it was because the man had hurt her feelings. Made her feel raunchy. Like trailer trash. Like the Katie Newman she could have been. Living hard and being easy. But she wasn't that person. She'd done better and she had standards. She didn't have to throw herself at a man to get laid. Usually, they came sniffing around her.

Morals and principles. Who needed them? Did anyone really pay attention to them in today's world? Please. Even the pious and righteous bent definitions to meet their needs. Kate believed in being honest. With herself and others. She wanted Rick. She liked the way he made her feel, even if it scared her a little. Okay, a lot. But she wasn't avoiding him or the feelings he stirred in her.

She was being true to herself.

She was being the Kate she'd chosen to be.

She had a full life. She had friends. She lived by her own rules and answered to no one. At least, she had until Justus had flipped the blackmail table on her.

"Katie Newman!" a voice shrieked from her left. "Holy heck! I haven't seen you since that Cowboy Mouth concert at Cooley's, where we danced on the pool tables."

Kate watched as the former head cheerleader for the Oak Stand Rebels nearly tripped on a large iron ore rock beside the path. Tamara Beach was as clumsy as ever. How she'd managed to nab the prime spot on the squad was a mystery. Could have been because her mother was the PE teacher and had counted the votes, but that was only Kate's guess. Tamara still had the naturally wavy blond locks that fell past her shoulders, but the boobs that sat high on her slight frame were absolutely store-bought.

"Hey, Tam." Kate hugged her then stepped back. "You look amazing. I like the rack."

Her former going-out buddy laughed. "Thanks, they're almost paid for. And you don't look too bad yourself. I'm digging the streaks in your hair, Katie."

"Kate."

"Oh, yeah, I forgot." She cocked her head like a terrier sniffing out a rat. "Oh, my gosh, you know what?"

Kate suffered a flash of dread. Tamara always had

something cooking. And whatever it was often got her into hot water. "What?"

"Crater Moon is playing at Cooley's tonight. You remember that drummer, right? He was so into you. You gotta come with me. Everybody will be there."

"Well, I—"

"You're staying for two weeks, right?" Tamara blushed, obviously realizing she'd admitted to knowing about Kate and the Mitchells. "What I mean is, I heard in town you were staying for a while. What's with that, anyway? You hate it here."

Kate felt Rick before she saw him. Again. He ascended the path to where she stood. "Umm…it's complicated. And kinda private."

Her friend averted her eyes and looked embarrassed. "Oh."

She hadn't really worked out what to say to people about why she was in Oak Stand. She thought that maybe she could get through the two weeks without having to venture out much. Not going to happen. She needed a cover story. Or maybe she would tell everyone to mind their own damned business.

"Well, what are you doing at Phoenix? Does it have to do with gang stuff or something?"

Kate shook her head. "No, I'm helping Rick with the center while I'm in town. Doing some…consulting."

"I thought someone said you owned a salon out in Vegas," Tamara said before catching Rick out of the corner of her eye. Kate prayed he wouldn't say anything that would call her bluff on the consulting thing.

He stopped beside her. She could feel his heat even in the cool breeze. "Hey, Tamara, did you bring the forms? I've got the planters ready to go."

"Silly man. All work and no play." She tapped him lightly on the arm and Kate could see her friend was into him. Of course she was—what warm-blooded single woman wouldn't be? "An awesome band is playing at Cooley's tonight and I'm trying to talk Katie, I mean Kate, into coming. You should come with us. It'll be cool."

He shook his head. "I got too much going on, but you girls go on ahead."

Tamara turned a full-wattage smile on him. "Oh, come on. This is your last chance. The guys arrive Thursday and you won't be able to get away. Dude, you never do anything but work."

Her pretty baby-blue eyes pleaded with Rick.

"Sorry, I can't," he said, sliding past them. "When you're done here we can look at those planters and see if they'll meet the green initiative. I want to keep that grant."

Tamara rolled her eyes as he turned his back to them and jogged up the path. "He's such a party pooper."

At that point, Kate had to wonder about Tamara's intentions toward Rick. Her former friend had always been open for fun with the right guy. She looked like she had her eye on Rick, and something about it made Kate feel a little sick. Tamara was a natural. Breezy manner, friendly smile and a string of broken hearts behind her, she partied, cajoled and danced her way through life. And had a lot of fun doing it. But he wasn't up for a casual relationship, was he?

Still, Tamara lived in Oak Stand. Kate didn't.

"So what's up with the grant and planters?" Kate asked, pulling the discussion away from Rick and going to Cooley's.

"Oh, I'm with the Farm Extension Bureau. I'm going to work with the clients at the center on nutrition and cultivation. We're doing outreach programs now, not just schools and stuff. We're actually going to help with a garden here as a sort of therapy. Rick was insistent on growing stuff."

"Oh," Kate said, trying to envision Tamara in overalls and work boots. Tam preferred less over more when it came to clothing. Case in point, she wore a thin long-sleeved T with a plunging neckline that hugged her generous curves.

"I always say, getting in touch with the earth is getting in touch with yourself." Tamara smiled as if she'd imparted the most sacred of insights, one that made Kate want to snort.

"Yeah," Kate said, stifling the need to make masturbation jokes. "I'm not sure about tonight."

Her taking off would likely make Justus hopping mad. Then again, the idea of a repeat of last night's dinner made her skin crawl. Besides, Rick had made her feel crappy about herself. As if wanting a man was a bad thing. She didn't have to sit around and moon over him like a lovesick calf. Nothing like hitting a bar to stroke her ego and take her mind off Rick, Justus and her flailing business.

"Come on, it'll be such a blast to hang with you. We used to have so much fun." Tamara's baby blues worked on Kate.

"Okay. Sure."

Tamara squealed and clapped her hands. "Yay."

"I don't have a car. Can you pick me up?"

Her friend nodded like one of those bobble-head dogs in the back of car windows. "I'll pick you up at 8:00."

Just enough time to have dinner with Justus and Vera. Damn. Another strained meal. Her stomach pinched. God, she wanted to go home to Vegas. Instead, she'd be hitting a honky-tonk.

"I'll be ready."

Chapter Ten

Cooley's stank of stale cigarettes and spilled beer. In other words, it smelled like a honky-tonk and was oddly comforting to Kate. Country music ricocheted off a tinny ceiling accompanied by the crack of pool balls and the laughter of folks unwinding after a day's labor. For a weekday night, things were hopping.

"Hey, there's Brent. He's seen you," Tamara said, pointing one French-tipped nail toward the crowded bar.

Great. The first guy she'd gone all the way with. Horny and hot, Brent Hamilton acted like God's gift to Oak Stand's womankind. She'd say he was delusional, but he did fill out a pair of jeans nicely. "Well, don't point at him."

She had to yell into Tamara's ear. The place was loud and redneck rowdy. Just the reason why Kate felt safe here. This place, she could manage. Justus, Rick, Oak Stand? Not so much.

"Let's get a table near the band," Tamara yelled.

As they slithered through the crowd, Kate felt the eyes of the establishment upon her. She caught the eye of a girl who'd grown up in a trailer down from hers. The eye of a guy who'd spilled Kool-Aid on her lap in the second grade. The eyes of guys she'd never met. Girls she'd never pissed off. Everyone watched her as she swayed and bobbed her way toward an empty table.

They may have looked because she'd painted violet streaks in her hair. Or because she'd pulled on a yellow satin halter top over skintight leggings. Or because her sweet Manolos made her look four inches taller. Thank God she'd squeezed them in her luggage at the last minute. They made her feel more powerful, like she could manage whatever came her way. She tossed her shoulders back.

"Hey, Tam. Who's your friend?"

Kate glanced over. "You know who I am."

Brent showed his polished veneers. "'Course I do. But it's been a while, Katie."

"Kate," she muttered under her breath as she sank onto a chair that had likely been used in a bar fight recently, if the torn seat and scratched legs were any indication.

"So what you drinkin', ladies?" Brent asked, spinning toward the equally brutalized bar. He waved old Bones Stewart over to fill his order.

"I'll take a Bud Light," Tamara called, raking her eyes up and down Brent like a prison guard about to do a cavity search. She lowered her voice. "Damn, but that's a fine piece of ass. Wasn't he your first?"

Kate sighed. "I don't want to talk about Brent."

Brent called over his shoulder. "Hey, Kate, pick your poison."

"Jack and Coke," Kate hollered before looking back at Tamara. "Have you two hooked up?"

Her friend shook her head. It caused her boobs to jiggle and three men standing at the bar nearly threw their backs out trying to get a second look. "Nah. He's my type, but it never worked out."

"Hmm. I thought he was like the DMV. You took a number and waited your turn."

Brent plopped a beer down in front of Tamara before pulling up a chair and plunking his tight buns on it. He slid a glass toward Kate. "Don't know why I asked. I know what you like."

His words carried extra meaning, but she chose to ignore him. Instead, she raised a toast. "When in Oak Stand."

The whiskey and soda tasted like a homecoming, especially with the Zac Brown Band blowing up the speakers and farm boys clad in tight Wranglers surrounding her. Kate Newman was finally home. Whether she wanted to be there or not.

"That's my girl." Brent didn't waste time. He was a man who always knew what he wanted. He liked whiskey, women and redneck honky-tonks. He was positively medieval. He might as well drag a heavy sword behind him. He'd look fine in a suit of armor.

Tamara edged forward, propping her cleavage on the table and twirling her platinum curls. "Brent, you wanna dance? I love this song."

He tore his gaze from assessing Kate and looked at Tamara. "I really—"

"Oh, come on, cowboy. I'll let you grab my butt." Tamara pulled Brent's hand from where it rested on the table and tugged hard with a won't-take-no-for-an-answer gleam in her eye. "Katie doesn't mind."

Brent's shoulders sank. She could see it in his eyes. He couldn't think up one good excuse not to dance. "Okay. Be back in a minute, Katie."

She watched as her friend pulled the former all-state quarterback to the crowded dance floor.

"Kate." She didn't have to mutter it this time. Rick had.

Her Latin fantasy took the chair Brent had vacated, and it both aggravated and thrilled her to her toes. She'd never envisioned him in a backwater dive. Something about him seemed not necessarily above such a scene, but surely out of place just the same.

"I thought you were busy." She swirled the whiskey in the glass. Didn't seem to be much soda in it as she tossed the last of it down. She could feel the warmth of the liquor flooding her body, making her feel loose.

"Yeah," was all he said.

She couldn't sit there and look at forbidden fruit without misbehaving, so she set her empty glass on the table. "You wanna shoot pool?"

His dark eyes met hers. She couldn't read them. "Yeah, sure. But I'm warning you. I'm good."

God, she so wanted to know how good Rick Mendez was, but according to him, that wasn't going to happen. So she'd have to settle for kicking his ass at the table. "I've never backed down from a challenge."

He grunted, which wasn't sexy. But somehow this man made everything tempting.

She rose and moved toward where the pool tables sat

in a section adjacent to the bar. Kate motioned Rick to get them a table while she collected another drink.

While waiting for her order she watched Brent dance with Tamara. Her friend practiced all the moves she'd seen in *Dirty Dancing* on the contractor. It would have been slightly pathetic if Brent didn't have a bit of a gleam in his eye. Tamara might get her hookup tonight, after all.

By the time Kate made it to the table where Rick stood twisting the chalk onto a battered cue stick, she'd nearly finished the whiskey sour she'd ordered.

"Here you go."

Rick took the drink. "Ginger ale? With a cherry?"

"I told Bones you like girly drinks."

He smiled and it slid down her body and curled around parts that were better left covered in public. "Ready to get your ass kicked?"

"That's my line." The rack was smudged from decades of use, but worked as well as the day Bones had bought it. She racked the balls and centered the faded cue ball on the mark.

"You wanna break?" she asked, finishing off the last of her drink.

His smile didn't curl anything this time—just made her wonder about the man sliding the stick between his fingers like he belonged on ESPN. "Are we playing for anything?"

She licked her lips, tasting the banana lip balm she'd applied before walking in the place. "You wanna play for…"

"A kiss."

"You think that's a good idea?"

He shook his head. "No, but it has to be something I want. You have to kiss me if I win."

"What if I—"

"You won't," he said, lowering his body toward the table. In one fluid motion, the balls spun to the corners in a dizzying explosion of color. Uh-oh. He hadn't lied when he'd said he was good. Suddenly she was happy. She rubbed her lips together again. She hoped he liked the tropics, because her kiss would take him there.

As Rick sank shot after shot, he silently beat himself up for coming to Cooley's and making such a stupid wager. He'd already stated his position earlier in the day, so why was he here?

Hours ago, he'd eaten his dinner and told himself that what Kate Newman did at Cooley's was none of his damn business. He wasn't going to think about her sitting on a bar stool, chatting with some rough-and-ready cowboy. He wasn't going to imagine her in someone else's arms, spinning around the dance floor or shrugging out of a tight shirt and jeans. Kate didn't belong to him.

But regardless, thirty minutes later, he found himself pulling on his "going out" jeans and digging cologne from the back of his bathroom cabinet. He'd actually debated which colorless shirt made him look better. Hell.

What was it about Kate that was different from all the other women he'd encountered in Oak Stand? He'd resisted every woman who'd come to him looking for a hard man and a good time. Why couldn't he resist this one?

He slid the stick between his fingers and took his shot. He missed.

Kate beckoned a worn-out-looking waitress toward her. "I'll have another whiskey sour while I beat this guy. And tell Bones to give me the good stuff, not that crap he used last time."

The waitress rolled her eyes but nodded.

Kate moved toward him, brushing against him as she eyed her shot. "Did you miss that on purpose?"

"Of course not," he lied, enjoying her bottom brushing against the fly of his jeans. His hands literally shook as he forced himself to remain cool and ignore the flare-up igniting inside him.

Kate lined up the shot and sank her striped three ball in the side pocket. She was good, but not good enough to beat him.

So he let her win.

And that seemed to tick her off. Her eyes glittered as she sank the eight ball in the corner pocket and dropped her cue stick in the stand between the three tables. She walked a little wobbly in her heels. She'd had way too much to drink.

She placed a finger in the center of his chest. "Why did you let me win?"

He regarded her like a chocolate lover would a box of Godiva. Sweet temptation stirred his blood, swirled around in his pelvis and heated him. "Because if I kissed you, I might not stop. And I really want to respect myself, Kate."

Her mouth opened. Then shut. "Then why the hell did you come here?"

He wished he knew the answer to that one.

Kate's face softened. A seductive smile hovered on her lips. She pressed the accusing finger against his chest and allowed her hand to slide to his shoulder. "So what would you do if I kissed you anyway?"

He looked around the crowded bar. Every now and then, people blatantly stared at the ex–gang member shooting pool with the bad girl come home. No one had bothered them during their game, nor had Tamara or Brent appeared. Just him and Kate, in their own little world. He moved closer to her, smelled the spiciness of her breath, the subtlety of her perfume. "I might slide my hands down to your tight ass and pull you up against me. Then kiss my way down that pretty neck till I get to those sweet little—"

She pressed a finger to his lips, silencing him. "Or?"

He forced a bark of laughter. He wanted her so bad. Just a taste. Electricity thrummed between them, and everyone else in the bar faded away.

Kate didn't give him time to answer. She lifted onto her toes and kissed him.

He closed his eyes and savored the feel of her body against his. He felt like a man dying of thirst tasting water for the first time. He knotted his fists before reaching for her waist and stepped back. "Don't."

"I guess now I know what you'd do." The edge in her voice smacked him.

He flinched. He'd made it worse. Now she was hurt and a hurt Kate seemed a most dangerous thing.

He directed his gaze away to the writhing dance floor. It looked like a full-on line dance was in progress. "How about we forget pool and dance?"

She shrugged. "Whatever."

Kate spun a little too fast on her high heels, teetering before correcting herself and heading for the dance floor without looking back. He handed the cue stick to a bearded guy waiting his turn and followed her. As he stepped onto the scuffed oak floor, a slow country song started. He thought it was Keith Urban. Haunting and seductive.

Shit.

"You two-step, cowboy?" Kate asked. But she wasn't asking him. She'd asked Brent, who was heading toward the bar and a smiling Tamara.

"You know I do." Brent's nostrils actually flared as Kate crooked a finger at him.

Kate looked Rick right in the eye and said, "Then let's get it on, if you're man enough."

Brent feathered his brown hair with one hand and grinned. "And you know the answer to that one, too."

Rick's fist knotted again but this time for a different reason. He watched as Kate pressed her finger into the cleft of Brent's chin, then smiled the kind of smile that would get a girl in trouble. Brent didn't waste time gathering Kate into his arms and sliding smoothly across the dance floor.

Rick stood there for a full minute, feeling like a loser, watching them sway and twirl around the floor before turning toward a now unsmiling Tamara.

He sat on the empty stool next to her.

"Vintage Katie," Tamara muttered. "You wanna make her jealous? I'm good at the two-step and better at making girlfriends mad."

"She's not my anything," Rick lied, trying to pretend it didn't bother him seeing Kate's whiskey-bright eyes glitter beneath the Christmas lights strung among the beams above the dance floor. Her hands laced through Brent's hair, and that action made his blood boil.

Suddenly, she and Brent disappeared. His eyes scanned the crowd until he found them, in the process of getting tangled in each other's arms, pressed against an old pinball machine.

Oh, hell no. He moved toward them, jealousy pecking at him like a hen at seed. No way he was going to sit there and watch her wrap herself around another man. Especially since she was doing it out of anger at him.

He grabbed Kate's arm as Brent lowered his head toward her. "Let's go."

"Hey," Brent said, lifting his head and tightening his hold on Kate's waist. "Back off, dude. The lady can choose for herself."

"Yeah, I can choose for myself." Kate's words were slurred.

Rick looked at her. "You're drunk."

She twisted her arm from him while at the same time moving away from Brent. "The hell I am. I never get drunk."

Brent eyed her and nodded. "Yeah, she's drunk."

Kate crossed her arms. "I hate this damned place. I hate everybody in it, and I don't need you two assholes to tell me what to do. I'm not that stupid poor girl anymore. I say who and when. I make my own decisions."

Neither Rick nor Brent responded. Kate's gaze roved the honky-tonk wildly as if looking for a way out. She looked on the verge of coming unraveled. "I want to go home."

"Let me take you," Rick said, taking her by the arm and giving Brent a look that brooked no argument. He didn't want to fight the man, but he'd do it if he had to. Brent had a good three inches and thirty pounds on him, but Rick had grown up on the streets. He fought dirty.

But Brent nodded. "Go with him, Katie."

Kate looked at Rick, eyes burning. "He doesn't want me."

Her words ripped through him and he felt as though he'd been kicked in the gut.

He was saved from answering by Brent. The man

stooped and planted a kiss on Kate's forehead. "Everybody wants you, Katie. Go home, sweetheart."

Kate couldn't even manage a wave to Tamara as they pulled away from Cooley's. "Why did I come here tonight?"

Rick shifted gears and ricocheted out of the gravel parking lot. "To get away from Justus. To get away from everything that makes you feel."

"Thank you, Dr. Phil," she said, slipping off her shoes. "I acted like an idiot."

"No one paid that much attention."

"Of course they did. Half that bar couldn't wait to watch me fall on my face. Or my ass."

Kate felt mooney. Light-headed. Of course, she *was* smashed. She could count on one hand the number of times she'd gotten drunk. Most of those times had been in college before she'd had the sense to know she needed to be in control. At all times.

"Don't you dare throw up in this car," Rick said.

"As if," she said, before hiccuping. God, was she drunk.

The moon played over the fallow fields, highlighting a random Angus cow or forlorn haystack. Trees flashed by in between fields and Kate felt miserable.

So she laid her head down in Rick's lap.

"What are you doing?" he asked. She felt his flinch.

"Resting."

He took one hand off the wheel and tugged at her shoulder. "Get up. You're going to hit the gear shift."

She looked up at him. His jaw was clenched. She liked the way it looked, so she reached up and traced the pulse throbbing there. "I won't hit it."

"It can't be comfortable lying over the console."

"I'm good." She slid her hand from his jaw to the collar of his tight T-shirt. It was gray and lifeless, like all the others he wore. But the pulse that beat beneath her fingers was very much alive. She smoothed the fabric over his chest. It was broad and hard, just like his stomach.

"God, Kate. Please."

She could feel his erection by her ear. She so wanted to touch him. Wrap her fingers around him. Her damned mouth watered at the thought. She slid her hand lower still.

His caught it. "Kate. Respect my decision."

She jerked from his lap and threw herself across the car to the bucket seat. Her side hurt from where it had pressed against the console. "You're a tease."

His fingers clenched the steering wheel, knuckles white in the faint moonlight. "I'm not the one touching and kissing and—"

"Bull. You show up at the bar, looking like a present for me, brushing against me and teasing me with the chance of a kiss. Then you chastise me for wanting you. For doing what I know you want me to do. What kind of game are *you* playing?"

He glared at her. "I'm not playing games. That was you sliding your ass against me, licking your lips and slithering all over me. Then you went off with some other guy to punish me."

"Why did you come tonight? You said you had things to do."

She knew he'd come for her alone, and that made her blood simmer. If he wasn't going to do anything other than make her want him so bad she lost all reason, did things she'd never consider, like drown a fifth of whiskey and seduce Brent Hamilton, why bother?

"I wanted to do what Tamara suggested—go out while I still had the chance."

"Right. Whatever." She folded her arms across her breasts and watched the road's broken yellow lines rush toward them as they headed for Cottonwood. If he wanted to lie, let him lie.

"Okay, fine. You want the truth? Well, here it is. I can't stay away from you." He turned his head to look at her. She saw naked emotion in his eyes. Desire. Torment. "I couldn't stop myself from going tonight."

"Then why are you stopping this from happening? Why can't we have sex, please each other? Life is tough. You gotta take pleasure where you can."

"I stopped living that way." He paused before letting out a breath. She could see he was grappling with the right words. "I can't go back to the man I was."

"It's not using me if I want it as bad as you do."

He closed his eyes briefly before refocusing on the highway. "So *you* want to use *me?*"

At that, she fell silent. Did she want to use him because she felt something for him, or because he was forbidden? Or maybe both? But deep down in places she suppressed, she knew that Rick meant more than a standard affair. Normally, that would make her run from him instead of run toward him.

The alcohol had dulled her senses. She wouldn't allow herself to feel more than lust or friendship toward Rick. She couldn't. She wasn't wired like other girls. "No. Maybe. I don't know. All I know is that it could be good between us."

He nodded. "No doubt. But you use sex as a weapon, Kate. It shouldn't be a tool to control people."

Even through the haze of whiskey, she felt as though she'd been slapped. His words fell hard against her, stilling her, making her face the fact she did use sex as a way to maintain control. She always had. Sex made her feel powerful. Loved. What a sad notion.

Before she could give it more thought, Cottonwood appeared like an apparition in the night. Rick hooked a right through the gates.

Silence reigned as the car hurtled toward the huge white house. Kate was glad they were almost there. She needed to get out of the damn car. Get away from Rick and his accusations. Away from the guilt he made her feel. Away from the doubt he'd awakened in her. At that moment, she really wanted to hit him.

When Rick killed the engine, the back porch light went on.

Kate blinked at the brightness.

"What the—" She started as a man in a wheelchair emerged in the glow of the porch light. "You've got to be kidding me."

The *Twilight Zone* theme song played in her head. Her bio dad was waiting up for her like she was some fifteen-year-old home from her first date?

Her anger at Rick boiled over onto Justus. She felt as if ropes had been placed on her and they were slowly and surely strangling her. Once again, another man tried to control her, tried to tell her who she should be, tried to layer guilt on her.

She tasted bitterness in her mouth as she climbed from the car. The world rocked a bit, so she waited for it to steady. It didn't. She moved toward the man in the wheelchair, nearly tripping on the stupid herb stuff planted between the pavers. She righted herself, but still listed. She looked Justus straight in the eye and in her best smart-ass voice drawled, "What's up, Pops?"

Chapter Eleven

Her father didn't look at her. He looked at Rick. "What the hell do you mean bringing her home at 2:00 in the morning in this condition?"

Kate didn't give Rick time to answer. "If I had my way, I wouldn't be home at all. I'd be in his bed. And, by the way, this is not my home."

She rocked a bit as the dark night swirled around her. Why the devil had she continued ordering whiskey? She stifled a belch as Rick shut the driver's door and came around to stand beside her.

Justus puffed up like a blowfish. "Right now, this is your home. And I am—"

"Not going to go there tonight," Rick finished, his voice soft but firm. He put a hand on the small of her back.

Before she could think better of it, she leaned into

him, allowed him to support her, even though it made her angry he thought he had to intervene.

"Kate, come inside," Justus demanded, banging his good hand on the wheelchair tray.

"Don't tell me what to do," she said, aware she sounded more like a teenager confronting her dad after a night of necking at the drive-in than a grown woman. Her stomach lurched against her ribs.

"I'll damned well tell you what I want to. I'm your—"

A brittle laugh escaped her. "You want to play daddy now? Tonight? I'm nearly thirty-one years old, Justus. Too late, buddy. You had your chance and you didn't take it. Or have you forgotten that day? That would have been a good time to play daddy."

Her mind tumbled back to the day he'd rebuked her in front of all those people. Pain struck fast and fierce, boiling up inside her, banging against her heart. She couldn't stop the rage. "How could you do that? I was *nine*. Nine years old. Do you know what it did to me? You are cruel and the worst person I can even—"

"Kate," Rick said. "Stop. It's not the time."

"I hate you," she said, narrowing her eyes at the man who'd hurt her so many years ago. "I will never be your daughter, so you might as well save us the drama, give me the money and let me go back to Vegas."

Kate could feel the contents of her stomach rising, burning a path up her throat, through her nostrils. As the hurt and anger from long ago came forth, so did the whiskey. She broke away from them and ran for the garden behind the house.

She made it in time to vomit on Vera's emerging flowers.

She sank to her knees and let her body rid itself of the poison.

Then, for the first time in a very long time, Kate cried. She cried for the little girl she'd once been, a little girl who had stupid dreams of a family, of a room with a bed that didn't poke her with its broken springs, of a dinner not served on a TV tray. Dreams of shiny dolls and brand-new books. Thanksgiving dinners and Christmas Eve services. Good-night kisses and baby brothers with toothy grins. Then she cried for the woman she'd become. A woman who held so fast to the pain of the past that she couldn't see the present with a man. Any man.

And she wept because she didn't know what else to do.

Jeremy was wrong. Kate the Great couldn't fix what was broken this time.

Rick glared at Justus. The bastard didn't know when to quit. And neither did his daughter.

"I don't want her around you," Justus said, rolling forward. His thinning hair gleamed silver in the light of the moon. Shadows withdrew and emerged again in wicked patches of darkness as tree branches swayed with the stirring of wind.

"You're telling me to stay away from her? You sent me to get her, if you recall."

"I remember," the old man said, halting his chair directly in front of him, "but that doesn't mean I want you sniffing around her. Anyone with eyes can see what's going on between you. She's not—"

"The sort of girl to be with riffraff like me?" Rick couldn't stop himself from baring his teeth at Justus. He wasn't good enough for the daughter Justus had thrown away? The irony didn't skip past him.

"Come now, Enrique, don't play the poor servant boy with me."

"Don't treat me like one."

"Just because you feel subpar does not mean the world views you as such."

The man's words seared Rick. "Who said I view myself below any man?"

Justus shrugged. "It's evident in the way you react. If you paint yourself in that light, you should expect to be treated as less than what you are."

Anger boiled over. The old man was cruel sometimes, but there was an elemental truth to his words. Rick had been raised to accept he was of the servile class. His people were washerwomen, maids, gardeners and migrant workers. It did not matter that he was born an American citizen. In many people's eyes he was an intruder, unwelcome and unwanted like weeds in the cracks of a sidewalk.

Justus's mouth tilted in a parody of the Cheshire cat, his hand mimicking the animal's tail as he flicked it toward Rick. "I don't cotton to stereotypes. I respect the man you've become."

"Justus, I—"

"No, we won't speak any more of it."

Rick glanced away toward the swishing bush next to the Japanese maple, accepting the truth in Justus's words. He knew the old man had a healthy dose of fear and admiration for him. Rick had earned it many times over, doing what many would consider fearless. Or stupid. Depended on how one looked at it. But he'd helped Justus correct his past mistakes. All because the man had cared enough to save a stupid gangbanger and give him a second chance.

And Rick had returned that favor. One night, a little more than two years ago, Rick had taken the gun from Justus's hand. Broken and beaten, the old man had wanted to face death more than he'd wanted to face life. Rick had pulled him back to the world Ryan had wanted to save. He'd given Justus something to cling to—Ryan's legacy. Phoenix. Now the man wanted more. He wanted a daughter who was too wounded to live up to what he wished.

"Kate isn't the right woman for you."

Rick jerked his head up. "Why the hell not?"

"Both of you have strong personalities. It won't work. You need someone soft. Like Vera."

"I'll choose the woman for me, and I'll be damned if you tell me who I can or can't have a relationship with. If I want Kate, I'll take her."

Rick would never admit he was trying like hell to avoid tumbling into bed with Kate. He wouldn't give Justus the satisfaction of knowing he wasn't going to take his relationship with Kate any further.

Kate couldn't be the right woman for him, no matter how well she fit against him, no matter how right it felt every time she appeared like a lovely blossom on a deadened tree. She couldn't be the right woman for him because she was leaving in less than two weeks. And two weeks wasn't enough time to take a risk. Two weeks wasn't worth compromising all that he'd become. Not for a few nights of pleasure.

So he'd be content to play the upstanding good guy, Kate's guide, her protector through the minefield of living with Justus. The ties that bound him would be ones of honor.

Not of selfish impulse.

There was no future with Justus Mitchell's illegitimate daughter. That much was certain.

Justus interrupted his thoughts. "Hell, I've never tried to tell you what to do, boy."

At that statement, Rick lifted one eyebrow.

"Okay, maybe a time or two, but I think it's a bad idea to see Kate as part of your future." Justus curled his left hand into a fist and looked at Rick as if the Lord had spoken.

"Maybe I should say the same to you."

Justus's bushy eyebrows knitted into a furious frown. "What do you mean? She's here, isn't she? She wants my money, doesn't she? Then she'll have to deal with me."

"Maybe so, but you're not mending any fences trying to control her the way you are."

"So what should I have done? Wired her the money with no questions asked? I wanted to have a chance to fix my past. Ever since I lost Ryan and found God, that's all I've wanted. Just to fix my past."

"Then why haven't you already fixed this with Kate? I ran all over Texas delivering checks to widows and selling land back to people you'd virtually stolen it from, but you don't bother to call your own daughter? What the hell did you do to her when she was a child, Justus?" Rick didn't understand this man, his motivations.

Justus's eyes shuttered. "That doesn't concern you. Let me fix this my way."

Rick knew it would do no good to continue arguing. "Fine, but remember this—Kate's like a dog that's been kicked, and you wore the boots. You can't expect her to come running to you and lick your hand like nothing happened. Your boot left a mark, old man."

Justus reversed his chair, settling it against the ramp

leading to the back porch. "Not much I can do about the past."

"No, not much any of us can do about it. Just move forward. But you can't control Kate." Rick caught a glimpse of Vera slipping out the door and heading for the garden. He pulled his keys from his pocket and turned toward the car still sitting in the drive with the headlights on.

He needed space. He needed to think. He couldn't do that with Kate around. Vera would take care of her tonight. Tomorrow, he might have his resolve back in place where she was concerned. Stress on the *might* because deep down he knew Kate had already sucked him in and he was losing the will to fight her deadly combination of vulnerability and blatant sex appeal.

No matter what he told himself.

Cool hands pushed the hair from her face as a damp washcloth appeared at Kate's elbow.

"Never as good coming up as it is going down." Vera's words held no judgment. For that, Kate was grateful.

"Tastes like I licked the bottom of someone's boot. Someone who works in a pasture." She took the cloth and wiped her face. Her stomach still rolled, but she felt enormously better.

"You can brush your teeth when you get inside."

"I don't want to go inside. I want to go back to Vegas and pretend none of this ever happened. This was a mistake." Kate couldn't believe she'd admitted to screwing up. Especially to the one woman who wished Kate would pack her bags and leave.

"I can't say I blame you. None of this has been easy, has it? Then again, once you start something, you can't leave it unfinished," Vera said. Kate immediately thought of Rick. If she left tomorrow, she'd leave things unfinished between them, too.

She turned to look at the woman who'd brought her small comfort. Vera wore cotton pajamas that likely cost too much to be worn kneeling on the dirty pavers of the garden. Her hair was loose about her shoulders, her face free of cosmetics, making her look both older and younger at the same time. Crow's-feet crinkled at the corners of brown eyes that were indecipherable in the faint light of the night.

"Must feel good to get it all out, though," Vera said, a soft sigh escaping her as she settled on her heels.

Kate wasn't sure whether she meant the liquor or the rage at her father. But either way, Vera was right. "Yes, it does."

Vera pointed to the crocus she'd baptized with Bone's cheap whiskey. "Ryan planted those when he was ten. Never know if they'll come up or not. Some years they don't."

Kate winced. She'd barfed on precious Ryan's flowers. "I'm sorry."

Vera shrugged. "Nothing the rain won't wash away. Organic, isn't it?"

Kate thought it rather weird they were talking about vomit being organic, but she went with it. "I guess. So, Ryan liked gardening? That's crazy for a guy."

Vera's lips twitched. "Well, he went through a phase one year. He'd attended a science camp and learned about botany. Growing things intrigued him. He went through the same phase again when Rick came to live with us— Rick worked as a gardener when he first came. That man took to the earth like no man I'd ever seen. It was odd, really. A gang member so angry with the world able to grow the most beautiful things you could imagine. Ryan tagged after Rick like a puppy. He loved that anger right out of him."

A lump appeared in Kate's throat at the thought of a boy loving Rick so much that he let go of the hate, that he began to dream about a future. "Ryan was special."

Vera nodded. Kate wondered if all Vera's thoughts wrapped around the past like a line anchoring a boat. "Yes, he was. More than anyone could ever know. You know, there are people who are born that way. Full of something so magical, so pure. He was like an angel. And I was lucky to be his momma."

Tears sprang to Kate's eyes. She could feel the sadness in Vera and something made her want to reach inside the woman and remove it. She touched Vera's hand, then wrapped her fingers around it so their hands curled together.

Vera flinched, but didn't withdraw. For the first time since Kate had stepped foot on Cottonwood, she felt something within herself shift. Click. A sort of rightness settled in her bones.

"I'd like to know more about—" she paused, the words getting clogged in her throat "—my brother."

Vera's eyes met hers. Honesty passed between. It was the first time Kate had admitted Ryan was indeed her brother. And Justus her father. No more pretense. Only truthfulness.

"You should know about him. It's a shame you never met him."

"I did. Sort of."

Like a puppy, Vera cocked her head. "How?"

"Shortly after my grandmother passed, I came to Oak Stand to settle some of her things, and he ran into me with his bicycle. Tore my new broom skirt." Kate frowned a little. She'd saved all her tips from the bar to buy that skirt from the boutique near campus. Sixty dollars had been a fortune back then.

Who was she kidding? It was a fortune now.

Vera smiled and clapped a hand over her mouth. "You were that mean girl?"

Kate laughed. "Well, I *was* mad. And the damn skirt looked like it had been shredded by a cat."

Vera laughed. The sound was soft against the night, and her face was framed against the fingernail moon. "He said a mean girl screamed at him. I remember that day. He'd gone with a friend to get an ice-cream cone at the Dairy Barn. Justus hadn't wanted to let him go because he'd just gotten that mountain bike and couldn't handle it that well. But Ryan insisted he could ride it fine."

"Yeah, right into me," Kate muttered, before smiling. "He was a cute kid. Hated him on sight."

Vera drew back, but then realized Kate was joking. "He cried because he tore your skirt. He was like that. Felt everything too much. It worried him you were mad, and he didn't know who you were. Took all the quarters he'd been saving for the arcade and said he was going to buy you a new skirt."

Kate shook her head, as something new lodged in her gut. Something called shame. Remorse. Or whatever a person called the feeling of hating a golden-haired, blue-eyed boy because his father loved him, then finding out the boy was truly worth the love. "I left that afternoon. Only came to pack some stuff and dispose of the rest."

"He said he'd find you. You had eyes the same color as his. I never made the connection, though I should have. I'd heard the rumors, but I didn't want to face them."

Kate didn't want to talk any more about the past tonight. She didn't want to push it with Vera. Didn't want to undo the good that had been done. "Almost everybody knew, Vera. No one else wanted to face it, either." She gave Vera's hand one last squeeze.

Vera sat stock-still and watched as Kate rose to her feet. "Well, it's late, and you need to brush your teeth."

"And grab a shower." Kate reached down to offer assistance standing.

As Vera took her hand, a fleeting peace brushed Kate, gentle as the wings of the dragonflies that often buzzed lazily along the edges of the East Texas ponds. Vera accepted. Vera adapted. Vera would heal.

Kate didn't believe in divine intervention—she was far too pragmatic. But something had happened between the two women. Like stones being pulled from a wall of doubt, they had made progress in opening the boundary that separated them.

Silently, they walked the twisting path of the garden, emerging into the porch light where Justus sat like a worn gargoyle. Kate didn't acknowledge her father, just glided past him.

There was honesty between them, too. But it hurt too much to acknowledge or embrace it. Anger still licked at her insides like the aftertaste of the whiskey, only harder to wash away.

Chapter Twelve

Days later, Kate sat on the back patio of Phoenix watching a clean and noticeably healthier Banjo chase doves in the brush. A cool breeze threatened the spiky locks she'd perfected around her face. She'd streaked her dark tresses with a deep red last night and liked how colorful it looked in the brightness of the day. She looked down at the planter at her feet. "Ugh! This soil keeps washing out of the pots. Why is it so light?"

Kate wiped her hands and frowned at the water spilling over the sides of the planter.

Random pots scattered the flagstone. Some were already filled, while others still awaited the tomato plants sitting in plastic cartons on the porch.

"Because we're using a moisture-binding potting soil. It'll help the plants stay succulent when summer gets here." Rick shoveled more soil into the pots. His tanned hands patted a hill in the center of one pot before cupping a hole in the center of the mound.

She and Rick hadn't spoken about the night at Cooley's even though she could feel the strings of tension tightening between them. She still wanted him with an intensity that surprised her, and he still fought against the magnetism between them, but they had other things to deal with. Rick's clients had arrived and Kate spent the past few nights making polite small talk with Vera and Justus at the dinner table. It was enough to set her on edge and make her grind her teeth as she slept. The only thing that got her through those evenings was the truce she and Vera had arrived at that night in the garden.

"My grandmother never planted anything until after Easter. It's already thundered in February, you know," she said, pulling a tender tomato plant from the plastic container.

"What does that mean, *bruja?*"

"Stop calling me witch," she grumbled, gently breaking apart the roots of the plant the way Rick had showed her earlier.

"You mean you don't know?" Georges, one of the clients, called from across the patio. "If it thunders in February, it will freeze in April, *cholo.*"

Kate smiled at Georges. He was the only guy who showed any openness toward the staff at Phoenix. The other four were eerily silent, almost sullen, as if they already regretted their choice to come here.

Carlos, Joe, Brandon, Georges and Manny had arrived by a church van, each hauling a makeshift suitcase and a scowl. Or at least that's what Rick had told her.

Only Georges had abandoned his serious demeanor for some lively teasing. He'd had Trudy pitching a fit when she'd found everything on her desk moved cock-eyed on the second day of GED classes. He'd also held an actual conversation with Rick, rather than merely grunting his replies.

"Well, that's why we're planting them in these containers. They'll be easy to move to the cover of the back patio if we get frost." Rick patted the soil around the plant Kate had set in the hole. He sat back and assessed the planting critically, narrowing his brown eyes as he studied his handiwork.

She watched as he rose and retrieved anther plant, handing it to Manny without a word. The plump gang member wrinkled his nose at the container.

"So why we gotta plant these things, anyway? This seems stupid if you ask me," Manny said, setting the tiny plants beside the wooden pot and studying the other members sprawled about doing much the same.

"I didn't ask you," Rick said, returning to her side.

Georges snickered. "He already told you, dude. We're gonna grow our own vegetables. It ain't that bad. You ain't shoveling horseshit or nothin'."

"Shut the f—"

"Guys, you'd do well to note there is a lady present," Rick cautioned.

"What lady?" Kate joked, looking around. She hit Rick with a smart-ass grin.

He rolled his eyes. "Seriously, let's start watching the way we speak to others. Part of this program is learning to present yourself as a new person. We're letting go of who we once were to find a new path."

"Now *there's* your horseshit to shovel," Joe said, tossing a trowel onto the patio. It clanked against the rock before scuttling toward Manny.

Rick stiffened beside her. She placed one hand on his forearm in warning. There was going to be resistance. There was likely going to be out-and-out rebellion before Rick could make any true progress.

"The trowel will probably work, though I notice Georges puts out a lot of bullshit. Might need a shovel for his," Kate joked, squeezing Rick's arm. She could feel him take a deep breath, feel his forearm relax under her fingers. She liked the way he felt, warm from the sun, strong from the labor he performed. He was no milk-white accountant in a knockoff designer suit. He was full-on man, and even though they were far from being alone, Kate felt a familiar heat surge inside her body along with the buzz of aggravation that it would go unfulfilled.

Georges laughed, interrupting her wicked thoughts. "You know it, muchachos."

Manny pulled a face and slid the trowel toward Joe. "Just plant the damn tomatoes, man."

Joe looked at the garden instrument, then looked away, his jaw set. "Whatever. I'm out."

He rose from the patio, hitched up his sagging pants and headed for the center, where Trudy stood at the side of the house, motioning a woman wearing a circus costume their way.

Rick sighed and pulled away from her. She felt the frustration coming off him in waves.

"Uh-oh," Kate said, watching as the woman in what was actually not a circus costume but a hideous Western skirt headed their way. "Betty Monk moving in at 12:00."

"Who's Betty Monk?" Georges asked, shielding his eyes against the rays bearing down on them.

"Yoo-hoo," she called, her brightly patterned skirt

swishing around her red cowboy boots as she balanced a basket on one arm. "Hiya, boys!"

Betty Monk was the coproprietor of The Curlique Beauty Salon in Oak Stand, where Kate had worked each summer to earn extra money. All that was left of the bouffant Betty used to wear were faded wisps of rose-colored hair held in place with Aqua Net above her penciled-on eyebrows and road-mapped face. Bright red lipstick matched the boots she wore, curving into a Texas-size smile.

"Look what I brought you boys—muffins. Right from the ovens of the Ladies Auxiliary," Betty said, shooing Banjo away as she maneuvered toward the patio.

No one said a word as Betty tousled Brandon's hair, which was as absent as her own since he wore a buzz. Brandon ducked his head and moved away, but it didn't deter Betty.

"Why, I'll be a monkey's uncle. If it isn't my favorite gal, Katie Newman. What in the blue blazes have you done to your hair, girl?" Betty handed Georges the basket. He immediately lifted the gingham cloth and peered within.

Kate brushed the dirt from her hands. "Hello, Mrs. Betty. The color is Fire two-oh-three, if you want me to do a little touch-up for you."

Kate gave the woman a brief hug, but the older woman wanted much more. She clasped Kate into a bear hug, which was remarkably easy for a woman who was descended from good Norwegian stock and stood five foot ten in her stocking feet. "The devil take me if I wear anything that bold, child. My color has been ravishing red for twenty-some-odd years, and that's what it'll stay."

Rick walked over and extended his hand. "Hello, Mrs.

Monk. I appreciate your being so neighborly and bringing us some home cooking."

Betty took his hand and gave it a hearty shake. "Some folks didn't want me to do it, but I'll be hanged if I listen to a bunch of narrow-minded deacons' wives. That Sally Holtzclaw is plum hypocritical, and I've just about—"

"What kind did you make?" Kate interrupted before Betty could dredge up every wrong done her by her archrival and former best friend, Sally. They'd been feuding for years, ever since Betty's design-challenged niece had reupholstered the Baptist church's choir chairs in teal satin, causing Sally to slip off the seat and show the whole congregation her girdle. One would think the two friends could have gotten past the bad feelings, but showing her undergarments to the township had stirred Sally to retribution. And so the battle had waged out of control for three years.

"Oh. I brought blueberry—Nellie's grandmother's recipe. Used the last of the frozen blueberries my grandbaby picked me over in Linden."

"Very kind of you," Rick muttered, looking a bit puzzled. It was a common reaction to Betty who name-dropped, subject-hopped and dredged the past with dizzying speed. Not many could follow her, let alone figure her out. Not even her dear departed Ed had tried. He'd always called her his Gordian knot. And he never claimed to be Hercules.

"Well, aren't you sweet." Betty beamed. "I've always liked you. You're a most handsome fellow, even with all those tattoos."

Rick looked at Kate before looking back at Betty. "Thanks, I think."

"No problem." Betty took Kate's elbow and moved her

out of the hearing range of the guys cramming muffins in their mouths. "Now, Katie, Nellie told me you're staying with Justus Mitchell. I guess that not-so-secret secret is out front and center. If that's so, why the devil are you staying with a man who never bothered to claim you as his own? I'm a forgiving woman, but even I couldn't cotton to pardoning that sin."

Kate wanted to laugh. Betty could meddle with the best of them, and after putting up with temper tantrums and tears from the many who'd unloaded their problems in her salon chair, she didn't mince words. So Kate shot her straight. "Who said anything about forgiveness? I want his money."

Betty cackled like the old hen she was and clapped her hands together. "Damn right. No one messes with my Katie."

Rick's eyes widened. "Are y'all related?"

"Not by actual relation," Betty said. "Here's the way it is, handsome—this little girl thinks she belongs only to herself, but she belongs to Oak Stand. To all of us."

Kate shook her head. She'd never felt she belonged in Oak Stand. She'd always felt second-rate. Nothing like the way she felt in Vegas. There she had control. And no one knew her past. But Mrs. Betty had meant her remark as a kindness, and it struck Kate with its tenderness.

"Whoa, these muffins are good," Georges mumbled, his mouth half-full.

"Of course they are. I made them, didn't I?" Betty said, moving toward him. "Now, let me show you the right way to plant tomatoes. You've got to have a little bit of bonemeal."

Her words faded into the background as Kate fought the dampness gathering on her lashes. Rick noticed and moved toward her. He took her hand and brushed some dirt from it. "I like your hair. It suits you. And I didn't know Oak Stand owned you."

Kate loved the feel of his hands on her. Loved it too much. "No one owns me. Especially not this town."

She stepped away from him, sensing her words had jabbed him, hurt him in some way. But what did it matter? He'd made it abundantly clear several nights ago when she'd thrown herself at him.

He didn't want her.

Just like Justus hadn't.

Just like Oak Stand hadn't.

She didn't belong here. She belonged in Vegas, with Jeremy and her friends. She belonged to a city that didn't sleep, where no one called her Katie.

She belonged to herself and she needed to get out of the place that made her feel as though she didn't.

But, as Vera had said, some things you can't leave undone.

Kate grabbed the empty cartons and headed to the side of the house where the garbage cans sat. From the corner of her eye she saw Vera pull up in a Lexus sedan. The older woman stepped out of the car, looking quite pretty with her hair tied in a low ponytail with a scarf and wearing a lime-green jacket over her factory-worn designer jeans. She carried a large bowl and a bag from a fancy gourmet store that was definitely not located in Oak Stand.

"Kate," she called, stopping on the front pavers. "Will you give me a hand?"

"I'm filthy," Kate called back, but walking toward her anyway.

"Just grab the sacks from the trunk, if you don't mind.

You can set them on the porch." She headed inside without waiting for Kate to agree.

"Fine," she said to no one in particular as she approached the car. The trunk was unlatched and she lifted the bags out and set them at her feet. Under the last bag lay a halter. She lifted it out. It was a strange item to be sitting in the middle of a perfectly clean trunk.

"That belonged to Ryan's horse."

Kate dropped it in the trunk, wondering if Vera had gotten the therapy she needed after Ryan's death. Carrying this kind of stuff was creepy. "Oh."

Vera's touch was a light caress on her back. "That was how he died. On his horse."

Kate had never thought to ask about how Ryan had died. Things had felt too heavy to think about much beyond the cold silence with Justus and the hot pandering for Rick. "He fell?"

Vera nodded. "Rick found pot in the ashtray of the Mustang. It wasn't Ryan's. Or at least he swore it wasn't, but Rick was hard on him. I guess because of his own mistakes. Ryan got angry because he didn't believe him and took off in a gallop on his quarter horse, Tolstoy. We don't know what happened really. Tolstoy came back and Ryan didn't. Rick found him crumpled in a ditch out by the ruins of the Spanish mission."

Sadness lurked in Vera's eyes, but she told the story in a matter-of-fact way. As if she'd told it the same way many times before.

"I'm sorry." It was all Kate could say.

Vera nodded, looking at the halter. "Justus shot that horse. Loaded the rifle, went out and killed him. It was Justus's way of dealing, as extreme as it was. But Rick…"

She sighed. "Rick went crazy. He thought it was his fault."

"Why?"

Vera shrugged and shut the lid. "He kept saying 'I should have believed him' as if that would have prevented it. But it wouldn't have. It was a freak accident. I guess I knew. What's that saying? 'Only the good die young'?"

"I'll probably live to a ripe old age then."

At this the woman finally smiled. "Me, too."

Vera didn't say anything else. She headed up the walk with the remaining bags, leaving Kate wondering what kind of help she'd actually been. She hadn't done a thing other than pick up the halter.

She glanced at the porch as Rick appeared.

Is that why he stayed under Justus's thumb? Guilt? Perhaps he couldn't cut the ties that bound him to the Mitchells because he felt responsible for Ryan's death. Which was ludicrous, but the mind and heart worked in mysterious ways.

Rick rubbed a hand across his chest and looked out at the horizon. Kate could feel his angst. His trouble. If she had to guess the source, she'd say things at the center, work with the clients wasn't going as planned.

Yeah, welcome to the club, buddy.

Chapter Thirteen

"We can't hold a car wash, stupid. It's February," Carlos said, leaning back in one of the chairs surrounding the dining table at Phoenix.

"But it's not cold outside when the sun's out," Georges said, spreading his hands. "You have a bad attitude, man."

Rick tried to be patient. The guys had only been here for four days and were still adjusting to one another. Two clients—Joe and Brandon—were from the Tango Blast organization, a relatively new albeit violent gang. They seemed the most dangerous of the group. The other three were Mexican Mafia, but from different barrios. They'd been low men in the gang and their personalities reflected their status. "We can disagree, but let's not name call."

Sullen eyes met his comment and worry settled in his gut. Nothing was working the way he'd envisioned it. He'd been a delusional fool to think the guys would accept him just because he'd been in their shoes at one time.

Not to mention he literally ached for Kate. He tried to stop himself from gravitating toward her, but time and time again, he found himself seeking her out, if only to soak her in as she teased the clients and did what he sought to do…bond with them.

Brandon spoke next. "Listen, not a car wash, man. That's, like, what the cheerleaders do in high school."

Joe grinned. "I took my mother's car for a wash every time. *Mochilas.* Tight asses and—"

"How about a detail place?" Brandon suggested. "We could wash, wax and buff that shit up."

Rick could see lightbulbs going off in their heads. He'd asked to meet with them right after their last GED class with the purpose of brainstorming ideas for raising money for the center.

The foundation had given the center enough money for the year, but the guys in the three-month program needed to earn their keep. Taking on responsibility was as much a part of their rehabilitation as therapy and education. Learning to work together to find solutions was key in getting them to accept a world where disagreements were met with honesty and compromise, not with guns and knives.

"That's whack, dude," Manny said, shaking his head. Tension thickened.

Rick slammed his hands on the table, breaking through the testosterone flare-up in the room and drawing their attention to him. "Actually, there's nothing like that in Oak Stand, outside of a do-it-yourself place on the outskirts of town. I'm good with cars myself."

"Yeah," Joe said, glancing out the back window to where the Mustang sat in the drive. "That's a sweet ride."

Rick could feel their interest. For the first time. "I

restored it. Me and a friend, that is. So I know my way around a vehicle."

The guys nodded.

"But we're too far out from town," Joe said. "Old ladies ain't gonna drive out here so this chunty can rag her car." He jerked his thumb toward Georges as he delivered the insult. Georges flipped Joe off.

Rick reminded them about using derogatory terms for the umpteenth time.

"Well, they damn sure ain't gonna let us drive their cars. They'll think we're stealin' them or something. We'll be laying the wax and hear sirens," said Joe.

Rick spent the next thirty minutes helping them iron out the particulars of the business. The guys were wary, but enthusiasm laced their words and several guys showed surprising entrepreneurial skills in their negotiations. Then he watched silently as they sketched out logos and talked about names for the business, one of which was Banjo's. Letting the dog stay had proven to be the right move. The guys loved the scrawny mutt. The dog was another piece in the puzzle for creating the right environment.

Rick drifted away from the table, leaving them to take ownership of the business idea. He'd follow up later and make a suggestion or two for drafting the plan, but he wanted to give them space. That seemed like the right move.

He entered the kitchen, set his mug in the sink and ran soapy water for the dishes stacked on the counter. Starting tonight, the clients would share in meal preparation and cleanup. Up until then, he'd borne the burden. For some reason, he hadn't thought much about feeding the guys. He'd spent much of his planning on the programs and supplies. Thank goodness, Vera and other townspeople had shown up with welcoming dishes. Another thing to tweak.

As he finished loading the dishwasher, Kate breezed in.

"Hey," she said, grabbing a kitchen towel and wiping the counters. "I finished organizing all of the paperwork into different files. When you have time, I'll show you how I set it up so it'll be easy to put your hands on what you need."

He watched her smooth strokes as she buffed the stove and knew exactly where he wanted to put his hands. And it damn sure wasn't on files. He looked at the half-eaten cinnamon roll sitting on a plate he'd missed on the far counter. It made him think of that morning several days ago. The morning he'd told Kate he'd made a vow. She'd teased him then about eating things that weren't good for him, and he'd replied that "some things were worth it."

He looked at the delicious woman bent over picking up a bread tie from the floor.

Wasn't Kate the same thing?

Decadent. Sweet. And absolutely worth it.

She turned and caught him watching her and the air crackled. "What?"

Laughter from the dining room jarred him from his wicked thoughts. It was getting harder and harder to drag himself from that place. And he knew his connection with Kate wasn't only physical. It was something more. "Nothing."

He took the towel from her and hung it up. "Actually, I do want to show you something."

She slid him a wicked smile. "Oh, really?"

He tried to ignore the stirring in his body and focus on where he wanted to take her. "Really."

He headed out the kitchen door past the guys at the table. Their discussion had grown pretty loud.

"That name is *chignon.* Beast," Brandon said. He leaned forward, forearms on the table in an aggressive manner.

Manny pulled his attention away from Brandon to look at Rick. "Yo, *chulo,* where you going with my *chica?*"

Rick shook his head. He was no player. Those days were long over. "Does she know she's yours?"

Kate rolled her eyes. "When will men ever learn? We ladies belong to ourselves."

"That's what we let you think," Joe said.

Rick told them they would return momentarily and the guys went back to arguing over a name.

He led Kate out the door and down the front steps. The wind announced another cold front moving in from the north, but the sun broke through the clouds to throw some much needed heat upon their shoulders. He headed down the sloping hill toward a small copse of woods that clung to the banks of a stream ribboning the property.

Kate didn't speak, just tilted her face up to the sun. He curled his hand and placed it in his pocket, so he wouldn't touch her, fall into her. His body was like a guitar string, tight and ready to be played by her.

But not now. There was something he wanted to show her, a secret place that he hoped would help her understand that someone had wanted her.

The pine trees didn't grow thick in the stand of woods. They towered above the dogwoods and redbuds, showing premature signs of awakening. Tangled graying vines curled around a small ramshackled fort built next to a huge pine tree.

"What's this?" she asked, approaching the weathered little building. She walked straight to the door hanging on rusted hinges.

"It's Ryan's fort," he said quietly, still feeling reverence for the secret place Ryan had hung out in.

She swung her head around. "Why would you bring me here? It's falling down."

He had good reason, but he wanted her to find out on her own, so he shrugged. Her brow furrowed as she turned and pulled the door open past withered dandelions blocking the threshold. The wood creaked and one board actually fell to the ground.

"Oops," she said, ducking her head to peer within.

"He built it himself with boards and scraps he found around Cottonwood. He'd started it before I came to live here. In fact, the day Justus pulled up with me sulking in the back of the truck, the roofers were accusing each other of misplacing boards and a box of nails. Turns out Ryan hauled the material almost two miles across the pasture on a four-wheeler they used on the ranch."

"I guess a lot of little boys want a fort," she said as she brushed a cobweb away and stepped inside. "I wonder why he built it so far away?"

"So nobody would find it."

She glanced out. "But you did."

"He showed it to me. You're the only other person who knows it's here."

Something flashed in Kate's eyes. He couldn't read it. She disappeared inside the fort, and he stood where he was. He wanted her to see something of her brother other than the portrait that hung over her as she shoveled peas into her mouth at dinner. He wanted her to feel like she had one tiny piece that neither Vera nor Justus held.

He wasn't sure why, but he knew that this would help Kate move toward a better place. He wished he'd thought of it earlier, but he'd been so wrapped up in all that had been going on that he'd forgotten Ryan's secret fort and all that lay inside.

Kate wondered if the structure was dangerous. A young boy had built it, so it couldn't be too sound. Yet it had weathered several years and still stood.

The tang of mold and decaying earth met her nostrils. The floor of the fort had been covered in an old piece of linoleum that curled at the edges. Faux wood. She and her grandmother had had the same pattern in the used trailer they'd rented in Happy Place Trailer Park—the name was a total oxymoron. Nothing happy about a run-down trailer park choked with weeds and soaked in poverty.

The fort walls were held together by exposed rusting nails. Large cracks allowed outside light to fall in bright slashes across the dirty linoleum. Two large sheets of plywood served as the roof and there was only one window, which had Plexiglas covering it. The contents consisted of one rickety TV tray, a camping chair and several boxes. One lone, faded poster of Angelina Jolie dressed as Lara Croft dated the fort as early 2000s.

Kate toed one of the boxes and a spider ran out.

She brought the heel of her sneaker down on it. One down, dozens likely to go.

She cautiously lifted the water-stained flap of the nearest box.

Baseball cards. Thousands of them. Most ruined by

the moisture. The Texas Rangers seemed to have been his favorite.

The next box held rocks. Nothing spectacular about them. Some were jagged with crystals, others were smooth and perfect for skipping across a still pond. A few marbles mixed within the depths. She decided to leave that box alone, for there was no telling what lurked beneath the stones.

A third box held a conglomeration of stuff: a yo-yo, a worn deck of cards with a casino logo on it, a watch that had stopped at 4:20, a bird whistle, an empty box of Hot Tamales candy and something that looked like a half-eaten Fruit Roll-Up. A couple of school papers littered the sides of the box. It appeared that at age nine or ten, Ryan had sucked at spelling but rocked fractions.

A large footlocker sat beneath the uneven window. It beckoned her like a topless dancer crooking her finger at a paunchy, bald guy.

Kate peeked out the door. Rick stood, arms akimbo, studying the writhing trees above his head. He was giving her time to get to know her deceased brother. To see the Ryan beyond the saint. But for what purpose?

She resigned herself to not knowing his motives and stepped toward the battered footlocker. She bent, flipped the unlocked latch and lifted the lid. The hinges creaked eerily. No spiders, but discolored paper hung from the inside of the lid. An address label affixed to the paper and scrawled in perfect penmanship declared the trunk to be that of Vera Horton.

Kate peered into its depths. A small stained bridle lay on top of a baseball jersey. Ryan had been number twenty-four for the Oak Stand Bears, no doubt his T-ball team if the size of the jersey was any indication. Beside that lay an elementary yearbook. She picked it up and leafed through it. Her brother had been in Mrs. Doyle's first grade class. One of his front teeth had been missing in the class picture, and it looked very similar to the one she'd taken at age six standing beside the same teacher.

She and her brother had shared the same homeroom teacher. Maybe Ryan had sat at the same desk she'd slumped in. Maybe he'd also hidden his pencil in the groove at the very back of the desk, hoping no one else would find it and take it.

She placed the yearbook back beside the jersey. Something pink caught her eye. An anomaly like something pink among baseball cards and disgusting boy stuff had to be explored. She tossed aside a baseball cap that matched the Bears jersey and froze.

She knew that backpack—it was hers. And it had been missing for so long she'd forgotten it.

She picked it up, brushing the cheerful face of Strawberry Shortcake.

It wasn't empty.

Hand trembling, she untied the frayed strings knitting the cloth opening together and tugged the backpack open. She pulled one item from the depths and cradled it in her hands. Carefully, she opened the journal to the first page.

Property of Katie Newman.

Beneath it, in childish handwriting, were the words: *my sister.*

Kate traced the spidery words then wiped the tears that dripped on her forgotten journal. Obviously Ryan knew a lot more about that mean girl who'd chewed him out for tearing her skirt than he'd let on. That he'd claimed—even in this silent, private way—knocked Kate on her proverbial butt. Especially because he would have had to dig it out of whatever moldering pile of crap it had been languishing in—he'd only been a toddler that fateful day she abandoned her prize possessions.

Damn Rick for pulling her heartstrings. He knew exactly what he was doing.

Kate shoved the journal into the backpack and dug around until she found what she wanted. She stared at the picture of her parents laughing into the camera for a moment before slipping it into her pocket.

She didn't even know why she wanted to keep it.

Chapter Fourteen

At Justus's request, Rick joined the Mitchells at Cottonwood for dinner that night. Upon his arrival, he'd dumped
his frustration about the center on Kate. It seemed San-
ford Stevens, the group therapy session leader, had requested that Rick not be present during his time with
the clients. It had frustrated Rick to discover he wasn't
needed at the center—he wasn't irate, but testy all the
same.

After his vent, Kate and Rick had joined Vera and
Justus in the formal living room for cocktails. Kate had
actually been glad of Rick's presence because the tension between her and her father had grown epic. Neither
of them could get past stilted formality with one another.

Kate was counting down the days to her return to
Vegas while dreading them at the same time. Her reasons
for feeling that way were murky at best, but she knew

they had mostly to do with Rick and her burning desire to be with him. And not only in the biblical sense. She wanted to be around *him* all the time.

It was all very strange.

Vera remained cheerful through the first course, though she cast worried glances Rick's way when he began cutting his filet into tiny little pieces while staring off into space.

"How are things progressing at Phoenix, Rick?" Vera asked, sipping her second glass of wine as she stared down at the dinner plate Rosa had set in front of her.

Rick muttered a terse "Fine."

"Well, are the boys nice?" Vera prodded.

"Yeah," Rick said, shuffling his green peas toward his mashed potatoes. Kate chalked his distraction up to his preoccupation with things not running the way he'd like them at the center.

"Well, that's nice. I hope they're adjusting to the quiet life. Is there anything more I can do to help?"

Rick shrugged.

"Why don't you answer her damned questions?" Justus exploded, throwing his fork onto the fine china of his plate. "I'm sick of this uncomfortable silence every damned night. The least you could do is carry the conversation, boy."

"Justus, watch your language, dear," Vera said, her hand trembling as she picked up her glass.

"I'll say what I want to at my table. And you stop drinking so much damn wine, Vera. That ain't gonna help one bit, woman. That boy—" he pointed his finger at the picture of Ryan, who looked quite amused at the whole situation "—is dead and he ain't coming back."

Vera burst into tears, Rick muttered a word that would make a nun blush, and Kate started laughing.

Justus turned his blue eyes on her. "What in the hell are you laughing about?"

"This is…this…is—" She snorted, before throwing a hand over her mouth. "It's the most dysfunctional family in the history of dysfunction."

Rick stared at her as if she'd licked acid tablets. "I'm not a member of this family."

Vera moaned and Justus cursed then asked for forgiveness with eyes cast upward.

"I mean, you guys are a bunch of loony tunes." Kate couldn't believe she'd lost control of her emotions. This afternoon had about broken her. Since she'd arrived at Cottonwood, she'd alternated between crying, cussing, laughing and throwing herself at a celibate guy—all indications that Kate Newman had lost her mind. Clearly she belonged at this table.

"I don't think feeling something means you're crazy." Vera sniffed as she shoved her half-filled glass of pinot grigio toward the Waterford saltshaker. "It means you're human."

"You're right, Vera," Rick said, his eyes connecting with Kate's. "Sometimes when you feel things, it's messy."

Kate felt his words. Knew he was talking to her, not Vera. But he need not have bothered. Didn't he know she knew things were messy? They were so messy she couldn't find a damn thing to hold on to.

"Thank you, Rick," Vera mumbled from the depths of her linen napkin.

"Oh, piss on it," Justus said, reversing his chair from the table. "I'm sick of holding my tongue."

He pointed a finger at Kate. "I don't know why I wanted you to stay here. You're more stubborn than any horse, mule or goat I've ever worked with. And that has been more than I care to remember. I thought I could make amends with you, but you won't even open your mouth and try. So I can't sit here another night and pretend." He rolled out the door.

"Justus, don't leave. We haven't had dessert," Vera called after him. He ignored her and kept rolling toward the elevator that would take him to his office.

Kate looked at Vera. Her misery was plainly evident on her face and Kate felt like shit for upsetting her. "I'm sorry."

Vera waved a hand before looking at the portrait of her dead son. "It's not just you. Justus hasn't grieved for Ryan properly. And I've grieved too much. I wish I could stop, but the hurt won't go away."

Kate looked at the picture of the boy who'd kept her journal hidden in a damp footlocker. His smile seemed so knowing. So like her own. "At least you let yourself feel. That has to be healthier than holding it in."

"Maybe," Vera acknowledged, turning to Kate. "But I've gotten so lost in the grief that I've forgotten how to live. I'm tired of merely existing. Talking about Ryan has helped me realize he'd never want me to ramble about this house, spending hours in the garden wishing for something that can no longer be."

Rick silently watched them. His eyes looked very much the way they had when she'd emerged from the fort earlier that afternoon. Satisfied. Like a general whose battle strategies were going according to plan.

Kate cleared her throat, thinking someone should say something. Something to affirm what Vera had admitted.

"From what you've told me, you're right. He'd be upset with you. But give yourself a break. You postponed your grief when Justus had his stroke, then you drowned in it. So now it's time to dry off and start living again."

Vera nodded, and reached over to grasp Kate's hand. Her touch was cool, but her eyes were finally warm. "Thank you, Kate. I know being here has been hard for you, but somehow, your presence has forced me to confront myself. You've unstuck me."

Kate gave the woman's hand a squeeze before withdrawing. The atmosphere felt too deep in the room. Stifling, the way it had after Jeremy had told her the IRS news. She had to get out to process. To think about how to handle her father. "I—I think I'm going to skip the cheesecake and take a walk."

She scooted back her chair and rose. Rick did the same. "Pardon us both, Vera. I'll join Kate on that walk."

She had thought she'd rather be alone, but when Rick stood, relief flooded her. Having Rick beside her was becoming a habit.

Vera nodded. "That's fine. I'll eat the cheesecake for breakfast." She dropped her napkin beside her plate then followed Justus's path, heading toward where her husband had likely gone to sulk. Kate and Rick slipped through the kitchen, complimenting Rosa on the meal, before emerging into the moonlight.

The night was slightly cool, and the stars twinkled like a string of Christmas lights placed for the benefit of the two of them walking the garden path.

"I had to escape," Kate commented after they'd walked for several minutes with no words between them.

"I know."

They walked for several minutes more, stepping off

the path and onto the land behind the house. A few Bradford pear trees showed off their snowy plumage against the dark velvet of the sky. Spring had arrived despite the cold front that had moved in a few days ago.

"You know, when I was rollin' with my gang, I tried like hell to be hard. That was living the gang life, to be hard." His words floated into the night, regret tinting them, making them sound prophetic. "That's why it's difficult to reach the guys at the center. Egos get in the way."

"Mmm," she said, enjoying his presence at her side. Had she ever taken a walk with a man beside her and felt comfortable?

"You know, I was never like that. Never hard."

Kate snickered.

"Ah, *bruja,* you know what I mean." There was a smile in his words. "I couldn't kick a puppy and laugh. I couldn't lift an old lady's purse when I knew it held her welfare check. I never got a kid to sell drugs for me with the promise of a pair of shoes. I tried to pretend I was a badass, but I wasn't."

She nodded even though he couldn't see her. And though she wore a sweater and jeans and wasn't cold, she moved closer to him.

"You are like me," he said, stopping and grabbing her hand. He brought it to his lips. His kiss was soft, and for a moment he became a Spanish courtier come to woo and win her. Kate was no romantic, but she couldn't seem to stop her heart from pounding, from wanting to feel his lips on hers beneath the fullness of the moon.

"How am I like you?"

"You got hurt early in life. Like me. So you build a shell. A tough, badass exterior. You try to be hard."

She shifted her eyes to his and he stopped beneath a

redbud tree that had started pushing purple blooms forth. "You think you're going to crack me or something?"

She tried to make her words teasing, but they didn't come out the way she'd intended. Emotion trembled in those words, as if she were daring him, no, begging him, to find the real Kate beneath the razored hair and too-tight clothes.

His mouth descended, hovering over hers. "I already have," he whispered against her lips.

She lifted herself onto her tiptoes and pressed herself to him as he claimed her mouth. She believed him. Maybe she'd been waiting forever for someone to find the real Kate.

The kiss was soft and sweet. And then it was not.

A rocket of passion exploded deep within her, filling her body with the sheer need to be claimed by Enrique Mendez. She wanted this man more than she'd ever wanted a man. And that wasn't romance, or lust, or anything other than the honest truth.

She opened her mouth to him and tasted him as she wound her hands round his broad shoulders. His mouth consumed her, hard, unrelenting.

Kate moaned, allowing desire to unwind within her, unfurl within every inch of her body. She reveled in wanting him. Loved the way he felt against her. So hard in all the right ways.

"I can't help it," he murmured against her lips, tilting his head so their foreheads met and their breaths mingled, frosty in the night air. "I've tried to resist you, but I can't. I want you, Kate, even if I'll have you only a little while."

She didn't answer. Merely pressed her lips against his once again. He lifted her against him, sliding her body along his so he could reach the pulse galloping out of control in her neck. Kate held on to him as he tugged at the neck of her sweater.

"Wait," she said, wiggling from his grasp. "You're serious?"

He dropped her to the ground. His chocolate eyes were dilated with desire and clouded with confusion. "Huh?"

Kate looked toward the house. Justus stewed inside. Vera could wander out to the garden for midnight prayer. Rick hadn't talked this through with Kate. This was bigger than mere sex. Kissing was one thing. Taking it to the next level was quite another.

"So you want me to leave?" he said, keeping his arms tight around her. His fingers played with the sensitive flesh beneath her sweater. The cool night air kissed her skin, but the cold didn't seem to reach her. Not with Rick touching her.

"Only if you take me with you," she said, half joking, half fearful he'd leave her standing here in the night wishing she'd kept her damn mouth shut.

His teeth flashed as he lowered his head to nuzzle her neck. "You're right. This is not the right place. I want to see you naked, watch you while I make love to you. I want to kiss every square inch of your body, love every hill, valley and plain."

Kate's insides turned to mush as her libido kicked into high gear.

Then he murmured next to her ear. "If I don't make love to you, I'll never get you out of my blood."

Kate stiffened. "Wait. You think having sex with me will cure you of this thing we have between us?"

He lifted his head. "Maybe. You make me crazy. I don't know how to make it better, but I know the vow I made years ago doesn't matter more to me than being with you."

Kate stepped back from him, ignoring her body as it protested the loss of warmth. She averted her eyes to the black horizon. "Look, I want you more than I've wanted any man. I'm being totally honest with you when I say that. I don't know if it's all this exploration of my past or if it's something more. All I know is that when I'm with you, it feels so…I can't even describe it."

She found his gaze in the darkness. She couldn't read his expression, but she could feel the desire still pulsing between them. "But even though I feel scared—not an emotion I ever admit to feeling to anyone—I want to respect the views you have on relationships. I'm not staying in Oak Stand. And I'm definitely not staying any longer than I have to at Cottonwood. I'm going back to Vegas. And everyone knows long-distance relationships don't work."

Rick's lips pressed into a thin line and it made Kate's heart ache. She couldn't allow him to give up something that made him who he was even though she reveled in how much he wanted her. She didn't want to be his mistake, the decision that would always haunt him.

"You amaze me, woman. So bold on the outside, but inside you're…tender," he murmured as he took her hand into his, cradling it much as he had on the plane. "When I was a boy, my grandmother gave me candies for being good in church. I loved them. They were hard on the outside, but sweet caramel on the inside. They were small, only a taste, but so very good."

He raised her hand and kissed it again, pausing to drop a kiss on the pad of each finger. The heat of his touch mixed with the seduction in his voice was kinky torture.

"Long-distance relationships start well, but don't end as well. That's true. I know you will leave, and I will stay here." He sighed as he imparted those words. "I can't leave this mission of mine. It is above me, and one commitment that I can't put aside."

Kate couldn't stop her shoulders from sinking. She understood. He was a man of honor. His principles trumped his passion.

"Still, I cannot ignore my body or my heart."

Her breath caught in her throat. "Your heart?"

"*Si,* my heart. I care for you, *bruja*. No matter what lies down the road, I will always care for you."

She didn't speak, only watched him. She didn't believe in love, but at that moment, she so wanted to think it could happen to her.

"You're like that candy, Kate. The memory of you will be as sweet."

The way he spoke told her he'd given the subject great thought. He'd weighed it in his mind. This was no rash decision. "I can promise you nothing but myself for the next six days."

"That's all I ask." He took her hand into his and brought her to him.

Kate kissed him, brushing her lips over his. Her heart swelled as she thought about how much he wanted her, how much he cared for her. She was humbled by this man. She turned her head and rested it upon his chest. "You are no longer the man you once were. There is nothing selfish about you, Rick. I've never met a man like you."

He lifted her face to him and placed his lips on hers once again, nibbling before demanding more. He broke the kiss and whispered against her lips. "Thank you."

Her answer was to brush her lips against his. He tasted

good, like all things spicy and forbidden. His tongue darted out to trace her bottom lip ever so slowly, a dance of seduction that took her breath away.

Then sped it up.

He slid his hands down her sides then around her hips, clasping her bottom and tugging her against him. He fit her like a tailored suit. Every seam met where intended. Perfect length, perfect cut. Rick had been designed for loving her.

He groaned against her mouth and took their kiss deeper. She could feel him losing control and thrilled in it. This man did not lose himself often. She would enjoy every minute of watching him surrender to desire.

"Let's go," he whispered, all the while letting his hands wander up her back then down again to her bottom.

She sighed against his mouth before trailing her lips down the side of his neck.

"Kate, we've got to get to my house. Fast."

"Yes, we do." She laughed huskily against his collarbone, before dotting teasing kisses along the hard ridge of his shoulder.

He lifted her up and tossed her over his shoulder.

"Rick!" she squealed.

He slapped her on the butt. "I don't like to be teased."

"Yes, you do."

"Okay, I do." His laughter floated on the crisp breeze. Her cheek bumped against the hardness of his back. She smiled. She felt so different, so not like herself. Three weeks ago she would have thought it uncool to have a guy tote her over his shoulder. So silly to giggle. To be happy. When had her world grown so narrow that she'd given up wanting to feel the way she did now?

And more important, what had changed?

She wasn't certain, but she knew at that moment she was the happiest she'd been in a long time. Rick was hers for a whole week. The possibilities seemed endless. Exciting.

"Hey, put me down." She slapped his bottom. "Though I must say, the view is nice."

"I'll put you down on my bed."

"Okay. That'll work."

Chapter Fifteen

Rick set Kate on the pavers, not caring if anyone saw him toting her around Cottonwood. He felt damn good. The thought of indulging in Kate had his pulse racing. He'd spent every night of the past week thinking about her. How her essence would curl around him, soak into him, as he made love to her. He'd lain awake thinking of her skin beneath his lips and he'd woken in the morning wishing he'd been able to live his dreams of loving Kate.

And the daytime wasn't much better. His body craved her touch. He wanted her so badly he felt like an addict. He'd break out in spontaneous sweats and once his hands had actually trembled. He'd had to thrust them into his back pockets to keep from sweeping her into his arms and covering her in kisses.

He called her *bruja* as a joke, but it was no laughing matter. Kate had bewitched him body and soul.

And that had made him think. About his vow and why he still clung to it. Was he the same punk-ass banger he'd been when he'd made that decision? No. The vow had been fulfilled. He was not the man he used to be. In fact, he'd gotten so far away from that man that he couldn't relate to the guys at the center. No, Rick Mendez had been different for a long time.

So he made the conscious decision to let the vow go.

To take the days he had left with Kate and enjoy them rather than suppress every impulse he had to grab hold of her and make her his.

Kate took his hand and smiled at him. She was so damn pretty. So vibrant. So much a part of his life already.

They walked to where his car was parked.

"Rick!" The door flew open and Vera's voice cracked the night. "Rick!"

He dropped Kate's hand and broke into a run toward Vera. Her voice told the story. Something was wrong. Very wrong.

"Oh, Rick, help! Something's wrong with Justus. I can't wake him!"

Wicked thoughts vanished as fear struck him. Justus had been upset at dinner. His color had been off. Why hadn't Rick seen what was right before him? Of course, he knew the answer. He hadn't been thinking with his head. He'd been thinking with a part much lower.

Vera grabbed his arm as he reached the porch and pulled him inside. "Oh, God, Rick. I think it's another stroke. He's unresponsive. He won't talk to me."

He pushed past Vera, and before rounding the corner, he turned to Kate. "Call for help and stay with Vera."

He left both women and pounded up the stairs, wary of what he might find.

Kate reached the porch in time to catch Vera before she collapsed with a sob. "Oh, no. No. I can't bear it."

Kate didn't know what to do. Her emotions had swung from happy to fearful, and Vera's crying didn't help. She dragged Vera to a kitchen bar stool and looked for Rosa, but Rick's grandmother had left for the night.

"Sit down and get hold of yourself, Vera."

The woman merely cried harder.

"Oh, for heaven's sake. You're a strong Southern woman. Start acting like it. Justus doesn't need you falling apart on him, so snap out of it, sister."

Kate slid her cell phone from her pocket and dialed 911. She gave the dispatcher as much information as she could before hanging up. She sat with Vera as the woman tried to reign in her emotions.

Finally, she wiped her eyes and straightened. "I'm strong."

"That a girl," Kate said, patting her stepmother's leg before jogging to the front door. It was a long jog. The house was too damned big. She yelled up the curved stairway, "I called 911. They'll be here soon."

Rick's head emerged. "Thanks. I'm bringing him down. Meet me at the elevator."

Kate glanced at the drive and saw the pulse of the ambulance lights in the distance. The low keen of the siren told her they were still on the county highway but getting closer.

The elevator car clanged into place, chiming as the doors slid open. Rick rolled the chair forward, carefully keeping one hand on Justus's shoulder as if he were comforting the man.

Her father looked horrible. His skin was pasty, making the partial paralysis of his face look more pronounced. A line of drool had formed a path from his mouth to the rigid collar of his pearl snap cowboy shirt. At that moment, pity and shame tumbled loose, smacking into her like a rock slide.

Had she been the cause of this?

Had her harsh words at the dinner table pushed him over the edge? The past week had been more than stressful. He'd gotten his wish—Kate had stayed at Cottonwood—but she hadn't made the stay easy. She'd been stubborn and testy at every turn, and though she'd made progress with Vera and had gotten to know her late half brother, she'd turned her back on any opportunity to interact with the man who'd fathered her.

Guilt pooled in her stomach, rising up, threatening to choke her.

Shit. She shouldn't have been so darned hard on him.

"Okay, Justus. Hold tight. The ambulance just pulled into the drive. I can see the lights from here," Rick said, maneuvering the chair Justus usually operated with his left hand.

To prove his point, the doorbell sounded.

"I'll get it," Kate called, leaping into action and skidding toward the front door, nearly crashing into the Remington sculpture planted right in the middle of the foyer.

She threw the door open. "In here. Hurry."

The paramedics bustled inside toting a bright yellow gurney and several medical canvas bags no doubt full of lifesaving paraphernalia. She hung back as one paramedic whipped out a clipboard and started asking Rick questions. The other bent over Justus and started taking his vitals. Kate clung to the doorknob, glad she had something to hold on to.

Vera appeared at Justus's side. The woman had run a comb through her hair, swiped a dash of lipstick across her lips and pulled on a velour jacket. Her expression was determined as she nudged Rick back and took her place beside her husband. The dampness in her eyes had disappeared, replaced with the starch of a true Southern belle.

Kate watched the paramedics lift Justus onto the gurney as carefully as if they balanced a serving tray of the finest crystal. After securing him, they rolled her way.

Kate caught Justus's eyes as he went past. Those eyes, so like her own, reflected sheer terror. He tried to say something as they lifted the gurney to clear the jamb. She stood stock-still, watching as they rolled the only blood relative she had from the mansion.

Justus struggled to speak again. "Ahhh...m...sah. Ahhhm sa...wee."

Kate pressed her hand to her mouth.

Dear God. Her heart squeezed so tight and hard that she could physically feel the intensity of it. She dropped her hand to her chest and tried not to cry.

Vera passed her, not looking her way at all. Did the woman blame her? Was she angry over Kate's reaction in the kitchen? Or was her mind wrapped around the fact that her husband might be dying?

Kate didn't know. Didn't have time enough to think about what needed to be said or done. Before she could move, the paramedics had loaded Justus into the ambulance and sped down the long drive.

I'm sorry.

Justus's words echoed and her head dropped forward as Rick's well-worn sneakers came into view.

"Kate?" His voice was soft, almost tentative. Not like him. But he seemed to know the emotion rollicking in her belly.

"What?"

"This isn't your fault." He placed his hands on her shoulders before sliding them down to cup her upper arms.

A single tear fell upon the mottled marble below. "I know."

He folded her into his arms. "No, you don't."

"I've screwed up, Rick. I messed this whole thing up. I so suck." She whispered this into the softness of his T-shirt. It was a muddy brown color and washed into softness. The front read Turkey Trot 2008. It was an absurd name for a five-k run. She didn't know why he wore it, other than it looked amazing stretched across his wide torso.

"You don't suck," he murmured against her curls, stroking her back. "This whole thing has gotten out of control. Justus, Vera, you and me."

Kate was silent, allowing Rick to shelter her in his arms. There was nothing left to say, no easy fix. "I should go to the hospital."

"Of course."

She looked at him. He seemed so grave. "I'm sorry about…you know…the other thing. About not going to your house."

He tried to smile. "Maybe it's best this way."

Pain zapped her right in the gut. She didn't want him to say they would have been a mistake, even if it were true. It hurt. She'd wanted to have that part of him, to

gather together the memory of his taste, smell, touch—
things to treasure in the empty days ahead of her. That
was how she now saw her life in Vegas—empty. Nothing was supposed to change. This two-week pause had
pivoted her into a new direction, one that had her looking hard at her old lifestyle and wondering what was so
terrific about it.

How had everything changed in only days?

But she had changed, and part of her was angry as hell
that coming to Oak Stand had caused it.

"Yes, you're right, of course." Her words were hollow.
She didn't believe them.

"Okay, let's get to the hospital."

Kate nodded and pulled herself from the sanctuary
of his arms. Life wasn't fair sometimes. And Kate was
getting rather tired of coming out on the short end of
the stick.

Nellie met them at the hospital in Longview, the nearest facility with emergency services. The place had a
smell that could only be labeled as death. Despite the ad-
mirable efforts of disinfectant and urine, nothing could
cover the scent.

"Oh, Kate," Nellie said, grabbing her and spinning her
into a hug. Nellie had seven inches on her, so Kate had
no choice in the matter. "Rick called me. How bad is it?"

"He's stable," Rick answered, something Kate didn't
appreciate. She didn't need a man to speak for her or
call her best friend, as if Kate couldn't handle herself.
"but they're worried about further damage to his organs.
Seems they don't always know the severity of the stroke
until several hours pass. Right now his body is still en-

gaging in small strokes, though they've given him medication to prevent that. He's having tests as we speak."

Kate looked at her friend. "Yeah, what he said."

Nellie's green eyes glinted. Even in such a grave situation, she knew Kate, and she knew Kate hated to be grandstanded by a man.

Rick issued a clipped "Sorry," before heading to triage, where Vera had left her jacket. He obviously figured out that she was aggravated. He was intuitive that way.

Nellie and Kate stood alone.

"Are you okay?" Nellie asked, tugging her away from the curtained bay where Vera sat waiting for the staff to bring Justus from the CAT scan.

"Yeah." Kate shrugged. "Sure. I'm dandy. The man I decide to blackmail just had a heart attack or stroke or something, and I'm fit as a filly."

"Come on, Kate," Nellie said, easing her friend into a plastic bucket chair. "You know this has nothing to do with you."

Kate shrugged. "God, Nell, everything is so screwed up. What am I doing?"

Her friend smiled. "I've asked myself that question about you for most of my life. Never could answer it."

Kate gave a harsh laugh. "I can't keep anything under control—my finances, my personal life, nothing. I can't even believe I'm admitting to being weak, but, shit, I am. Me. I'm falling apart. That's not supposed to happen."

"It happens to the best of us, Kate. You opened a can of worms when you wrote that letter demanding money. That gets icky."

She looked at Nellie. "No, shit."

"But the upside is that you're finally dealing with your past. You've needed to do that for a long time."

"Why?" Kate stomped her foot like a petulant child. "A month ago everything was good. I was an almost-successful business owner whose only sin was dressing too outlandishly, spending too much money and killing the occasional houseplant. My life was platinum. Now it's, like, crappy tin or something."

Nellie laughed but still shook her head. "Maybe, but you've been avoiding dealing with yourself for a long time. Coming home is about more than Justus. Or Rick."

Kate's head snapped up on its own volition. "Rick?"

"I'm no dummy. I have eyes. And this guy is different from any of the others. You're not keeping him at arm's length."

"He doesn't seem to let me. He's always there whether I need him or not," she groused, rubbing at a pull in her sweater. "And for some reason I don't want to keep him away."

Nellie smiled.

"Don't do that."

"Sorry, but you've always had a bad attitude about falling in love. Almost as bad as the attitude you have about Oak Stand," Nellie said. Her green eyes shot to Rick as he stepped into the bay where Vera sat waiting for word on Justus.

"Well, yeah. Every time I come back I'm reminded of who I am. Or more like who I'm not. I'm no founding father's great-great-granddaughter. I'm trailer trash, remember?"

"Oh, please. This again? Let me get out my hammer so I can hack away at that enormous chip on your shoulder. Screw that, I need a jackhammer."

"Easy for you to say, Nell. You weren't the resident charity case." Kate felt her ire grow. It was bad enough she sat in a cracked hospital chair wearing a cheap sweater while lusting after the only man who made her so crazy she'd thrown herself at him to no avail. It was bad enough she'd blackmailed her biological father into another stroke and made Vera cry so many tears she'd needed a hydration IV, but Nellie had to lump in her dissatisfaction with Oak Stand, too.

Give a girl a break.

"You weren't charity, Kate. The people in this town loved you. Why can't you see that?"

She blinked at Nellie. "Did you swipe pills from behind the nurses' desk? Are you hallucinating? People in this town don't think much of me. Get real."

"You are so full of crap, Kate Newman. This town loved you. Still loves you. Did you think people took care of you and your grandmother because they didn't care? Don't you think they knew your mother had left you to go off with some other man? And that the man who'd fathered you had turned his back on you?"

"Exactly. Charity."

Nellie shook her head, her disgust obvious. "You look at it from your point of view, not from the people who loved you. Listen. Do you really think the dress that fit you perfectly showed up in the thrift shop two weeks before prom by accident?"

"Huh?"

"Betty Monk ordered that for you based on the one you circled in that damn teen prom magazine. Think she did that because she didn't like you?"

Kate felt her heart tighten. "What?"

"And remember that trip we took with the church? The one where they suddenly had a spot open? You think that wasn't planned by the Ladies Auxiliary for months? And that time you got sick and had to go to the hospital? Dr. Grabel helped pay the bill. He gave you more than suckers, Kate. Left and right, the people of Oak Stand loved you, even when you acted like a bitch."

Nellie rose, pulling her purse onto her arm. "I swear, if I didn't love you so much and if you weren't in this mess, I'd kick your butt up between your shoulder blades."

"Nell—"

Her friend lifted a hand. "Don't. Just know this. Betty Monk used to always say 'It takes a town to raise a child.' And she said that long before Hillary Clinton did. And she meant you."

Nellie didn't wait for Kate to reply, she stomped down the hall, never looking back.

At that moment, Kate hated Nellie. Hated her friend for being so damned brutally honest at a time she needed someone to lie to her. She needed someone to tell her everything was going to be okay.

The curtain to the bay opened and Rick stuck his head out. He was checking on her.

Kate bowed her head into her hands.

Chapter Sixteen

Rick watched Kate with a feeling of trepidation. Kate's head was bowed and Nellie had left. His Kate looked so forlorn sitting by herself. When her gaze met his, he saw the raw emotion and despair. Things were starting to come unraveled, and there wasn't a damned thing he could do about it.

Destiny twined about Kate, wrapping her in its embrace, chipping away at the protection she'd built around herself.

He felt the same pull. He had known from the moment he'd first laid eyes on her in Vegas that it was inevitable he'd get tangled in Kate. Something had propelled him to her, and he'd been helpless to stop it.

Perhaps the incident with Justus had been part of destiny's plan, a nudge to remind Rick he was not in control. None of them were. Hadn't he seen that firsthand? His plans, promises and vows had twisted and turned upon themselves. He was no longer centered. The gang members resented him, Kate hovered out of his grasp and now Justus lay fighting for his life.

It made him want to hit someone. Equally strong was the longing to wrap his arms around her and love her for all she was worth.

Life was contradictory sometimes.

"You think he'll be okay, Rick?"

Vera's words cut through his distraction. He should be thinking of Justus. "I don't know."

Vera pressed her lips together and stared at a sign that demonstrated what to do if someone were choking. She looked as if she might need the procedure herself. But then she literally shook herself, and her eyes grew determined. "He will be okay. He has to."

He wondered if it might be better for Justus if he succumbed to the stroke this time. The man had been through so much. Rick didn't know how much more Justus's body could take. But the old man was a fighter. No way he'd leave this life easily. "You may be right. He's a tough old bird."

As he reached out to take Vera's hand, a nurse stuck her head through the curtain. "Mrs. Mitchell?"

"Yes?" There was a hint of misgiving in Vera's response.

"I have some forms for you to fill out. I know it's not the best time, but it will hasten the process in moving Mr. Mitchell to Dallas if need be. Do you mind coming with me for a moment?"

Vera cast a glance at Rick. He nodded. "I'll stay and wait. Go ahead."

She gathered her things and followed the nurse toward

the admitting desk. Before she disappeared, she asked. "You have my cell number?"

He gave her a reassuring nod. "Of course."

Then he was alone with his thoughts. Not a good place to be. Not when the person who dominated so many of them sat just down the hallway. Alone. He should go to her, but knew she needed a moment to gather herself. His instincts about Kate came naturally. He got her in a way no one else did.

Man, he was screwed.

Because he knew he'd fallen hard for Kate. Ton-of-bricks hard. No way around it.

"Hey."

The object of his affection poked her head around the curtain. She looked as though she'd been kicked. Her hair stuck to her head in a couple of places, mascara was smudged beneath her hauntingly beautiful eyes and her normally stylish clothes were wrinkled.

"Hey, yourself," he said, sitting back and crossing his foot over his thigh. "No word yet."

"Oh," she said as she stepped inside the bay. "Where's Vera?"

"She went to fill out some paperwork. They may not admit him. They may transfer him to Dallas instead."

A different nurse appeared outside the curtain and looked at Kate. "Mrs. Mitchell?"

"No." She shook her head. "She's—"

"Down the hall," Rick finished for her, mentally kicking himself. He could tell it had bothered Kate when he'd answered for her with Nellie. He glanced her way. She didn't seem to care this time. The life seemed to have been sucked right out of her.

"Oh, well." The nurse hovered, hesitant.

"But I'm his daughter," Kate said. She bit her lower lip and he couldn't tell if she was nervous, or regretted admitting the fact for the first time in a very public way.

"Okay." The nurse smiled at Kate. "We're going to admit Mr. Mitchell for the night and make sure he's stable. They're taking him to intensive care as we speak. You can go up. Visiting hours will be over in fifteen minutes, but you might catch a moment with him."

"Go check on him, Kate. I'll get Vera," Rick said, rising.

Kate's brow furrowed. "Maybe I should find Vera and you can go up."

The nurse patted her shoulder. "Don't worry. He'll likely be sleeping. They've given him a sedative."

He couldn't tell what she was thinking. Maybe no one ever knew what she was thinking. Kate, the enigma.

She looked at him. "Come when you find Vera."

He nodded as the nurse disappeared.

They were alone. He moved toward her, brushing her hair from her forehead. "Are you sure you're okay?"

Her gaze moved from his. "Sure. I'm dandy."

He pressed her to him, tucking her head beneath his chin, wrapping her in his arms. She felt so good there. So right. "It will be okay, Kate."

She relaxed against him. "I don't think so."

He tilted her chin so she was forced to meet his gaze. Tears shimmered in their blue depths. "It will."

She blinked. "No, it's about as bad as it can get. My best friend is pissed at me. Vera's ignoring me. My father had a stroke because I acted like a shit. And, you, well, you make me confused and comforted and happy and scared all at the same time. Life is pretty much sucking right now."

He gathered her to him again. "It could be worse."

She nodded against his chest, wrapping her small arms about him and squeezing. "Yeah, I could be living in Oak Stand working at the Curlique for peanuts. Be fat and pregnant. Or on the Junior League board."

He sighed against hair that vaguely smelled like coconut. "Funny—what sounds good to me sounds like hell to you."

She snorted. "You obviously haven't met the Junior League."

"Oh, I've met them. Some of them have a secret desire to dabble with a tatted up bad boy. Not so different from you."

"I want to do more than dabble with you."

"Do you?"

Kate looked up at him. "I think so. But I can't, can I?"

She slid from his embrace, leaving him with questions and a small burgeoning of hope.

Kate walked through the doors of the intensive care unit like someone walking her last few yards. She didn't want to face what was left of the man who'd sired her. But how could she not?

She couldn't tuck her tail and run. Not after she'd played a part in putting him here. So she pushed through the heavy doors that guarded the gravely ill and looked for a nurse.

"Excuse me." She noticed a flash of blue scrubs behind the curved nurses' desk. A petite woman with braided hair popped up from where she'd been digging in a drawer.

"Yes?"

"A nurse downstairs told me they'd brought, uh, my father here. Justus Mitchell."

The woman dropped the chart she had in her hand onto the cluttered counter. "You've only got—" she looked at her watch "—ten minutes." She swept her hand toward the row of small rooms adjacent to the nurses' desk. "He's in number five."

Kate hesitated.

"Well, come on." The nurse shook her beaded corn-rows. "You got to pick up your feet, child."

She followed the nurse to the room that beeped with equipment. The nurse shifted a tray out of the way. "Don't mind the machines. They beep all the time."

"Oh," was all Kate could manage. Her gaze was rooted to the man in the bed. He looked fragile. Small. Insignificant. So unlike any way she'd ever seen him.

"Ten minutes. That's all." Then the nurse left Kate alone with her father.

Kate didn't know what to do. A lone chair was in the corner. Perhaps she should sit and wait on Vera. She sat, but it didn't feel right. She was too far from the bed. Wasn't it good for the sick to know someone was close by?

She pulled the chair across the floor, wincing as it scraped against the shiny waxed tiles. She parked it in front of the blood pressure monitor and resumed her seat.

Justus stirred.

Tentatively, she reached out and patted his arm. It felt awkward, but she did it anyway. She was lame at giving comfort, but she owed it to him.

He opened his eyes and stared at her.

Kate drew back. She could tell he didn't recognize her.

He groaned, swiping at the oxygen tube over his nose.

It registered with Kate as she swatted his hand that he could at least move that part of his body.

"Don't," she said. "Leave that. It's helping you."

He made one more attempt at removing the tube before dropping his hand onto his chest.

"Good. That's good," she said, using a voice she might use with little Mae.

"Katie?" he said, quite plainly.

"Oh," she responded, tucking his hand beneath the sheet and giving it a pat. "You recognize me."

He didn't say anything, just watched her as she settled into the chair. Sitting with a man she half hated as he lay helpless in the bed was uncomfortable, to stay the least.

Several seconds ticked off the clock on the wall before she could look back at him.

"Katie," he said again.

"What?"

"I—I—" Huge coughs racked his body. He pulled his arm from beneath the covers and grabbed her hand.

"Let me get you some water," she said, pulling her hand from his and searching for one of those little plastic pitchers they kept in hospital rooms. She didn't see even a cup. "Let me get the—"

"No," he barked between coughs. "I've got to—"

"Don't be stubborn. You're ill." Kate started for the open doorway. Surely that nurse could hear him.

The nurse met her at the door. She held a pitcher. She ignored Kate as she slid into the room.

"Awake, Mr. Mitchell?"

Kate wanted to tell her she was the queen of the obvious, but figured the nurse wasn't the kind to fancy a smart-ass.

"Katie," Justus said again, between gasps.

"Don't worry about the girl right now. She's over there. Take a little sip of this." The nurse placed a bendy straw between Justus's cracked lips. He sucked at the straw like a dying man. Then it struck Kate. What if he was dying? What if he didn't recover?

"There now. Not too much, Mr. Mitchell," the nurse said, removing the cup and placing it on the rolling table. She looked at Kate. "He can have another sip if he needs it, but let's not give him too much. I don't want him getting sick."

Kate nodded but said nothing as the nurse walked out.

Where the hell were Vera and Rick?

Justus blinked at her.

She had nothing better to do than sit down and wait, so she did. She tried not to focus on Justus, but she couldn't get away from him. She could hear him breathing, smell the Aramis cologne, feel his presence surround her even as silence descended upon her like a shroud.

"Katie."

She finally met his eyes. Fell into them. The pain there, the pleading.

"I need to tell you—"

She lifted a hand and patted the shoulder beneath the worn hospital gown. "You don't need to talk. You need to rest. Vera will be here in a moment."

He shook his head. Irritation evident in his eyes. Oddly, it made her feel better.

"No Vera. Need to talk to you." His words were labored, but he looked damned determined.

"I—" she started then snapped her mouth shut. She couldn't stop him. He'd say what he had to say. But part of her didn't want to hear it. Didn't want him to take away the anger, the part of her that made her Kate Newman. She didn't want to revert to being Katie. But this had been his intention all along. This was what her coming to Texas was about. Justus had regrets. About her.

He wanted forgiveness, and she wasn't sure she could give it to him. She thought about Nellie's words how the people of Oak Stand loved her. Kate had been wrong about them. Could she have been wrong about Justus?

She'd been a child. Had she seen only what she wanted to see?

"Okay. Tell me what you need to tell me."

It took several moments before Justus began to speak. "I'm sorry for—" he passed his good hand over his eyes "—that day."

Kate felt like she'd been thrown from a car with each one of his carefully articulated words. She hadn't expected him to pull no punches right out of the gate. "Oh."

"I was wrong." His words fell on her, heavy, sorrowful and Kate's memory tumbled back to *the day*.

It was the day she'd replayed in her mind for years. The day he'd taken away her childhood, balling it into a wad and tossing it into a corner like a broken toy. It was the day she'd started hating him.

And he'd deserved it.

Chapter Seventeen

Kate was nine years old the afternoon her mother packed her bags. Not once as she'd tossed her cheap clothes and cheaper jewelry in an old suitcase had she bothered to look at Kate where she sat on the woven couch with the stained arms and missing buttons. Hadn't bothered to offer anything other than "I deserve better than this life." Hadn't bothered to admit she was being the most irresponsible of women, leaving her child with her mother, choosing a man over the little girl she'd given life to.

Kate had watched her mother throw her suitcase into the trunk of the slimy insurance agent's car, heading for a new job in Southern California. Her mother's promises of the beach and Disneyland rang in Kate's ears. She knew her mother lied. Kate would never spin in teacups or dip her toe in the Pacific—at least not with her mom. Her mother had driven out of the trailer park with a toot and a wave. Kate climbed onto her pink bike, the one with the cool water bottle Santa had brought her for Christmas, and pedaled toward Cottonwood.

If her mother didn't want her, her father would.

She was a good kid. She could do long division and climb trees all the way to the top. She didn't eat much and her long hair looked like an Indian princess's when she braided it. She could make her own bed, fold her own clothes and knew how to make grilled cheese sandwiches and peanut-butter cookies. He'd love having her in that big house, even if he was married to someone else.

She'd taken her time getting there. After all, she needed to study this new world she'd be entering. Cows stood around munching on grass. She didn't know much about cows, but she could learn. Her real father had lots of cows and lots of oil wells. She didn't know much about oil, either, except people used it to run their cars and lawn mowers.

By the time she'd reached the gates of Cottonwood, she'd drank all the water she'd put in her water bottle and had to go to the bathroom really bad. When she finally made it up the long drive, she saw a lot of cars in the yard adjacent to the huge white house. Cadillacs, Mercedes and Beemers—all the cars her mother drooled over in the TV ads. Around the back of the house was a white tent with big signs. She'd seen the signs all over town. They were for the governor's race.

Kate dropped her bike beneath a willow tree and pulled off her backpack. Her back was sweaty and her hair had come out of her braid on one side of her head. Grams had brought home leftover French fries from the diner for lunch and Kate had dropped ketchup on her shirt, but it didn't look too bad. Plus, her jeans were practically new and her knockoff Keds were clean and bright.

She smoothed her hair behind her ears and walked toward the people talking and holding glasses that sparkled in the light. They wore pretty clothes like the people on soap operas. She didn't see her father.

She knew what he looked like. He drove through town in his convertible sports car sometimes. He wasn't young, but he wasn't too old. He always wore a cowboy hat and his laugh was really loud. Her mother said he was a force to be reckoned with. Kate didn't know what that meant, but he had to love her. She was his kid.

She wove through the crowd, accidently stepping on one lady's high-heeled shoes. Some people looked at her funny, probably because there weren't any other kids here. She ducked under a man's arm and there he stood. Her father.

He wore dark pants and a light-colored cowboy shirt. A big straw hat perched atop his head. A broad forehead stretched above his brilliant blue eyes. Eyes just like hers. People gathered around him, smiling and nodding as he said something. Probably told a funny story. Kate smiled. He was handsome and rich. And he belonged to her now.

She threw back her shoulders and ran to him.

"Daddy," she called, her shoes slapping the temporary floor beneath the tent. "Momma's gone, so I have to live with you now."

He paused, the drink in his hand halfway to his mouth, and stared at her. His face looked the same way Grams did when a roach crawled across the floor in their cramped kitchen. Like he wanted to squash her.

She stopped about ten feet away from him.

All the people who were talking to him looked at her. It grew very quiet.

Her father set his glass on a nearby table. "Who let you in here?"

Kate could feel the butterflies in her tummy thrash around. Something was wrong. Didn't he know her? He'd sent her a bunny last Easter. Sent it home with her mom. Momma said he thought she was pretty. That he loved her. He was just too busy and important to mess with her.

"I—I— My mom left and went to California. I have to live with you now since you're my dad." Her voice trembled. She didn't want to cry. She had to go to the bathroom real bad and he was supposed to be happy his little girl had come to live with him.

"Who sent you here?"

"I— No one. I just came."

Everybody was watching her. One woman giggled behind her hand. Her fingernails were long and painted shimmery pink. Kate looked at all the adults. They seemed confused and embarrassed.

Her daddy looked mad. "Well, you can go back to where you came from. No one asked you to come here, girl."

Kate grabbed her stomach because it hurt, like the time Tommy Tidwell had kicked her during recess. "But—"

"Don't you argue with me, missy. Turn right around and leave. Right now."

Kate took a step backward. Then another. She couldn't believe it. He was mad at her. "Don't you want me?"

His eyes got all cold and icy looking. "I have a wife and son. You are not my child. I don't know who gave you the idea that you belonged to me, but you don't."

He pushed through the crowd. "Excuse me, Governor, while I deal with this, will you? I'll return in a moment."

His grip was steel on her arm. He dragged her through the crowd, avoiding their eyes but never loosening his grasp on her. She felt her sneakers slide a few times on the grass. Finally, they were beneath the willow tree where she'd left her backpack and bike.

He released her. "Get back on that bike and get off my property. You have embarrassed me in front of the most powerful people in Texas, girl."

"But my momma told me—"

"I don't care what that woman told you. You don't belong to me."

His words felt like bullets whizzing through her body. They hurt and made her feel like she might sink down and die. Tears streamed down her cheeks, she couldn't stop them. They dripped from her chin as she picked up the handlebars of her bike.

She glanced once more at the man. His face was red like he'd been working in the sun. His eyes looked weird.

"You will never belong to me," he said.

Kate slid onto her bike and pedaled away as fast as she could down that hard-packed drive. She imagined that she was escaping from a bad man. A boogey monster. She pedaled until her legs burned, right out the gate, all the way down the county road until she couldn't see that big white house anymore. Then she jumped off her bike and ran. Ran till her lungs burned. Ran till she couldn't run anymore. At some point, she realized that she'd peed on herself. Her legs were wet and her new tennis shoes squished as she ran. But she didn't care. Nothing mattered anymore.

She finally collapsed near an old wooden fence that

had been nearly eaten through with termites and lay beneath the brilliant blue sky.

She'd left her backpack. It had her opal ring and fairy journal in it. It also had the bunny he'd given her. And the picture of Justus and her mom at the state fair in Dallas, the one where her mother's hair looked like the girl from *I Dream of Jeannie*. All her good stuff had been in there. And now it was gone.

He'd probably throw it away like it was junk. Just like he'd thrown her away.

She hated him.

She'd always hate him.

The erratic beeping of the heart monitor pulled Kate from the memory into the present.

That same man lay before her, broken and weak.

She met his eyes once again. He'd killed part of her that April day. Taken away her innocence and made her hard. Made her rebellious. Determined. Guarded. Everything that constituted who she now was.

She'd lost her mother, her father and her dreams that day.

But she'd forged new ones. Ones that she still clung to. Dreams of Fantabulous. And independence. Dreams that felt cloudier by the day. Who was she if she didn't have her anger to protect her?

She looked away.

"I'm sorry," he said again. "I shouldn't have done what I did. I hurt you."

Anger boiled inside her. Even as he lay so vulnerable and sick, she wanted to hurt him. Make him pay for the act he'd perpetrated on a nine-year-old girl.

At the same time, as much as she longed to hold on to that kernel of hate, she wondered if perhaps it was time to let it go. To let the resentment slip into the past and take the hurt with it. Then, perhaps, she'd have room in her heart for better things. Things like faith, hope and charity.

Rick's image appeared.

And maybe she'd have room to fall in love.

"Yes, you did hurt me. I was young. I didn't realize the way the world worked." Kate sighed, finally glancing at him.

"I—I was a bastard. Mean. I hurt you out of pride. Damned pride." She could hear the disgust in his voice and wondered how long he'd felt that way.

Kate pressed her fingers into her eyes. She was tired of crying, but when she pulled her hands away, they were wet. "I shouldn't have gone to Cottonwood that day. I didn't know. I thought…" Hell, did it matter anymore? Was she any different than any other kid who'd been unwanted by a parent?

A choking noise came from Justus. She jumped up to fetch a cup of water, but his good hand caught her and pressed her into the chair. For someone who'd suffered another stroke, his grip was firm. Her eyes jerked from his hand to his face.

He was crying.

"I tried to forget about you. Tried to pretend you weren't my kid. But the wee hours of morning bring truth when they bring the sun. You can't hide from your mistakes at dawn." Tears slid down his weathered cheeks and dropped onto the sheet. He made no attempt to brush them away. His good hand was on her arm, gripping her the way he'd done the day he'd dragged her toward that pink bike beneath the weeping willow.

"I'm so very sorry, Katie. You were just a little girl.

A little girl who wanted to be loved. I still see your face. See how hurt you were. It haunts me."

His words surrounded her, settling around her shoulders, pressing her down. And as the regret in his voice penetrated her heart, a flood of sadness, anger, need came gushing forth. "So why did you wait? Why did you ignore me all these years?"

His eyes shuttered. "I'm a fool. I didn't want to face you. I was about as ashamed as a man can be. And I was scared you wouldn't talk to me. When your letter came, I—" He paused. "I couldn't ignore what I needed to do."

She dropped her head. "It feels too late, Justus."

"No, don't say that. It's not too late for forgiveness. Even Jesus forgave while nailed to the cross. Please, Katie. I'm a foolish, unworthy man."

A sob rose in her throat, overpowering her. She let it loose. Let the storm that had gathered inside her for over twenty years come forth. Her body fell forward onto the bed as she shook with the emotion he'd unleashed within her.

And in that small room surrounded by the machines that monitored her father's vital statistics, Kate cried like she'd never cried…not since the day her father had denied her in front of a crowd of Texas's most influential. All the frustration, loneliness and hurt spilled out onto hospital sheets that smelled of bleach.

She cried until her nose ran and her head throbbed. At some point, she realized her father stroked her head soothingly.

"Shh, my Katie, shh," he said, his voice still heavy with the tears he'd cried.

But Kate couldn't stop. The emotion flooded her again

and again until finally she stilled beneath his hand, exhausted and replete.

"It's okay, Katie," he said, patting her head in an awkward manner. "It's okay."

She lifted her head and looked at him square in the eye. "I forgive you."

And as she said the words, she meant them.

No more hanging on to the hurt of the past. No more hating Ryan because he'd had what she didn't. No more hating Vera because she'd stolen her mother's dream. No more hating her mother for being so weak. No more hating Oak Stand. Kate was just plain tired of being so angry about her past. It was time to let it all go.

Her father's hand slid to hers and he gave it a squeeze. She watched as his eyes closed and his face grew slack. His breathing rose slow and steady. He looked at peace.

And he was very much asleep.

Kate removed her hand from his and wiped her eyes. She turned toward the table for a tissue to mop her face, and that's when she saw them out of the corner of her eye.

Rick and Vera stood in the doorway.

Vera had tears streaming down her face, and the man who'd stood beside her over the past week had suspicious moisture glinting in his own brown eyes.

No words were said.

Vera simply held out her arms.

Kate didn't think twice. She rose, took three steps and fell into them. Vera wrapped her arms around her and held her, murmuring soothing endearments into her hair as she stroked her back.

Kate didn't bother to think about the fact that Vera was mad at her. Or the fact that visiting hours were over and the no-nonsense nurse had her arms crossed and foot tapping.

She let her father's wife hold her.

Because Kate thought that she might have finally found a family.

Chapter Eighteen

Rick's car ate up the highway as they traveled back to Cottonwood. It was two o'clock in the morning. Kate was utterly exhausted, yet, at the same, tingling from the enormity of what had occurred.

She stifled a yawn and glanced in the little mirror clipped to the sun visor. Yikes. She barely recognized the person staring back. Her eyes were swollen from the crying, her nose red as Rudolph's and her hair vaguely resembled a dust mop. Outwardly, Kate was a mess.

But inside, she was as still as a pond in August.

It felt good to rid herself of the turbulent emotion that had rocked so steadily inside her for so many years. She looked over at Rick, at the way the light played on the hollows and planes of his face, and her heart moved in her chest.

And that was a first for her.

She'd always figured the heart that she'd protected for so long had shrunk until it was a wizened little seed like the ones they'd planted at the center. But now it had awakened and throbbed within her. Aching and tenderly new.

She didn't say anything. Just slid her hand beneath the one Rick rested on the gearshift.

He looked at her.

The air crackled and the mood changed.

No sorrow or tears. Only potential.

"I've got to go by the center and check on things. I called the doc and he stayed for a while. Said he was making headway."

"Good. That's good." She studied his face again. What did he want? Where could they go from here?

"Do you want to go home with me?" His words were quietly spoken.

"So I won't be alone?"

A smile touched his lips. "Yeah, that, too, I guess."

Kate paused. Did she really want this? Her body did, had already reacted to his words, tightening and anticipating. But she didn't have the luxury of being impulsive with Rick. He was too important to her. "I thought we'd agreed it would be a mistake."

He nodded. "I know, but like everything with you, Kate, I can't fight myself. I can't let you slip through my fingers and not grab hold of some piece of you. That feeling hasn't changed."

He tore his eyes from the lonely road and looked at her. His dark eyes were almost mystical. "You'll go back to Vegas, but I want the memory of your skin on my lips. The memory of your smell, the sounds you make when you come, the feel of your hands on my body. I'll keep those memories."

"What if you hate me afterward?"

Another little smile. "I could never hate someone as incredible as you, Kate."

She worried her lip as she turned her head and looked out the window. He'd once said she used sex to gain control. Was she doing that again? Trying to recapture herself after pouring everything out in that hospital room? Reestablishing what she'd always been so that she didn't have to deal with the woman she'd become? A woman who could forgive and maybe love.

She wasn't sure.

She hadn't been sure about anything since she'd left Vegas…was it only a little over a week ago? Seemed impossible she'd experienced all she had in the course of such a short time. But there was one thing that was certain, and that, too, hadn't changed since Vegas. She wanted Rick. Body and soul. And that scared her so badly she didn't want to think about it.

"Rick?"

He tightened his grip on her hand. "Yeah, babe?"

Could there ever be a future for them? She couldn't believe she even batted around the thought of commitment. It had been her long-established belief that love was for other people. Not her. Was she contemplating letting herself go there? Long-distance relationships were hard for even the most stable of couples. *Stable* and *Kate* were never used in the same sentence. "Never mind."

His hand tightened on hers. "Stop overanalyzing. Tonight we won't think. We've done too much of it. No mulling, debating or talking ourselves out of it. Tonight we do. Even if in the light of day, it seems certifiable."

"No regrets?"

He shook his head. "I'm not a selfish boy anymore,

remember? This is not about fulfilling a need, this is about being with you."

Her heart swelled and contracted. She nodded because tonight was different, almost magical, like destiny was at work again, binding them together.

His thumb stroked her hand in small circles. This time it did not soothe, it stirred.

Moments later, they entered the drive to Phoenix. The lights blazed in the house. There was life there now and it made Kate's heart glad to know the guys within were on the same path she'd walked. Letting go, nourishing their hearts with forgiveness, growing, becoming something they'd never thought possible.

"Wait here. Won't take but a moment."

So she did. And she didn't think about anything other than the way Rick would feel against her. His mouth. The inked breadth of his chest. His calloused hands clasping her hips. His eyes as he slid into her.

By the time he'd jogged back, she'd worked herself up to a fine level of anticipation. Anticipation for hot sex. No thinking. Only doing.

"Okay, everything's good." He slid behind the idling car's wheel and put the gear into Reverse before he even shut the door. Maybe he'd been thinking the same thoughts she had.

The short ride to his cottage was silent, each of them soaked in the thought of each other.

Rick shut off the car and reached for her.

She was ready and straddled the console to get to him. Her mouth met his as her hands sank into his short hair.

"Oh, yes," he breathed against her mouth before sliding his lips down her neck. His hands were just as busy, running up and down her back, cupping her ass before sliding up again.

With one hand she groped for the door handle. She had to get closer to him, feel him between her thighs, and she couldn't do that in the position they were in.

Rick dragged her over his body and out the door that fell open. He stepped out, breaking neither the hold he had on her ass nor the kiss he'd deepened so that she groaned with need. And then they fell onto the cold grass.

"Oh!" she said, landing on his body.

He laughed and rolled her over so he cradled her in his arms. Then he went back to consuming her with his mouth.

She sighed and ran her hands down the muscles of his back. He felt so damn good. So hot. Her body throbbed, pulsed, even, on the cold, slightly damp ground.

She didn't care if her butt grew numb from the cold. Not when one of his warm hands shoved the hem of her shirt upward then followed the path he cleared. All the way up to where her small breast waited beneath the lacy bra. The sweater was Target, but the lingerie was Parisian. And sexy. That's how she rolled.

His fingers plucked her nipple before his hand curved round the flesh that barely filled his palm.

"We've—" He groaned as her hand closed over the hardness lurking behind his fly. She stoked him through his jeans, enjoying the nice length straining against the denim. Very nice indeed. He ripped his lips from her collarbone. "We've got to get inside. Now."

She smiled. "Yes, we do. No free shows for your boys up there."

He lifted his head and smiled at her. In one motion, he leaped to his feet and held out a hand.

Kate took it then, as suddenly, she was in his arms, like Scarlett in Rhett's as he strode up the grand staircase. Except Kate wasn't fighting Rick, and she was no spoiled damsel. She was a willing participant, so she wiggled loose and swung her legs so they fell. Then she twisted and encircled his waist with them. "Better," she whispered against his lips as she rocked her hips so his hardness rubbed right where she needed it.

"Mmm…" He groaned against her mouth, grasping her hips and helping her with the delicious friction she was creating with her movement. "My keys…"

He pressed her against the door. The cold windowpane hit her back. She squealed.

"Sorry," he said, setting her on her feet. "I don't know where my keys went."

They both looked back at the red Mustang. The door was open, the interior light was on and the keys dangled in the ignition.

Kate pointed. "I found them."

"Hell," he muttered. He jogged to the car, grabbed the keys, pressed the lock down and shut the door with his foot. He returned and gathered her against him as he jabbed the key into the lock.

One twist and they tumbled into blessed warmth.

The house was dark, lit only by moonlight. And it felt appropriately intimate. Rick slammed the door, grabbed her hips and pulled her to him. "Do you know how much I want you, Kate?"

Her hand found him again beneath the zipper of his jeans. He was as hard as she'd left him. "I'm getting an idea."

She dropped little kisses along the stubble lining his

jaw. "Remember that day you brought me here? When you took the shower?"

"Yeah?" he whispered, sliding his hands so they cupped her ass. He pulled her firm against him.

"I've been dreaming of you beneath the water. Imagining the water sliding over your chest."

"You want to take a shower?"

Her answer was to kick off her shoes and grab the hem of her sweater. One tug and it went over her head.

His laugh was throaty. "I'm taking that as a yes."

He, too, started shedding his clothing, tossing the Turkey Trot T on the floor, revealing to her for the first time the ink that marred the smoothness of his chest. He had no hair, just smooth brandied skin with whorls and images that didn't matter to her now. She'd have time to explore those later. He toed his tennis shoes off and unbuckled the belt at his waist.

Kate kept her eye on him as she shimmied out of her jeans and pulled the angora socks from her feet. He dropped his jeans to the floor and stepped from them, clad only in tented boxers with little hearts on them.

She paused, standing in her expensive lilac lace underwear.

Rick couldn't stop himself from growing even harder when he saw Kate framed in the seductive moonlight in the most amazingly delicate and sexy bra and panties. She was like a sea nymph risen from glittering depths.

Then she became a siren, reaching behind her back and unhooking her bra. She dropped it to the floor and tugged the matching panties down.

He couldn't even swallow. She was magnificent.

Lithe with hollows that rounded out to softness, Kate was all he'd ever imagined in a woman. She was perfectly proportioned with sweet upturned breasts, a sculpted stomach, trim thighs and graceful little feet. Even her bright red toenails were perfection.

"Well?" she said, and looked at his boxers. "Are you going to do the honors? Or shall I?"

He grinned. "Never afraid, are you."

She cocked her head and lifted her eyebrows. "Are you telling me you got something in there I should be afraid of? 'Cause that's getting my hopes up."

Rick slid his boxers off and tossed them over the sofa.

"Oh, yeah. I'm afraid," Kate said with a smile.

He couldn't wait any longer. He grabbed her hand and tugged her behind him toward the single bathroom in the house.

Luckily, the cottage was small and it only took a few steps. He turned on only the inset light above the shower so that they were bathed in a soft glow, reached in and started the water, then used his hands to check out the hills and valleys of Kate's body.

And she did some exploring of her own, sliding her hands across his body like a sculptor molding her subject. She knew how to tease, build anticipation, move him to greater need.

Soon steam curled around them as the tension reached new heights.

"In. Now." Kate pushed at his stomach before sliding her hand down to grasp the length of his erection.

"Mmm?" he murmured against the sweetness of her upturned breasts. The nipples were small and shell-pink. He sucked one into his mouth just as he swept the hand stroking her hip around her bottom, reaching through to stroke the slick heat between her thighs.

"Eek," she yelped, widening her legs before sighing.

He smiled against the sweetness of her breast before catching her nipple between his teeth again and tugging. He increased the rhythm of his fingers, teasing her, driving her crazy.

"No. Now." She pushed against him, more insistent this time. And he complied, mostly because he loved the idea of soaping her up and running his hands over her skin.

He opened the glass door and stepped inside the tumbled stone-tiled shower. It wasn't very big, but wrapped in each other's arms they didn't take up much space. Kate's mouth met his as the warm water coursed down their bodies, washing away the uncertainty, melting away the questions, leaving only him and Kate and the magic that pulsed between them.

He couldn't get enough of her. Her hands were everywhere, frenzied and insistent.

"I can't wait," she groaned against his shoulder before nipping the skin there with her perfect little teeth. She lifted on her toes and hooked a leg around his waist.

"Kate, we can't have sex without a condom."

She dropped her leg and peered up at him with dazed eyes. "Huh?"

He ducked his head and allowed his mouth to explore the tenderness of her neck before working his way to her ear. "We need a condom."

She rubbed her hands down his back, stroking him as she rubbed her belly against the length of his erection. "Oh."

Rick grabbed the soap and spun her around, lathering up. He gently but quickly scrubbed her back, paying special attention to her delicious derriere. He finished the job on the rest of her body, giving her a sensual washing that left her nearly mewling. She slumped against the gray tile and watched as he made short work of washing himself. Her eyes were a caress and by the time he'd rinsed, he was as hard as a poker.

Kate reached out and grasped his erection. "You could put someone's eye out with that."

He laughed. "Oh, I'll put something out all right."

Her eyes glittered with humor and desire. "That doesn't even make sense."

"Yeah? You do that to me." He pulled the door open and stepped onto the gray mat, grabbing a fluffy towel. Kate stepped out and he didn't give her time to dry off. He did it for her. A brief rubbing before capturing her lips again.

Man, she tasted good. Sweet, sweet, with a hint of spice.

She wrapped her arms about his damp shoulders and met the stroke of his tongue with her own. "Please, Rick. The bed. Now."

She didn't tease him this time. Simply flew by him as she ran toward the bed.

He laughed and padded to his room. He found her in the center of his bed, sprawled, digging through his nightstand. She pulled out a strip of condoms and waved them in the air. "I thought you weren't planning on having sex until you were committed."

He climbed onto the high mattress and crawled toward her. "I was never a Boy Scout, but that doesn't mean I don't follow their motto."

She fell back against his pillows, arching her back, thrusting her pink-tipped breasts into the air. "Watch out for bears?"

"You were a Boy Scout?" He tugged her knee so he

could walk his fingers up her thigh toward the sweetest temptation he'd known in a while. She had a small tattoo of a butterfly on her hip. He tapped it with one finger.

Kate laughed, then sighed as his fingers found where she needed him most. "Nope. I just taught them real survival skills. Like how to get to second base or how to sneak bourbon from the family liquor cabinet."

"My wicked Kate," he whispered against her lips before tracing her bottom lip with his tongue. She widened her legs to give him better access. He didn't waste time accommodating her. Soon she was writhing, sighing and reaching out to touch him, stroke his shoulder, glance his jaw, tug his hair.

"Please, no more," she said, twisting away from him.

"I can't wait anyway." He grabbed the condoms from the hand she'd pressed to the quilt, ripped one open and quickly did the honors.

She raised on her elbows and watched as he sheathed himself with the condom. Her eyes were liquid pools, pulsing with desire. He knew he could get lost in them.

He rose onto his knees and moved toward her. She welcomed him, parting her thighs, and Rick knew it was a picture he would savor in the wee dark hours of the night when the taste of her skin had faded from his memory.

He entered her swiftly.

"Ahh." She threw her head back and clasped his shoulders. "Rick. So good."

He agreed, but couldn't find the words. She was so hot and tight and it had been so damn long for him. He established the rhythm, capturing her head between his hands, holding her so he could cover her mouth with his. His tongue met hers as he plunged into her again and again. Soon he was lost in the magic of making love.

To his beautiful, wild Kate.

She slid her arms from his shoulders to wrap around his neck. Jerking him toward her, she twined her legs about his waist, locking him in place, causing his chest to brush the tips of her breasts. He could feel her tightening around him, could feel his release building.

"Oh," she breathed against his mouth. Their bodies moved faster. He tilted her hips so she could take him deeper. He watched Kate as she caught her bottom lip between her teeth. Her eyes were closed, her face screwed up in concentration.

Her hands slid to his ass as she urged him to increase the tempo. He obliged, driving into her, moving her across the bed, bumping her head against the pine headboard.

He felt her tighten around him. Then her eyes flew open.

He caught her scream with his mouth as he tumbled over the edge to join her. Wave after wave of pleasure seized him, pounding into him. Until it finally subsided.

He fell to the side, pulling Kate on top of him.

She panted as if she'd run a race, and for a moment they lay utterly still.

"Wow," she breathed against his chest. "That was fantastic."

He chuckled as he smoothed her raven hair. "Yeah, pretty damned awesome."

She lifted her head. "I mean it was fantastic. Like something I'd never felt before."

He grinned. "You say that to all the fellows."

She shook her head and he could see she was serious. "No, what I meant is that has never happened before."

The realization smacked him in the head. "You mean you've never come before?"

Heat stole across her cheeks. His wild, cosmopolitan Kate had never had an orgasm? Something akin to self-satisfaction stole across him, swelled inside him.

"I've come before. Just not with a man." She sounded defensive. And embarrassed.

He dropped a kiss on her upturned nose before capturing her sweet little bee-stung mouth with his. "Well, then. I'm assuming the other has been battery-operated?"

She smacked him on the arm before rolling off him. "Smug, aren't you?"

He smiled. "No, honored."

She ducked her head and rested it upon his outstretched arm.

"Hey," he said, tugging a dark blade of her hair. She looked up and the honesty in her blue eyes rocked him. This was Kate naked, literally and emotionally. "Guess what?"

"What?" she whispered.

He lifted himself upon one elbow and tugged her to him, nipping her silken shoulder. "My batteries don't ever run out."

She laughed. "That's an upside."

"Better believe it." And then he kissed her.

Chapter Nineteen

Rick kept kissing her for the next five days. In the kitchen of Phoenix. On the back patio of Cottonwood. Below the statue of Rufus Tucker in the center of Oak Stand. And around the corner of the Longview Regional Hospital stroke center, where her father was recovering.

No matter where they were, Rick didn't pass up the opportunity to pull her into his arms and let her know he wanted her. In fact, they made out like teenagers every chance they got. It would have been embarrassing if it hadn't felt so good.

For once in her life, Kate enjoyed being someone's— dare she say it?—girlfriend.

It was a title she'd never tolerated before. Oh, sure, she dated, even went out for second and third dates, but never had she wanted to feel like part of a couple with someone. Surprisingly, she liked it, so she indulged the little fantasy she'd created in her mind. The one where she was normal, like any other girl. The one where she didn't go back to Vegas. Where she expected a happy ending. Where she planned for weekend getaways, a princess-cut ring and a white lace veil.

The whole thing was a sham.

But she went with it anyway, mostly because she didn't want to think about this being a fling. She didn't want to think about her and Rick being over in less than twenty-four hours. She only wanted to savor the time she had left with the man who made her feel comfortable in her own skin.

With him, she didn't have to think. She simply was.

"Penny for your thoughts," he said, jarring her from her musings as they drove down Interstate 20 in his Mustang for yet another visit with Justus. It would probably be her last—her flight left tomorrow afternoon.

"Not even worth a plug nickel," she said. "What is a plug nickel, anyway?"

"Something people use to fool vending machines, I think."

They'd spent so much time on this stretch of highway that the landmarks were familiar. She'd miss sitting beside him while he took the twists and bends of the road. She'd miss a lot of things.

But she wasn't supposed to think about that.

"Nellie said she'd take me to the airport. I think it might be for the, um, best." The words rushed from her mouth. Damn. She didn't want to bring up leaving. Why had she?

"Why?" The word was spoken softly, shaded with hurt.

"I—I'm not sure I can—" She was afraid she'd say

it—that she wouldn't be able to get on the plane. That she wanted to stay with him and pretend to be something she wasn't—a daughter, a sister, a girlfriend.

But she was none of those things. Not really. She was Kate Newman. And Kate Newman was a Vegas business owner. A hard-ass ballbuster with an attitude and towering stilettos. She was a good time party girl with no ties, no mortgage and no dependents on her tax form. She was an island and she didn't need anyone.

His eyes met hers. "That's fine. For the best."

Silence fell, hard and bitter.

A lump formed in Kate's throat, and she stared out the window at the scenery whizzing by. The past few days had been wonderful. Why had she ruined it by bringing up her flight tomorrow? She was a dumb-ass.

Just this morning she'd awakened to find him watching her sleep. She'd always thought that was something a character did in movies or words in a song by Aerosmith. Honestly, it had always seemed a bit hokey. But Rick's soft brown eyes had caressed her, reflecting the morning light and something she couldn't quite grasp. He'd given her a sheepish grin.

She'd stretched. "Are you watching me sleep?"

"Maybe."

"Why?" She'd curled her toes into his somewhat scratchy new sheets.

"It sounds lame, but you're always moving, always running that smart-assed mouth. It's nice to watch you curled up, like a little girl. You look almost innocent."

She smiled. "After last night, you know that's not true."

Rick wouldn't let the tender moment go. "I thought I'd take a mental picture."

Something sweet filled Kate at his words. And she'd taken a mental picture herself. Rick, bare-chested in a pair of striped pajama pants sitting in a rustic rocker framed against an awakening sky. His hair clipped short, his jaw whiskered with stubble, his feet crossed and propped on the end of the bed. The sun behind him cast shadows on his face, but she could see his eyes, see the way they moved over her and loved her.

She patted the still-warm spot next to her. "How about creating a mental video?"

He smiled and unwound his body, joining her. He pulled the quilt to their chins, tucking her close to him, spooning her. One hand curled round to rest securely on her ribs, and they lay together, each feeling the other's heart beat.

Her invitation had been for pleasure, and he gave her that by holding her in the still morning light.

She'd never savored such feeling before, simply being held in the arms of a man, and it surprised her how much she loved being secured in his warm embrace. Such ease. Such comfort.

The exact opposite of what she felt now as they approached Longview, caught in that horrible moment of regret. A moment she'd prayed wouldn't come.

"I didn't mean I didn't want you to take me. I just don't know if it would be a good idea. I don't think—"

He held up a hand. "Not a problem. I know the score, Kate."

He sounded hurt. That big guy who had sent shivers down her spine the first time she'd seen him in the post office. He'd been almost threatening, and she remembered how she'd hurried to her car, thinking him dangerous. And now here he sat, vulnerable, because of her.

"Rick, I have to go back. I don't have a future here." She touched his shoulder and felt him stiffen.

"That's nice. Remind me of why I should have said no to you. No future. Exactly."

"I don't mean with you, I mean here." She waved her hand at the outskirts of Longview. A feed store with gleaming orange tractors lined up like toys on a shelf. A run-down gas station. A fast loan place. A nail salon. It was a far cry from the glitz of Vegas. "I have a business, friends, a life somewhere else. I can't throw who I am away because I have a hunch."

He whipped his head around. His eyes sparked. "That's what we are? A hunch?"

Kate sighed. She wasn't going to win. She'd hurt him, and for that, she was sorry. But she wasn't staying in Oak Stand. She wouldn't go back to being Katie Newman. She wouldn't embrace a life she didn't want. "No, we are what we agreed to that night on the way home from Longview. We're a moment in time. I thought we said there would be no regrets."

He didn't say anything else. His face hardened as he stared at the traffic. Minutes later, the facade of Longview Regional peered gloomily at them as they entered the drive. Or maybe it wasn't the hospital that was depressing, it was the rotten mood in the car. Unspoken words. Fissures in the foundation of something fleeting.

"I'll drop you, then park," Rick said, swinging toward the entrance to the physical-therapy wing.

"No, just park. I'll walk with you," she said.

His foot hovered on the brake, slowing them, but then the car shot forward.

"Fine." He narrowly missed a pickup truck as he turned into the parking lot.

"Rick." She placed a hand on his arm.

He flinched. "What?"

"Let's not ruin it."

His dark eyes flashed as they met hers. He stopped the car in the middle of a row. "So we're gonna pretend that everything's okay? That you aren't leaving? That you aren't throwing us away?"

She drew back as if he'd slapped her. "What?"

"You know damn well what." He ground the words out between gritted teeth. She could feel his anger burgeoning, crowding the interior of the vintage car.

A horn sounded behind them. Rick's car blocked the row.

"Shit," he said, stepping on the accelerator, jerking them forward. He rounded another row. There were no parking spots. Again, he spun the wheel and gave the car gas. It leaped to life, roaring down the next aisle.

"Please," she said. "Calm down."

"Ha. That's funny coming from you," he said in a not-so-friendly way.

So this is how it would end. Badly. Meanly. God, she hadn't wanted it to be this way, but had known it would be hard to pretend parting didn't hurt. That hearts hadn't gotten knocked around and bruised. "Insult me if it makes you feel better. Maybe you can learn to hate me so it won't be so bad."

He finally found a spot and swung the car into it, braking hard, jerking her forward. "Maybe so."

Kate pressed her hands over her face before dropping them in her lap. "Why are you doing this?"

He turned so his broad shoulders were squared with the door. They were wonderful shoulders, covered with looping ink, strong, capable of carrying burdens. How many times had Kate leaned on them over the past two weeks? How many times had she clung to them as he'd taken her to heights she'd never explored before? Now they tensed. "Because you are a coward."

She could feel the color leave her face. "Bullshit. I'm not a coward."

He shrugged. "I call 'em like I see 'em."

He pulled the keys from the ignition, climbed out and walked away.

Kate felt blindsided by his anger. She'd always been straight with him. Never misled him. He knew she wasn't going to stay. No way in hell did she want to go back to what she'd been, even if she had a better understanding of exactly who that was. She couldn't take those steps backward, she'd worked too long and too hard. Fantabulous waited. Her clients waited. The IRS waited. It was time to return to the reality of her life.

How could he not understand?

She climbed from the car, wishing she could call Nellie and head to the airport right now. She even rooted around in her bag for her cell phone before realizing there was no way around saying goodbye to her father. No way of avoiding Rick's uncomfortable anger.

And no way of ignoring the twangs of hurt vibrating in her heart. These past two weeks had taken a chisel to the flinty emotions once cemented inside her, chipping them away in big chunks. The problem with a heart that had been emptied of bad stuff was the space made for good stuff. Really good stuff. Hopes and dreams had found their way in, filling her up, making her think of possibilities instead of doom.

She'd been foolish to fall in love with Rick.

And that's what she'd done. Allowed herself to fall

head over heels. She'd never thought it possible. Almost didn't believe in the shifty emotion, even though she'd seen people immerse themselves in it completely. And not only had she opened her heart to Rick, but she'd made room for Vera, Justus and Oak Stand. She was consumed with lots of tender, new emotions. And she wasn't sure she could sort through them. Wasn't sure if they could be enough to pull her from her past life. From all things she'd wanted for so long.

The hospital doors swooshed open and she stepped into the chilly interior. Hospitals always seemed to be cold and sterile, no matter how many prints of flowers lined their halls.

Rick wasn't waiting.

Kate gave a mental shrug and headed to the bank of elevators that would take her to the Stroke Center on the second floor, where her father would be cranky and weary in a bed outfitted for his rehab.

She made it to her father's room without seeing Rick. The door was half-open and she could hear Vera placating Justus.

She tapped on the door and pushed it open. The arguing stopped.

"Kate." Vera smiled. "I wondered when you would be by. Is Rick with you?"

She shrugged. "He's here somewhere. I don't know where he went."

Her father stilled and managed a lopsided smile. "Hello, Katie. Glad you came to see me before you left."

She still didn't feel exactly comfortable with the man she'd so recently forgiven, but she was trying to be nicer. More open. "Hello, Justus. How are you today?"

"Tired of them jerking me left and right, pulling me this way and that like I'm a piece of taffy."

"In other words, you're feeling normal?"

Vera laughed. "Didn't take you long to figure him out, did it?"

"Not really," Kate said, stepping into the room. Flowers covered every surface. She moved a planter from a guest chair and slid it next to Vera. "It looks like a flower shop in here."

"Yes, Justus has many associates." Vera looked around the room at the tulips, daisies, yellow roses and bluebonnets perfuming the air. Obviously, everyone thought the Texas state flower appropriate. "We should see if there are other patients who might be cheered by a few bouquets. Or a nursing home perhaps?"

"I'll check on it," Rick said, entering the room with a cardboard tray of coffees.

"There you are," Vera said, taking the coffee from him. "Kate said she didn't know where you were."

Rick didn't look at her. "She wouldn't."

His words were heavy with meaning. Vera's brow crinkled, but she didn't say anything, just shifted her gaze from Rick to Kate.

Kate tried to smile, but it felt pained. Shit.

Rick took a cup and positioned himself against the hospital wall.

"Thank you for the coffee," Vera said, moving the cardboard tray from Justus's reach. He'd inched his good hand toward the cup. "None for you, dear."

"I'm sick of juice. Feel like a toddler with all the grape juice they push my way," he grumbled, his blues eyes narrowing as he studied Kate and Rick. "What the devil is going on with you two?"

Kate stiffened and Rick shrugged.

"Nothing," Rick said. "Having some trouble at the center with one of the guys."

This was news to Kate. She echoed his response. "Nothing."

Her father opened his mouth to say something, then snapped it closed. He looked at his wife and Kate could see something pass between them. "What's the problem at the center? Thought things were going fine."

Rick stared out the window, meeting no one's gaze. "Nothing I can't handle. Just got my thoughts tied up."

Silence pressed down, interrupted only by the chirping of one of the machines hooked to Justus. Seconds ticked by, but it seemed like hours.

Finally, Vera waded into the tension. "Justus should be released the day after tomorrow. His regular physical therapist has been briefed and the doctor says they can find no significant damage from the last stroke."

"That's good," Kate murmured.

"When will you come back?" Justus asked. She jerked her gaze to her father. His blue eyes pinned her against the striped wallpaper behind her.

"Well, I—" Kate paused.

"She's not coming back." Rick's harsh words echoed in the small room. He'd turned to glare at the Mitchells. "She did what you asked. Stayed two weeks. The money is hers."

Justus didn't react.

At that instant, Kate wished for a natural disaster to sweep through and save her from the sheer hell of the moment, but the sunshine beaming in from the window declared it impossible. So she closed her eyes and tried to propel herself through space to Vegas. Or the Bermuda Triangle. Or anywhere other than here.

"I never said I wouldn't come back." She opened her eyes. "But I need some time. A lot has happened, stuff I haven't even had time to process. I need a little space."

Vera nodded. "I understand, Kate. What I think Justus is trying to say—" she patted his shoulder "—in a rather abrupt manner, is that we hope you will choose to be part of our lives…even if it's in a small way."

Kate pressed her lips together and nodded. Rick had spun toward the window and no longer looked at any of them. His muscles were bunched beneath his long-sleeved T-shirt, and her hands itched to soothe them, to ply the muscles beneath her fingers, make him calm and at peace. But she couldn't. His anger at her would have to burn itself out. And that might take longer than a day. Or a week. Or a year. He might never get over his anger at her.

There would be no more tangled sheets with Rick. No more sweet kisses and wisecracks. What they'd shared was what she'd intended all along—something wonderful but temporary.

And it was time to go home to Vegas, to move forward.

She looked at her father. Her eyes softened. "I'll be back, Justus. But this time, I'll come on my own terms."

He nodded.

Rick walked out.

Kate looked from Vera to Justus, at a loss for what to say about Rick's behavior.

A nurse came in with a big bouquet of red roses. She nudged a box of tissues aside and set the vase on the bed-side table. "There. Happy Valentine's Day!"

The lush roses were in full bloom, beautifully signifying the day for love.

Irony sucked.

Chapter Twenty

Kate's condo smelled like rotten Chinese takeout.

She'd forgotten to take the garbage out before she'd left Vegas, and so her homecoming was none too pleasant. Not that she'd expected it to be. But after the rollicking roller coaster of emotions she'd been on, a clean house would have been a small solace.

No balm for her heart.

And no more Chinese takeout for a while. Bluck.

Kate parked her rolling suitcase in the foyer and surveyed her domain.

White fluffy rug centered on slate floor. A Driade couch in fuschia, matching striped armchairs, funky George Kovac floor lamps and a glass sculpture made by her friend Billie filled the room. Very sleek, very modern, very designer.

And, oddly, not so welcoming.

Kate kicked off her flats and padded to the kitchen to remove the offending smell. Her answering machine blinked with messages, her one houseplant had died and she'd left a yogurt carton in the sink. Thank God she didn't have a pet.

After setting things right, she grabbed her purse and looked for her cell. The check for fifty thousand dollars stared at her from the gaping opening of her bag.

She pulled it out, studying the tight signature of her father, looking at the zeroes following the five.

She'd gotten what she'd set out for…and more.

So why didn't she feel victorious? Of course, she knew the answer. But she didn't want to think about him. Couldn't do that yet. Not when she felt so raw. And vulnerable.

She grabbed her phone, then stuck the check to her fridge with a magnet right beside the appointment for a dental cleaning she'd missed while in Texas. The check seemed to mock her, so she turned it over.

She punched out the numbers she'd dialed a million times. Jeremy answered on the second ring. "Let us make you Fantabulous."

"Too late. I'm already there," Kate said.

"Kate! You're back already? Why didn't you call? I would have picked you up, chickadee."

She smiled even though it was hard. Her face felt tight. She was a patched piece of plaster, praying the cracks didn't give way to crumbled dust. "I took a cab. Knew you were busy."

"Well, get down here, girlfriend. I've got something to show you." Jeremy sounded pretty cheerful, considering the last time she'd spoken with him Victor hadn't been doing well.

"I'm gonna take it easy this afternoon. I'm pretty tired—you know how flying makes me."

"How many pills did you pop? You've got your clothes on, don't you?"

Kate laughed. "The cabdriver wouldn't have picked me up if I hadn't."

"You'd be surprised," he said. Laughter sounded in the background and she could hear Jay-Z playing. Singing about concrete jungles. Places so different from gentle rolling hills and open patios where people grew tomatoes in old whiskey barrels. "Okay, sugar, tomorrow it is. You've got two on the books."

Kate frowned. Only two clients? Usually she was booked solid when she returned from a trip. But then again, business had been slow. She could sleep in, so it was all good. "See you then."

She hung up and faced her empty apartment…and her wounded heart. Her place looked lonely. Sad. Empty.

The phone vibrated in her hand as Sade erupted. Her friend Trish.

"Hey, lady," Kate said, tracing her finger over the dust on her glass table. She dropped into an acrylic chair shaped like a stiletto.

"Marshall's guest deejaying tonight at the Ghost Bar. Wanna?" Trish sounded like she always did. Smooth as Scotch. Totally unruffled. Marshall Wainwright, aka DJ Rain, was her current flavor of the month.

"I don't—" Maybe going with Trish would make her feel better. Get Kate back into her old vibe. She looked around the silent room. "Okay, sure."

"You want me to swing by and pick you up? I'm not going home with Marsh. I've got a deposition at 9:00."

Trish was an assistant district attorney for Carson

County. She kicked serious butt in the courtroom, intimidating defendants like a hawk would a hapless mouse. She had an outstanding conviction record and was on the fast track to the top. She wouldn't jeopardize a case even for the wickedly sweet Marshall Wainwright, who played a thug DJ but was really from the wealthy suburbs of Chicago.

"Okay, um, sure." Kate glanced at the clock on her state-of-the-art stove she'd never used for anything other than boiling water for tea.

"You sound strange. What did they do to you down there in Texas?" Trish didn't miss a thing. Not the slightest hesitation or inflection.

"They put me in cowboy boots and made me do the two-step," she replied, trying to sound like her old self.

"Yeah. Whatever. I'll be there at 9:00," Trish said, sounding much more like she was saying, "I'll interrogate you at 9:00."

"Ciao," Kate said, but the line was already dead.

She rose with a sigh and retrieved her luggage. A hot shower would melt away the travel stress and a little nap would rid her of the vestiges of the Xanax she'd taken in Dallas. She had a new baby-doll dress to wear tonight, not to mention a pair of Stuart Weitzman strappy sandals that made her legs look longer. Sure. She'd be back to her old self in no time.

"Kate the Great is back in the house," Jeremy called out the next morning when she dragged herself in clutching a triple mocha latte and a bag full of clean towels she'd had at her condo for over three weeks.

"If you can call physically being here *back*," she muttered, heading toward their shared office and dumping the towels in a side chair.

She slipped off the dark glasses she wore to hide her swollen eyes and glanced in the mirror above her desk. Ouch. She looked like reheated oatmeal. Pasty, lumpy and unappetizing.

She couldn't go out into the salon looking the way she did.

She grabbed the tackle box she kept her lures in. No plastic worms or bright wooden fish with hooks. No, this tackle box contained a palette of lip glosses, concealers, mascaras, sparkling eye shadow and various liners and brushes. These were the real lures in life.

While she tried to hide the damage done from a late night—too many beers and a crying jag—she berated herself for going out with Trish.

It had been miserable. She'd sat on a stool in a corner, swilling beer and watching happy people get their groove on. The whole time, all she could think about was how this used to make her happy, and how it now seemed so stupid.

People pumped their hands in the air to the beat of the music, shot neon-colored liquor from test tubes and prattled about their Facebook status and how much they'd lost doing P90X. Thirty-something men wearing too much cologne roved in packs and behaved like a bunch of frat boys on spring break. Women her age, wearing cheap clothes that barely contained their store-bought boobs, tottered on heels that were too high and actually invited the wolf pack to sample the wares.

She'd spent the whole night drinking and wondering if her life had always been this way.

But she knew the answer deep down inside.

Vegas hadn't changed. The club scene hadn't changed. She had.

That hacked her off so much that she'd drunk too much. One Newcastle after another flew through her hands until she could see two Trish's when her friend finally came to tug her to the dance floor. But Kate wouldn't go.

And that pissed her off *even* more. She was supposed to get her groove back, put Rick behind her and move forward. Instead, she'd sat like a lonely sourpuss, warding off gelled-up dudes with a get-away-from-me death stare. She'd felt like a bitter, washed-up old maid. And in her beer-soaked mind, all she wanted was the man she'd left behind.

For this—thumping music, lukewarm beer and an empty bed.

She was a dumb-ass.

Jeremy stuck his head in the office, jarring her from her sad-sack memory. "Hey, you. What's going—"

He paused when she turned around. His waxed and perfectly tinted eyebrows crinkled. "Jeez, doll. Have you been crying?"

"No." Her response was too quick.

Jeremy moved inside the office and draped an arm over her shoulder. "They made you do line dances down there, didn't they? It's okay. We can get you some therapy."

Kate smiled. She had to. Jeremy was one of her best friends. "No. No line dances."

He dropped a kiss on her head. "Then why's my Katiebug so sad?"

Just him calling her *Katie* made tears spring into her eyes.

"Oh, God. Did they make you wear Wranglers? Because Wrangler butts drive me nuts, but not on women." He was trying to make her smile again. But this time she couldn't. She actually felt her chin wobble.

"I fell in love," she said.

Jeremy clutched his chest and fell into the chair holding the bag of towels. He yelped, hopped up, tossed the bag, then swooned again. Then he pulled her onto his lap and wrapped his arms around her. "That's great, Katiebug. Really great."

She laid her head on his shoulder. "No, it's not. It's impossible."

"Why?"

"Because my life is here. I have everything here. How can I be in a relationship that's a thousand miles away?" She wiped her cheeks so she wouldn't get Jeremy's Oxford shirt damp.

"Hey," he said, shifting her so he could look at her. "I want to show you something."

He patted her back, indicating she had to get off his lap. She stood and he walked to their none-too-tidy desk and pulled an envelope from under the blotter. He handed her the letter.

She read it and then looked up at him and repeated the same word she'd said to him over a similar letter a little over a month ago. "How?"

"My father gave me the money my grandmother had left me. Money he'd hidden. It was over seventy-five thousand dollars."

"Oh, my God!" Kate lowered the letter. Her mouth fell open as she looked at her friend. She was absolutely shocked. And he beamed at her, like a proud schoolboy. "Your father *talked* to you?"

"Better than that, knowing you were facing your past gave me the courage to face mine. I invited my father to lunch, and though he's no card-carrying member of PFLAG yet, he's offered to start therapy with me." He turned his hands over and shrugged. "It's a start."

She hurried around the desk and enveloped her friend in a hug. "I'm so happy for you. I can't believe it!"

He wrapped her in his thin arms. "I can't, either, but I'm happy about it. And the salon is okay. Better than okay."

Kate untangled herself from her friend and looked at the letter she'd dropped on the desk. No more bankruptcy. No more IRS threats. Fantabulous would stay fantabulous.

"I still can't believe it. I didn't even have to go to Texas after all." Her heart beat as though she'd run a race. Why? She wasn't sure. She stared at a picture of her wearing a wig and sparkly dress. Jeremy had taken it on New Year's Eve before they'd gotten the first IRS letter. She looked happy.

The room fell silent for a moment.

She looked at her friend. He stared at her measuringly. "Maybe you did have to go, hon."

She sank into the chair they'd vacated moments before.

Jeremy fell into the desk chair and folded his hands on the desk like a high-school counselor. "Maybe all this was meant to be. A way for me to reconcile with my father. A way for you to face the past you've been running from all these years."

Kate stared at a dust bunny huddled in a corner. "Maybe."

"You said you fell in love, but you've changed more

than that. I can see it in your eyes. The way you hold yourself. You seem vulnerable and, I don't know, deeper."

She shrugged. "I went through a lot of shit down there. A lot of stuff I needed to go through, I guess, but it changed me. I don't feel the same."

He nodded. "Let me tell you something, my dear friend. I'm learning that life is too damned short to waste time on things that don't matter. You know?"

Victor's cheerful face flashed into her mind. Jeremy likely didn't have much time left with his partner. No time to waste. "I get you, Jer, but I can't pursue something that's not right for me. My life is here. In Vegas. I can't throw everything I've worked so hard for out the window like it's nothing. It means something to me."

"Sure it does." He nodded, picking up her glass paperweight. The one Nellie had sent her. "But, you see, Victor is my life. I'd choose him over my career, my house, my car, anything. I'd throw everything aside if I could have him forever."

Kate lifted her head and met his eyes. She could see he meant what he said. What could she say to something like that?

He continued. "If I could go back in time, I'd toss out all those wasted years of clubbing, buying designer clothes, vacationing in St. Barts—all that stuff I thought was important—just to hurry up and get to the part where I had him in my life. He's made me so much more than I ever expected. And the thought of not having him with me makes me so ill that I can barely get out of bed in the morning. No way would I ever let anything stand between us."

She looked away because she didn't want to see his pain, didn't want to witness his grief. She was afraid she might find herself in his eyes. Knew she'd already found herself in his words. "I don't know. I don't know what to do. The salon—"

"Is a place. It's not a person, Kate."

"But it's mine. It's what I worked for. What I dreamed about."

He shrugged. "Then, darling, you've got to decide if it's enough."

He shoved the rolling chair back and rose. On his way out of the office, he gave her a sympathetic pat on the shoulder. But he didn't say anything other than, "By the way, Mandy wanted to know if she could buy into the business. She's brought in more new customers in the past two weeks than we've had in three months. Feels like destiny knocking, doesn't it?"

And he left.

Kate pressed her hands to her eyes and rubbed. God, she wished she could wipe away her thoughts. Her head pounded from her hangover, her thoughts whirled faster than the bike spokes at the Tour de France and her heart plain ached. Her throat clogged with unshed tears.

Damn. She hated herself for being weak. For not being the Kate she was a month ago. For not being able to pull out the emotions rolling inside her, shove them in a box and hide them underneath her bed.

She opened her eyes and looked around her office. At the mosaic tile mirror she and Jeremy had attempted to recreate from a *Design Star* episode. At the bookcase she'd found on the side of the road the one time she'd managed to drag her friend Billie to a garage sale. At the mug that read I Fix $8 Haircuts she'd been given by a stylist before she moved to Rhode Island with an accountant she'd met at Cirque du Soleil. At the ratty plant in the window, the stacks of catalogs on the desk and the framed picture of her, Nellie, Billie and Trish taken the night Nellie had met Jack at Agave Blue, his former nightclub.

Her world had seemed so full.

She looked at the bag she'd dropped beside the chair next to her favorite catalogs—Neiman's, Nordstrom's and Saks. An awesome pair of bright pink Christian Louboutins seduced from the front cover of the Neiman Marcus spring collection.

She sighed and pulled the check her father had given her from the depths of her purse. She'd stuck it inside that morning, intending to head to the bank. She studied all those zeroes and thought of what they could buy.

She had to decide where her future lay.

Should she stay in Vegas?

Or should she carve out a new future in the piney woods of East Texas with Rick?

One way seemed smooth and safe.

The other very uncertain.

She was in the city of second chances. A city of risk takers. Of rebels. Of the brokenhearted.

But could Kate really roll the dice on her life?

Chapter Twenty-One

Over two months later, Kate considered how silly her powder-blue VW bug looked parked next to the huge pickup in front of Phoenix. Especially with one of her George Kovac modern lamps looming in the backseat over a motley assortment of boxes and bags. Kate took a deep breath and pulled her canvas bag onto her shoulder. She hadn't had time to bring a covered dish for the postgraduation party. Hell, she couldn't cook anyway. She'd stopped and picked up brownies at Whole Foods before rolling into East Texas.

Her stomach felt fluttery, but she was resolved.

She'd made her decision. For better or worse.

She had no clue if Rick would have her. Or want to pursue anything other than friendship with her. He'd once said right before they'd made love that he would always be her friend. Always care about her. Well, she was about to test the truth of his words.

She approached the center, which was now awash in flowering Hawthorne bushes. Only one person stood on the porch—an older Hispanic man, who held a cigarette between his lips and nodded when she smiled at him. Heck. Even her smile felt nervous.

"They're in there. Already started," he said.

Kate nodded and opened the door.

The first sound she heard was her heart thumping against her ribs. Then she heard a woman singing a Barbra Streisand song that she could never remember the name of but had to do with love being like an easy chair. And she realized it was Vera singing.

The vaulted main room of the center was filled with folding chairs placed in five even rows, on either side of a center aisle. Every chair was filled, and a few people stood at the back. Justus's wheelchair was parked at the end of the last row, and though she could only see the side of his face, she could tell he was enchanted with the way his wife sang the ballad. Everyone's attention was on Vera, who was the only person to see Kate slip inside.

Her stepmother's eyes widened only slightly, but she kept right on singing.

Kate eased into a spot at the back between a teenage boy with a tattoo of a skeleton on his forearm and a woman with curly black hair, who smelled faintly of clean linen. The woman smiled at Kate. The teen looked at her then returned his attention to the moose head hanging above the mantel.

The center's graduates sat in the front row. They all wore white dress shirts and ties and, to Kate, seemed to hold themselves proudly. She scanned the crowd for Rick but didn't see him. She saw Nellie, Jack, Tamara, Betty Monk and even Sally Holtzclaw, but she didn't see the man she'd missed so much it had physically hurt. She'd been a mess, popping antacids for weeks, although the negotiations over Fantabulous, clearing out her life in Vegas and summoning up the courage to take this enormous leap of faith contributed to the acid churning.

She was midair and it was time to stick the landing. She just needed to find her spotter. And he wasn't anywhere to be seen.

Vera wrapped up the song with a soft, emotional note. The crowd clapped politely as she stepped from the platform that had been erected where the huge dining-room table usually sat. Outside the bay windows, Kate could see Banjo lying on the patio next to a barrel of tomatoes they'd planted nearly three months ago. Bright red plums perched among the spring green branches of the plants. All around the East Texas countryside, winter had melted into a cacophony of greens, each shade doing its best to one-up the other.

Vera patted her husband as she passed him, but she didn't stop. She came straight to Kate, slipping in between her and the teenager, earning a disdainful frown from the youth.

She took Kate's hand and squeezed it.

Justus swiveled his head to find his wife, but found Kate instead. The emotion that swept over his face wrung Kate's heart. She had vowed she wouldn't get overly emotional with her father. They both needed slow and steady. But they did have the start to a new relationship.

A microphone crackled then whined. The interference stopped when Rick stepped onto the stage and moved behind the podium.

Kate's heart paused. She grasped Vera's hand even harder, earning a smile from the older woman.

He looked amazing, if a few pounds lighter. His hair was still military short, his shoulders still broad beneath the navy sports jacket he wore over a light blue button-down and striped tie. He looked just about as good as any man Kate had ever seen.

"Thank you, Vera." His gaze sought the woman beside her, and just like Justus, he found Kate instead.

If lightning could have struck, it would have.

That's how powerful the moment felt. Like sheer electricity had zapped the air between them. Rick stopped and stared.

Many in the room swung around to follow his gaze.

"Kate," Rick said into the mic, still obviously stunned she was here.

Manny waved at her and she waved back, and the moment was shattered. Rick cleared his throat and recovered.

"Now I will read the names of those who are graduating from Phoenix today." His voice swelled with pride as he read each graduate's name and accomplishments. Every so often he'd look toward her and each time she could see his questions.

After the participants in the program received their certificates of completion, Justus rolled forward. Rick handed the microphone to her father and helped him steady it before he spoke.

"Today is a day of new beginnings, but it is also a day for remembering the past. What will be and what is no more. My son, Ryan Talton Mitchell, was the inspiration for this center. His belief that all people hold a piece of goodness, a desire to do right and a need for a second chance is the seed that grew into the fruit that is this center. He is no longer with us…"

Her father's words fell off for a moment.

"But his influence lives on in his words and his works. He believed in the power of love. And so do I. Today, I would like to present to Enrique Mendez, a man who is like a son to me, the deed to the land on which Phoenix stands. It is a gift from the Ryan Mitchell Love Foundation."

Applause sounded as her father handed a paper to Rick. Rick bent to shake Justus's hand and someone snapped a picture.

Her father rolled away as Rick returned to the podium.

"Now, before we indulge in the cake and punch so graciously provided by the Oak Stand Ladies Auxiliary, I would like to invite anyone present who would like to say a few words to do so."

No one moved a muscle. Not even the graduates. The air was static once again.

Kate dropped Vera's hand. "I'd like to say something."

Rick watched as Kate made her way to the stage. She looked different. Her hair was longer, cut in a flattering fringe around her face. No flame-red or violet-blue streaked it. Just lovely raven locks framing a pert nose, lush lips and determined chin. And those eyes, man, they sparked, tugging new life into his blood, suturing the heart that had been gashed when she'd walked out of his life two months ago.

Her skirt swished around her trim ankles as she stepped onto the platform.

As he handed her the microphone, her hand brushed his. He felt a jolt to the center of his gut. Yep, he was a goner for Kate Newman. Stick-a-fork-in-him-done kind of goner.

She gave him a mysterious smile, then turned to face the audience.

"Hello, everyone. My name is Katie Newman. I'm Justus's daughter and Ryan's sister. I wanted to tell these guys how proud I am of them." She swept a hand over the area where Georges, Manny, Joe, Brandon and Carlos sat. "I know what they feel this day. I know this journey has been hard but worth it, mostly because I've taken a similar journey over the past couple of months, so if you all will indulge me for a moment."

"Go ahead, Kate," Georges called out with a grin.

"Okay." She sighed. "Facing your mistakes is hard. I was born here in Oak Stand and spent most of my life trying to get out. I was ashamed of who I was. And like these guys here, I resented many of the people who tried to help me, and I hated those who didn't. Over the years, I built up anger and fear inside me. I only took comfort in the material things of this world, and I tried to control my life by never being weak. Never opening myself up to anyone."

Rick watched her as she said those words. Her eyes shimmered under the recessed lighting. Her hands trembled only slightly.

"Over the years, I've hurt people who loved me." Kate looked at Nellie. Her friend was waving her hands in front of her eyes, as though trying to hold herself together. Jack wound an arm around his wife that she shrugged away, handing him a wiggling toddler.

"And, on this day of new beginnings, I want to say I'm sorry for not seeing the big picture earlier." She looked at the graduates. "Sometimes it's hard to ask for help. I'm glad you guys took that first step. And I'm glad I did, too."

She shifted her gaze to the crowd. "This town held me up, just like they are holding Phoenix up. I never saw that. Never noticed who I had become. I closed myself to love."

She stopped, pressed her lips together and glanced at Rick before continuing.

"Several months ago, I met myself. I came to terms with who I am. I discovered a brother I never knew, a stepmother I didn't like and a father I didn't think I could forgive. I was wrong. Just like I was wrong about this town. And for the very first time in my life, I fell in love."

Her words stunned Rick. Something rose and expanded in his chest. His wounded heart came to life and thumped against his ribs. He was certain everyone in the room could hear it, could see his emotions coming undone.

Tears fell from Kate's eyes, but she didn't stop to wipe them from her cheeks. They dripped off her chin onto the floor.

"My heart, which had been full of bad things, is now full of something I never thought I could feel."

A sob tore through her, but she pressed a hand to her chest and fought through it. "I went back to Vegas, but it wasn't the same. I wasn't the same because love had changed me. I don't know what my future holds, but I want it to play out here."

She finally wiped her face and smiled. "I can't believe I'm about to say these words, but, I've finally come home."

Nellie stood and whooped. Big Bubba Malone did the same. Betty Monk merely lifted her hands in a praise-Jesus gesture.

Jack shouted, "It's about time!"

Her father and Vera held hands and beamed as though life had finally found them again.

Kate looked at the graduates. "I didn't mean to steal your thunder because this day is about you and your journey. But I took that journey with you guys, whether you realized it or not. I'm proud of what we've become together—people who have risen from the ashes. We are new again."

The center erupted into applause, many of the audience standing.

Rick watched Kate as she turned to him.

"Rick?"

"What, baby?"

"I love you," she said right into the microphone.

Those words were the sweetest he'd ever heard. And Kate taking that chance on him was the most profound moment he'd ever experienced. There was nothing to do but welcome his Kate home with a kiss.

"I love you, too, baby," he whispered before he covered her lips with his. He picked her up and spun her around and around until the edges of the world blurred and there was only this incredibly brave woman in his arms and a future laid out in front of them like the sweetest gift.

Applause continued, stomping occurred and hands slapped him on the back. Banjo barked.

But nothing registered.

There was only Kate.

"Thank you," he whispered against her lips.

She smiled against his lips. "For what? Donating the fifty thousand dollars to Phoenix?"

He squeezed her tighter. "No. For coming home."

Epilogue

One year later

The music sounded as Kate stood facing the French doors leading out to the balcony. She pressed her dress against her thighs and breathed a simple prayer, "Please."

She wasn't exactly clear what she was praying for. It might have been for the dress to stay put. The wind was blowing pretty hard and the bodice was strategically draped. Or it might have been for the grace she needed to descend the stairs. She'd counted them. Twenty-six.

Nellie appeared at her elbow and handed her a clutch of roses. "Don't fall. I'll be in front of you."

Kate rolled her eyes. "Oh, thanks for the concern for the bride."

Her friend grinned. "Well, you're not always graceful. Plus, I'm eating for two now."

Kate assessed her friend's expanding bump. Nellie was five months along and the dress had had to be altered. Could her friend stand the shock? "Yeah? Well, so am I, sister."

"Holy shit!" Nellie screeched before clapping her hand over her mouth and glancing out to the balcony. "You're serious?"

Kate nodded and smiled. "But *I* still fit in my dress."

"Oh, my goodness," Nellie breathed, jerking Kate into a hug. She sputtered against the flowers pinned in Kate's hair, and gave a suspicious sniffle. "Have you told Rick?"

"No. You're the first to know. And it really should have been him, but the devil inside me pops out sometimes." She pushed Nellie from her and wagged her finger at her. "Not a word."

Her best friend made the lock-and-key motion and picked up her bouquet. "Of course I won't tell."

Kate smiled at her friend before punching her on the arm. "So don't trip. I'll be right behind you and I'm eating for two."

"Whatever."

The music swelled louder and Billie squealed. "That's it. The cue!"

Trish appeared behind her, looking particularly regal in her seafoam-green bridesmaid's dress. Her coffee-colored skin looked lustrous, and Billie, newly married herself, looked fresh and innocent in her pleated dress of peach. But Kate knew firsthand her artisan friend was anything but innocent—Billie had thrown the bachelorette party, complete with a male stripper and penis-shaped cookies.

"Okay, let's rock this wedding," Kate said, giving Nellie a wink. The daffodil dress looked good against

Nellie's tan skin and caramel-streaked hair. Her friend always looked radiant when she had a bun in the oven.

Trish opened the doors and the sound of the stringed orchestra floated inside. The sun broke through the clouds as she descended first, elegantly gliding down the curved stairs of Cottonwood like an African princess greeting her subjects. Billie followed, looking petrified and stiff. Nellie started out the doors behind Billie, but paused and caught Kate's arm.

"I love you, Katie."

"Love you, too," Kate said, trying not to mess up her makeup with the dampness misting her eyes. Then she pushed Nellie toward the doors. "Hurry up."

Jeremy emerged from around the corner. He'd been waiting outside, looking splendid in an Armani tuxedo. He'd tucked an outlandish peach handkerchief in his pocket. It perfectly matched the roses she held. "Let's go, doll."

And he offered his arm.

Kate took it and they emerged to a gorgeous spring day. The notes of the cello were plaintive on the breeze, but the violins livened up the traditional wedding march. Kate kept her eyes on Rick as she descended stairs that swept round the front of Cottonwood. From her vantage point, if she looked across the pristine lawn past the crowd of people sitting in white chairs, she could just glimpse the gates of the estate. The same gates she'd once sat outside of on a pink bike, picturing herself doing exactly what she did today.

Only her dress wasn't fluffy and she didn't wear a veil. Her gown was a gorgeous, tight Vera Wang. And her father wasn't escorting her.

But he would.

Justus waited at the foot of the steps. Jeremy handed her to him, and she tucked his hand into the crook of her right arm.

Vera had tied a white satin bow to the back of his motorized wheelchair. Together they faced the audience assembled. Kate watched as Vera, the stepmother of the bride, stood; a tender expression lit her face. The rest of the guests rose, and together, she and her father started up the white runner that led to Rick and her future. Her father's hand trembled on her arm and she tore her gaze from Rick to glance at him. He smiled, squeezing her arm and looking as proud as any father.

Finally, they reached Rick. He looked nervous, so she smiled. She didn't feel nervous at all. Certainty had made a home inside Kate Newman.

The pastor who'd dunked Kate beneath the eternal waters when she was eight began the service, talking about forgiveness, commitment and love. Three things Kate already knew about.

"Who gives this woman in marriage?"

"Her father," Justus said quite solemnly.

Then he put her hand into Rick's.

And gave Katie Newman the family she'd always wanted.

* * * * *

***

Just for an instant, Gabriel worried about putting Michelle
in the line of fire, considering his line of work. He had
enemies. Dangerous enemies who wouldn't hesitate to
threaten anyone close to him. Of course, there was his
sister, Sara, but she'd lived in Wyoming for the past few
years, away from him, on a ranch they co-owned. Now he
was putting her in jeopardy along with Michelle.

But what could he do? The child had nobody. Now that
her idiot stepmother, Roberta, was dead, Michelle was truly
on her own. It was dangerous for a young woman to live
alone, even in a small community. And there was also the
question of Roberta's boyfriend, Bert.

Gabriel knew things about the man that he wasn't eager to share with Michelle. Bert was part of a criminal organization, and he knew Michelle's habits. He also had a yen for her, if what Michelle had blurted out to Gabriel once was true—and he had no indication that she would lie about it. Bert might decide to come try his luck with her now that her stepmother was out of the picture. That couldn't be allowed.

Gabriel was surprised by his own affection for Michelle. It wasn't paternal. She was, of course, far too young for anything heavy. She was a beauty, kind and generous and sweet. She was the sort of woman he usually ran from. No, strike that, she was no woman. She was still unfledged, a dove without flight feathers. He had to keep his interest hidden. At least, until she was grown up enough that it wouldn't hurt his conscience to pursue her. Afterward…well, who knew the future?

***

Don't miss TEXAS BORN
by New York Times *bestselling author Diana Palmer,*
the latest installment in
THE LONG, TALL TEXANS *miniseries.*

Available October 2014 wherever
Harlequin® Special Edition books and ebooks are sold.

⊕ HARLEQUIN®

SPECIAL &EDITION

Life, Love and Family

Coming in November 2014

THE SOLDIER'S HOLIDAY HOMECOMING

by *USA TODAY* bestselling author

Judy Duarte

Sergeant Joe Wilcox is back where he never expected to be—Brighton Valley, which he left long ago. He's in town because he promised to deliver a letter for a fellow marine to Chloe Dawson, who broke his late pal's heart. But before he can do so, Joe is struck by a car and gets temporary amnesia. Joe can't remember who he is, but he's intrigued by the lovely Chloe. Can the soldier and his sweetheart find happily-ever-after just in time for Christmas?

Don't miss the latest edition of the *Return to Brighton Valley* miniseries!

Available wherever books and ebooks are sold.

HARLEQUIN®

SPECIAL EDITION

Life, Love and Family

THE LAST-CHANCE MAVERICK
The latest edition of
MONTANA MAVERICKS: 20 YEARS IN THE SADDLE!
by *USA TODAY* bestselling author

Christyne Butler

Vanessa Brent might be a famous artist, but not even
she can paint a happy ending for her best friend.
Following her late BFF's instructions, Vanessa moves
to Rust Creek Falls to find true happiness, which is
where she meets architect Jonah Dalton. He's looking
to rebuild his own life after a painful divorce, but
little does each know that the other might be
the key to true love.

Available October 2014
wherever books and ebooks are sold!

Catch up on the first three stories in
MONTANA MAVERICKS: 20 YEARS IN THE SADDLE!

MILLION-DOLLAR MAVERICK
by Christine Rimmer
FROM MAVERICK TO DADDY
by Teresa Southwick
MAVERICK FOR HIRE
by Leanne Banks

www.Harlequin.com

HSE65843

HARLEQUIN®

SPECIAL EDITION

Life, Love and Family

Coming in October 2014
THE EARL'S PREGNANT BRIDE
by *NEW YORK TIMES* bestselling author
Christine Rimmer

Genevra Bravo-Calabretti might be a princess of
Montedoro, but that doesn't mean she's doesn't
make mistakes. When one night with the devilishly
handsome Rafael DeValery, Earl of Hartmore,
results in a surprise pregnancy, Genny can't believe
it. Meanwhile, Rafe is determined to make her
his bride. Will the fairy-tale couple get a
happily-ever-after of their very own?

Don't miss the latest edition of
***THE BRAVO ROYALES* continuity!**

Available wherever books and ebooks are sold!

HSE65842